Gypsy's Kilt

To Eva,
Magic and
Miracles... always

To gain everything she had ever wanted...

she had to lose everything she had ever known.

Gypsy's Kilt

Jennifer Ensley

To all the dreamers out there, the romantics, the visionaries, the believers of magic… I bow to you. This book was written with you in mind. Namaste, kindred spirits. Keep the unexplainable, secret… the supernatural, wondrous… the bizarre, astonishing… and the Fairytales, ever enchanting… Always.

❀ *Gratitude!!!*

All works by Jennifer (JK) Ensley are available in print at Amazon.com, Createspace.com, and wherever books are sold. eBooks available in all formats and for all devices. Audio books available through Audible.com, Amazon.com, and iTunes.

Also by Jennifer Ensley/JK Ensley

Forgotten Grace

A Dance with Destiny Series:
Cursed by Diamonds
Blessed by Sapphires
Enthroned by Amethysts
Destroyed by Onyx
Protected by Emeralds
Redeemed by Rubies

Short stories

Dark Games

Chapter 1

The rhythmic tick of an old grandfather clock... the soft clinking of the spoon as she mindlessly stirred her English tea... the sweet smell of the gentle summer rain.

Gypsy watched as tiny, misshapen drops slowly converged on the windowpane, finally gaining the needed momentum to race down the cool glass. Yet, she wasn't focused on the *rain*, on the clear streaks now lacing intricately down that old window. She was concentrating on the *flow*, on the tiny trickles that disappeared once stretched beyond their limit.

The clock's ticking grew louder, echoing through her drifting mind. Those clear raindrops began to thicken and darken... taking on the crimson color of her haunted memories...

Her *initial* recollection of that fateful day was the heat against her back—the warmth that cold, black pavement had saved up during such a pleasant, sunny day. Then... the flow.

She watched as the thick red liquid pooled—swelling like a grotesque cinnabar ink blot bubble—before eventually seeping down into the tiny cracks and fractures of the asphalt. Lying there, she gazed blindly into the surrounding lights, not truly seeing them, focusing instead on the thin, wispy strands sticking up from the midst of that growing red pool before her.

Is that... hair? But... why?

Calmness had claimed her. Gypsy didn't hear the yelling, the honking horns, the sound of twisting metal and broken glass. All was silent, surreal, almost deathly quiet.

She tried to reach for that crimson puddle, reach for the now sodden strands slowly becoming lost within it. She *tried* to reach, yes, but her fingers merely twitched. They refused to obey.

Smells, distinct odors began to invade her floating senses— hot tar, gasoline, human sweat, musky cologne. Then, the most potent smell of all overtook her... blood. The sweet, sickening stench pulled her mind back to a chaotic reality, back to the horrible sounds that had seemed so far away, back to the awful, gut-wrenching pain.

"Lass? What are ye doing up there? Lass? Lass? Gypsy! Are ye well, Kitten?"

As her eyes slowly closed, the past melted away and Gillis's voice helped steady her in the present.

She turned toward him. "Gills? You up already?"

"Already?" He snorted out a laugh. "Gyps, it's nearly half past five. We better get a move on if we want tae be set up in time for the party."

"...Party?"

"Aye, Lass—party. They booked the back room for seven p.m. on the dot. Ye'll only have aboot an hour by the time ye get dressed. Hurry up." He clapped his hands. "Move yer arse, Lass." He reached for the door. "I'm gonna make sure the bar is stocked and ready. If yer nae down there in twenty minutes, I'll drag ye down those steps myself."

She smiled. "I'll be there, Gills. Don't get your skirt all twisted in a knot."

He stopped short and turned back to face her. "Aye, Lass... it's nae a skirt. I'll remember yer words taenight when yer feet are tired and swollen and yer whining for my loving attention."

"I didn't say skirt. I said kilt. You misheard."

"Dunnae play with me, Gyps. Now, come on. We've a long night ahead of us. Dunnae make me punish ye afore it even starts."

Gypsy chuckled as she hopped down from the banister railing and ran towards her room. Gillis was right. Now was not the time to be lost within the past.

The veterans were coming in for their monthly get-together. She would have her hands full. The Vets were her favorite customers, the best of the bunch. They had perfect manners, always helped her serve the beer, and never walked out without a "Thank you, Ma'am" *and* a nice tip. She loved those honorable, scarred men... but even *they* wouldn't abide her acting like an airhead ditz. Work was work, and she loved it.

"Dwelling on the past will give you wrinkles," Trace would always say when he would catch her furrowing her brows, a vacant look in her honey-brown eyes.

Yet, Trace wasn't around right now. He was overseas, and work was what kept her from dwelling on that sad fact. Alas, when the night came and the crowds had gone home, her mind was hell-bent on reliving the past... whether she was conscious or no.

———❦———

Her dreams always took her back to ten years earlier...

That constant, irritating beeping sound was the first thing she remembered. It permeated her subconscious, slowly pulling her back into reality. Then, there was the odd *swoosh* of the oxygen pump.

Where am I?

Mumbling, incoherent voices now invaded her tranquil thoughts.

She tried to speak, but her throat was on fire—no voice would come. She tried to open her eyes. It was no use. She tried to raise her arm. Nothing happened.

Gypsy slowly drifted back into her comatose dreams.

When next she woke, there was a young man sitting beside her bed. His jet-black hair and bright blue eyes were a beautifully striking combination.

She tried to smile, but couldn't.

The young man had her hand clasped in his, his lips pressed firmly against her fingers, as he stared blindly out the window.

Such a pleasant face... but, he looks so sad. Why is he crying?

She slowly drifted back into darkness.

Gypsy was now standing in an empty void, the intermittent flashes of light only accentuating her solitude.

Then, she was lying on her back... looking into the warmest chocolate-brown eyes she had ever seen. Slowly, the outline of his face came into view—handsome, boyish features framed by sandy-blond hair.

"Are you an angel?" she asked.

The handsome young man smiled a dreamy, heart-stopping smile. It made her feel warm... all the way down to her toes.

"And here I thought *you* were the angel," he whispered.

3

She remembered smiling, remembered the way the corners of her mouth tugged up at her cheeks.

"Look at that," he said, brushing her hair back from her forehead. "You really *are* an angel. Don't you worry now, beautiful angel… help is on the way. You stay with me. You hear me, Angel? Stay with me. Come on. Open those gorgeous eyes for me."

Again, when Gypsy closed her eyes in her coma-induced dream, she opened them into what must only be reality.

It was dark outside the large window, but a soft glow filled the room. She tried to pinpoint the light source, but found it too difficult to move her head.

Gypsy tried to focus her mind, concentrate on her body.

Come on, toes. Where are my toes? Come on you little buggers. Wiggle. Wiggle. Ahh… there you are.

She glanced down at the foot of the bed, watching as the small bumps under the covers slowly moved back and forth.

Hello there, little piggies. You have to be attached to some feet, right? Let's see if we can't get them moving as well.

As soon as she moved her left ankle, excruciating pain shot up her leg. Gypsy closed her eyes and held her breath until it subsided. Only when she looked back down did she notice the sleeping man at her side—head and shoulders resting upon the edge of her bed.

Hello, Blue Eyes. I remember you from earlier. Too bad those amazing azure orbs are closed now. Where did you get all that gorgeous raven hair? Huh? I wish I had hair like that. And look at those long eyelashes. It's a shame—such lovely things wasted on a boy who probably wishes he didn't even have lashes like that.

She glanced up at the sterile white ceiling, but could garner no clue as to her whereabouts.

I don't know the room. I don't know the boy. Hmm…Think, Gypsy. What is it that you do know? Well… I know not to try and move my ankle again. Soooo… there's that. Let's see. What else should I try to move? Oh yeah, fingers. Fingers? Where are you? Right hand. Oh, please let me have fingers on my right hand.

It was like she had to literally *force* her consciousness down her right arm, inch by inch. With the awareness came some pain and discomfort, but nothing she couldn't handle. Besides, anything would have been better than the weighted numbness she was now enduring.

Ahh… there you guys are. Hello. Wakie, wakie. Now, count with me. Yep, pointer finger working perfectly fine. That's one. Middle finger… oh yeah. That's two. Gotta have a working middle finger.

She chuckled in her thoughts. She tried to smile, but found *that* particular task to still be an impossibility.

Okay, where was I? Ring finger… check. Pinkie… owwie zowwie, that smarts. But at least it's working. That makes four. Alrighty then, Mr. Thumb… please still be attached to my body. I would be lost without you. Yes! Whoo hoo! Right hand is a-okay and ready for business. Now, hows about Lefty?

Gypsy went through the same process of slowly waking up her left arm, but found trying to move the fingers on *this* hand to be much more of a challenge.

What's the deal? They feel bound, trapped. Do I have a cast on?
She sent her consciousness back up her arm.

Nope. Cool air and prickly goose bumps from my wrist to my shoulder. Soooo… what gives, Lefty? You just wanting to be a jerk today? Is that it?

She tried to move all of her fingers at once, ball them into a fist. When she did, the sleeping young man jerked upright in his chair.

Ahh, so that's it. You were holding my hand, keeping me from wiggling my digits. Aww… how sweet. Hello, Blue Eyes. Nice to see you again.

The boy stared at her face, blinking, as those sparkling eyes of his grew wider and wider. He suddenly jumped up and ran out of the room without a word.

She tried again to smile. *Well, perhaps I look a fright. Heh, what a way to have to wake up. Sorry about that, Blue Eyes. Hope I didn't scare you too badly. Now, let's see what else I can move.*

Her concentration was quickly interrupted by bright lights and many frantic voices.

Ugh! Get the hell out! I was doing just fine on my own.

Of course they couldn't hear her. Gypsy knew she wasn't actually speaking. Then she was gagging. Her parched throat hurt like mad. A sudden fit of coughing shook her whole body. She gasped for air.

"…Water," she rasped.

No quicker than the word had slipped out, a tiny straw was placed to her lips. She didn't get as much as she wanted before it was all too soon removed.

The poking and prodding and questions seemed to go on forever. As soon as the bright lights were blessedly turned off and a soft glow was all that illuminated her room, she drifted back into her dreams. Blondie was there—hovering over her, gorgeous chocolate eyes sparkling like the heavens.

"There you are, Angel," he whispered. "I've been waiting for you. I have so much to tell you, so much to ask you. We share a destiny, lovely lady, one which we will walk together... always."

Gypsy smiled. "I think I'd like that. You make my dreams a place I never wish to leave. Why don't you smile at me like that when I'm awake? Why can't I gaze into your mesmerizing eyes when I open mine?"

"You can, *if* you really want to. Try it, Angel. Open your eyes and look at me, look at your future. I'm waiting."

When Gypsy finally *did* open her eyes, a young man in a wheelchair was by her bed. His warm smile was the one from her dreams.

"Hello, Angel," he whispered.

His gentle voice healed everything that was hurting on her insides. She couldn't help but return that enchanting smile.

"Hello, Chocolate Eyes. I've been dreaming about you."

"Then we are of like-mind. I've been dreaming about you, too." He squeezed her hand. "I will probably always call you Angel, but... would you think me too forward if I asked for your real name?"

She shook her head, still smiling. "It's Gypsy... Gypsy Rodden."

He chuckled softly. "Of course it is. You are a Gypsy if ever I've seen one. It's nice to finally hear your voice, it alone has healed me."

A single tear trickled back to soak her hair. "I felt the exact same way when you first spoke."

"Is that right? Well then, let's hope our rare connection does nothing but grow with time." He softly stroked her cheek, lightly running his thumb across her parched lips. "It's nice to meet you, Gypsy. My name... is Trace."

A relieved laugh escaped through her tears. "Hi, Trace. I... I think I love you."

He smiled again. "I already know I love you, and I have for weeks now. I was just waiting for you to wake up so I could tell you."

Then... she woke for real.

Chapter 2

Ugh! Why am I so flippin' nervous? What have I got to be nervous about? Nothing, that's what. I killed that interview. Killed it. Nailed it straight in the head.

Gypsy sighed as she glanced down at her watch, while her heels clicked happily down the quieted hallway.

Right on time. She smiled and tugged on the front of her suit jacket. *Jeez... Is this like the longest hall in the history of ever? Last door at the end. Yep. I see you. I'll get there, eventually.*

She stopped short and looked down at her shoes, double-checking to make sure there was no dust or street-gunk on her favorite Jimmy Choos.

Is my watch ticking? Why is it— What the— Did I just never notice that before? Naw. Wristwatches don't tick. Jeez, girl... get a hold of yourself.

She took a deep breath before rapping twice on the solid wooden door.

"Enter."

His deep voice reminded her of a Sociology professor she had her freshman year of college. It made a knot form in the pit of her stomach, just like Dr. Black's always had.

Gypsy gripped the cold metal knob and took another deep breath.

Her first interview had gone unexpectedly well. She thought back to a week earlier...

The meeting with that group of four men—wearing overly stern expressions—had ended with collective smiles and firm handshakes. She was poised, confident, maintained eye contact, respectfully addressed each questioner before giving a self-assured, intelligent answer. Gypsy had left that solid cherry boardroom with her shoulders back and her head held high. The confident ring of her high heels echoing off that creamy marble floor had caused the initially snotty-acting receptionist to look up at her and smile.

Gypsy returned the gesture with a respectful nod before pushing open that heavy glass door, smiling like a Cheshire cat as soon as the sun hit her cheeks.

She was still fist-pumping the air when she entered the locker room at the gym.

"Wow. Somebody looks like they're having a good day."

Gypsy turned toward the petite brunette and addressed her with a dramatic bow via response. The lady chuckled.

"One for the diary, Saline," Gypsy said with a smile. "One for the diary."

The brunette sort of snorted. "I didn't know you could smile like that. Normally, you scare the hell outta me."

"Ahh, Saline." Gypsy slammed her locker door before snatching up her gloves. "That's because I come here to train. If you ever see me smiling like this out in the ring... run."

Saline chuckled. "Like a bat out of hell, Gyps." She slapped Gypsy's shoulder as she headed for the door. "Like a bat out of hell."

Gypsy was still all smiles as she put in her ear buds, pulled on her gloves, and headed for the small punching bag—*Come With Me Now*, blaring in her head.

Yes, that had been one hell of a day. Gillis had even been able to talk her into swapping shooters at the bar that night. Even though she knew better than to go up against a Scotsman in a drinking game, she had been too high on life to back down. Of course, she'd paid for it the next day... but not that day. *That* day... she was undefeatable.

Gypsy smiled to herself as she gripped tighter to that cold doorknob and thought about what had happened only a couple hours ago...

When the callback had finally come from Bishop, Grey & Sweet, she had bounded down the stairs, pounced on Gillis's broad back, and happily sang her news in his ear.

"So, does that mean ye got the job, Lass?"

"Nope. It was a callback. Not a job offer."

"Then... what are ye singing aboot?"

"Apparently I was so *awesome*; the Big Man himself wants a face-to-face."

"Who's the Big Man?"

"The first name on the building. Duh, Gillis. What? Don't they have law firms in Scotland?"

"Aye, they have 'em, alright. A bunch of nutters—the lot of 'em."

Gypsy chuckled. "Yeah, we are."

"What time do ye have tae appear before Big Man Bishop? Do ye have a wee bit tae spare?"

"Spare? For what?"

"For a cuddle or two. Maybe three. If ye'd let me, I'd tame ye, Lass. Well and good."

"Hands off my ass, Gillis. Unless you want a roundhouse to the side of your head."

"Aye, but yer arse is so firm, Gypsy. Give me a chance, Lass. Let me warm that cold heart of yers."

She jerked her hips, twisting away from him. "Roundhouse, Gillis. I ain't kidding."

"And I'm nae the nutter here, Gyps. There's nae enough room behind this bar for ye tae get yer leg up that high."

She playfully stuck her tongue out at him as she went back to balancing the till.

"I'll make the deposit on the way there. You need me to take anything to the bank for you?"

"Nae, Lass. I'm good. So… what time? Ye nae said."

"Five o'clock. I'll be back before we open. I'll just skip the gym tonight. Sound good?"

"I dunnae like it."

She glanced at him. "Don't like what?"

"The fact some man wants ye tae come tae his office at closing time."

Gypsy snorted. "Hmpft. My guess—they never get to leave at five anyway. That's probably just when their day starts to slow down."

"But if yer so *awesome*, ye'd think he'd have a bit more respect than tae call ye tae come oot at closing time. Like I said… I dunnae like it."

"Fine, Gillis." Gypsy pulled a card out of her pocket and slapped it down on the bar. "Here's the address. If I'm not back at a respectable time, bust through the doors and start yelling my name."

"If ye think I wulnae do it, Lass, yer wrong." He winked at her. "Besides, Trace hired me tae take care of ye. And that's what I'll be doing."

"No. Trace hired you to run the bar in my absence. You're not a bodyguard. You're a business associate."

He placed his hand over his heart. "Aye... ye wound me, Lass—a gash deeper than a broadsword."

She chuckled. "You're an idiot."

"Guilty as charged, my wee darlin'."

Gypsy headed for the door. "Wish me luck, you big goofball."

"Have ye got yer cell?"

"Yep. It's in my bag."

"Have ye got yer bag?"

"Yep," she said without checking, then turned back to face him. "Dammit," she grumbled under her breath.

Gillis was smiling, dangling her purse over the end of the bar. She scowled as she snatched it and headed back towards the door.

"Dunnae forget tae stop at the bank."

"I won't."

"Do ye have the deposit?"

"Aww... Bloody hell! Just hand me everything I've forgotten and stop gloating."

He only chuckled when she snatched the deposit bag *and* her portfolio out of his hands.

"Good luck, Gyps."

***

She took another deep breath before finally twisting that cold metal knob and entering Mr. Baron Bishop's giant office.

"Mr. Bishop, it's nice to finally get to meet you."

Gypsy had blurted out her greeting as she'd opened the door. Now, she stood blinking—staring at a large mahogany desk with a black leather chair behind it... an *empty* black leather chair.

"Sit."

She jumped at the sound of that deep, commanding voice, and then glanced toward the man standing in front of the large window completely covering one wall of the enormous office. He was gazing silently out at the city below—hands clasped loosely behind his back.

"Sir?"

"Did you not hear me? Sit."

Her jaw immediately clenched. She raised a single eyebrow as she glared at his shadowed profile.

I'm not a dog, asshole, she thought. *Just who the hell do you think you are?*

Her inner angel quickly answered, *He is Baron Bishop, you idiot—the man you are begging a job from.*

I don't beg, her inner demon countered. *I don't beg. I don't kneel. And I damn sure don't sit.*

The tall man turned his head slightly. Not to face her, no, but definitely capturing her in his peripheral.

If he listened closely, Gypsy was certain he could hear her teeth grinding together. She glanced back at the imposing desk with the two high-back leather chairs facing it. They were placed at an angle, each facing slightly toward the center of Mr. Bishop's desk. Gypsy's gaze slowly went back to the silent man. He hadn't moved.

She sighed inwardly, lifting her chin as she deliberately walked to the chair farthest from the door. She gave a sharp tug to the bottom of her suit jacket as her knees unwillingly bent until her bottom touched the subtle leather.

I don't sit.

Her inner angel giggled softly. *Today you do.*

She heard the man huff out a… What was it? A grunt, or a laugh? Gypsy wasn't sure. She remained silent—hands in her lap, back stiff—and waited.

He didn't speak for several more moments.

I'll give him two more minutes—one hundred and twenty seconds. That's it. If the interview doesn't start by then, I'll politely see myself out and the Big Man can kiss my lily white ass.

Liar.

Shut up, Angel.

The sweet side of her inner conscious only giggled again.

Gypsy almost growled… aloud.

"Interesting," the man said in a low voice. "Tell me. Why did you choose *that* chair?"

She didn't turn to face him. He hadn't granted *her* that respect, and she wasn't going to return a gesture she hadn't been given. Not to *this* man.

This is why you still don't have a job, her inner angel chirped.

Yeah, and why you spend half your life in that stinky old gym, the demon agreed.

Ganging up on me, huh?

She almost snorted, but then remembered Mr. Bishop was waiting for an answer.

"This happened to be the chair facing me. That's all."

"And yet... it is *not* the chair facing *me*."

"No," she said calmly. "You would have to dangle one on the outside of the building to accomplish *that*."

His silence returned.

Gypsy sat there, waiting. Without truly meaning to, she inhaled deeply and let the breath blow out noisily through her nose.

"Do I bore you, Ms. Rodden?"

"No. I'm just normally hyper. That's all."

"I see. So... I bore you."

She shrugged her shoulders. "I do not know you, sir. And such being the case, I do not have the pleasure of knowing whether *you* personally bore me or not. If you were asking me if this interview was boring... then, yes. Pretty. Darn. Boring."

The corner of his mouth turned up slightly. Gypsy didn't notice the gesture, seeing as how she was facing in nearly the opposite direction.

The awkward silence returned. She used the *dead-air* time to glance around the room. There were several framed diplomas hanging on the walls, and some rather expensive artwork as well. A mahogany bookcase filled with large legal tomes and various plaques and awards, all but covered the back wall.

Where are the pictures? she thought. *There's nothing personal in here at all—no kids, no wife, not even a pet. Ugh... This office is as sterile as his attitude is.*

Gypsy thought back to her meeting with the four junior partners. The questions had been expectedly probing. Not uncomfortably so, no. Just... business-like and appropriate. She had responded to each of them with a conversational vibe, letting her answers lead the men into a more relaxed, comfortable back-

and-forth type of atmosphere. It had been fun, enlightening—two things this second meeting was definitely *not*.

Ugh! I hate this whole mind-game crap. I'm outta here. There's no way in hell I can work for a man who doesn't even make eye contact.

Gypsy sighed as she reached down for her bag and slowly stood to leave. She only glanced back up as she took her first step toward the door… and almost ran head-first into the imposing man's dark burgundy necktie. When she stepped back from the sudden shock, Mr. Bishop grabbed her arm.

Gaining her footing, Gypsy jerked free and glared at the man.

"I see. So… you don't like to be touched," he said.

"Not when it's inappropriate, no," she snapped.

"Very well." He straightened back up. "Next time… I will let you fall."

"Hows about *next time* you don't sneak up on me?"

Baron raised a single eyebrow. His dark blue eyes were piercing, cold.

"I do not *sneak*."

She narrowed her gaze, studying his stern features. He was handsome. Not in an oh-my-god-that-dude-is-hot kind of way. His was a more regal, elegant type of handsome. Her searching gaze stopped on his mouth, fixating on the two elongated dents framing either side of his thin lips.

"Were you going somewhere?" he said.

Gypsy followed his icy gaze down to the small purse dangling from her fingertips.

"Yes. I was leaving."

"Leaving?" That piercing glare of his was now boring right through her. "Where were you going?"

"Home. That's normally where I go when I'm done for the day."

"And yet… you are *not* done for the day. Our agreed upon appointment has not reached its conclusion."

"Be that as it may, you seem busy—a bit lost in thought. I felt this interview was more than just a little bothersome to you. So, I chose to spare you the pain of it and just go."

The cold look on his face didn't change. "This is not an interview. You have already been interviewed by highly capable people. Oh, and… do not lie to me, Ms. Rodden. I can *always* sniff out a liar."

Gypsy bristled. "I do not lie, Mr. Bishop. I don't like the taste it leaves in my mouth. And what do you mean, this is not an interview? If you have nothing to say to me, why did you ask me to come in?"

"Yes, you did lie. And stop grinding your teeth. You have been doing that since you first entered. I find it irritating."

Gypsy took a deep breath and then smiled sweetly. "I was not grinding my teeth when I first entered. That didn't start until you demanded I *sit*. Now, tell me. What did I lie about?"

"You were not leaving for *my* comfort. *That* was a lie."

"Humft. You caught me." She let her fake smile quickly fade. "That's what I get for trying to be nice."

"Well, stop it." He moved back to his spot near the window. "Nice doesn't suit you. Come. Join me, Ms. Rodden."

She stared at his sleek, black, perfectly coifed hair. Gypsy rolled her eyes before taking a place not too far from him, gazing out at the slowly dimming skyline.

"Searching for your Zen?" she mumbled.

The corners of his mouth turned up, ever so slightly. "I like to spend a few moments at the end of the day… unwinding, yes."

She cast him a sideways glance and half snorted, half chuckled.

"And what was that vile noise for, Ms. Rodden?"

"The dimples."

He turned to face her properly. She mirrored him.

"I never would have guessed those two lines on your face were caused by dimples."

His small smile melted back to his normal stoic expression. Gypsy didn't bat a lash at his emotionless response.

"Oh? And what else did you think could have caused them?"

Gypsy held his unwavering gaze and didn't falter. "I thought, perhaps they were scowl scars."

His brows barely lifted. "Scowl sc—"

Mr. Bishop turned back to the window. He didn't speak, but he did smile. Well, a little. After a couple more quiet moments, he finally broke the silence.

"Can we start over, Ms. Rodden?"

She smiled. "I'd like that."

"As would I." He turned to her, extending his hand. "I am Baron Bishop. It is nice to finally meet you, Ms. Rodden."

Gypsy took his proffered hand, matching the strength of his handshake appropriately.

"Nice to meet you as well, Mr. Bishop. But what do you mean, *finally?*"

He smiled then, almost showing his teeth. She smiled too… at the sight of those deep dimples.

"Ever since you walked out of here last week, your name has been floating from office to office. You impressed the right people, Ms. Rodden. I have yet to hear the end of it. Your paperwork had already been sent to HR by the time you walked out the door and started punching the air like you were in a Rocky movie."

She blushed. "You saw that?"

He barely nodded. "Yes. You knew you had killed it, didn't you?"

"Yeah." She smiled again. "I had a feeling."

"Please." He motioned with a wave of his hand. "Have a seat. Make yourself comfortable."

Gypsy only inclined her head toward him before seating herself in the exact same place as before. She was surprised when Mr. Bishop sat down in the seat slightly facing hers, not the one behind his desk.

He smiled softly at her obvious shock. "As I said before, Ms. Rodden, *this* is not an interview."

Then what the hell is it? Gypsy didn't respond aloud, only stared at him.

"Are you comfortable? Would you like something to drink?"

Drink? Her demon snorted. *Not bloody likely.*

"I'm confused… not thirsty."

He smiled. "You don't have to be thirsty to have a drink."

Wait… her angel timidly whispered. *What's going on here?*

"Why did you call me in today? I mean, *really*. Why am I here? Did I get the job?"

"Ms. Rodden, you had the job before you walked out the door."

"So…" She narrowed her gaze. "When was somebody gonna tell *me* that?"

"That's what I'm doing now. It has been my habit, since the day I founded this law firm, to personally hire every lawyer I bring on board. My days soon became far too full to actually participate in the recruiting or interviewing process, but I still make time to welcome the new guy—tell them I wish to hire them… face to face."

"And… that's what *this* is?"

He gave her a little nod via response.

Gypsy closed her eyes, furrowing her brow as she pressed against her temples. When she looked back up, she was once again met with his piercing gaze.

"Is there a problem, Ms. Rodden?"

"Nope." She shook her head. "We each have our own way of doing things. This just happens to be yours, I guess. Although I will admit… this is the absolute strangest, most awkward way I could possibly imagine receiving a job offer."

"Is that so?"

She nodded. "Yes, it is. Tell me, Mr. Bishop. Do you actually find my reaction to be so odd? When faced with such a scenario, how have your other hire-ees responded?"

"I have never set up a scenario such as this with anyone else I've hired… prior to you."

"Wha— But I thought you did this with all the other lawyers."

"No. I said I met them and offered them a position, personally. I never insinuated that I invited them into my private office before they had officially joined my team."

"Then why—"

"I met Stanson on the golf course. Landry and I went out for sushi. I met Grey while we were in law school together. And Sweet… Sweet met me at the range—a little target practice."

Gypsy just sat there, staring at him.

Baron cleared his throat, then sighed. "The truth is, Ms. Rodden… I have never hired a woman before. I wasn't certain where you would feel the most at ease."

"So… you invited me to your private office—after hours— and began barking out commands before even turning to face me?"

"When you put it that way…"

"Yeah. Ranks right up there in the top three of a *Worst Ideas Ever* list."

He smiled. "The top three, huh?"

She nodded. "Well… it was actually just in the top ten."

"…Until?" he said, coaxingly.

"Until you sat down uncomfortably close to me and asked if I wanted a drink." Gypsy snorted out a laugh. "I was just waiting for that corny 70's bow-chicka-wow-wow music to start playing in the background."

He almost chuckled. "So… you think I'm *that* guy."

"No. Well, I'm not real sure yet. Let's just say… the needle hit red on my Totally Creepy Meter a while ago."

"Creepy?" He did chuckle then. "I have been called many things, Ms. Rodden. I do not believe *creepy* has ever been among them. Apologies. I have obviously handled our first meeting improperly. Yet, you did say we could start again." He stood, offering her his hand. "Ms. Rodden, have you had dinner?"

Dinner? her demon said, before huffing and crossing his arms.

Wait… I'm still confused, her angel whispered. *Dinner and drinks and now holding hands… Seriously? What's going on here?*

"Okay, listen." Gypsy stood, ignoring his proffered hand. "I get that I am the first female you have ever invited to join your team. I also understand this meeting has become completely unsalvageable—for both of us. Be that as it may, you are still making this feel like some sort of weird one-sided date or something."

"That was never my intent."

"Yeah, I know. But since I hope I will not be the only woman lawyer you ever hire at this firm, let me give you a free lesson."

He raised a single eyebrow, skeptically. "Lesson?"

She shrugged. "Lesson, pointers, advice, whatever. Women are just people, too, Mr. Bishop."

"Meaning?"

"Meaning… sushi would have been great, or even the drink. But only during lunch—never after hours. The truth of the matter is, Mr. Bishop, the best way would have been like this." She spread out her arms to encompass his large office. "Here… in this room… with you behind *that* desk… during the day while other people are working and running the halls."

"No." He shook his head. "That is not how I do things. I am not interested in credentials at this point. By the time I am ready to meet someone, all that tedious stuff has been taken care of. Besides, I am too busy during the day and there are too many distractions going on around the office. I want to *meet* so that I can assess what kind of person you are outside of all this." He waved his hands, repeating her action. "I like to get a better feel for what kind of person you are before signing you to my roster."

"Now *that* is much better." She smiled. "I like it when all the cards are on the table. Makes for a much better game, don't you think? Levels the playing field a bit."

"I see. So… you tricked me."

"I did not trick you. I… broke you."

"Hmpfts." Baron slid his hands in his pockets. "I wouldn't say you *broke* me, Ms. Rodden, but you did force me to play my hand much sooner than I should have."

"Lawyers…" She smiled with only one corner of her mouth. "…never trust 'em—total jerks."

"Yes, you are quite right. The good ones are always the slick ones. The great ones… well, they are the ones who can do it with a charming smile on their face."

"Aww, you think I'm charming. That's so sweet." She stepped around him and headed for the door. "Now, if you will excuse me."

"Our meeting isn't over."

"Apologies, Mr. Bishop. I didn't realize how late it had gotten. I'm due at work."

"Work?"

"Yes, and if I'm not there in about twenty minutes… I wouldn't be surprised if some loud, cursing Scotsman in a kilt didn't try to bust in here. I mean, I told him he could, but I was only teasing. Still… Gillis is sort of a wildcard. I'm never really sure what he will say next. Or *do*, for that matter." Gypsy mumbled that last part.

"He is your husband?"

"Heh. Nope. He is my *partner's* friend. Well, Gillis is my friend, too. But he was hired to basically keep an eye on me."

"Because your *partner* doesn't trust you?"

"What? No. My *partner* and I trust each other completely, unwaveringly."

"I see. You must love each other very much—you and your partner."

"Our love is so strong... it cannot be put into mere words."

Baron smiled. "She is one extraordinarily lucky lady."

"Huh? Who is?"

"Your partner."

"My part—" She gazed into his piercing navy eyes. "My partner is a dude—Trace. What in the world would make you think otherwise?"

Baron furrowed his brow. "Normally, when someone has a *partner*, a life partner... they are of the same sex."

"Trace is my life partner, that's true, but our relationship has nothing to do with *sex*."

They both stared at each other, both confused, both at a loss as to what should come next.

Gypsy nervously cleared her throat. "Alrighty then. Well, I will wait for your call. Just let me know when you want me."

Baron placed his hand on the door when she turned to open it.

"Tonight."

She looked up at his large hand, and then turned to meet his unwavering gaze.

"Tonight what?"

"I want you tonight."

"Umm... Maxing out the Creepy Meter again."

"Ms. Rodden, this meeting has been the most baffling one I have ever tried to conduct."

"Tell me about it," she mumbled.

"I want my questions answered tonight. I wish to see a glimpse of who you truly are... tonight. Instead of revealing a piece of yourself, you have stepped farther into the shadows than I care to follow."

Gypsy let out a sigh, pressing her fingertips to her forehead.

"...You still interested in that drink," she said.

"I thought you said you had to work."

"We can kill both of those birds with the same stone."

20

Chapter 3

When Gillis heard the door open, he called out from behind the bar.

"Gyps? That better be yer sweet wee arse coming in here."

"Yeah. It's me."

"I was just aboot tae come get ye."

"I figured as much."

"What's wrong, Lass?" he said, glancing up at her deeply furrowed brow. "Dunnae tell me it's over afore it started."

"We didn't get to finish." She headed straight toward the stairs. "I'm gonna go get changed. Mr. Bishop agreed to continue our intervi—I mean, *meeting*—here. I gave him the address. If he comes in before I get into uniform, just serve him a drink or something."

"Aye, now *that* I can handle." He smiled. "What does Mr. Bishop look like?"

"Oh, you'll know him when you see him, Gills. Trust me."

Gillis didn't respond, but he did bend down when she bounded up the stairs... trying at another peek up her skirt.

He chuckled, shaking his head. "I'll nae tell the lass she bares her arse every time she does that."

———◆———

Baron Bishop looked up at the glowing sign before he hit the button, setting the alarm on his Mercedes.

"Gypsy's Kilt, huh?" He smiled with only one corner of his mouth. "Just like she said, it's hard to miss."

She hadn't told him the name of the pub, only the address. When he had questioned her further, Gypsy only smiled and said, "You'll know it when you see it. It's hard to miss... if you know what, or *who*, you're looking for."

That was just it. Baron did know *who*, but didn't know *what* he was looking for. Now that he had found it, her words made perfect sense.

⁂

"Aye, ye must be Bishop."

Gillis grabbed a towel, wiping the cold water off his hands before extending one to the tall, handsome looking man in the smart business suit.

"And you must be the Scotsman."

Their hands clasped firmly, both men's knuckles going white from the exchange. Although pleasant smiles adorned their faces, the cold glare coming from each told a whole different story.

"Aye… the Scotsman, I am. Gillis McCullough's the name."

"Baron Bishop. Nice to meet you, Gillis."

"Likewise. Have a seat and I'll fix ye right up. Gyps went tae change. She'll be back in a jiff. What'll it be?"

"I was warned that if Ms. Rodden didn't return soon, you would be busting down my door."

"Aye, and that'd be the truth of it." He chuckled loudly. "Now, hows aboot ye pick yer poison. I wanna have ye all set up afore Mistress Manic returns."

"Mistress?" Baron's eyebrows lifted slightly when he said the word.

Gillis didn't like the man's subtle reaction, not at all.

"It's just what we call her when she gets all stressed oot."

"We?"

"Aye. Trace and myself." He sat the glass of honey brown whiskey down in front of the other man. "But only us. Dunnae let her hear that from *yer* lips."

Baron half smiled at the large Scotsman's intended warning, but did not respond.

Gypsy's voice wafted down to them as she quickly descended the stairs.

"I had to skip the gym today, Gills, and now my back's killing me. You know how I get when I miss a day with Old Mack. And to make matters worse… my awkward meeting with *the Pope*

22

only added to the knots in my shoulders." She bounced up to him and spun around so that her back was facing him. "Will you loosen me up a bit?"

Gillis glanced sideways at Baron. He realized Gypsy hadn't yet noticed the other man, and there was no way in hell Gillis wasn't going to take this perfect opportunity to mark his territory.

"Come here, Lass. I'll loosen ye up *more* than just a bit."

She giggled. "Can you do it without being gross and inappropriate?"

He began massaging her tense shoulders. "I've nae had any complaints on *how* I do it. Relax a little, Kitten. It feels like yer back is full of golf balls."

"I know, right? It's killing me."

"Dunnae tell me Old Mack has tae work these oot every day."

"No. I hit Old Mack's table *after* I've had a good workout. Like I said, I missed the gym."

Gillis brushed her long hair across one shoulder, then leaned down and softly kissed the nape of her neck.

"Ye need tae breathe with me, Kitten. Yer heart's racing." He wrapped his arms around her. "Lean back. Find my breath. Slower… Slower… Aye, that's a good lass. Now, stay with me." He tried her shoulders again. "Good. That's much better. Keep breathing with me… Good."

When Gillis lightly kissed her neck again, Gypsy felt his lips part into a smile. She couldn't help but smile in return.

"I like it when ye mind me, Kitten."

Her smile grew wider. "Then you'd best savor the rare opportunity."

"Aye… like a king's treasure." He gently leaned her forward. "Brace yerself, Lass. I need tae work on ye from behind."

Gypsy chuckled as she grabbed hold of the edge of the bar.

"Can't you do *one* simple thing without making it sound so disgusting?"

"I can do *many* things, Kitten. By the time I'm done with ye, there'd nae be one of them ye'd call disgusting."

He kissed her between the shoulder blades as he continued his therapeutic ministrations.

"You are a total pervert, Gills."

"Aye, but ye already knew that, Kitten."

"It *is* one of your many charms, I suppose."

"That it is, Lass. Now, tell me. When did ye meet with the Pope?"

She snorted out a sardonic laugh. "Mr. Baron Bishop. Bishop—Pope... get it?"

"Aye, I get it."

"I had to keep telling myself not to call him that out loud. He's not the most open book I've ever tried to read. I don't think he would appreciate my particular brand of humor."

"Is that right? Tell me true, Kitten. What did ye think of him?"

Gillis glanced back toward the other man.

Baron didn't move, didn't make a single sound. His cold gaze was locked on the side of Gypsy's smiling face.

"The truth?"

"Aye, Kitten. Always... the truth."

"Cold," she whispered.

"Cold?" Gillis growled under his breath. "Was he mean tae ye?"

"Not really *mean*, no. He was cold, distant... acted completely above me."

Gillis chuckled then. "Well, Kitten, he does own the place. *He* is the top."

Gypsy playfully bumped back against the teasing Scotsman with her rear-end. Gillis grunted and sucked in a sharp breath, gripping her shoulders ever tighter. He held her like that until she apologized.

"Sorry, Gills." She snickered. "I didn't realize you were nearly *excited*."

He lightly swatted her bottom. "Aye, ye *did* realize it. Dunnae play dumb with me, Kitten. I get excited when I'm *nae* touching ye. Try and imagine my torture right now." He smiled when she giggled again. "Now, tell me how ye were trying tae top the top."

"It wasn't like that, Gillis. I swear. I was *not* trying to top from the bottom. It's just... When I walked into his office, he didn't even turn to look at me. It's like he was saying I wasn't worth the effort or something. *Then* he started barking commands."

"What did he say?"

"He told me to *sit*." She snorted. "Like I was a damn dog or something."

"Yer nae a dog, Kitten."

She chuckled. "I'm not a kitten, either."

"Aye, that'd be the truth of it. Yer more like a tiger or a panther. Nae... more like a wildcat—a mountain lion."

"Ain't that the truth? I'd come closer to roaring instead of purring."

"I can make ye purr, Kitten."

She giggled softly. "Keep working with those magic hands and you just may."

"I'll do my best. Now, tell me more aboot yer Pope."

"Well... he's sexy as hell. *That's* for sure."

Gillis slapped her bottom, pretty hard this time. Gypsy only laughed.

"Well, he is," she said. "I gotta give the man props, Gills. He's got this air about him. His movements are... refined... elegant. Let's just say, the Queen wouldn't object to having tea with that princely-acting man. But still... he's cold. I thought at first his eyes were black. But when I looked at them in the light... I realized they were blue. Well, a deep rich navy color. Oh, and his nose... I wanted to touch that gorgeous nose of his."

"Long and sharp—just like ye like 'em?"

"Yeah. I'm a sucker for a nose like that." She *almost* purred. "I couldn't help but imagine the way it would feel... gliding slowly down my tingling spine."

A visible tremor ran through her.

Gillis chuckled. "Aye, and ye call *me* the pervert."

"I know." She groaned. "Ugh... I am so horrible. I can't believe I let myself picture that... with a man I was hoping to work for, no less."

"Just imagine it, Kitten—one of those closed meeting rooms with everyone sitting around the long table... chilled air blowing down from above, keeping the room at proper *brain functioning* temperature... yer cold Pope standing there with his hands in his pockets... yer hungry gaze pulled tae his sexy profile." Gillis chuckled when she let out a soft moan. "Ye'll have tae start wearing a bra, Kitten."

"No. No bras."

"Then everyone in that meeting will know." He leaned over and kissed her back. "Know exactly what that perverted wee mind of yers is playing aboot with."

She giggled. "Oh, and I didn't even tell you the *best* part."

He growled against her spine. "If ye say the man had dimples, I'm gonna take ye upstairs and claim ye right now."

She giggled again. "Not just dimples, Gillis. The *perfect* dimples—surprise dimples—the ones you aren't expecting. The smile comes and it's like... surprise."

"So he smiled at ye. Made yer heart race, did he?"

She snorted. "Hell, I had to force myself not to pant. I probably drooled a little, too."

Gillis laughed that deep, soothing laugh that always put her at ease.

"So, Kitten... ye like yer Pope, do ye?"

"No."

"Nae?" Gillis suddenly went rigid, then glanced back at the other man. "What do ye mean, nae?"

"I mean... not even no, but hell no."

"Kitten, wha—"

"Did you not hear the part where I said he barked at me— *demanded* I sit?" She snorted. "Hell, Gills. I wouldn't be surprised if he expected me to crawl behind his desk and curl up at his feet— lick my paws and call him Master."

Gillis slapped her butt again. "Here now, Lass. Stop it. I thought ye said he was sexy. The nose and dimples are yer ultimate weakness. Tell me how ye didnae like him."

"I also said he was cold. Did you miss that part, Gills? Hell, I think Vlad the Impaler was *sexy*. That doesn't mean I want him over for dinner."

"Shut it, Gyps."

"I'm serious, Gillis. You know how I like to look—devour a man like that with my eyes, drink in and fully appreciate every last drop of his strong, silent profile. It's like gazing at a perfect statue."

"Aye, as long as he doesnae speak."

She smiled. "True. They look so mouth-wateringly delicious... standing there all soundless and perfect. Then they gotta ruin the whole thing by opening their damn mouth."

"Ye are one twisted wee mountain lion. There's nae denying that, Kitten."

"Yeah, your bad habits have rubbed off on me."

"Nae true, my wee darlin'. Ye were at *least* this messed up when first I met ye."

"True." She smiled. "Anyway, it doesn't matter—the fact that his looks made me go weak in the knees. He was a total ass."

"Perhaps it's best we stop talking now, Lass."

"Well, you asked for the truth."

"Shush now, Gypsy."

"I mean, I respect the fine sculpting skills of those twisted ancient Romans, but that doesn't mean I want a plaque of an overly endowed gladiator's dangly bits hanging on my living room wall."

"Stop!"

Gillis grabbed her hips and gave her a good jerk. Gypsy cried out in pain. She would have gone down on her knees, had he not caught her.

He pulled her back against him, whispering into her hair. "Forgive me, Kitten. I didnae mean tae be so rough. I wouldnae hurt ye for any treasure in the world. I'm sorry, Lass."

"You didn't hurt me, Gills. I'm not as delicate as that."

"Then... what's wrong? Dunnae tell me the shadows came."

"Shhh... Don't even whisper about the shadows. No. *This* pain... it came from the Pope."

Gillis glanced back at the silent man. "Are ye sure?"

She nodded. "Yeah. The Pope's got one major dark secret, Gills. When I walked in his office... it felt like a dagger pierced me to its hilt. I couldn't even breathe for a couple heartbeats."

Gillis felt her begin to tremble. He embraced her, trying to keep her coming chills at bay.

"He said he needs to get to know me, Gills. That's why I invited him over here. But... there's no way in hell I can actually work for that man, not if I've gotta live with *this* much pain. I mean... I left his office quite a while ago. Why's it still this damn bad?"

Baron gently set his empty glass down on the napkin. The soft clinking of the ice cubes caused her to glance down the bar.

"Blood-dee-hell... Gillis, I hate you."

"Dunnae speak such lies, Kitten."

"Don't call me that. Not when you've pissed me off. Bad boys don't get rewards."

"I was just doing what ye would've done, Gyps. Cards on the table... right?"

"You suck." She sighed and tossed her apron on the counter. "Fine. Might as well get this over with before opening time."

"I'll take care of the prep." Gillis patted her back. "Ye've got thirty minutes afore the Vets show up."

"Aww, hell. I forgot about the Vets."

Gypsy walked around the bar and slowly made her way up to Mr. Bishop. She couldn't look him in the eye. She glanced up, yes, but couldn't hold his piercing stare.

"Mr. Bishop, I—"

"Nice uniform."

The imposing man ran his fingers down the side of her short kilt. Gypsy twitched.

"You know the Creepy Meter we were talking abou—"

"You can still say that after I just heard all the *creepy* thoughts floating through your mind concerning *me*?"

She blanched. "I would never have shared that with you, sir... never. It was inappropriate, vile, and completely unprofessional. Those were private thoughts only. Had you not just heard them for yourself, you would *never* have received improper vibes from me. I promise. That's not the way I work. A boss is a boss."

"And a statue is a statue."

She blushed. "Sincerest apologies for objectifying you in such a tasteless manner, sir. I wasn't lying, no. I *do* admit to being that twisted, yes. But... those words were certainly not meant for *your* ears. Perhaps I'm not cut out to—"

Mr. Bishop then leaned in toward her so quickly, Gypsy jumped and tried to move away. She didn't get far. Baron's large hand was at the small of her back, halting her escape. She watched in horror as he leaned ever closer, a tiny smile revealing that gorgeous dimple on the left side of his nearing mouth. She squeezed her eyes closed.

No. No. No. Don't do it. Please. Holy crap! This can't be happening. Dammit. And I wanted that job sooo bad.

Gypsy let out a tiny squeak when the sharp tip of Mr. Bishop's perfect nose grazed her cheek before he whispered close to her ear.

"I wish to enter into a contract with you, Ms. Rodden."

Gypsy froze—her eyes flying open at the same time her jaw dropped.

"A c-contract?"

"Yes, Ms. Rodden." His lips barely brushed her ear as he spoke. "We will discuss the details in full… when your work here is done."

"B-but the bar doesn't close until three."

"I will wait."

"For eight hours? But, Mr. Bishop—"

Her voice caught when the tip of his nose once again grazed her cheek. She shivered.

Baron leaned back against the barstool and smiled.

He did that on purpose. Her inner angel was stomping around, yelling out in disgust.

Of course he did it on purpose, the little devil cooed. *He knew how much we would like it. See? Look at that satisfied smile he's wearing.*

"Eight hours of golf or eight hours of watching a woman at work. It is still a meeting, all the same. I said I wanted to know the real you. What better place than a bar that bears your name… and *hints* at your pleasing attire?"

"But what about tomor—"

"Tomorrow is tomorrow. This is the day scheduled for our meeting, and this is the day it will happen. Besides, it wouldn't be fair if you didn't give me another chance."

"What? Another chance?"

He nodded. "It would be a travesty to let you walk away from my firm… knowing that you hated me."

"I never said I hated you."

He lifted a single eyebrow and sent her a knowing look. "It was implied."

"No. You've got it all wrong." She looked away. "I didn't mean—"

"Gypsy."

She froze again. Hearing him say her first name like that… it was unsettling.

"Look at me."

She begrudgingly obeyed.

"You spoke the truth of your heart—spoke it in confidence… and to your dear friend, no less. Own your words, Ms. Rodden."

"Fine." She sighed loudly. "It's true. I meant every single word I said."

"*Every* word?"

"Yes, sir." Gypsy lifted her chin and looked him in the eye. "I own them all."

He smiled. "Good. And… I find this extremely refreshing—having all the cards laying face-up in front of me. Wouldn't you agree?"

"Pfft… normally," she grumbled.

"And just for the record…"

He leaned in to whisper in her ear again. She didn't jump away this time.

"…I think *your* nose is perfect."

Gypsy felt the heat now radiating off her cheeks. When Baron chuckled softly, she knew *he* could feel it as well.

Chapter 4

"Right this way, sir," Gypsy said, smiling. "I'll be taking you to the back room. I believe your name is the last on my list. Come, Sergeant Stewart. Your comrades are eagerly awaiting your arrival. Watch your step. Just there. That's right."

She pushed open the door and was met with a rousing cheer for the older man still holding her bent arm. She couldn't help but smile—watching the closeness they seemed to still share.

"It is comforting, is it not?"

Gypsy jumped when she heard Baron's deep voice right behind her.

"Did you need something, Mr. Bishop?"

When she turned to face him, she realized he was holding two full pitchers of beer.

"Gillis sent these." Baron carefully sat them down on the little table near her station. "I'll go get the rest. I am all but certain they would much prefer *you* pour their drinks."

"Wow... Thanks, Mr. Bishop."

"It is my pleasure, Ms. Rodden. Go now. Mingle with your veterans."

He smiled before turning to leave.

Ho-lee hell...

Stop it, Gypsy, her inner angel demanded.

Perfect dimples, the demon prodded.

"Yeah." She sighed. "Perfect."

When Baron returned to the back room with more beer, his jaw clenched at the sight of several older men checking out her bottom and asking her to dance. Gypsy laughed off the flirtatious passes, but did agree to a couple short spins around the small dance floor. When she glanced his way, smiling and waving, Baron couldn't even force out a fake smile.

"Okay, gentlemen, looks like your refreshments have arrived. Please help yourselves while I try to get an ETA on your *real* entertainment. It appears they are running a bit late. Be back in a flash."

Boos accompanied her departure.

"Thanks for all the help, Mr. Bishop." She relieved him of the fresh pitchers. "I don't know what I would have done without you. Did either one of the other girls show up?"

"No," he said, still glaring at her semi-rowdy customers. "Gillis said to tell you... 9-1-1 Mistress Manic."

"Aww, hell. What now?"

Baron continued to stare at the room full of men as she hurriedly delivered the beer and then ran past him. When he followed her back into the main bar, the ten or twelve lone customers Gillis had been waiting on were now joined by about twenty loud young men. There wasn't an empty seat in the house.

Baron quietly walked up behind Gypsy, not realizing she was actually on the phone.

"I know you weren't scheduled until nine, but if you can make it in the next fifteen minutes there'll be another hundred dollars for each of you. That amount will drop by half every five minutes until it is gone. I will make it worth your while, but only if you're willing to hustle. When I hang up the phone, the timer starts, ladies."

Gypsy whistled at Gillis. "Fifteen, starting now."

She tapped her watch. He nodded.

"Hey, fellas!"

The collage-aged group turned her way.

"Is what's on tap good to get you started?"

As soon as the young men yelled out their confirmations, Gillis began filling pitchers and setting them up behind the bar. Gypsy grabbed the first two and was talking to someone as she passed Baron. Only then did he notice the headset stuck in her ear.

"If your skinny little ass isn't sashaying through that front door in the next ten minutes, you can forget about picking up your last paycheck. I'll drop it in the post on Friday week... No, you better not show your face around here if I don't see you in the next ten minutes... What do you mean, why? I think you already know the answer to that, Sheila. I'll kick your ass seven ways to Sunday. Ten minutes—clock started when you said hello."

By the time Gypsy got to the waiting tables, she had a smile on her face and was back to being the polite hostess.

Baron had to admit… he was impressed. He found himself smiling, even though he was still a bit perturbed by what he had witnessed in the back room. He was admiring her profile, enjoying her laughter and professionalism even though he was certain her stress level must be near its breaking point. He grabbed the next two pitchers and went to join her.

When Gypsy turned to reach for the mugs Gillis had readied for her at the far end of the bar, one of the louder frat boys slipped his hand under her kilt. Baron froze, anger stealing his breath.

Gypsy didn't miss a beat. She simply twisted away from the groping boy as she spun back towards the tables and started handing out the frosty mugs.

Baron delivered the beer, but stood beside the offending young man, glaring down at him. The boy paid him no mind.

"I've got two more ready for ye," Gillis called out.

Baron was hesitant to leave her side, but knew Gypsy would be burdened with the task of retrieving the fresh pitchers if he did not. Before he returned, the belligerent young man was at it again.

"Is it true what they say about Scots—that they go all natural under their kilts?"

He was sliding his hand up her inner thigh as he was speaking.

"I wouldn't know." Gypsy twisted away again. "I'm not Scottish."

"Aye, but I am, lad," Gillis called out. "Try lifting *my* kilt and see what ye find."

The boy's friends laughed and teased him, but he would not be dissuaded.

"Come on now. Just let me have a *little* peek."

Gypsy didn't respond as she kept pouring the beer. Yet, the young man wouldn't stop. He hooked his finger under the hem of her kilt and taunted her as he slowly lifted it up.

She didn't make eye contact with him as she spoke. "You'll find nothing but trouble, there, boy."

"Yeah? And what if trouble is exactly what I'm looking for?" He slowly ran his bent knuckle up the outside of her leg until he felt a strip of leather. "Hey, what's this? A garter belt?"

He jerked her kilt on up to get a better look.

"No," Gypsy said, still keeping her cool as she served the drinks. "It's my thigh strap."

"Thigh strap for what?"

"My blade."

Baron had almost made it back to the tables. He didn't even see Gillis jump over the bar. The imposing Scotsman now stood beside Gypsy, her assailant's wrist grasped firmly within his large hand. Still, Gypsy never missed a beat as she emptied the third pitcher into the glasses.

The young man jerked away from Gillis, knocking his chair over as he leapt to his feet.

"Thanks, Gills," she said with a smile. "I can take it from here."

Gillis smiled at the boy. "Ye stood a better chance with me, lad. Best cool yer knickers afore she gets really pissed. See that smile she's wearing?" He snorted out a laugh. "It ain't cause she's happy."

The flustered young man jerked down on the front of his shirt as he stuck out his chest.

"I'm not scared of that," he said, motioning towards her thigh. "What's some little three inch knife going to do?"

Gypsy turned to face him then. "Oh, you'll feel me. I promise."

She glanced toward Baron standing frozen behind the boy, cold blue eyes shining like black stars.

"It looks like the rest of your order has arrived, gentlemen." She served them the new pitchers, then sighed. "If you need anything else, I'm just a shout away. Name's Gypsy."

The doorman came in. "Ms. Rodden, the entertainment's here."

She glanced down at her watch. "Take them around to the side and show them in the back room. I'll be right there."

"Yes, Ma'am." He nodded before turning to go.

A young redheaded lady almost plowed into him as she burst through the door. Gypsy glanced back down at her watch.

"I hurried as fast as I could, Ms. Rodden."

Gypsy motioned with a nod toward the locker room. "Go make yourself presentable, Sheila. We'll talk later."

"We're almost oot of limes," Gillis called out.

"I'm on it," Gypsy said as she grabbed the young man's arm who was still standing there with his chest stuck out. "Come with me, Hotrod."

"Get your hands off me."

He tried to jerk free. Gypsy only dug her nails in deeper as she led him to the very last stool at the far end of the bar.

"I said, let go of me."

"Doesn't feel good, does it?"

The young man only glared at her as she shoved him into the seat. He started to speak. She stopped him.

"Shut your damn mouth and open up your bloody ears for a minute. I showed you the courtesy of saying this out of ear-shot of your buddies over there. Show me the same respect by paying attention."

The boy snorted, but didn't speak.

"I am going to bestow a favor upon you—a priceless life lesson you weren't expecting, but definitely need."

He turned away, but she grabbed his chin. He didn't try to fight her this time.

"What's your name?"

"Blain," he mumbled.

"Tell me, Blain. What would you do if you were at work—"

"I go to school."

Baron noticed Gypsy's jaw clench tightly, before slowly relaxing. He moved closer.

"Very well. Tell me, Blain. What would you do if you were in *class* and some man slid his hand between your legs?"

The boy furrowed his brow. "Some *man*?"

"Yes." She nodded. "Some man."

"B-but... you're a girl."

"Does being a girl make me less of a human?"

"N-no."

"Very well, then. We are both humans—you and I—are we not, Blain?"

He gave her a quick nod. "Yes."

"Then let me go on. What if you—as a human—were doing your best to pay attention in class when some *man* slid his hand between your thighs and asked for a little look-see?"

"I'd punch his lights out."

She smiled. "*I* am a human as well. I was trying my best to do my job when some man slid his hand between my thighs. Not once, but twice. How should I have reacted?"

Blain didn't speak. He looked down at his hands, unable to meet her gaze.

"Look, Blaine. I know what it's like to be young and dumb and out partying with your friends. Been there. Done that."

She gently lifted his chin and smiled at him. He blushed.

"Now, let me speak to you not only as a fellow human, but as a woman as well. You are a handsome guy—athletic build, sun-bleached hair, perfect teeth. You are attractive by any woman's standards. But know this. *No* woman wants to be violated like that. No man or woman wants to be touched without permission. Am I right?"

He nodded slowly, his green eyes now sparkling as he almost smiled.

"If you truly want to pick up a *worthy* woman, you can only do so by acting like a worthy man. If that little trick you pulled on me actually worked on some girl, she's the very one you *don't* want crawling up in your lap." Gypsy scrunched up her nose and chuckled. "Trust me. She'll leave you with something ya can't wash off."

They shared a quiet laugh as Gillis sat a full frosty mug down on the bar beside them. Gypsy handed it to the young man.

"Here ya go. This one's on the house. Go on back and join your friends. Enjoy your youth, Blain, but never forget to show respect."

He stood up to leave, but then turned back to face her.

"Thank you, Ms. Gypsy. Sorry I treated you like that." He blushed again. "I won't forget what you said. I want to be as lucky as *that* guy someday." He motioned behind her with a tip of his mug. "Because I want a woman just like you."

Gypsy turned around to find Baron Bishop standing not too far behind her. She just stood there, staring up at him.

Gillis plopped his elbows down on the bar near them.

"Why's the Pope yer boyfriend and nae the handsome Scot who protected that sweet arse of yers?" He tossed a hand towel over her head. "Limes!"

"I'm on it."

———⟨◆◆⟩———

Baron watched as Gypsy came back from the storeroom with her arms loaded down. A pleasant, closed-lipped smile adorned her lovely face as she deftly quartered the limes, a few lemons, cut two oranges into super thin slices, brought out some more cherries, and then filled up the salt and sugar dishes.

"I'm gonna check on the Vets, Gills. If Tam shows up, send her packing before I see her. Tonight... I'd snatch that cow bald, sure as the world."

"Ye got it, Kitten. Here's four more for the back."

Gypsy grabbed two pitchers just as Baron reached for the others.

"I feel bad making you help out like this, Mr. Bishop. I'll pay you a fair wage when the rush is over."

He smiled. "I will not accept your money, Ms. Rodden. The gift this particular meeting has given me... it's worth more than gold."

She chuckled as they made their way to the back. "Gift? What gift?"

"Watching a confident, capable woman doing what has to be done with a smile on her face... even though she's stressed out and in physical pain. I am in awe of you, Ms. Rodden."

Gypsy stopped and just stood there a couple heartbeats. Her words started coming out before her brain had fully reconnected.

"I have been in awe of you since I saw you standing in front of that large window... how the waning sunlight seemed to make you glow." She quickly sucked in her breath. "I am sooo sorry I just said that," she half whispered, biting down on her bottom lip to keep any other horribly embarrassing truth from just spilling out.

Nice going, her devil mumbled.

Her inner angel only tried to muffle his laugh.

When Baron smiled down at her, a thousand butterflies threatened to fly up from her stomach and burst through her clenched teeth.

"One more thing, before we join your throng of veteran fans." He leaned in, purposefully brushing his nose along her cheekbone. "I love it when you blush like that," he whispered. "The color… suits you *perfectly*."

⋯⊰⟨⟨◆⟩⟩⊱⋯

By the time two o'clock rolled around, most of the patrons were making their way home, or waiting on various cabs and other transportation. Gillis took advantage of the lull by catching up on the dishes while Gypsy wiped down the tables and Sheila kept up with drink orders.

"Last call, boys," Gypsy chirped.

Her announcement was met with groans and mumbling. She jumped a little when she suddenly felt the gentle warmth of a hand pressed against her lower back.

"Gypsy, honey?"

She turned to find one of her regulars, and an attendee to tonight's veteran celebration, standing beside her.

"Yes, Harold. Did you need something?"

"I just wanted to thank you, Ms. Gypsy. The band you got tonight, they were perfect. They sang all the old stuff. We liked that. Also… they were pleasing on the eyes as well." He chuckled softly. "You always go above and beyond for us, Ma'am. And, well… I just wanted you to know how much we appreciate it."

When he kissed her cheek, Gypsy felt him slide something in her apron pocket.

"Oh, no, Captain Bennett. That's not necessary. I love when you all get together. I'm just proud you choose *my* place to do it."

He patted the wad of money now filling her pocket. "It's a gift from the guys. They wanted you to have it. We love you, Ms. Gypsy. We all do."

She smiled graciously. "And I love you all right back."

When she turned toward the next table, she almost bumped into the young college man from before. She glanced down at the scratches on his bicep, just below where his t-shirt had protected him from the rest of her nails.

"Oh, Blaine... I'm so sorry about that."

He followed her gaze before blushing brightly. "I'm glad they're there. I earned them."

Gypsy only smiled.

"Coach is sending the team bus to pick us up."

"Yes, well, I think that would be best. Tell your coach I said thank you."

"I will."

He glanced behind her, then quickly back down. Gypsy furrowed her brow, tilting her head slightly.

"Blaine, is there something else you needed?"

"No, Ma'am. It's just..." He slowly looked back up, meeting her questioning gaze. "I wanted to know how serious you were."

"Serious? About what?"

He fidgeted with his hands before continuing. "I haven't had a hard crush on anyone since I was in grade school and Jenny Landon walked into class wearing a pink dress... perfect blonde pigtails hanging down to her waist. You know what I'm talking about?"

She smiled. "Yes. I can remember what that kind of love feels like."

"Yeah, well..." He glanced over her shoulder and then right back into her eyes. "I hadn't felt anything like that since third grade... until tonight."

Gypsy didn't speak, didn't know *what* to say.

"That's why I asked... if you were serious."

When she opened her mouth to speak, Gypsy felt the warmth of someone's chest against her back a split second before Baron Bishop lightly ran his hands down her arms.

"We are extremely serious," he said.

Baron's deep voice vibrated against her. She almost shivered.

Blaine glanced down at Gypsy's hands. She was almost positive they were trembling.

"But... she isn't wearing a ring."

Baron gently pulled her back against him. "I'm hoping to make things more official *after* closing time."

Gypsy swallowed hard, but kept her gaze locked with Blaine's.

The young man smiled. "She's the kind of woman you can't easily forget. She grabs hold of something deep down inside of you."

"Yes," Baron whispered. "I know exactly what you mean."

"I'll be back, Ms. Gypsy," Blaine said through a shy smile. "Consider me a regular from now on."

She smiled softly. "That is very kind of you, Blaine."

"And I have no intention of stopping…" He nodded toward her clasped hands. "…until I see a ring on that finger."

"But… I'm so much older than you."

"So what."

"So what? Blaine, you've got some of your most incredible years just ahead. Don't waste them on the likes of me. Find an amazing young girl to start your life with."

"I already have." He smiled sweetly. "And if that cold-eyed man holding you isn't quick about it… I'll make you fall for me just as hard as I fell for you." He winked. "I can be quite charming… when I want to be."

When Baron slid his arms around her waist, Gypsy almost protested.

"Challenge accepted, young Blaine," he said with a smile. "But know this. Whether Ms. Rodden realizes it yet or not… She. Is. Mine."

When the young man walked off, Gypsy waited for Baron to release her. He did not.

"Umm… Mr. Bishop, that whole Creepy Meter thing we were talking about before—"

"How can you still be on about that? We have moved way past perfect strangers, have we not? I would consider us friends by now."

"Yes, well… friends or not, you are still my potential employer, Mr. Bishop. And such being the case, *this* sort of closeness is completely unacceptable."

He stiffened with her words. Gypsy quietly waited until he finally released her.

"It is as you say, Ms. Rodden. My apologies. I forgot my place."

She smiled softly. "No worries. It's been a long day... for both of us."

⸺◈⸺

When the bar was finally empty and the till reconciled, Gypsy fell against Gillis's chest, draping her arms over his shoulders as she sighed wearily.

"I am done for, Gills. You're gonna have to carry me to bed. I can't take another step."

"As ye wish, Kitten. Climb on up here."

"Bed?" Baron stood up. "But... we have yet to finish our meeting."

She groaned. "Aww, come on. Seriously?"

He nodded. "Although we have spent the last several hours together, we have yet to actually speak properly. Now that your day has wound down, I would like to talk with you."

"Can we do it upstairs?"

"Upstairs?"

"Aye, we live up there," Gillis added.

"You *live* upstairs? Together?"

Gillis chuckled. "Nae as *together* as I'd like, mind ye. But she's one tough cookie tae crack."

Gypsy turned around with a smile. "I would be honored for you to visit my home, Mr. Bishop." She motioned for him to follow her. "Come on up and make yourself comfortable."

At the top of the small flight of steps, Baron was surprised by what he saw. The brightly lit marble landing was cut short by an immense metal door. He watched closely as Gypsy placed her palm to the black screen mounted on the wall.

A soothing computer voice surrounded them. "Hello, Gypsy Rodden. Please proceed with voice activation."

"Hey, House. I'm home."

"Welcome back, Ms. Rodden. State the number of guests."

"Two."

"Guest one, proceed."

Gillis lifted her out of the way as he placed his palm where hers had been.

41

"Hello, Gillis McCullough. Please proceed with voice activation."

"Aye, Lass. I'm home."

"Welcome home, Mr. McCullough."

"Guest two, proceed."

When Baron only stood there, speechless, Gypsy lifted his wrist and gently placed his palm on the blackened screen.

"Guest two… unknown. Please state your name."

When he glanced at Gypsy, she smiled and motioned for him to answer.

"Baron Bishop."

"Hello, Baron Bishop. Will data be saved for future access?"

"Nope," Gypsy replied.

"Future access for Baron Bishop… denied by Gypsy Rodden."

He could hear the tumblers start turning over within the thick metal door as they waited for the green light to come on.

Baron brushed her hair back before leaning down to whisper in her ear. "So… I have been denied by Gypsy Rodden."

She chuckled. "Well, I'm all but certain you didn't want your fingerprints and voice waves to be permanently stored within my security system."

"Security system, huh? Seems like some awfully high level clearance stuff just to get into a simple apartment. Tell me. Why fingerprint data *and* voice activation?"

She shrugged her shoulders. "So someone can't kill me and just chop off my hands to gain access. Oh, and the voice activation notices the slightest fluctuation in sound waves. Meaning, it can tell if I'm under duress. Like… if some dude has a gun to my back and is *making* me talk."

"I see. So… I take it you don't have many uninvited guests."

"Nope. None at all."

"What if I choose to stop by unannounced?"

"You'll have to text me first. From the inside, you just gotta turn the knob."

"Is that so?"

"Yeah. I'm trying to keep people out. Not lock them in. *That* would be called a prison."

Gillis chuckled. "Aye, or a dungeon."

She snickered. "Of which I have neither."

"Pity," Baron whispered as he stepped into her home… and was struck speechless.

Gypsy smiled. "Not what you were expecting, huh?"

"I wouldn't expect a place like this no matter how strange a door I had to walk through. You may not know this yet, Ms. Rodden, but I am a man who is extremely hard to impress."

"Yeah, I figured that," she mumbled.

"Yet *you*…" Baron glanced sideways at her. "You seem to be able to do so with ease."

Gypsy inhaled deeply, puffing out her chest and stretching her arms wide. "You feel that, Gillis?"

The Scotsman rolled his eyes. "Feel what, Kitten? The power?"

"Yes!" She exhaled loudly. "I *love* the way it feels coursing through me. Kneel at my feet, puny mortals."

Gillis tossed her a beer while she still had her arms spread.

"Put a cork in it, Goddess," he mumbled.

She gasped as she barely caught the bottle before it slammed into her stomach.

"Ye want a beer, Pope?"

"That will be fine, yes."

"Bottle alright? Or do ye need a mug?"

"A bottle is fine."

Gypsy twisted off the beer cap, held it between her thumb and middle finger, then snapped. The spinning little metal disk flew across the room and hit Gillis squarely between his shoulder blades. He stiffened before slowly turning around.

"Ye remember what I told ye would happen the next time ye did that, Kitten? Dunnae play dumb with me, Lass. As soon as yer company's gone, I'm gonna bend ye over my knee."

"Please. Don't let my presence interfere," Baron said. "Commence with her punishment. I will wait."

Gypsy snorted. "You wish. On your best days, neither one of you could hold me down unless I allowed it."

"Ye may be right, Kitten. But there's two of us here now. Wanna try yer luck?"

She sighed as she collapsed into a large fluffy chair. "It's almost four in the morning. I don't feel like playing anymore. Come, Gillis. Service me."

Baron only managed to pull his stunned gaze from her profile when Gillis handed him the beer.

"Sorry, mate. She gets like this in the wee hours. Have a seat. Let me see tae my mistress afore she starts pouting."

Baron Bishop didn't speak, but he didn't sit down, either. His breath caught when Gypsy suddenly stood and reached up under her short kilt. He heard the unmistakable sound of tearing velcro. Tiny beads of sweat popped out on his forehead. His knuckles went white as he gripped the beer bottle ever tighter.

"I hate that damn thing," she said, tossing the black thigh strap with the tiny knife onto the coffee table. "Trace must have been out of his mind when he thought of that."

"Aye, but it saved yer wee arse tonight, did it nae?"

"Nope. That was all you, my brawny Scotsman. Come on, Gills." She plopped back down on the chair. "You're taking forever."

"And yer whining like a spoiled wee bairn. Ye still have yer apron on tae boot."

Gypsy sighed. "Ugh…"

She untied the fully stuffed black garment and turned it upside down. Money spilled out all over the white rug.

"Nae too bad, Kitten. Looks like yer still keeping all yer men happy."

She half grinned. "Of course I am. It's what I do best."

"Is that… your tips?" Baron asked.

"*That* is, yeah." She pointed to the pile of paper money. "*This*…" She picked up a neatly folded wad of twenties. "…is a special gift from my Vets." She quickly counted it. "Four hundred even." She tossed it to Gillis. "That goes in petty cash. I got out four hundred earlier to cover the extra I promised the band."

He only nodded as he opened a white metal box on the counter and tossed it inside.

"Tell me," Baron said softly. "Why did you let those veterans fondle you, but not the boy?"

Gypsy shot him a venomous glare. "The veterans did not *fondle* me. They may look and they may whistle, but they *never* touch. They know how to show respect even while having a good time. In turn… I dote on them, dance with them, laugh at their jokes. Nothing is more sacred to me than a man or woman who has given up the best years of their life so that I can live as freely as I wish."

"Apologies. My words were not meant as an accusation— curiosity only. So… what do you do with all of this high praise and worship money?" He motioned with a nod to the bills scattered upon the floor.

Gypsy smiled and then lifted the corner of the large white coffee table. Her thigh strap skidded off onto the floor. Baron's eyes went wide at the large chest hidden underneath. It was filled to the brim with neatly stacked bills and bags of coins.

"Surprised?" she said through a smirking smile.

Baron only nodded in response.

"Heh… Big enough to hide a couple of bodies in, right?" She winked and smiled again.

"Gyps, yer an idiot." Gillis snorted. "I dunnae think the *size* of yer secret honey-hole is what surprised him."

She only laughed as she quickly sorted out the different denominations into their proper places.

"It's aboot full again, Kitten. Yer gonna have tae break down and take it tae the bank, sooner or later."

She sighed and fell back into her chair. "I just don't feel like it, Gills. Now, come. Service your mistress. I have *need* of you."

"Yeah, yeah. Dunnae go and get yer knickers in a knot. I'm coming."

When the large Scotsman kneeled in front of her, removed her boots and began massaging her feet, Baron slowly released his held breath. He wasn't certain if he was relieved, or disappointed. What *had* he wanted to see happen? He wasn't completely sure.

"Hey, Gills," she whispered softly. "I love you. I'd never make it without you."

"I'm the one who'd nae be able tae make it, Lass. If I lost my wee Kitten, I couldnae go on."

He lightly kissed her lips, then gave her a big hug. Gypsy winced at the contact, sucking air in through her teeth.

"Sorry, Kitten. I forgot aboot yer hip. Here… let me have a look-see."

Gillis carefully slid the band of her kilt down to expose the dark purple spot near her left hip bone. He placed a tiny kiss beside it.

"This one is as bad as I've seen in a while, Kitten."

"I know." She brushed away a tear. "It hurts like hell. And it's only gotten worse as the night went on."

They both turned to look at the cold-eyed man who was intently watching their tender exchange.

Baron's chest tightened when his gaze locked on the large bruise Gillis was lightly circling with his fingertip. He thought back to her earlier confession... *It felt like a dagger pierced me to its hilt.* When he realized they were both staring at him, Baron spoke.

"You two share the most unique D/s relationship I have ever seen. I've been studying the dynamics of it from the moment I first saw you together. Still... I haven't quite figured it out. It is both enchanting, as well as discombobulating."

Gypsy cocked one eyebrow. "Our what?"

"Your D/s bond. Never have I seen the like."

"What the hell is a D/s bond? You mean... like a video game or something?"

Gillis snorted out a laugh as he buried his face between her breasts.

"What? What's so funny?"

"He's nae talking aboot a video game, my wee darlin'. He means a Dom/sub relationship. He is trying tae figure oot who is the Dominant and who's the submissive."

"Submissive?" She looked from her dear friend to her potential boss. "You mean like... that bondage sex stuff?" She snorted out a laugh. "Yeah, like I'd ever bend over and let some dude whip me."

"Then... *you* are the Dominant," Baron said. "I sort of thought that was the case."

Gillis and Gypsy immediately looked at each other, before bursting into laughter.

"Then... I am mistaken?"

Gypsy gasped. "Wait. Hold on. Hold on. Let me catch my breath." She sighed happily. "Whew... That was the funniest damn thing I've heard in ages."

"What my rude wee Kitten is trying tae say is... Nae. We dunnae have a D/s relationship."

"Yeah. In fact, our relationship consists of no sex at all—kinky *or* otherwise," she said.

"Well now, Kitten. There was that one time when we were trying oot all those new martini flavors."

"That doesn't count." She scrunched up her brows, half pouting. "I don't even remember the whole of it."

"Remember it or nae, ye couldnae sit down that next day withoot making a funny squeaking noise."

"That's not fair." She playfully hit his chest. "And besides… I could barely sit down for *two* days, I was so sore."

"Aye, ye should have let me work ye through the pain, Lass. I remember well how I made ye purr, whether *ye* do or nae."

When he started to tickle her, Gypsy winced again. Gillis looked at the bruise, and then to Baron Bishop.

"What was it that made ye think we had a Dom/sub connection?"

"Many things," Baron said. "For starters… the way you have pet names for each other that no one else calls you by. It was obvious they weren't simply nicknames."

"Yeah." Gypsy snorted. "If any other man called me Kitten, I'd throat-punch him."

"He not only called you Kitten…" Baron said. "…he has referred to you as Mistress on several different occasions. Then, there's the way you almost purred when he slapped your bottom."

"That wasn't a purr. It was a laugh."

"Nae, Kitten. I make ye purr. Admit it."

Gypsy giggled.

"It wasn't just those common things, either," Baron continued. "It was the way you seemed to be constantly connected to each other—the way you shared breath to relax, each knowing what the other needed almost before they did. It happened all night long. You share an unspoken spiritual connection. You orbit each other, move in unison. Then, there were the more obvious references… topping from the bottom, demanding he service you, him threatening to punish you. The list goes on and on."

"But…" Gypsy furrowed her brow. "Us *vanilla* people can have strong connections as well."

"This is true. Apologies. I realized my mistake as soon as I began to question you. By then, the *kitten* was out of the bag, so to speak."

"Tell me true, Pope," Gillis said. "Do ye have a D/s relationship with some lass?"

"Not currently. No, I do not."

"A lad, then?"

"No. That is not my preference."

"But ye *are* a Dom, are ye nae? I mean, there's nae way in hell a man with eyes like yers would submit tae anyone."

Baron sat down and elegantly crossed his legs as he leaned back, draping his arms across the back of the couch.

"Although I do not make it a habit of speaking about it in the vanilla world… Yes, I am a Dom."

Gypsy let out a tiny cry and grabbed her hip. Gillis held her hand while the dark spot slowly faded back to its normal light brown color. Once again, Baron was struck speechless.

"Thank you, Mr. Bishop," she said, sighing. "Thank you for revealing your secret and relieving my pain."

The man furrowed his brow. "What are you implying? Are you saying that *I* was the one to cause your injury?"

"It's nae an injury," Gillis said softly. "It's a birthmark… of sorts."

Gypsy nodded. "Yeah. But it only ever acts up when I'm in close proximity to someone who is desperately trying to hide something from me."

"Explain," Baron said flatly.

"Well… it doesn't work just because someone is hiding something or just has a secret. It only happens when they are trying to hide it from *me*."

"Meaning?"

"Meaning…" Gypsy sighed. "If you have a secret, it's yours. Plain as that. But let's say for some reason you don't want *me* particularly to know that secret… then *this* happens." She motioned to her now normal-looking birthmark.

"That is simply ridiculous," Baron grumbled under his breath.

"Aye, mate. Ye saw the proof of it with yer own eyes. Did ye nae?"

Baron didn't answer the man.

Gypsy smiled. "It comes in quite handy—being a lawyer and all. I can tell when someone hasn't laid all their cards out on the table, when they're hiding something from me."

"How can that ever be a good thing—walking around in pain all the time?" Baron's voice seemed strained.

Gypsy's smile softened. "It's okay. It doesn't hurt *all* the time. For instance… the further I move away from the person, the more the pain fades. Like… if a client is hiding something from me, I would know—physically. The pain would remain until I convinced that person to confide in me, or until we finally parted."

"Aye, but it comes right back as soon as she's around that person again."

"Yes." Gypsy nodded. "If they have not told me their secret—revealed all their cards—the pain will return each time the person does."

"I see," Baron mumbled. "So that's why you said you wouldn't be able to work for me… if you had to live with that kind of pain."

"Aye, now yer getting it, Pope."

"It's just because it's so different with a client, as opposed to an employer," she said. "The client will eventually walk out of the office. The boss… I'll see him on a daily basis."

Baron only stared at her, still unsure if he could possibly believe what it was he was hearing.

"One thing I dunnae get, though."

They both looked to the Scotsman before he continued.

"It only ever bothers ye if it sort of concerns ye. Right?"

Gypsy nodded.

Gillis looked then to Baron. "Then why is the fact that he's a closet Dom, something he'd want tae keep from ye? It's nae like ye'd care what kind of freaky sex yer boss was intae. I mean… ye'd only just met him, had ye nae?"

"I am *not* a closet Dom," Baron said. "I practice freely and openly. As I said before, it is not always something immediately noticeable to the eyes of the unlearned."

"Aye, but why did ye care if my wee Kitten knew? If yer so open and free with it—"

"I was *not* trying to hide it."

"Aye, but her hip says different."

Gypsy stared at the handsome man with her favorite kind of dimples, and nervously waited for his answer.

Baron took a drink of beer, then blew out a long breath. "Today may have been the first time Ms. Rodden had laid eyes on me, yes." He met Gypsy gaze. "But the same does not hold true on my side."

"And how's that?" Gillis furrowed his brow. "Are ye a stalker?"

"Nothing of the sort." Baron kept his gaze locked with Gypsy's. "I saw Ms. Rodden when she showed up for her initial interview. I found her... intriguing."

"I don't remember seeing *you*."

"You did not." He smiled softly. "Normally, I don't get involved in that stage of employment. Yet, your credentials were quite impressive on paper—graduating with honors from Oxford. And then when the whole office started buzzing about the brunette with long curls and extremely high heels... I had to see for myself."

"My heels aren't *that* high."

Baron cast her a sideways glance and half smiled, displaying one of those dimples that nearly made her swoon.

"They *are* that high, Ms. Rodden. It doesn't appear so to you because you are on the short side."

"Hey!"

Gillis muffled a laugh.

"I watched the entire thing," Baron said.

"The entire what? Interview?"

He nodded. "Yes. I watched you work those four cocky hard-asses over until they were putty in your pretty little hands. Before you even made it out the front door, they already had an office pool going over which one would *bang* you first."

"Heh." She snorted. "Like I'd ever sleep with a man I could physically beat the hell out of. I will *never* be that desperate."

Baron smiled. "I thought as much."

"Oh, really?" She chuckled. "And why's that?"

"When you left... I followed you to the gym."

"Wha— You belong to Tony's?"

"No, Ms. Rodden." Baron shook his head. "But Tony *is* an old friend of mine."

Gillis made a deep growling type noise. "So ye *are* a stalker."

"Calm down, Mr. McCullough. I was not stalking your lovely friend, there. I was merely trying to discover her interests. As I have already explained to Ms. Rodden, I like to meet with each potential candidate on a more personal level before I offer them a contract. Seeing as how Ms. Rodden would be the first female attorney to join our ranks, I was uncertain how to proceed. I followed her to try and get an idea. I already knew I wanted to hire her, I just wasn't entirely certain exactly how that meeting should be held."

"And what did following her tae the gym reveal tae ye?"

"Well… when I saw her pummeling that punching bag, I no longer harbored doubts concerning whether she could handle herself around so many hungry men." He smiled softly. "She will be commanding their respect in no time."

Gypsy didn't speak. She was too busy playing out different torture scenarios concerning those *hungry men* he had just mentioned.

"I sorta get what yer saying, Pope. But what I still cannae figure oot is… why ye felt the need tae hide yer sexual fetishes from my wee Kitten."

Baron didn't respond.

Gillis smiled down at her. "Seems ye have another admirer, Gyps. I dunnae believe those other men are the only ones trying tae figure oot how tae slip inside that wee skirt of yers."

"That's not true," Gypsy protested, turning toward the man who would soon be her boss. "Tell him, Mr. Bishop. Tell him he has it wrong."

Baron remained silent.

"He cannae, Lass. If he wasnae entertaining thoughts of what he'd like tae do tae ye, why would he care if ye knew his secret? Why would ye have been in so much pain?"

She only stared at the elegant looking man through pleading eyes.

"Fear not, Ms. Rodden," Baron finally said. "I have no ill intentions concerning you, nor will I delve into the taboo no-no's of employee and employer relationships."

She smiled, relieved.

"Aye, is that so? Then tell me. Why did her pain only get worse as the night wore on? The longer ye were with her, the darker her mark grew. What was playing aboot in yer twisted wee mind while ye watched her working the bar?"

Baron gazed into Gypsy's honey bourbon eyes. "You must forgive me, Ms. Rodden. You are an extremely attractive, confident woman… and I am merely a man. Yet, no matter my private desires concerning you, what I said before holds true. You have nothing to fear from me—sexually or otherwise."

When she smiled that time, Baron could see the relief sparkling in her lovely warm eyes.

"Thank you, Mr. Bishop."

He only nodded toward her via response.

"Heh." Gillis chuckled. "It's nae like ye can hold fault with the man for playing oot fantasies aboot ye, Lass. Remember, he heard ye admit tae all those wicked wee thoughts ye were having aboot *him* as well."

Gypsy only blushed.

"Now then," Baron said, sitting his beer down and looking around their unusual home. "I wish to know more about this incredible little hide-a-way you've got here. How in the world did you come by it?"

"Aye, we built it."

"You built it? You mean… by yourselves?"

"Well, not wholly," she said. "We bought the building, then gutted it and made it our own."

"You and Gillis?"

She nodded. "And Trace. We had to hire a few of the bits done. But we did what we could ourselves—save money."

"It belonged tae my uncle," Gillis added. "It was a six story apartment building with a bar down below. When he decided tae move back tae his home country—"

"We jumped at the chance," Gypsy said.

"Aye. We kept the pub as it was."

"Yeah. But we saved the rest for ourselves. First, we gutted it—floor to roof."

"I can see that," Baron mumbled, tilting his head for a better view.

"The first three floors we just left completely open," she said. "It's where we live—our commons area. I *love* how big and open it feels."

"Those two giant curved staircases, there." Gillis nodded to the center of the room. "Those were a gift from Trace tae Gyps. She kept going on and on aboot some old movie she'd seen."

Gypsy smiled. "Yeah… but they tie in beautifully to the surrounding walkway up there."

Baron followed where she was pointing out the glass railing completely encompassing what used to be the fourth floor of the building. Each of the top three floors had a walkway with matching glass railing going around the *left-open* part of that floor—just above where they now sat.

"We had tae leave some bits for structural purposes," Gillis said.

"And to meet the fire codes," Gypsy added.

"Aye. And where those two ridiculously large staircases meet in the center down here on the first floor…" He pointed. "…that's where the elevator tae our bedrooms is located."

Baron looked at the glass elevator that ran from floor to ceiling. Although the part where they were now sitting was completely open—six stories high—the back half of the large room was only three stories high. Above that, the elevator went up to three different sets of double doors, one on each floor of what used to be the top three floors.

"You mean… your bedrooms are an entire floor of an apartment building?"

"Well, just half an entire floor." She pointed up again. "We left this whole half open to the roof. Remember?"

"Still, that is an extraordinary amount of space for a single bedroom."

"I know. It's awesome." She giggled. "Trace lives there at the bottom—those first set of doors. Gillis is all the way at the top. And *my* room is sandwiched in-between them, on the fifth floor. There… in the middle."

"I see."

When Baron looked back at her, Gypsy was smiling at him. Her sparkling eyes pulled a matching smile from him in return.

"Even though they didn't say it out loud, they put me in the middle so it would be harder to get to me. You have to get past Trace if you're coming from down here."

"And I've got the roof covered," Gillis said. "She'll nae be having visitors withoot it being public knowledge."

Baron's smile widened. "That's good to know, but probably unnecessary." He motioned toward the front door. "Who could possibly get inside?"

"That was Trace's idea," Gypsy said. "He was working in a lab near here—that's where he got a job when we first moved back to the States. When the lab moved, the city decided to tear it down and build a shopping mall, I think. Anyway, *that's* where the high security clearance door came from. I think it was where they kept the alien cadavers or something."

Gillis pinched her. "Yer an idiot, Kitten."

Gypsy chuckled.

"That door isnae all we got from that lab."

"Yeah. We were super lucky. The elevator, most of our appliances, the interior doors, the trim work… even some of our furniture came from there."

"Aye. As long as we had the muscle tae move it, it was ours for the taking."

"The whole back side of these bottom three floors—back behind the staircase—that's where the main kitchen is, the laundry room, workout stuff, a couple of guest bathrooms… you know, stuff like that is located."

"But Gyps insisted on having that breakfast nook over there in the corner." Gillis glanced back to the fridge where he had gotten the beers when they'd first entered. "She likes things handy."

"Well, that's because the real kitchen is *huge*."

"Nae. It's because ye cannae reach the cabinets."

She blushed. "Yeah… that, too."

"Trace spoils ye, Lass."

"No. He just didn't wanna have to come downstairs every single time I wanted to make a cup of tea."

"Because yer just a wee bairn who can't even reach her own teacup."

When she punched him, Gillis only laughed.

Baron couldn't help noticing how the two of them smiled at each other as they walked him through their happy memories together.

"Where is this Trace?" Baron asked. "I have yet to meet him."

A shadow suddenly fell over Gypsy's smile. Tears fast filled her honey-colored eyes.

"He's away," she whispered. "…Like always."

"He's a doctor," Gillis added, wiping her cheeks as she stared blindly toward the ceiling. "He's in the— Wait. Where is he right now, Gyps?"

"Africa… last I heard."

"Aye, Africa. He's hell bent on saving the world, all by himself."

When Gypsy sniffed, Gillis softly kissed her forehead.

"If ye think me and Kitten are close, Pope, ye should see the two of them. It's like they occupy the same space—one always shadowing the other. Nae one can make her smile like Trace can." He kissed her again. "He owns yer heart. Ain't that right, Kitten?"

She only nodded in silence.

"So... Trace is your boyfriend?"

"Nae. Naethin' as mundane as that," Gillis answered in her stead. "It's more like... they share the same soul. I cannae explain it. Ye've just got tae see it with yer own eyes. They wake at the same time, sleep at the same time, order each other's food. They eat off the same plate, use each other's toothbrush... they even piss in front of each other withoot batting a lash. I've seen them carry on entire conversations withoot saying a single word. They just look intae each other's eyes and bam... they come up with the exact same decision. It's eerie. When they're together, they give me the creeps."

Baron was listening to everything the other man was saying, but his gaze and his thoughts were all on Gypsy. When she looked the way she did now—full of obvious sorrow and pain—it tugged at his heart, made his chest hurt.

"They have cell phones, but they dunnae need 'em. I've seen Trace tear oot of here like a bat outta hell, only tae return a while later carrying Gypsy caused she'd crilled her ankle in those damn shoes she wears. Once, the two of us were oot getting supplies... he liked tae have killed the both of us—turning around in the middle of the highway like that. He raced right up ontae the curb ootside Tony's place."

"What happened?"

Gypsy looked over at Baron. "I broke my hand... punching on the large bag."

"Pfft." Gillis snorted. "Ye broke yer wee pinkie. That's all."

"But... how did Trace know?" Baron asked.

Gillis shrugged his shoulders. "Like I said, they're creepy... linked in some cosmic way the rest of us cannae understand."

"Like twins?"

"Who knows?" Gillis shook his head. "They ain't kin... but they're still the same person."

Baron could no longer stand her constant, silent tears. He cleared his throat and determined to change the subject.

"Ms. Rodden?"

Gypsy glanced toward him.

"How is it you came by a law degree from Oxford, when your accent clearly marks you as Southern?"

Her tears came in earnest then.

"Will you excuse me, please?" she barely managed to say.

Baron quickly stood when Gypsy jumped up and ran toward the back of the large room, ducking behind one of the winding staircases before disappearing entirely.

"Let her be, Pope. She'll be fine. She just needs a minute tae herself. That's all."

"I didn't mean to—"

Gillis held his hand up, ceasing the other man's words. "Ye didnae do anything wrong." He glanced to where she had run off to. "And I'll tell ye for why. It'd be too painful for her. She wouldnae mind ye knowing this bit aboot her, she'd just nae be able tae get it all oot."

Baron quietly sat back down and waited.

"It all started back in their first year of college. They went tae the same university, but it was a big place. They didnae know one another. Gyps was on her way back from an evening class. A drunk driver ran the red light and hit her."

"Was she driving?"

"Nae. Walking."

Baron suddenly had a painful lump form in his throat, one he couldn't swallow down.

"She was crossing the street when he hit her. Nae one is certain the real damage caused by *that* collision, because the impact knocked her oot intae the intersection."

"…No."

Gillis solemnly nodded. "Aye. Right oot intae oncoming traffic. As soon as her wee body hit the pavement, a motorcycle ran over her… here." He motioned across his lower stomach with a wave of his hand. "The poor lad nae seen her coming. Their impact threw him a ways on oot past her—messed him up pretty bad. *That* lad happened to be Trace's roommate. They were oot riding taegether. When Trace saw the accident, he jumped off his bike. Just jumped off… let it slide on its side through the intersection."

"Was he hurt?"

"Nae. He jumped off tae protect *her*—threw his body over hers. He told me once... he didnae even think aboot it. His body moved on its own. His buddy was lying in the street a few yards away, but that girl was all he could think aboot. He would die afore he let one more thing touch her." Gillis sighed and shook his head. "The EMTs had a hell of a time trying tae convince him they werenae going tae hurt her. When they got tae the hospital, Trace swore they were all family—got his roommate *and* the girl in the same room. After each had gotten oot of surgery, that is. His buddy had a couple broken bones and some serious road rash, but Gypsy was hurt real bad. I cannae remember how many bones he said were broken. Alls I remember... was the internal damage."

Baron's jaws began to ache. When he realized he was clenching his teeth, he had to keep telling himself to stop. Gillis brought him a fresh beer, then sat down beside him.

"Well... seeing as how Trace had convinced the staff they were all siblings, the doctors immediately came tae him when she needed blood. And... as strange as everything else aboot their bond, they were a perfect match. Aye, but blood wasnae all they ended up needing. Afore it was all said and done, Trace had set himself up tae be her personal living donation bank. They took some blood, some skin, even one of his kidneys. Aye, nearly had tae cut him in two tae get it."

Baron felt his strength slowly leaving his body. He slumped back against the couch.

Gillis paused and glanced towards the back of the room before continuing.

"When Trace finally came around from surgery, Gypsy was in a coma and his buddy was sitting beside her bed holding her hand. The lad had cried himself tae sleep right there... and there he stayed. Trace and Gyps were the ones sharing the room now, but his buddy nae left her side. When the doctors were certain Trace was coherent enough tae understand them, they told him the bad news."

Baron's eyes widened as he sat up straight.

"Nae matter what all Trace was willing tae give up for her, the one thing she now needed... he didnae have—female stuff. The motorcycle had crushed all her internal girlie bits. She had undergone a complete hysterectomy while they were in there replacing her kidney."

Tears dripped off Baron's chin. He didn't even bother wiping them.

"Trace's buddy… he lost it when he heard the news— blamed himself for the whole thing, seeing as how it was *his* bike what had crushed her. They've been a part of each other from that day 'til this… spiritually *and* physically."

"That's… the saddest thing I've ever heard."

"Aye, it is." Gillis sighed. "When they finally got oot of the hospital, they had tae get an apartment taegether—the three of 'em. Trace and Gyps couldnae sleep unless one was touching the other… like babes in the same womb. The buddy doted on her day and night. Oot of love or guilt… who knows? But the three of them were inseparable. When Trace received an invitation from Oxford School of Medicine, the buddy asked his parents tae set up a trust for Gypsy's schooling… seeing as how she'd only been able tae afford college through grants and scholarships. The lad's parents did it withoot hesitation. After that, he seemed satisfied… found his peace, I guess. Anyway, Gyps got accepted tae law school there and they left the States on the same plane… side by side."

"So they left for England… just the two of them?"

Gillis nodded and smiled. "Bound for Oxford… and a brand new start. Trace became obsessed in his research. He desperately tried tae find a way tae give her back what she had lost… give her the joy of knowing wee bairns, of being able tae one day feel the tiny miracle growing in her tummy."

"He found nothing?"

"How can ye repair what nae longer exists?" Gillis shook his head. "Nae. He nae found the answer, but he nae gave up. Still hasnae, I suppose. I believe he roams the planet now—helping poor unfortunate woman—as a sort of penance, ye see… taeward Gyps."

"And in so doing… he must separate from the one woman who treasures and needs him above all."

"Aye." He sighed. "It was always just the two of them. I didnae know 'em back then. I lived in Aberfoyle, Scotland. When my uncle decided tae move back home, his best friend mentioned it tae Trace. He was one of his professors—asked what part of America Trace was from, then asked if he'd be interested in buying a pub." Gillis chuckled. "I met the two of them because I offered tae come over and help them get started. And... I nae went back home."

"Why did you choose to stay?"

"At first, it was the weather. Have ye ever been tae Scotland, Pope? After living oot here in California, I couldnae imagine having tae go back tae all that rain and cold."

"...And?" Baron prodded.

Gillis blushed slightly. "And... I fell in love with the wee Kitten. We all three just blended taegether like we'd been born that way. I dunnae have the connection *they* share, nae, but we are perfectly matched tae one another. I dunnae know how else tae explain it. We love her. We protect her, dote on her... a bit too much, most times. Yet, it goes deeper than that. We're like family... but so much more."

"Hey! Who wants some watermelon?"

Both men jumped when she suddenly came back into the room, smiling like nothing had ever happened.

Gillis chuckled. "Bloody hell, Kitten. Ye gonna start on the watermelon *now*? Ye need tae get that sweet little arse off tae bed."

"Yes." Baron stood. "I probably should be going."

"It's Saturday," she said dismissively. "You don't have to work. Please? Just a little?"

Baron smiled. "Of course, Ms. Rodden. I would love to have some watermelon with you."

"*Aye, he* might nae have tae work on Saturdays, but *we* do, Lass."

"I know. I know. I'll go to bed soon. I promise." She got the large pink bowl out of the fridge and plopped down beside Baron. "Salt or no?"

He chuckled. "Whatever you prefer."

Baron reached over and gently took a lock of her hair between his fingers. Gypsy flinched from the familiar acting touch, but once her heart slowed back down, she sort of enjoyed how calm he was making her feel.

"Watermelon at five in the morning," Baron half whispered. "Strange breakfast or healthy breakfast—I cannot decide."

She giggled softly. "Watermelon is good no matter the time—God's perfect gift."

"So… you like watermelon, I see."

"Aye, the lass would live off of it if she could."

She smiled. "Yep. Watermelon—better than roses for saying I'm sorry."

"Better than roses?" Baron chuckled softly. "If a man were *truly* sorry, he would say it with diamonds."

"Pffts, whatever." She motioned toward Gillis. "There's nothing better than pretending that old softie over there hurt my feelings. He always brings me watermelon… and a new video game if I act *real* hurt."

"Old softie, aye?" Gillis snorted. "Yer spoiled. What I *should* do when ye pout like that, is turn yer pretty arse pink with the palm of my hand… then give ye something that's nae where near *soft*."

"Pervert."

"Aye, that be the truth of it."

They both looked at each other and just smiled. Baron didn't miss the sparkle they exchanged.

"Why do you not have sex with Gillis?"

The Scotsman half choked on his beer.

Gypsy looked to him, then back to Baron.

"Y-you mean… have sex with him *now*?"

Baron smiled. "No. I mean have sex with him… ever. You obviously love the man. Why do you withhold your passions?"

"I do love Gillis." She turned back to the now blushing Scot. "Just look at him. Not only is he the most tender, sweetest man on the planet… he's about as sexy as they come—broad shoulders, chiseled abs, ruggedly handsome face. Oh, and that accent. Girls get wet just listening to him talk."

"Yes," Baron said. "These things are all obvious. So tell me. Why do you withhold your love from him?"

"Ugh… you make it sound like I'm some sort of prude or something. Like I have this *thing* against intimacy."

"Do you not?"

"No." She would have crossed her arms, had she not been holding the big bowl of watermelon. "I'm not a prude. And I'm not scared, either. I date."

"Is that so?"

"Yes. I've dated lots of guys. Tell him, Gillis."

He snorted. "Aye, she dates. Her favorites are those pretty wee ninjas."

Gypsy rolled her eyes. "Just because they are Asian doesn't make them a ninja."

"So... you like Asian men?"

"Aye. Those *lovely* wee Japanese lads are her favorites."

"That's not true, Gills. Stop teasing me."

"Then tell me, Ms. Rodden. If you have no problem with intimacy, why do you run from that handsome man over there?"

She sighed. "I guess... I guess... I withhold my love for Gillis *because* I love him so much."

"...Kitten," he whispered softly.

She blushed and looked away.

Baron continued to stroke her hair, coaxing her to go on. "Explain that to me, lovely lady."

Gypsy swallowed hard. "Just look at him. He's perfect."

"Yes, he is. And so are you."

"No. I would never do that to Gillis. He deserves someone better than me. If I give in to that temptation... he may never find the woman who's *truly* meant for him. He'd quit looking. I know he would."

"What if he has already found the woman who's truly meant for him? What if that someone... is you?"

"No." She shook her head. "It's not me. I know this."

"How, lovely lady? How do you know you are not his perfect mate?"

"I know because I am... because I am..."

"Because you are what?"

A single tear slid down her cheek. "Because I am... broken."

Silence filled the room.

Gillis wanted to scoop her up in his arms, but knew he would never be able to hold back his burning tears if he touched her now.

"With perfect genes like his..." she barely whispered. "...he should be allowed to pass them on."

"Lass, look at me."

Gypsy hesitated a moment, then complied.

"Yer nae broken, my wee darlin'. Yer absolutely perfect in every way. Kitten... ye are a treasure withoot equal." He smiled. "Now, forget aboot all those nasty things ye are wanting me tae do tae ye right now, and enjoy yer watermelon."

She snorted out a muffled laugh and then stabbed a piece with her fork.

"Here." She held it up to Baron. "It's awesome. I've already had some. Sweetest one I've bought all year."

He furrowed his brow as he looked down at the fruit-laden fork.

"What's wrong? Don't you like watermelon?"

"I do."

"Then open up."

"You mean… let you feed me?"

"Oh, don't be such a baby. Open up and say ahh."

He smiled softly, then opened his mouth. She gently placed it on his tongue and waited anxiously for his response.

"You are quite right, Ms. Rodden. It is delicious."

"I know, right? Here. Have another."

Baron didn't hesitate this time. He accepted the third proffered bite before speaking.

"So… you prefer Asian men. Why is that?"

"Because they are so elegant and lovely," Gillis said in a high-pitched voice before snorting. "She likes 'em dainty."

Gypsy looked at Baron and sort of rolled her eyes. "He's just trying to tease me again. I do not *prefer* dainty men."

"Well then, what *is* your preference?"

She shrugged her shoulders and continued feeding him. "I don't really have a preference, I guess. I mean… I'm not prejudiced or racist or even nationalist. I like *all* men. I find beauty in many different forms. I have dated American guys, of course. I've gone out with a couple of Australians, an Italian, a Canadian, tons of Brits. I have dated several Japanese men, yes. And… umm…"

"Dunnae forget that dark-haired man ye drooled all over."

"Oh, yeah… Manuel." She giggled. "He was a total fox. Looked just like Antonio Banderas. I wanted to *devour* him."

"Aye, and she fancied this Russian brute down at the gym."

"A Russian, huh?" Baron smiled. "I haven't met many *dainty* Russian men. Tell me, Ms. Rodden. Was he gentle with you?"

Gypsy shook her head and looked away.

"She cannae answer that one, Pope. She ran every time he came near her. He even showed up at the bar a few times, all brimming over with testosterones and that gruff accent. I hated it. He sounded like… Dasvidania, beautiful flower."

"He called me his beautiful *lily*." Gypsy chuckled. "And he didn't sound *anything* like that."

"Aye, she squeaked like a wee mouse every time the man got close tae her. He touched her hair once and I thought she was gonna jump clean oot of her skin."

"Were you afraid of him, lovely lady?"

Gypsy shook her head. "I wasn't *afraid* of him. I just… didn't feel worthy."

"And why is that? You are more than worthy for any man."

"…Russian women." She blushed. "I think Russian women are some of the loveliest in the world. They look like… like fairies or something. He could do better."

"Aye, Lass. Ye *are* an idiot."

"I must concur with Mr. McCullough on this one. You are as lovely as any fairy could hope to be. Here," Baron whispered, taking the readied fork from her hand. "My turn."

"Oh…"

Gypsy hesitated, not sure what to do.

"Open up. Turnabout is fair play, Ms. Rodden." He smiled. "Trust me. It's delicious."

"I know it is. I had some earlier," she mumbled softly, before slowly opening her mouth and accepting the juicy bite. "Mmm… sooo good."

"Yes, it is. Now, tell me more about these many boyfriends. Did they not please you?"

"Pffts." Gillis snorted. "They were nae *boyfriends*. When she says they dated, she means they went oot tae dinner a couple of times *if* the guy was lucky."

"I see. So… you denied intimacy to them as well."

She blushed again.

"Here. You've got a little…" Baron slowly slid his thumb along the bottom of her lip and put it to his mouth. "Yes… delicious," he whispered.

"And *that's* my cue tae go." Gillis stood up. "I cannae take anymore of this. I'm hitting the sheets. Ye two be good wee bairns now. Hey, Gyps."

She turned to look at him.

"Dunnae do anything with yer Pope ye wouldnae do with me."

She blushed. "You're such a pervert, Gills."

"Aye. All men are, Lass."

When the elevator doors closed, Baron leaned over and whispered into her curls.

"He's right, you know… all men are."

Chapter 5

They hadn't been alone for much more than half an hour when Baron felt her slumping against him. He was explaining how he had initially started his law office and what direction he had planned for the firm's future. When he got the part concerning full partnership responsibilities, her head fell over against his shoulder. Instead of waking her, he slowly stood up and lowered her onto the couch.

Baron gazed down at her sleeping face. "You are too unguarded, Ms. Rodden," he whispered. "I wonder... if you could look into my eyes now, would they still seem cold to you?" He smiled softly. "No. You would not see the ice, lovely lady. Now... now they burn."

Gypsy mumbled incoherently as she drew her knees up, curling onto her side. His breath hitched when her balled-up fists neared her mouth. He thought (he hoped) she was going to suck her thumb. She did not, only mumbled again.

"I know now why your Trace installed that front door." He knelt down beside the couch and brushed her hair back from her face. "I know why he built you this magnificently gilded cage and set a formidable watchdog as your roommate. It was to keep out men like me."

She rolled over, facing the other way. His gaze lingered on the curve beneath her t-shirt marking the tip of her shoulder blade. Baron reached for her, but didn't touch her—his hand hovering a fraction above her ribcage. He watched as her side slowly rose and fell—coming so close to his waiting palm, and then retreating as she exhaled. His intoxicated gaze outlined the soft curve of her back, the dip at her waist, and then the rise of her beautifully rounded hip. Baron Bishop drank in every last inch of her... and found not a single thing that displeased him.

"Physically, Ms. Gypsy Rodden... you are the sub of my dreams." He twisted one of her loose curls around his long, thin finger. "Why did you have to touch my heart, first? I had imagined you to be the *perfect* little plaything. Why did you mess that up? Why did you creep inside of me—lay claims to parts I have not yet explored? Tell me, lovely lady. How did such a sassy, confident, defiant little girl... steal away my will to tame you?" He sighed and glanced up toward her bedroom doors. "It would be ungentlemanly of me to go... or to stay. No matter the case, your competent watchdog would surely try to throttle me if I left you all alone down here like this."

When Baron slid his arms under her, Gypsy curled up against his chest and mumbled again.

"Perhaps I should just steal you away." He held her like that a few moments more, drinking in all that he desired... but could never have. "How long do you think it would take Gillis to find us, hmm? How long would I get to lock you away—caress your creamy skin, kiss those beautiful pink lips—before he busted down my door and reclaimed you? Two days? Three?" He sighed again as he headed toward the elevator. "Even if it took him years upon years... it would not be long enough. So for now, tiny angel, I will leave you in his capable care." He stepped through the sliding doors. "Until I can find a way to make you mine."

⊰⟨◆◆◆⟩⊱

Baron gently laid her down and pulled her covers up. Gypsy greedily snagged them, wrapping them over her shoulder as she curled back into a ball. He smiled softly, trying to think of an excuse to stay... knowing he could not.

A shadow fell across the room. Baron's peripheral caught the darkened outline of the tall Scotsman now leaning against her doorframe. He dared just a few more heartbeats in her presence before he joined the other man outside the room.

"Fell asleep on ye, did she?"

Baron only half smiled by way of response.

"I cannae for the life of me figure oot why she wants tae pursue her career. We have our hands full with the pub alone. She's nae hurting for money. The lass has all she needs." He snorted softly. "She told me... My soul begs me tae do it, Gills. Aye, *my* soul tells me she will wear herself oot—run down like one of those twirling dolls in a jewelry box. I dunnae like it, but I wulnae stop her."

"You mean… she plans to keep running the pub?"

"Aye, she does. What ye saw tonight, she'll be doing that six days a week. Same as always. The only difference will be… instead of sleeping, she'll be bouncing around yer office."

"I didn't realize… I will have to consider this when drawing up her contract."

Gillis didn't say anything more as the two men silently made their way back downstairs.

"Mr. McCullough?"

Gillis stopped and turned toward the other man, crossing his arms over his broad chest.

"I wish to be her Trace," Baron said.

"Eh? What the hell are ye on aboot now?"

Baron held out his arms, glancing around the room. "This is his version of her Fortress of Solitude, is it not?"

Gillis only cocked a single brow. He didn't speak.

"He has thought of everything he possibly can to protect her in his absence. I wish to extend her fortress to encompass my office as well. *I* will be her Trace when she walks out that door."

"Ye dunnae get it, Pope. She's full of spit and fire, that one. She doesnae need a gatekeeper. Do ye think he keeps her locked away because she's fragile? Nae. It's because she's precious… more precious than even his own life." He shook his head. "Ye've got it all wrong, Pope. Gypsy is a grown arse woman—able tae take care of herself, and mean as hell when she's cornered. Nae. She doesnae need yer protection. Yer respect—heh, she'll demand *that*. But if she thought for one minute ye were treating her as anything other than the fierce woman she is, ye'd see her claws… up close and all personal like."

When the other man looked away, obviously confused, Gillis sighed.

"Listen, Pope. This place isnae for that sexy wee fireball upstairs, nae. It's for Trace, for *his* peace of mind. And nae matter what's playing oot behind those cold eyes of yers… ye'll nae be her Trace. Nae tae me, and nae tae Gypsy, either."

Gillis smiled when he saw Baron's jaw clench.

"If ye truly want tae be the man she can count on ootside these walls, then ye have tae let her be."

"Meaning?" Baron's deep voice betrayed his obvious frustration.

Gillis smiled again. "Ye gotta give her room, let her use her wings. Nae worries… she's good at flying. Trust her. Respect her. Support her. Help her grow. If ye ever hope she'll one day look at ye with those mesmerizing eyes she saves only for Trace, ye'll have tae be her *best* friend… in every possible sense of the word. It's painful, aye, painful as hell. But it's worth it. Trust me."

⸎

Later that night, Baron sat outside Gypsy's Kilt, his white knuckles grasping tightly to the steering wheel. Gillis's words had been running through his mind all day, and it pissed him off. Not necessarily at the Scotsman himself, no, but Baron Bishop had never allowed *any* man to tell him what he could and could not do… what he could and could not have. How in the hell was he supposed to be best friends with a woman? He didn't even know where to start.

He finally got out of his car and made his way into the pub. It was crowded, yes, but not crazy like it had been *last* night. Gypsy was running full force—serving up drinks and liberally sprinkling that amazing smile of hers upon all who were there.

Baron noticed Blaine was back, but this time he wasn't surrounded by all his frat buddies. This time, he had chosen a lone seat at the bar. The boy wasn't unnecessarily bothering Gypsy, but he did have his eye trained on her at all times.

Baron overheard a few businessmen talking about what they would like to do to their *hot little waitress*—how much she could endure from each of them. He started toward them before he even realized his feet were moving. Yet, he didn't get the chance to confront them. Blaine beat him to it. Such a simple thing, yes, but it made Baron's blood boil up to the surface.

Who does that little shit think he is? Does he actually believe he is capable of teaching grown men… not to be men? What a trifling little idiot.

When he neared the bar, Baron overheard Blaine telling Gypsy what the men had been saying and to be careful around those guys.

68

Gypsy smiled and said, "Blaine, honey… this is a bar. What did you expect? The alcohol is flowing and their testosterones are through the roof. Don't worry about it. They're just a bunch of men trying to compare the size of their dicks. But there's not a one of them at that table who actually has the balls to act on anything they're saying. Trust me. I've been doing this for a long time. I can tell these kinds of things. Besides, they're just human—no different from the rest of us. I mean, look at you. Only a day ago *you* were swinging yours around in front of your comrades. It's human nature. Hell, when I go out with the girls from the gym, we say a heck of a lot worse than that. Jeez, Blaine, I am the world's worst at objectifying a good looking man—undressing him with my eyes, thinking about all the ways I could use him, all the things I could make him do. But it's all talk." She smiled. "As long as it's all talk and daydreams, it's all good. How you *behave*… now, *that's* a whole other matter."

"But I don't even like them talking and thinking about it," Blaine grumbled.

"That's very sweet of you." She placed her hand on his shoulder. "Thanks for looking out for me and defending me. Don't ever stop. Okay?"

When Gypsy lightly kissed his cheek, the young man's face turned ten shades of crimson.

Baron felt a darkness rising within him. He turned to go, almost plowing over the redheaded waitress who had shown up late the night before—Sheila.

"This packet is for Ms. Rodden," Baron said. "Will you please put it safely behind the bar and tell Mr. McCullough to see that she gets it?"

And with that, the irate Dom, and Gypsy's future boss, stormed out of the popular pub and headed home.

⬥⬥⬥

"Come. Service me, Gillis."

"Aye, Mistress. It'd be my pleasure, as always."

Gypsy yawned as he loosened the laces on her boot.

"There's a package for ye on the table, there."

"A package? From whom?"

"It seems the Pope dropped by this evening with yer contract."

"The Pope? Mr. Bishop? Did you speak to him?"

"Nae. I didnae see him. Sheila ran intae him at the door. He said tae make sure ye got that."

"Hmm... Wonder why he didn't stay?"

Gillis removed her other boot and continued with his nightly massage. "Cause ye need yer sleep, Lass. Ever heard of wearing oot yer welcome?"

Gypsy yawned again. "Yeah... I suppose you're right."

"I'm always right, Kitten. Mind me, and ye'll be just fine."

She barely made it up to her room before collapsing into a deep, much-needed sleep.

When Baron exploded inside of her, he felt his built-up tension slowly seep away. He collapsed onto the floor, utterly spent.

The pretty blonde did not look him in the eye when she spoke. "Have you decided to change my name, Master?"

He furrowed his brow, not even glancing her way. "What are you talking about?"

"My name—the one Master gave me. Normally you call me Pearl. I love it when my master calls me Pearl."

"Well, what else would I call you?"

"Tonight... Master called me Gypsy."

He glared at the young woman's bent head. "What did you just say?"

"I love whatever my master wishes to call me. I am grateful for the new name... *and* the desirous way my master kept repeating it."

Baron stood, a snarl turning up one side of his mouth. "Kneel before me—arms spread, chin on the ground, eyes closed. Stay like that until I tell you otherwise. And, *Pearl*, never question your master again."

"Yes, Master."

The young woman flinched when Baron slammed the bathroom door.

"Whatever my master wishes," she whispered to herself. "If you would only let me stay…"

Tears trickled down from her closed eyes, yet a lovely, contented smile remained upon her perfect lips.

***

When Baron stepped out of the shower, he swiped the steam from the mirror and was disgusted by what he saw.

"Who the hell are you?" he grumbled at his reflection.

He came back into the living room to find his sub still kneeling as he had left her.

"You may rise."

She dutifully did so, head still bowed.

"Do not worry. I am not angry with you, Pearl. Go and get ready for this evening's gathering. Sir Lucas will be at the party. He still wishes to try you out as his sub. What do you think about that?"

"If Master wishes me to please Sir, it will be my honor to do so."

"Our contract was a temporary one, Pearl. If you wish to serve Sir Lucas, it will be by your own choice, not by my command. Do not forget. This evening will mark the end of our time together. When we arrive at Master Lebeaux's, you will join the other uncollared subs. It will be your choice alone if you wish to offer your collar to another Dom. Do not make a decision based upon me. You know the rules. When a temporary contract is up, the same Dom can accept your collar again *only* if he wishes to make your mutual arrangement a more permanent thing. This is set up for *your* benefit… as a sub."

"May I speak, Master?"

"As you wish."

"If I presented my collar to you at the close of the gathering, would you accept it?"

"I would not. I have told you before, Pearl. I do not wish an extended contract with *any* sub. You have served me well. I will give my highest recommendations concerning your abilities. Don't be sad, Pearl. You are at the top of the list. There are many Doms who wish to see you kneel down before them. Tonight… *you* hold all the power."

"Master?"

"Yes, Pearl."

"Will you accept a collar from another sub this evening?"

"That is none of your concern. Don't be so presumptuous. You should know your place by now."

"Apologies, Master."

"You are forgiven. Now, go get ready. We will leave in one hour."

"Yes, Master."

⚜

"Hey there, sleepyhead. Glad tae see yer finally up and aboot. What are yer plans for this evening?"

Gypsy yawned. "I dunno. It's Sunday, right? After the gym, I'll probably just come back here and veg out—play some video games or something. What about you?"

Gillis smiled. "I've got a hot date."

"Pffts. Bless her heart. I wish you the best."

"Aye, Lass. Ye sure know how tae cut away at a man's heart."

"Oh please. You're the lucky one. *You've* got a date."

"Ye could have as many dates as ye wanted."

"No thanks." She downed her orange juice. "I'm good."

"I saw that horny wee frat boy sniffing around again last night."

She snorted. "Yeah… as if I had the time to raise him up proper. He's pretty cute, but *way* too young. I'd feel like I was doing something illegal."

Gillis chuckled. "What aboot yer steely-eyed Pope?"

"Who? Mr. Bishop? As if."

"He likes ye, Kitten."

"As a potential lawyer, yeah."

"Nae. I saw the way he was looking at ye."

"So did I." She visibly shivered. "Like he could eat me whole, bones and all."

"Aye, that be the truth of it. He's a dark one—yer Pope. Ye called it right, Lass. There's something aboot him that's… unsettling."

"I know, right?" She jerked on her tennis shoes. "So, what's this hot date like?"

"Aye, she's a foxy wee minx, she is. Cute as a button one minute, then sexy as all get oot the next."

"Wow. Go on. I want to hear more about this magical creature."

"She makes me stiff in my nether regions just looking at her. Sweetest wee arse I've ever seen."

Gypsy giggled. "You are *such* a pervert. So, where are you going? What have you got planned?"

"I'm going tae meet her at her house. She'll be free in a couple of hours. I thought I'd stop by the game store and pick up Diablo IV."

"What? It's out now?"

"Aye, been oot for a while."

"Wow… How'd I miss that?"

"Ye've got too many irons in the fire, Kitten."

"So… you're telling me you've found a girl that will let you come over and pile up on *her* couch, and she'll even play video games with you?"

"Aye. I have."

"Well hells bells, Gillis. Marry the girl. You'll never find another one like her."

"I know that. Eh, I've asked her tae marry me many times afore."

Gypsy turned to him then. Gillis laughed at her confused look.

"What? Dunnae believe me? It's true. I've already asked her tae be mine. She denied me. Hell, I had tae get her drunk off her arse tae even get a little."

Gypsy grabbed one of the red accent pillows off the couch and threw it in his face. Gillis burst out laughing.

"You jerk."

"Aye. Ye wouldnae have me any other way, now would ye, Kitten?"

"Are you being for real? Are you really going to get Diablo IV?"

"Aye. And I'll be right here waiting on the couch for yer return."

She huffed out a laugh. "Hot damn! I've got a date with a sexy Scotsman and an Xbox full of demons. Call me the luckiest girl on the planet."

"Hows aboot a kiss? Ye know, tae seal the deal."

"Hows about... *if* you beat me, I'll give you that kiss. But don't forget. I. Am. Diablo!" She flexed her biceps.

He chuckled. "Yer an idiot, *that's* for sure. Ye cannae even play as Diablo."

"Come at me, Tyrael—Angel of Justice, Aspect of Wisdom. I. Will. Crush. You!" She roared as deep and menacingly as she could.

Gillis was still laughing as she walked out the door.

Baron couldn't have been more disinterested in this formal gathering had he tried. His mind wasn't on all the lovely subs in the other room. He was too distracted. By what... he wasn't quite sure.

"Master Baron, why are you not partaking of the delicious bounty, presented for us this fine evening?"

Baron turned toward the dark-skinned Dom standing to his right. Jacob Quintal—Lord Jacoby, as he preferred to be called—had been a friend of Baron's since they had first entered this alternate lifestyle at about the same time. They had much in common and often recommended subs to one another.

"You will get wrinkles if you keep frowning like that," Lord Jacoby said.

"I always frown like this."

"You always frown, yes. But not like this. Tell me. Was your sub not to your liking?"

"I have no complaints concerning my last six months with Pearl. She is an exquisite creature, in every sense of the word. What she is not... is *the one.*"

Lord Jacoby laughed. "Ahh... but for our distinguished Master Baron, the Creator has yet to make *the one.*" He placed his hand on Baron's shoulder. "Just look at them—properly displayed for our enjoyment. I believe I will go have a taste of that enchanting redhead Master Leiben has just uncollared. I hear her throat is expansive and deep—eighth wonder of the world, so they say. I will try her out before committing." He patted Baron's shoulder. "If I know you, and I do, you will gravitate over to the exquisite blondes now available. Enjoy yourself, old friend. I will see you at the ceremony."

Baron watched as the lovely redhead obediently kneeled down in front of the imposing Lord Jacoby. He scanned the room once more, unsure why his heart simply wasn't in it this time. In truth, Baron lived for these gatherings—a fresh new sub to do his bidding—a delicate creature he would care for, lavish unparalleled affection upon, take to the heights of ecstasy. He was a true Dom, all the way to his core. He didn't feel whole without a lovely submissive he could caress at his leisure. And... his subs loved him, they all had. Baron had a way of making a woman feel worshipped, like a true goddess... all while she was on her knees, willingly obeying his every command.

Sir Lucas approached him then. "I see you have uncollared your lovely *Pearl*. She is even more beautiful than I recall. Careful, Master Baron, you spoil your subs. It makes it harder for the rest of us—having to live up to the godlike power of the gentle Master Baron Bishop."

Baron half smiled. "You will have no problem pleasing Ms. Jessica Lamont. She is a very willing sub—always eager to please her master. She will love you."

"I plan to see that she does," Sir Lucas said. "I have already taken the liberty of delighting in the fruit of her womanhood this evening. Tell me. Has she always been so good at controlling her climax? Or was that *your* doing?"

"As I said before, she is a very willing sub. I merely took her to places she hadn't yet realized she could go. I pushed her limits... and she rose to the occasion. Every. Single. Time."

"I see." Sir Lucas glanced back over at the enchanting, timid-acting blonde with her head bowed. "Perhaps I will leave our contract open. If we are both as satisfied as we just were in the blue room, I will keep her... permanently."

"You will not be dissatisfied," Baron said softly. "She is a rare find."

Sir Lucas snorted. "Apparently not rare enough for *your* defined palate."

"I am… still searching, yes."

Lucas laughed. "When you find this fabled unicorn, I should like to meet her. A woman capable of enticing the great Master Baron would certainly be an extraordinary creature to behold."

"When I find her…" Baron glanced sideways at the other Dom. "My *unicorn* will not be on display."

Sir Lucas slapped his shoulder. "Always a pleasure, Master Baron… always a pleasure." He pointed then toward a young brunette bowing next to Baron. "I believe someone is trying to get your attention."

Baron glanced toward the lovely woman holding tight to a plate of ripe strawberries.

"He prefers blondes," Sir Lucas whispered to the woman as he left them.

Baron stood silently for a few moments, but the fair-skinned brunette didn't move.

"You may speak," he said, dryly.

"I noticed you haven't eaten anything, Master Baron. I wish to serve you."

He studied her a moment before saying, "You may look at me."

When the girl lifted her head, displaying light hazel eyes, Baron's displeasure was obvious. She quickly bowed her head again.

"What is your name?"

"Remy Rothbroc… Master."

Baron looked down at the bright red strawberries and then to the woman's round breasts.

"You may serve me… Lily."

The girl's smile was hard to hide, she beamed with excitement.

"Thank you for bestowing me with such a lovely name, Master. Are strawberries to your liking?"

"I prefer… watermelon."

<hr>

"How the hell are ye so good at this, Lass?"

Gypsy jumped up, throwing her arms up in the air. "Hell yeah! Eat *that*, Gills!"

"Yer like a bloodthirsty warrior... wrapped up inside a deceptively feminine package. Yer a *trap*, that's what ye are. A wicked we trap."

She looked back down at him. "You're just jealous of my awesome fighting skills *and* mad because you didn't win that kiss."

"Damn straight." Gillis chuckled. "Alright now, that's enough killing demons for one night. Ye've got work in the morning. Hop on. I'll give ye a ride tae bed, Kitten."

Gypsy giggled as she climbed up on his broad back, but was yawning before the elevator doors even slid closed.

Chapter 6

Gypsy pulled open the heavy glass doors and entered Bishop, Grey & Sweet first thing Monday morning. She marched up to the overly attractive receptionist just as the lady put her coffee mug to her lips.

"Hello. I'm Gypsy Rodden. If you would be so kind as to show me around a bit, there'll be an awesome lunch in it for you."

When she smiled, the other woman's eyes went wide.

"Ms. Rodden… I wasn't expecting you so soon." The lady quickly stood. "The invitation to lunch is appreciated, yet unnecessary. Please, come this way. Mr. Bishop has requested your presence immediately upon your arrival."

Gypsy followed the curvaceous young woman down the halls.

Damn. If all the secretaries and assistants have bodies like hers… this place is a man's dream come true.

The elegant blonde pushed open a door, bowing slightly. "He is expecting you, Ms. Rodden."

When Gypsy entered Mr. Bishop's office, the regal man was once again staring out the large window. To her surprise, he actually turned to face her… with a smile.

Holy hell, he's gorgeous.

Calm down, girl, her angel complained.

"Expecting you, yes," Baron said through his smile. "But not for a few hours yet. Why so early, Ms. Rodden?"

At the mere mention of time, Gypsy found herself having to suppress a yawn.

"Sorry," she said, covering her mouth. "But since it's Monday, and I didn't actually have to work yesterday, I thought I'd get a jumpstart."

"Even though your regular day with this firm doesn't begin until noon?"

She yawned again. "Stop mentioning the time, will ya? You're killing me."

"Your dedication is admirable, but wasted." He smiled again. "You don't have to impress me, Ms. Rodden. You have already accomplished that... on many different levels."

"Thanks for the compliment, sir. But if you don't mind me saying, your arrogance is astounding. I wasn't *trying* to impress you. I just need to get a feel for the place before work actually starts. You know... where my desk is, the break room, the copy machine, where I'm supposed to pee. Stuff like that."

"Yes, I know... stuff like that. Please, have a seat, Ms. Rodden."

Before she could do so, Baron sat down in the same chair he had during their initial meeting. Gypsy sort of snorted out a laugh before doing the same.

"For you to be a Dom, I seem to have trained *you*. Quite easily, in fact."

"*Now* who is arrogant?"

Gypsy only smiled and shrugged her shoulders.

"I am glad you are here early, Ms. Rodden. I want to lay out some ground rules."

"Rules?"

He nodded. "Things that were not mentioned in your contract—rules just for the two of us. I trust I can expect your discretion, if the case need be."

"You can always trust me, Mr. Bishop. I am true to my word and my oath."

"As I expected. First, let's start with names."

Gypsy furrowed her brow. "Names?"

"Yes. Ms. Rodden and Mr. Bishop are perfect for business situations. Do you have a problem with that?"

She shook her head, but was totally confused.

"As for other situations, ones not related to business, I will let *you* choose."

"...I don't understand."

"I do not wish to keep our formal titles outside of work. And... if we need to speak of things not related to work while we are here, it will be our own little clue—help our brains to switch gears while the conversation seems to flow on naturally to all who might hear. Understand?"

She shook her head. "Not even a little."

Baron smiled again.

"Umm… Are you just doing that because you know how I feel about your dimples? I feel like you are. I feel like you're about to make me agree to something that I probably shouldn't. You're using my weakness to top me, aren't you?"

"Is your hip hurting?"

"…No."

"That's because I'm trying to keep my cards on the table with you, Ms. Rodden. The relationship we now share goes far beyond anything I have with anyone else at this firm. You and I know some rather intimate things about each other. The conversation we just had only emphasizes what I am saying."

She continued to look at him, confused.

"You mentioning your weakness for my dimples… me making reference to your hip. Those are little things, yes, but completely natural and normal for us now. Tell me. What would the others think if they heard us speaking this way?"

"If you hadn't shut the door, I would never have said those things."

"And yet… I *want* you to. I want you to be as free with me here as you were with me Friday night. I want you to be completely natural around me."

"But work is not—"

"Gypsy."

She froze, loving the way her name sounded in his deep, masculine voice.

"I *need* you to be natural around me… *need* it." He leaned back, straightening his shoulders. "My request was not for your comfort alone."

"Wow, Mr. Bishop. I'm… I'm speechless."

He raised a single brow. "I highly doubt that."

"No, I'm serious. The guts it took for someone like *you* to say something like *that*… just… wow. I am honored, truly. If you can muster such strength—strength enough to be vulnerable—I respect it and return it… with pleasure."

"Stop doing that. Stop using your openness as I use my dimples."

"Why?" She snorted out a laugh. "Does it make you melt?"

"…Yes, it does."

Gypsy hadn't been expecting *that* response, certainly not from *him*.

"I wish to maintain the closeness we now share," Baron said. "To do that, we need to decide on appropriate names for one another."

She rubbed her hands together, smiling mischievously. "Like super secret spy code names or something?"

"Super secret, yes, and since they will be our *code* to one another, that term is also appropriate. But they need to be something no one else would even bat a lash at."

"So... we can't be Diablo and Tyrael?"

"No, Ms. Rodden. If you wish us to play about with names such as those, it will have to be far from *this* place."

"Yeah, I know. I was only teasing."

"First names should be sufficient. I can tell you like it when I call you Gypsy."

"You noticed that, huh? Yes, well, as much as I enjoy *my* name dripping from *your* lips... I could never return the favor."

"I see. So calling me Baron is too intimate a thing for you, is it?"

She only blushed and nodded.

"Very well. It would probably raise a few eyebrows as well. In truth... I quite like the way you call me Sir."

"Sir?"

He smiled. "Yes. When *you* say it... it takes my mind far away from business."

"So... Sir does the same thing to you—"

He leaned toward her. "As me saying Gypsy does to you," he whispered.

Goose bumps ran down her arms. He noticed.

"When we wish to speak concerning anything outside our caseloads, you will start your sentence with Sir. I, in turn, will do the same by starting with Gypsy. This shouldn't call any added attention to our exchange. How do you feel about it?"

She squirmed in her seat a little. "I think you are topping me again."

"Gypsy, I will *always* be the top."

She visibly shivered. "Apparently Sir does *not* affect you the same way Gypsy affects me."

He smiled again. "Trust me... it does."

"Okay, I can do this." She smiled. "Actually, it makes me feel like we are... friends."

His smile softened. "Good. That was my intent. I wish us to be friends, Gypsy. Now, as for work... I am putting you over our Asian market. Any cases pertaining to our Eastern clients will immediately be transferred to you."

"Wow... That totally rocks my face off, Mr. Bishop. Scoring an entire continent on my first day—epic win."

"I trust you will not actually speak that way with clients."

"Of course not. I'm a total professional when I work. But the way I talk—like what I said just now—that's the *real* me. I'm only like that around Trace and Gillis, though."

"And now... me."

She blushed. "Yeah, I guess you're in the elite group now, huh?" She chuckled. "I never would have imagined that."

"Do not think the honor is lost on me. It is beyond value."

"Yeah, whatever." She blushed even brighter, then cleared her throat. "So... the Asian market. Why me? I don't speak the language, not any of them. I am much more familiar with Europe."

"Two reasons." He held up as many fingers. "The time difference works well with your alternative work schedule. And secondly... you have a ridiculously strong sense of professional morality."

Gypsy cocked her head to the side. "Umm... huh?"

"You refrain from allowing personal relationships within your work environment. Yes, I know that should be a standard type practice, but the reality is... it isn't. I truly respect that in you. And because of your ethical—yet outdated—sense of morality, I won't have to worry about you swooning over those *lovely* men you hold in such high regard."

"Ouch..." Gypsy blanched. "That... really just happened, didn't it? You *really* just said that."

"Ms. Rodden I—"

"That was harsh, Mr. Bishop... and wrong on more levels than I can even call to mind at the moment. Firstly, thank you for the noon to five work day. And secondly... what the hell? Are you implying I'm the kind of person who jumps into bed on a whim?"

"I was *not* implying such."

"Yes, you were. I am offended to my core. If you want me to take care of your Asian clients simply so I don't *screw* them, does that mean the rest of the world is free game? What a pompous jerk." She jumped up. "I seriously don't need this crap. You're not the only law firm in town."

Baron grabbed her before she reached the door, embracing her from behind.

"Shhh, lovely lady. Calm down."

"Don't call me that," she hissed through gritted teeth. "And get your filthy hands off me."

"Gypsy... be calm. Listen to me. I have obviously explained myself improperly, since you have taken such offense. That was not my intent. Forgive me. The fault is mine. Give me a moment to explain myself. Please."

He felt her relax, just the slightest bit.

"Thank you," he whispered into her hair. "This is going to be harder for me than I thought. I want to be completely honest and open with you. I respect you, Gypsy. Yet, I have a hard time remembering to rein in my demands. I will admit... I have to keep telling myself—you are my equal, not my sub. You *know* who I am, Gypsy. Allow me just a fraction of leeway. Don't be offended so easily by my words. With your help... I will learn how you wish me to treat you, to speak with you. Give me time... please."

"You and I, Mr. Bishop, are obviously cut from extremely different cloths. You can *say* respect all you want. The word itself means nothing."

"You are correct."

"Tell me. How many of your attorneys have you sat down with and told them not to *bang their clients?*"

He sighed. "...None."

"And why is that?"

"I assume they know better." He squeezed her tighter. "That's not to say that you—"

"Stop. Right. There. Take your hands off me before I return the favor... with hostile intent."

She didn't turn back to face him once he had released her.

"I understand you have a skewed perception concerning women. No... I don't *understand* it, yet I do acknowledge it. I thought I could move past it, live with it. That was before I realized you don't see me as anything more than one of your subs."

"That's not tru—"

She held up her hand, ceasing his words.

"In your mind... I am your submissive. Unwilling and untrained, yes, but a submissive all the same. The only difference that stands between *our* relationship and what you have with *them*... is the sex. Can you not see that? Can you not see how frickin' twisted your little game is?" She grasped the doorknob. "We are not friends, Mr. Bishop. Not because I wasn't willing, but because you are incapable of such a thing. Apologies, but I don't believe this will work out. Good luck in your search for... whatever the hell it is you're looking for."

"You just put a hurting on that bag, Gypsy girl."

"Oh, hey, Tony."

"Hey yourself." He handed her a towel. "Anybody I know?" He pointed toward the large punching bag. "Someone needs to give them a heads-up on what's coming their way."

"Naw." She snorted. "Just working off a little steam. That's all."

"Want some ring time?"

"If you're offering, then hell yeah."

"That's my girl." Tony smiled. "Let me grab my pads."

Gypsy rehydrated before stepping between the ropes.

"We don't get to do this much. Thanks, Tony. I really appreciate it."

"That's because you aren't normally here before nine in the morning. What's with that, Gypsy girl? Why aren't you in bed?"

"Eh, just had something that needed to be done."

"Did you take care of it?"

"Yeah, it's all good now."

"If someone is messing with my Gypsy girl, you just tell old Tony about it. I'll take care of it."

She smiled. "You're an angel, to be sure. But like I said, I handled it. One less problem. One less worry. One less piece of shit meant to hold me down."

"Heh. That's my girl." He lowered the pads. "You've lost weight. I don't like it."

"No I haven't." She looked down at herself. "I've been this size since... forever."

"Your cheeks are gaunt."

She put her gloves to her face and rubbed.

"You ready for the table? I'll mix you up some protein while you're in the shower."

"Wait. You mean Old Mack is here in the mornings, too?"

"Normally, yeah, but he's off this week. Poor Old Mack. He's half broke down as it is. He needed a break. No, I'm trying out a new guy. He came highly recommended. Why don't you give him a whirl and tell me what you think?"

"Sure thing." She chuckled. "I'm a massage connoisseur."

———<◆◆◆>———

Gypsy finished her chocolate-flavored protein shake before climbing up on the table.

"Bleh... I hate that stuff."

She was slowly succumbing to the affects of her messed-up sleep schedule—her eyelids growing heavier by the heartbeat—when the gentle scent of jasmine filled her nostrils. It brought a warm smile to her face. The soft sound of flutes began to gently waft around her.

"I am glad my preference is to your liking," a man softly said, dripping warm oil down her spine.

Gypsy didn't open her eyes as she spoke. "I love jasmine. It is an unexpected change. I'm used to Old Mack telling me war stories... smelling of ben-gay and worn leather." She inhaled deeply. "This may be a bit *too* exotic for my palate. It is luxurious, yes, but I don't workout at Tony's for the ambience." She snorted. "I guess I have a pension for man sweat and Axe body spray."

"Ahh... but you are such a lovely creature. You should treat yourself to the finer things in life. A woman with skin as soft as yours..." He moved down from her shoulders, spreading the flowery oil down her sides. "...should be properly worshipped."

She grunted. "Keep talking like that and you'll never get this gig. Tony's *peculiarly* distinguished clientele probably won't be able to appreciate it. Your divine touch... it will be lost on them. If you truly want to fill in for Old Mack, you gotta get rougher... dig in a little deeper."

"Force doesn't always yield the desired results. Often... *digging deeper* can cause irrecoverable damage." He moved on to her legs. "Are you saying my touch is too gentle for you?"

"No. Not me. But I am not the majority around here. If you're auditioning for the position of masseuse in a boxing gym..." She half laughed. "...your transcendent touch might make the guys uncomfortable, make them question their sexuality."

"And if I were auditioning for you alone." He made it down her left arm and began tracing little circles across her palm. "Tell me how you would rate me."

Gypsy smiled. "I cannot grade you properly until you have completed the exam."

He moved around to the head of the table, then leaned down and whispered near her ear, "Then I shall do my utmost to leave a lasting impression."

He grasped her just above her hips, pressing firmly as he moved back up her sides, catching her arms and pulling them toward him. After he had made it all the way to her fingertips, he gently folded her arms above her head, and then moved down to her feet. She groaned.

"Stop before you spoil me."

"But... that is my intent."

She only smiled. Gypsy could easily drift off to sleep at this very moment. If he would stop talking, she'd be snoozing already.

"Did you know there are pressure points in the hands and feet that affect every part of the body?"

He lifted her foot and blew gently across her arch. Gypsy gasped.

"Everything from your sinuses to your pelvis," he continued. "I can ease your headache or stimulate your cervix. If there is anything that ails you... *I* am your cure."

Gypsy quickly jumped up then, wrapping her towel around herself. "Alrighty then, audition's over. I'd give you a ten if you were applying for concierge at the Oriental Love Motel... and a low two if you're shooting for a fulltime position *here*."

She turned to go... then saw the man for the first time. Gypsy did sort of a shuffle-step before she froze.

"Y-you're... Asian."

He smiled then. "Hello there, Doll Eyes."

Holy hell, Gypsy. Look at him. Look at that divinely delicious man, her inner demon cooed sweetly. *Have you ever seen the like? Gray, almond-shaped eyes, rich chocolate-colored hair, skin as flawless as a lotus blossom… damn. Tell me, girl. How are you still standing upright? His smile alone made your knees tremble. I know. I'm in here with you.*

Shut up, you wicked little devil. She steadied herself against the table. *Come on, Angel. Help me out here.*

Umm… I'm voting with him this time. This one is exactly what the doctor ordered. Be gentle with him, Gypsy… or not.

Gypsy growled inside her head, but as far as speaking out loud… it wasn't even close to possible.

"I was watching you workout earlier." He moved beside her and gently brushed back a strand of her hair. "It is rare to see such a tiny woman… with so much fire. It reminded me of a story my mother used to tell me when I was a small boy—The Slight Samurai, Musashi."

"The *Slight* Samurai?" she barely whispered.

The man nodded. "He was very thin, just a wisp of a man. No one took him seriously. Musashi roamed from province to province, crossing the lands of all the great Feudal Lords. But no matter how well he swung his blade… he could never procure a retainment—a great dishonor for a samurai. So, he remained a lowly ronin, minus a master."

"That's so sad. Why would seeing me bring such a story to mind?"

"Because of how the story ends, Doll Eyes."

"And… how *does* it end?"

"Have dinner with me and I will tell you."

"I-I can't. I have to work."

"Such a shame." He gently ran his fingertip down the side of her face. "Another time, perhaps?"

Gypsy swallowed hard. "I don't think so. My nights are pretty full. If you'll excuse me—"

"Your nights are too full for a single meal?" He smiled sweetly. "Careful, Doll Eyes. Careful you don't set your life up so that one day… one day when you slow down and take a deep breath… you find yourself all alone."

She could feel the burn of her coming tears. His words had pierced her in the very place she tried to always keep hidden. She pushed past him and ran for the locker room.

Tony called out to her before she headed outside, but Gypsy didn't turn to face him. She ran out onto the sidewalk… and then just kept running. She didn't stop for a breath until she made it all the way inside The Kilt.

Gillis heard when her shower came on. He wondered why she had come home early from the office, but he didn't bother her. Then, when he heard her bitter sobs, he just sat down on the floor outside her door… and waited.

Chapter 7

Mondays were normally pretty slow at The Kilt. This one proved no different. Gypsy went through the motions like an obedient marionette, one whose strings were being manipulated by an unseen force. She didn't even have to send out a last call. By the time two o'clock rolled around, the place was already empty. She just locked the doors and silently headed upstairs.

"Are ye nae gonna tally the till, Gyps?"

"Tomorrow. I'll do it tomorrow."

"Ye'll nae have time tomorrow, Lass. Ye'll be lucky tae make it back here before serving time."

"I'll do it tomorrow," she whispered, not even glancing his way.

By the time Gillis made it upstairs, he heard the lock engage on her bedroom door. She had dropped her apron on the floor near the coffee table—tips spilling out onto the rug.

"Aye, my wee Kitten didnae even take her boots off. Well, that'll be enough of this shite."

He jerked a business card from his wallet and started hammering away at the flat buttons on his phone.

⊰⟨◆◆⟩⊱

Gillis McCullough was leaned back with his feet propped up on the bar when Baron Bishop started banging on the door.

"Aye, yer too late, Pope," he said as he flipped the lock.

"Too late?" Baron pushed his way inside. "What do you mean, too late? I rushed over as soon as I got your message."

"I mean what I said. Yer too late. Her savior arrived less than half an hour ago. Ye'll nae be speaking tae the lass now."

"Her savior? Wha-what are you talking about? Where is she?"

"She's with Trace."

89

"Trace? But… but I thought you said he was in Africa."

"Aye, he was. He took the first flight oot this morning. It took him over seventeen hours tae get here. But he's home now."

"I don't understand. Gypsy never mentioned him coming home today."

"And that's cause she didnae know. Neither of us did."

"Then… why?"

"He said he felt her pain. He was in the middle of seeing patients when he said it felt like his heart tore clean in two. He jumped in his car and drove straight tae the nearest airport withoot another thought. He's up there with her now."

"Wha— His *heart* broke? But… what does that even mean?"

"I was hoping ye could fill in that wee bit for me."

"Me? But—"

"What did ye do tae my Kitten, Pope? Dunnae be denying it. Ye hurt her… hurt her bad. I didnae like ye from the start, but the lass was smitten with ye. Aye… I spoil her. I know that. I should have made a fuss aboot her going tae work for ye, but I let her have her way. Now look what's happened. First day on the job with ye and she comes home—early, mind ye—crying."

"Crying?"

"Aye, and she acted like a wee zombie all night at the bar, then locked herself in her room withoot even making oot the deposit *or* taking off her boots."

"Wait a minute. Just… give me a minute to catch up." Baron took a deep breath, gladly accepting the whiskey Gillis had poured for him. "She came into the office this morning, yes."

"…And?"

"And like I always seem to do… I offended her. That was not my intent. I swear it. I just… I just don't know how to talk to that woman."

"Ye talk tae her like ye *should* talk tae any other woman. Gypsy's nae the problem there, Pope. Ye are."

"I know. I know that." He sighed, collapsing into the nearest seat. "I was trying to be completely open and honest with her, Gillis. After I saw what pain my *secrets* had left her in on Friday, I vowed never to repeat that same mistake again." He released another weary sigh and rubbed his brow. "As soon as I realized

how my *honesty* had offended her, I apologized immediately—
begged her for another chance."

"...And?"

"And... she wished me luck and walked out the door. She
wouldn't even look at me."

"What time was this?"

"Before nine. Why?"

"She didnae make it back *here* until half past one."

"What? But... where did she go for *five* hours?"

"I cannae say. I only know when she returned. As soon as
the lass came in, she went straight tae her room. Then, she sat in
her shower for nearly an hour... bawling her wee eyes oot."

"Bawling? But why?"

"Ye tell me why. Enough with all yer damn questions,
Pope. I called ye down here for answers, nae the other way
around."

"Gillis?"

Baron jumped to his feet when the sandy-haired man
spoke. He hadn't even heard him come down the stairs.

"Make up some of those special watermelon margaritas.
Just... fill up a pitcher, if you would."

When Trace silently began getting a couple of glasses down
from the rack, Baron cleared his throat.

"How is she?"

Trace turned, purposefully slowly, toward the other man,
his level glare as cold as any Baron had ever seen.

"What concern is it of yours?"

"I am Baron—"

"I know who you are," Trace said. "I also know all her ties
to you have been severed. The bar is closed. You have no reason to
be here. Kindly see yourself out. Gillis?"

The Scotsman turned toward Trace when he addressed
him.

"Why didn't you tell me about her fairy saddle acting up
again?"

"I sent ye a message as soon as she told me."

"And you're saying she has walked around in that kind of
shape for the last four days?"

"Nae. It went away that same night... when the Pope over
there confessed he was a Dom."

Trace turned back to Baron. "A Dom? Why would something as ridiculous as that cause her so much pain?"

When Trace narrowed his gaze, Baron Bishop mirrored him.

Gillis chuckled. "Is it nae obvious? The man desired her—was playing oot twisted wee fantasies aboot her in his mind. Nae worries. When he confessed, the mark faded."

"Then why is it now as bad as I have ever seen it?" Trace asked, keeping his cold glare locked with Baron's.

"It left that same night. I watched it with my own two eyes." Gillis growled threateningly. "Aye, what did ye do tae her this time, Pope?"

"It wasn't me," Baron answered coolly. "Like I said... I hid *nothing* from her. Why do you think she stormed out of my office like that? I was honest with her... held nothing back."

Trace sighed. "Then I'll just have to wait until I hear back from Nasaka. I called him on my way to the airport... the moment I first felt her shattering." He paused a couple more heartbeats. "But... I haven't been able to reach him since."

"Who's Nasaka?" Gillis grumbled. "Dunnae tell me, another wee Asian."

Trace almost smiled. "When *you* say it, Gills, you make it sound so awful."

The Scotsman only snorted.

"He is Japanese-Korean-American. I met him while I was setting up that clinic in Australia. He is into all of that strange Eastern/alternative medicine/feng shui stuff. When I mentioned Gypsy's fairy saddle, he knew exactly what I was talking about."

"What's a fairy saddle?"

Both men turned toward Baron, yet remained silent for several more heartbeats. Gillis finally spoke up.

"It's what my Gran calls that mark ye seen on her hip Friday night. Ye must have seen the like afore, Pope. Most people have them on their face, somewhere on their head. But they can be anywhere. My brother had one right between his eyes, just there." Gillis pointed to the bridge of his nose. "When he was a wee bairn, crying for all he was worth, it would go from brown tae pink tae red tae purple. Quick as a whip. When he got older, ye only ever noticed it when he got mad. Most folks didnae even know he was marked by the Fae. Nae 'til he got good and pissed."

"Marked by the Fae?"

Trace sighed and shook his head. "That's just what they believe in Scotland. Well... most of Europe, actually. The people of old believe a child born with such a mark had been touched—or cursed, whichever the case may be—by Fairies. They think that person holds some sort of fated destiny."

"Dunnae say it like it isnae true," Gillis grumbled. "I know better."

Trace half rolled his eyes and smiled. "It isn't wholly a European superstition. Hindus believe it is the revealed form of the Third Eye—a gate linking that person to *inner realms*... visions, clairvoyance, spiritual connections and the like. Nasaka, he is Buddhist. He tells a story about one of their Kami, a goddess who fell in love with a Fox Spirit—pretty much the same as a European fairy."

Gillis snorted and mumbled, "How in the bloody hell is some made-up *Fox Spirit* comparable tae the Fae?"

Trace stood there for a moment, silently staring at the still-grumbling Scotsman... before shaking his head and continuing. "Anyway, the goddess also fell in love with a mortal man and bore him a child. Needless to say, the Fox Spirit didn't take kindly to it and attacked the babe, biting through the child's main chakra point in his stomach. The goddess saved the child, but the Fox's curse mark remained. It is said that people born bearing such a mark can feel the pain of coming betrayal. Just like the pain the Fox Spirit felt when his lover betrayed *him*." Trace sighed as he reached for the now full pitcher of her sweet pink nectar. "Medically speaking, I believe it is simply a variant of a port-wine stain—a birthmark that's color can be affected by stress, hormone changes, and other various problems of the like. Since Gypsy's main source of hormones was destroyed..." He paused, swallowing hard. "...who knows *what* affects the visual change in color? It remains an enigma—a mystery as deep as the woman herself."

"And yet..." Baron waited until Trace finally made eye-contact with him. "...a port-wine stain would not cause such pain."

"Yes, which is why I called Nasaka. I am not a learned idiot, Mr. Bishop. I have seen too many mysterious, unexplainable things—things that would make your toes curl, things that would make my Oxford professors piss their starched pants. Yes, I have learned to accept *many* things... and learned to deny nothing.

Anyway… Nasaka lives in LA. I knew he could get to her before I could. But what, if anything, actually transpired between the two, remains to be seen. Gypsy claims not to know the man and Nasaka cannot be reached at the moment. If I didn't wish to drag Tony out of bed at this hour, I would ask *him*."

Gillis furrowed his brow. "What's Tony got tae do with any of this?"

Trace shook his head. "Something crushed her early this morning. Well, I guess at this point…" He glanced at his watch. "…it would have been yesterday morning—Monday. Anyway, I felt her soul cry out in pain. That's all I know."

"Yesterday morning?" Gillis turned to Baron. "Aye, so that would be the something *ye* did tae her when she came intae work."

Did my words truly crush her that badly? …Why? he thought. *How could that simple request—asking that she not get involved with anyone in Asia—cause her to crumble to the point of sending this man running back to her from the other side of the world?* Yet, Baron did not speak.

Trace glared at the cold-eyed man before continuing. "When I realized what she was feeling, I knew Tony's would be the first place she would go. I sent Nasaka *there*. Now, if you will please excuse me… I have a heart to rescue."

Chapter 8

Gypsy came bopping down the stairs, all smiles.

"Wow! Look at ye, Lass. *That's* my old Gyps."

"Told you I would have time to balance the till."

"Aye, that ye did. But ye didnae tell me ye'd given yer Pope the boot. I'm proud of ye, Kitten."

She shrugged her shoulders. "Eh, it wasn't a good fit. I'll find where I belong, one day."

"Ye belong here, Kitten, with yer devoted Scotsman by yer side. We were doing fine—just the two of us. Stay with me, Lass. I'll see tae yer heart."

She was giggling as she made out the deposit. "I know, Gills. You're the one man who has never lied to me, never left me."

"Hey," Trace said, emerging from the stairwell. "I've never lied to you. Have the two of you gotten so close, there's no room left for me?"

"Aye, only in my dreams, Brother… only in my fondest, most delicious dreams."

Gypsy lunged for Trace as he walked toward her. He wrapped her up in his arms as he kept on walking, stopping only when they reached the end of the bar and could go no further. And there they stayed—surrounded by each other—as the rest of the world faded away.

Gillis glanced up at the clock when he heard someone at the door. "Eh… that'll be trouble coming. It's still an hour afore opening."

Neither Trace nor Gypsy acknowledged he had even spoken. Gillis knew they wouldn't, knew what it was like when they were together. He flipped the lock, still grumbling.

"Pub hours are seven tae three, Pope. Ye know that."

"I need to see her. You know *that*."

Gillis stepped aside. "Fat lot of good it'll do ye. Trace is home. There'll be nae talking tae Gyps. Nae while he's around."

"Are you saying he won't let me see her?"

"Nae. Alls I'm saying is... she'll nae even notice ye are there. Come on in and have a drink. See for yerself."

Baron slowly swallowed another mouthful of the smooth scotch, his gaze transfixed on the silent duo.

"Why does she shake her head every once in a while?" he asked.

Gillis glanced over at the couple, then back down to his prep work. "They're talking."

"Talking? But... they haven't said a word since I got here."

"That's what I've been trying tae tell ye. They can... I dunnae know... *commune* withoot speaking. Ye can see it on her face. Watch how she'll smile, then her expression will change and he'll brush away her tears afore they even fall. I told ye afore... it's weird."

"Weird would be... sporadic, unexplainable coincidences. This? This is beyond bizarre. I've never even *heard* of anything like this."

"Aye, and that's why I couldnae explain it."

Gillis growled when he heard the door open.

"Bloody hell. I forgot tae lock it back. Who could be coming in here at half past six on a Tuesday?"

Baron didn't answer the Scot. He was lost in the vision of what was *Trace and Gypsy*. He was mesmerized by their strange bond. They truly did seem to occupy the same space. They moved together, shared breath. His hands gently caressed her back, while hers remained steady upon his chest. Their eyes didn't just sparkle, they sang—a heavenly song shared only by the two of them. Trace would nuzzle his nose in her hair, kiss her forehead. Gypsy would occasionally blush and bury her face against his chest. Neither of them acknowledged Baron, Gillis, *or* the stranger who had just entered the pub.

"I dunnae give a mule's arse *who* ye are, wee ninja!"

When Gillis raised his voice, Baron finally noticed the two men arguing on the other side of the bar. Yet, the entwined couple remained unfazed.

"I'm here to help," the man was saying. "Now… if you would kindly move out of my way…"

"If ye want past me, ye'll have tae move me. Think ye got it in ye, lad?"

The stranger just threw up his hands, rolling his eyes as he turned from the enraged Scotsman and walked over behind the entranced Gypsy. He reached across the bar, brushed her hair over her shoulder, and then lightly pressed two fingers to the nape of her neck.

Gypsy let out a tiny yelp… and their magical spell was broken.

Trace smiled as he looked down over her shoulder. "Hello, Nasaka. Glad you could make it."

⚜

"If ye want warm sake, there's a sushi bar aboot four blocks down that way. Knock yerself oot."

"Calm down, Gills," Trace said softly. "Nasaka is a bit of a trickster. He's just trying to get a rise out of you."

"He'll get a helluva lot more than a rise, if he isnae careful."

Trace chuckled. "Let me formally introduce everyone. This is the friend I was telling you about—Taka Nasaka."

At the mention of the man's full name, Gypsy and Gillis shared a chuckle. When Trace cleared his throat, Gypsy immediately bit her bottom lip and looked down, duly chastised.

Baron's breath caught at the sight—her blush-tinged cheeks, the way she immediately inched closer to Trace and squeezed his hand. No matter how defiant and strong-willed this lovely woman was, next to her Trace… she was the perfect sub. Baron's chest tightened.

"Taka," Trace said. "I believe you know my angel—Gypsy Rodden. This large man with the short temper and thick accent is our dear friend Gillis McCullough."

"And that man over there…" Gypsy said in a small voice. "…the one with the cold eyes and perfect features, that's Mr. Baron Bishop of Bishop, Grey & Sweet."

When Trace wrapped his arm around her waist and gave her a little squeeze, Gypsy curled up against his side. Baron didn't miss Trace's sideways glare, *or* the way the sandy-haired man's jaw suddenly clenched. Baron had to smile.

"Now," Trace continued. "Let's get down to the business at hand. Firstly, why didn't you return any of my calls?"

"I am not disputing the fact that the world normally revolves around you, Dr. Feelgood." Nasaka smiled as he spoke. "But I was booked up solid. I had clients back-to-back all day yesterday *and* today. And since there was no real emergency, I came when I had the time to sit down and talk."

"How can you say there was no emergency? She is in severe pain." Trace gently stroked her hair. "She's been crying since the moment I arrived."

"I can see that," Nasaka said. "But she's not crying now. Other than the puffy red eyes, she looks completely fine to me."

"Does *this* look fine to you?"

Baron clenched his teeth when Trace pulled her t-shirt up and her kilt down, exposing her left hipbone.

"My, my, my. That's a lovely little fox bite you've got there." Nasaka rounded the bar and came to join them. "Hello again, Doll Eyes."

Gypsy blushed and looked away. The sight of it made Baron flinch.

The feng shui doctor knelt down in front of her and lightly ran his fingers across the dark purple mark.

"He nibbled on you real good, didn't he, Doll Eyes?"

Gypsy didn't speak.

Nasaka sighed and stood up. "Yeah, that's one serious curse mark. No wonder she's in pain. Her chakra is completely disrupted."

Trace narrowed his gaze. "And would you like to explain to me exactly what happened?"

Nasaka held his hands up. "Trace, dude, that wasn't there yesterday. She was fine when I got to the gym." He gave Gypsy a tiny wink. "And even better when we were through. Right, Doll Eyes?"

Gypsy's cheeks grew redder and she pressed closer to Trace.

"I would have spent more time with her." Nasaka shrugged his shoulders. "But when I started on her feet… she nearly jumped out of her skin. I promise you, Trace. She was in no *physical* pain when she walked out of that gym."

"And what's *that* supposed to mean... no *physical* pain?"

Nasaka shrugged his shoulders again. "We talked a bit." He reached for her then, tenderly brushing her hair back. "I might have hit on a nerve when I warned her not to set her life up so that she ended it all alone. But that wouldn't make the curse mark act up. This lovely little lady has nothing to fear from me. I would delight in telling her *all* my secrets."

When Gillis growled, Baron almost joined him.

Nasaka smiled at the two men before going on. "No... whoever—or whomever—set the fox to chewing on her hip... she met that person *after* she left the gym."

Trace turned to Gillis.

"Dunnae look at me, Brother. She was already crying in the shower by the time I found her. She didnae even mention her hip. She *always* tells me when it's acting up... always."

Everyone turned to Baron when he cleared his throat to speak.

"I thought the pain faded when the perpetrator left her presence. Had it been Nasaka, or even me, why would the pain still be so intense that it made her cry all night this past night? We haven't even been around her since early yesterday."

Gillis grabbed her hands. "Hey, Kitten. Did I do something tae harm ye?"

Gypsy shook her head, but didn't speak.

"Gypsy, honey, look at me." Trace turned her back to face him. "When did the pain start?"

Again, she shook her head and looked away.

"Tell me, Gypsy."

She remained silent.

"Damn..." Trace sighed as he wrapped her up in his arms. "How did you know, my love? I wasn't even thinking about it. *You* were the only one on my mind... not her. I swear it, Gyps."

Gillis furrowed his brow. "...Trace? What are ye saying, Brother?"

Baron snorted as he slid his hands in his pockets, sending Trace an icy glare.

Trace glanced at the smirking Dom, but didn't respond.

Gypsy pulled free of the man she loved above all others. No longer able to hold her silence, she burst into audible tears before ever making it to the stairway.

Gillis hung a *closed due to illness* sign on the door before joining the others upstairs.

"I met her while setting up this latest clinic," Trace said. "I didn't pay any attention to it at first, but somewhere along the way... we fell in love."

Gypsy whimpered with her next shaky breath.

Trace looked at her, trying hard to hold back his own tears. "I didn't know it would affect you like this, Gyps, or I never would have allowed it. You are more important to me than any other person on this planet. You know that."

Gypsy was slumped down in her favorite chair, staring blindly up at the ceiling.

"Doll Eyes?" Nasaka said, glancing upon her tear-stained face while massaging her palm. "The bond you and Trace share is not in question here. It is obvious to all. Yet... do you wish it to be different? In your heart... do you want Trace to love you like a woman, like a wife?"

Trace didn't wait for her to answer. "Consider it done." He knelt in front of her, hovering over her, kissing her face. "If I knew you desired me, Gypsy, I would have married you the day we got out of the hospital." He smiled. "Why didn't you tell me you loved me *that* way? How could you even hide such a thing for so long? I'm sorry I didn't notice, Gyps. I am so very, very sorry."

"Calm down, Trace, and give her some room. You're making my job ten times harder than it should be." Nasaka turned her chin so that she was facing him. "Tell me true, Doll Eyes. Do you love Trace like you would a husband, a lover?"

Another silent tear ran down her face as she barely shook her head.

Trace sighed before collapsing onto the couch, burying his face in his hands.

"I don't understand," he groaned. "I have confessed everything to her—the fact that I fell in love with a woman, and also the fact that I have and always will love *her* above all others. Why is she still in pain? Why has the mark not diminished?"

At the mention of her curse mark, Nasaka began caressing it while he continued to massage her palm. "Because, Trace… you're not just some regular person. The deceit—betrayal—goes much deeper. You two not only share a spiritual bond, you share a physical one as well. Your blood pumps through her veins. Your skin covers the back of her neck, one elbow, and a large piece of her thigh. And… it's *your* kidney that has kept her alive all these years. You can't expect her mark to react the same way with you. It's just not possible. Hey… Look at me, Doll Eyes."

When she slowly turned toward him, Nasaka smiled at her and waited until she tried to do the same.

"What I said before, at the gym… *this* is what I was talking about. I saw something disturbing in your aura. I didn't know what it was. Not then. But I do now. Answer me true, Doll Eyes. Have you blocked out all other meaningful relationships in your life? Have you denied your heart from loving?"

Her sudden, bitter sobs caused Trace to cry out as well.

Nasaka gently stroked her hair. "Did the possibility that Trace would one day find love… did that never cross your mind?"

She shook her head.

"Aww, Doll Eyes. You were saving all your love for a man you knew you would never marry. In so doing, you are purposefully writing the very destiny I only just warned you about. Eventually… every man in your life is going to fall in love with a woman who is going to love him right back. One day you'll wake up… and they will all have moved on with their lives. Remember what I said… take care that you don't set things up to ensure you end up all alone."

"I can't take anymore of this," Trace said, jumping to his feet. "I refuse to let this happen. She *won't* be alone. I won't allow it. Whether she will marry me or not, doesn't matter. I'm moving back home. We will spend the rest of our lives together, Gyps. We don't need anyone else. Just you and me, Angel. Right?"

We can't let him do that, her inner angel said.

He will throw away his whole life for us, the demon whispered.

I know. Gypsy bit her bottom lip. *I love Trace too much to crush his dreams like that.*

Baron kept his gaze fixed on her the whole time. He swallowed hard when he saw the dull, dead look now shadowing her lovely brown eyes. It sent a shiver down his spine. He was so absorbed in her pain; he didn't even realize she was reaching for him. When the silence now filling the room finally registered, Baron focused on her trembling, extended hand. The Dom was on his knees beside her before he even told his body to move.

"Does the job offer still stand?" she whispered.

"It will always stand… for you."

Gypsy smiled, but it was a weak, hollow smile. "Can it be amended?"

"Anything you want. Just name it."

"I want my office in Asia," she said, in barely more than a whisper.

"Will you split your time between there and here?" he asked.

She nodded.

"Done," Baron said with a smile. "Just give me time to find a proper translator, one who can remain at your side. Once that is done, we will fly over together—set up everything you'll need."

"Well, look no further," Nasaka said. "I speak Japanese, Mandarin, Cantonese, Taiwanese… *and* a few others."

"Aye… so nae only are ye a witch doctor, yer a damn polyglot as well?"

Nasaka winked at the large Scotsman.

"That settles it," Gillis mumbled. "I hate the pretty wee ninja lad."

Trace jumped up. "No, Nasaka, you can't!"

Nasaka glanced at him. "And why not?"

"Because you're happy here. You've got a thriving business in LA. Your family is here. Your friends are here."

"Yes, and they'll still be here when I come back. But for now… I want to join Doll Eyes on her magical new journey."

Baron cleared his throat. "Do we have a contract then, Ms. Rodden?"

"Yes!" Gypsy wrapped her arms around Baron's neck. "Yes, Mr. Bishop. We have a contract."

He embraced her fully, standing up with her still wrapped in his arms.

"Gillis, do something," Trace demanded.

"Me? What the hell am I supposed tae do? If she wulnae listen tae ye, there's nae a bloody chance in hell she'll hear a word *I* say."

Baron squeezed her tighter, burying his nose into her hair. "Are you still in pain, Gypsy?" he whispered.

She shook her head. "It's easing off now. Just hold me like this a moment longer and it will all be gone..." She paused. "Unless this is too inappropriate."

He squeezed her tighter. "Gillis is right. You *are* an idiot."

Baron smiled when she giggled.

"I will hold you as much and as often as I need to, Gypsy. As long as you return the favor."

"Meaning?"

"You will hold *me* when I need it as well."

"Deal," she whispered softly.

Trace walked over and lightly touched her back. "That'll be enough of that. The man offered you a job, Gyps, not a free trip around the world. You don't owe him *this* much thanks."

At Trace's words, Gypsy slackened her hold... but Baron only tightened his embrace—digging his fingers into her sides, burying his nose against that tender spot where her neck and shoulder meet. A shiver ran down her spine.

"I-I'm sorry I suddenly hugged you like that," she said. "I guess I got a little over excited."

She placed her hands on his shoulders and tried to pull back.

"You remember the promise you only just made?" Baron whispered.

Gypsy froze, unable to speak or move.

He ran his sharp nose up the side of her neck. "The one where you promised to hold me when I truly needed it?"

She barely nodded her head, only once.

"I *need* it, Gypsy. I need this just a moment longer."

She relaxed as she slowly slid her arms back around him.

Baron's breath hitched at her sudden compliance, her sudden *submission* to his needs. He shuddered.

Gypsy felt Baron's lips part into a smile against her tingling skin a heartbeat before he whispered there. "...Gypsy."

Goose bumps ran across her entire body. He felt her slowly melt against him.

"...Sir," she whispered.

Gypsy had barely managed to whimper out the small word, but Baron's breath caught at the sound of it. He softly groaned.

"Whoa!" Nasaka yelled. "Stop. Right. There." He physically separated the two. "*That* was headed in a very bad direction." He turned toward Baron. "Your aura is consuming hers, almost devouring it. Back up, the both of you."

Trace pulled Gypsy to his side and felt her trembling. He glared at the other man. Baron didn't back down, he matched the good doctor... dagger for dagger.

"Aye, Gyps?"

She glanced over at Gillis when he spoke.

"Looks like ye were spot on aboot him wanting tae gobble ye up... bones and all. But ye were wrong aboot the other."

She furrowed her brow. "The other?"

"Aye." Gillis nodded. "He's nae the Pope, Lass. He's the big bad wolf."

When Gypsy looked back to Baron, he was smiling with only one corner of his mouth—that single perfect dimple taunting her there. She swallowed hard. He noticed.

"This is astounding," Nasaka said, looking from one man to the other. "You each have extremely powerful, yet extraordinarily different chakra forces surrounding you. Doll Eyes, you're no exception. But the thing I find *most* fascinating is... the way *hers* responds to each of *yours*. I mean, I assumed the assimilation of her fierce aura by Trace... was simply due to their highly unique bond. Now, after seeing her succumb to Mr. Bishop as well—"

"I didn't *succumb*," Gypsy said.

"Aye, Lass. Ye succumbed."

She growled at Gillis. "I don't want to hear anymore about this... this... ridiculousness."

Gillis only smiled at her, sending her a teasing little wink.

"Seriously." She balled her hands into fists. "People can't *see* auras, and crap like that. It's all utter nonsense. And I, for one, am done with it. Like I said, I don't want to hear any more about such drivel."

"Very well, then. You won't have to," Nasaka said. "I mean, believing in lie-detecting fox curses is sooo much easier than believing in the fact that people's emotions can take on a physical, colorful manifestation."

Gypsy rolled her eyes at the man.

Nasaka clapped his hands together. "Well then, let's see now... On the surface, things seem to be working out quite nicely here. But... I like to put my mind at ease—helps me *and* my patients all stay on the same page. Okay then. Trace..." He turned toward the man as he spoke. "I'm assuming you understand that Gypsy has, or is, working through her reservations concerning your future bond with another woman."

Gypsy visibly flinched.

"Come now, Doll Eyes." Nasaka smiled. "You were doing so well just a moment ago. Don't worry. You will never sever your bond with Trace, not completely. But you were doing the right thing by stretching it. It's healthy—helps you grow. You took a giant leap in the right direction. Do not falter now."

Trace pulled her closer.

"Careful, Dr. Feelgood. That isn't fair to the lady." Nasaka took her hand and gently drew her to him. "You are used to the comfort and security you give each other. Don't get me wrong. It's a beautiful thing, one which we all hope to have some day. But right now, you're being selfish, Trace—feeding off the love of a woman you will one day part ways with."

Burning tears once again filled her tired eyes.

"Shhh, Doll Eyes," Nasaka whispered. "It's alright. Smile. It's time for you to fly."

Gypsy numbly made her way over to Gillis. He wrapped her up in a big hug and kissed the top of her head.

"C'mere, Kitten. I got ye. Everything's gonna be okay now."

"But... what about you, Gills?" She sniffed. "What about the bar? If I go away, what will happen to you, to us?"

"What do ye mean, what'll happen tae us? Naethin', that's what. Yer nae leaving forever, Gyps. When ye get back home, I'll be here waiting for ye."

She brushed away her tears and finally managed a real smile. "Just like old times?"

"Nae. Even better."

"Whoa, whoa, whoa." Nasaka approached them. "What just happened? Your auras were perfectly in-tune. Now... now they are polar opposites. What's going on here?" He looked at Gypsy. "Doll Eyes?"

"…Yes?"

"Tell me exactly what you were thinking, the exact image that was running through your mind as you two were talking just now."

"Umm… I was just thinking normal things. Things like coming home to Gillis and playing video games, working the bar together, watching scary movies together, sharing this home and laughing our heads off."

"I see." He looked then to the Scot. "And, Gillis, what were you thinking? Please be as honest as she was. If you try to hide something, you'll give her over to be feasted upon by that wicked little fox."

Gillis looked down into Gypsy's eyes and tried to smile. He couldn't.

"When I said things would be even better than they were afore… I saw ye doing all those things ye just mentioned, but doing them *with* me, nae beside me. I saw ye finally loving me back, Gyps. The way I want ye tae. The way a man needs a woman tae love him." He sighed. "I saw ye looking up at me, Kitten, smiling and gasping as I moved within ye. I *need* that, Gyps."

"…Gillis."

"And there it goes again." Nasaka shook his head. "Your connection is obvious—deep, trusting, loving. But when you communicate with each other, you only hear what you want to hear. Your souls are not *listening* to one another."

"Aye, wee ninja lad. I think we hear each other just fine."

Nasaka only sighed and tried to walk away. Gypsy grabbed his arm.

He smiled at her. "What is it, Doll Eyes?"

"I'm afraid."

"Of what?"

"I'm afraid… if I do this…" She glanced toward Baron. "…if I take this leap…" She sniffed. "My little family here… will splinter."

"Aww, Doll Eyes." He tenderly stroked her cheek. "Leaping… is the only way you learn how to fly. Your little family here will never fault you for taking flight. And that man over there…" He motioned toward Baron. "…he's the one who can give you wings."

Baron gently took her hand. "Ms. Rodden, you are *entitled* to this, to this life. The only limitations you have… are the ones you place upon yourself. Remove those assumed limitations, Gypsy." He smiled softly. "You are so worth it."

"You're using your dimples again, aren't you?"

"Are they working?"

She blushed. "…Yeah."

His smile widened. "I can't wait to see you fly."

Chapter
9

"So… what do you think?"

"What do I think?" Gypsy scanned the room once more. "I think I'm in love. This place is ridiculously perfect."

The wonderment sparkling in her warm eyes captivated Baron.

"I hoped you would like it." He took a step closer. "I wanted this to feel like home."

"Yes." Nasaka nodded approvingly. "We will be more than comfortable here."

"We?" Baron furrowed his brow. "Yes, well, I am trusting that both of you realize how inappropriate a relationship between—"

"Mr. Bishop!"

When she snapped out his name, Baron forcefully swallowed back his coming words.

Gypsy narrowed her gaze. "I will *not* walk down that path with you again. Apparently you think of me as your daughter or little sister or something."

"No!" He bit his lip and turned away. "I have *never* considered you as such."

"Then quit acting like my dad."

Baron gritted his teeth. "I am not—"

"The reason we came to Tokyo in the first place—the *only* reason—is to do business," she said. "And while you have procured an ideal home for us, I have no intention of *playing house* with Nasaka. Just… don't go there."

She waited a moment, but he didn't respond.

"I do not speak the language, Baron." She sighed. "I can't even order food for myself. The fact that I *need* him goes without saying. If I was planning on having sex with him, I would have done so in America. I didn't have to fly to the other frickin' side of the world to have my way with Dr. Magic Hands over there."

108

Nasaka chuckled. "Doll Eyes has a point. Although I do not like to define my sexuality with such narrow boundaries, as far as women go... she is definitely my type. Had she shown the proper interest, I would have taken her at the gym that day."

"Nasaka..."

"Yes, Doll Eyes?"

"Would. You. Please. Shut. Up?"

"Ahh... I do love your fire, Doll Eyes." He chuckled again. "But can't you see? Your boss needs more assurance than just your denial that we will not develop a physical relationship."

"He has no right to need such assurances," she hissed.

"Calm down. Calm down." Nasaka laughed nervously. "Your chakra is looking pretty scary right now. No... what Mr. Bishop needs, is assurance from *me*." He turned to the brooding man. "It is not an unfair request, Doll Eyes. If the man wants to know of my desires, I am more than willing to share them with him."

Baron cut his eyes toward the smiling, pretty Asian man.

"I like sex, Mr. Bishop... many different forms of sex. It feels good. I like to feel good. As long as they are from legal age to not yet dead... sex is a possibility. There is great beauty to be found in *every* stage of life. Age is not a factor... nor is gender or nationality or even fetish. I happily partake of them all."

Gypsy growled. "As long as you try to at least keep it within the same species *and* behind the closed door to your own room, I care not if you *partake*. What I do care about... is that the two of you felt that the mendacity of such a conversation was even bloody necessary."

"See what I mean?" Nasaka laughed and flipped up one of her curls. "If you haven't yet noticed, this lovely little doll-eyed beauty standing next to me is a bit more on the *reserved* side. And while I would like nothing more than to expand her climactic horizons, I would never *force* her in anything. No, dear Mr. Bishop, this one... heh, her vanilla little knees are locked tighter than the Emperor's treasure vault."

Gypsy crossed her arms. "We're in Japan, asshat," she mumbled. "They have no Emperor."

Nasaka raised a single brow, sardonically. "Umm... Yeah, they do. As a matter of fact, Japan is the *only* country with a ruler still titled Emperor."

Gypsy paused, furrowing her brows. "Wait… Are you being serious right now?"

"Yes, Doll Eyes. I'm being completely serious."

"Huh… Wow… Well, is he like the Queen, then—just a figurehead?"

"Since the Postwar Constitution, yeah, pretty much. But the Emperor of Japan is more like the Queen and the Pope—the *real* one—mixed together."

Gypsy gave him an incredulous look. "So… he is the ruling monarch *and* the heavenly sovereign?"

"Of the Shinto religion, yeah. They say his family is directly descended from the sun-goddess, Amaterasu. Well, that's the legend, anyway."

"…Wow. I didn't realize. Hmpft."

"And not only that," Nasaka said. "He lives right here in the heart of Tokyo."

"*Here?*"

Taka nodded. "What did you think the Tokyo Imperial Palace was, Doll Eyes?"

"A tourist attraction."

"Nope." He sort of snorted, amusedly. "That's where the Emperor lives. Who's the asshat now, lovely lady?"

"Apparently, we *both* are," Gypsy mumbled.

"Apparently." He lightly yanked on one of her curls.

She slapped his hand away. "Stop changing the subject, Taka. I was good and pissed. Still am."

He winked at her. "Threw you off your rant, huh?"

She almost snarled at him.

Nasaka only chuckled again and walked off to explore the rest of the house.

Gypsy was glaring at Baron when he turned back to face her, but the uncharacteristically vulnerable look now clouding his normally cold eyes caused her anger to falter.

"I would ask for your forgiveness once again…" He sighed. "But what I truly need from you is… *understanding*. We will continue to have this same *mis*understanding until you can actually see who I truly am. Will you give me at least that?"

She didn't respond.

"Gypsy…" he whispered, in that deep, mesmerizing voice.

She sucked in a quick breath.

"You allowed me to see the *real* you. Please... allow me the opportunity to do the same. The only way you and I are going to see eye to eye... is if we walk side by side."

"Meaning?"

He smiled. "Meaning... I walked beside you. I experienced who you were at the pub *and* who you were at home—when your guard was down. Allow me to give you the same such prying glance. After that, if you still cannot understand where I'm coming from, I will... step back, so to speak."

"You mean... you'll quit acting like some psycho, overprotective father figure."

He clenched his teeth. "If that is the way you have to put it... then, yes. I will stop."

"Fine." She sighed. "I don't feel like fighting anyway. We only have a couple of days here before we fly to Shanghi. I want to explore a bit... while I have someone other than Nasaka to show me around."

Baron smiled. "Are you asking me out on a date, Ms. Rodden?"

She blushed. "Please don't get creepy again."

"I wouldn't dream of it," he whispered as he placed his hand on her lower back and led her out the door.

Gypsy inhaled deeply. "Mmm... What is that?"

Baron leaned forward, pulling her hair back with his chin. She shuddered when the tip of his nose brushed against her ear.

"You have to guess, sweet Gypsy. What kind of game is it if I cover your eyes and then simply *give* you the answers?"

"It's a spice," she said.

"Go on..."

His warm breath against her neck made her shiver. He smiled.

"Umm... Mr. Bishop?"

"What we are doing now has nothing to do with work. So tell me again, Gypsy. What were our personal, *intimate* names we agreed upon?"

"...Sir?"

"Ahh… You have no idea the pleasure I receive when *that* word drips from *those* lips."

When Gypsy stiffened, Baron couldn't help but chuckle.

"I'm glad you're enjoying yourself, *Sir.*"

"I am. I only wish I could say the same for you."

"How can I possibly enjoy myself when you are touching me, teasing me, bringing your lips so close it completely steals my breath? I can't even think straight. I get dizzy when you're holding me like this."

"…Gypsy."

Baron slowly removed his hand from her eyes. She blinked down at the pretty little lotus-carved candle he was holding under her nose. She turned around, looking up at him.

"Why did you stop the game? You didn't even let me have another guess."

"I thought I was making you uncomfortable."

"Uncomfortable as a boss, yes. As a man… you are sensual beyond explanation." She chuckled. "I'm gonna start calling you Baron Von Dreamy. Look at my arms…" She held them out to him. "…they're covered in goose bumps."

Baron glanced away, trying to hide the flush he could feel covering his cheeks. "Don't say such things."

"What?" She snorted out a laugh. "So *you're* the only one who gets to tease?"

He looked back at her. "You were only teasing?"

"I was teasing you *back*, yes."

He made a little huffing sound. "You shouldn't allow your lies to sound so sweet."

"Oh, it wasn't a lie. Jeezy peez, Mr. Bishop, you are certainly trained in the art of completely melting a woman."

He smiled with only one corner of his mouth. "So, I melted you?"

"Yeah, duh. I'm only human, after all. So stop it… Baron Von Creepy."

"Creepy? I thought you said I was dreamy."

"Yeah, in a creepy oh-my-gawd-what-is-he-going-to-do-next kind of way." She grabbed his hand. "Come on. There's so much more to see."

Baron could tell by the way she was holding to him, there was nothing deeper to be gleaned by her natural touch. Still, he fiercely held to her hand and didn't let go.

"Oh, Baron. Look at that. Have you ever seen anything so pretty? Ugh! I want one... bad."

But Baron was no longer listening to her. The fact that she had so casually just called him by his first name, had completely shaken him up inside. He stared at her smiling profile—stunned, entranced.

"I wish *I* could wear something like that," she mumbled.

When he didn't respond, Gypsy yanked on his hand and turned to face him.

"Are you even listening to me?"

He glanced to the colorful dresses in the window display, then back down into her smiling, bourbon-colored eyes.

"The emerald one would suit you perfectly."

"Yeah, right. Look at this butt." She slapped her hip. "You can't have curves and wear dresses like that."

"It is called a cheongsam. It is actually Chinese in origin. Come." He guided her inside the small shop. "I will prove you— *and* your butt—wrong, sweet Gypsy."

When she stepped out of the dressing room, Gypsy sighed, disappointed.

"See? I told you. It's way too tight around my breasts. I can barely move my arms." She looked in the mirror, turning from side to side. "My butt sticks out too far... it makes the side-slits come up dangerously high."

When Baron didn't respond Gypsy turned to look at him, but found him already standing against her.

"B-Baron?"

He didn't say anything. He simply placed his hands on her shoulders and stared at their reflection. Then, he said something Gypsy couldn't understand to the sales lady who had come running over to help them.

"Ahh... I see," the lady said with a nod before turning to Gypsy. "Tatas are too big. No problem. New style. Just in. Will look so beautiful."

Gypsy just stared after the lady as she ran into the back, quickly speaking words Gypsy knew there was no way in the world she would ever be able to understand.

"Did she... Did she just say... my *tatas* were too big?"

"Hmpft, your tatas are perfect, sweet Gypsy. As is the rest of you."

She glanced back at the mirror when he spoke. Baron's deep blue eyes sparkled behind her.

"M-Mr. Bishop?"

"Don't worry. They are bringing you another cheongsam. One that will accommodate your... tatas."

Gypsy furrowed her brow. "That's not funny. My breasts are completely normal sized."

"Ahh, but the cut of the clothing here speaks differently." He gently pulled her hair back. "Personally... I think you look incredible. Even better than in your kilt."

"Even better than in my kilt, huh?"

"Yes." He winked at her in the looking glass. "And as far as business goes, lovely lady... this dress look would definitely help *any* negotiation to swing in your favor. Can I ask something inappropriate of you?"

"Pfft. Go ahead. You always do."

Baron leaned in closer. "Promise me you won't wear a cheongsam in front of anyone else."

"Why?"

He lightly brushed the tip of his nose across her ear. She gasped.

"I want this vision all to myself," he whispered. "Save it for me, Gypsy."

She nearly shivered. "Why do you keep doing that—touching me with your nose?"

"...Because you like it."

She chuckled. "You are an evil man. Such unseemly behavior warrants an equally unseemly punishment."

"Punishment?" He smiled. "You are the first to dare try. Tell me, sweet Gypsy. What horribly unseemly thing did you have in mind?"

"Torture." She smiled when she heard his breath hitch. "I am going to buy a cheongsam in every color—a different dress for each day of the week."

"Wha— Why would you do that?"

"To ensure that our clients—and everyone else in this insanely large city—don't have to constantly see me wearing the same one. Because, you know… that's just tacky."

He squeezed her shoulders. "You wouldn't dare."

She sent him her best sarcastic look. "Oh yeah? Well then, challenge accepted."

The shop owner came running back over, arms loaded down with colorful silk.

"New style," she said, smiling. "See? No back."

⁂

Baron actually growled when she stepped back out in front of the mirror.

Gypsy smiled at her reflection. "This… fits… perfectly."

And it did. This new style was different only in the fact that it was minus the short sleeves and the back down to just below her shoulder blades. It still had the same high collar and those beautifully ornate buttons that started at the base of her throat, curved around her right breast, and trickled all the way down past her waist. She could now move her arms without restraint, and the open back meant no more squished tatas.

She turned to the smiling, expectant woman at her side. "I'll take them all, please."

"Ahh, very good."

When the woman clapped her hands, two other ladies started wrapping up the lovely dresses.

"Oh, and can I have the hangers as well?" Gypsy asked. "I've only just arrived. I haven't had time to procure the basics just yet."

The owner only stared at her a moment before looking to Baron, who apparently repeated what she said because the lady smiled again and nodded her head.

"We're leaving out in two days," Baron said. "Don't you think that was a bit rash?"

115

The irritated tone in his voice caused Gypsy to smile. "It's not like I'm gonna drag a suitcase all around the globe. The house belongs to Bishop, Grey & Sweet, does it not?"

He only glared at her. He didn't speak.

"Since about half my life will now be spent *there*, I'll be stocking my closets and traveling with a carry-on."

"What if I forbid it?"

She shrugged her shoulders. "It's *my* money. Forbid all you like."

Baron only stood there, scowling.

Gypsy chuckled. "I assume you are well acquainted with *passing out* punishment—seeing as that's one of your *things*—but apparently you need some work in the *receiving* punishment department. I'll be happy to help you out with that."

Baron only sighed and shook his head.

"What?" Gypsy went back to admiring her reflection. "You don't like hanging out with another Dom?"

He rolled his eyes. "That would be Domme, not Dom."

"Domme Gypsy—I kind of like the sound of that. It's got a certain mysterious *ring* to it."

He clicked his tongue against the roof of his mouth. "You have no clue what you're even talking about."

"True." She smiled. "But I prefer you call me that, anyway."

"Never gonna happen."

She chuckled. "So says the pouty Master of Darkness."

"I knew you would be difficult, but you are proving positively incorrigible."

"Then stop trying to *train* me. I know what you're thinking. I'm not a *complete* idiot. I thought I'd made myself perfectly clear—I will *never* be a submissive."

"I would never want you to be," he mumbled under his breath.

When she started back to the dressing room, Baron grabbed her arm.

"Leave that one on."

She looked down at the beautiful, emerald-colored silk. "Why?"

"There's something I want to show you. That dress will be perfect."

"But… my shoes don't match."

"Easily remedied."

He motioned to all the heels lining the back wall and then headed that way.

Gypsy paid the owner and was about to collect all of her lovely new items when Baron returned.

"Here. Try these on."

She smiled. "And just how did you know my size?"

"I've had a great deal of experience picking out the right attire for the right woman."

Baron handed a business card to the cashier and said something as Gypsy walked back to the mirrors. She was admiring the sexy green shoes when he joined her.

"I've gotta hand it to you, Mr. Bishop. These are perfect."

"One final touch," he said, lifting her hair, loosely twisting her curls up before securing them atop her head with exquisite jade chopsticks. "My gift to you," he whispered. "As are the shoes."

"Wow…" She turned from side to side. "I look… stunning."

"Yes, you do."

"But I thought you didn't want anyone seeing me in this dress. You've gone and made it ten times worse."

Baron smiled. "Since you are incapable of minding me, I've decided to show you off. Come. Your packages are being delivered to the house. The only thing you need to concern yourself with… is whether Nasaka will try them all on before we get back."

Gypsy was still giggling as he led her back out onto the street.

———— ❦ ————

"What *is* this place?"

Baron leaned over and whispered, "It's a secret."

"Yeah. I already know *that*. You've been hiding something from me since I stepped out of that dressing room."

"Wha—" He grabbed her hand. "Are you in pain?"

Gypsy nodded. "Yeah, but I figured if I came along… you would make it go away." She gave him a weak smile. "I trust you to make it all better, Baron, to make that little devil of a fox go back to sleep."

He wrapped his arm around her waist and quickly pulled her into an alley.

"Listen to me, Gypsy. I would *never* do anything to hurt you. Do you believe me?"

She barely nodded.

"Damn…" He sighed. "Surprising *you* is going to be much harder than I thought."

"Yeah." She glanced down. "The only surprises I've ever received are the spontaneous kind. If you plan something and try to hide it…" She shrugged her shoulders.

"Hey, look at me." He tilted her chin up. "I promised you a glimpse into *me*, didn't I?"

She didn't answer.

"I was afraid if I told you where I wanted to take you… you would flat out refuse."

"Why?" She furrowed her brow. "Is this place not a club? The lights outside… and the music vibrating through this wall—"

"Yes." He smiled softly. "But it's not just an ordinary club. The party *we're* attending… it is by invitation only."

"Wha— So we were invited here?"

"Well, *I* was. You're my plus one." He winked. "I didn't mention it earlier because I knew you would shoot me down. But when I saw you in this dress… I *knew* you could pull it off."

"Pull what off? Baron, if you're leading me into darkness, the only proper thing to do is to give me *inner* enlightenment."

"It's funny you should put it that way." He smiled. "There are places for… people like me, all over the world. *This* is one of those places."

"A club?"

"Of sorts. The party we are attending is not a public affair. Vanillas can't just walk in off the street. It's not permitted… even as a guest."

"But… how do you expect me—"

"They know me here, Gypsy. That's one thing we have working in our favor."

"And the other?"

"…You."

"Me? But how—"

"You've got this, Gypsy."

"No way in hell I've got this, Baron. If you think for one minute I'm going to walk into a club with my head bowed and two steps behind you… you've lost your bloody mind."

He chuckled. "As if I would ever expect *that*. No, Gypsy, I mean you've got this on your own."

She tilted her head. "Huh?"

"Just be yourself. Trust me. You've got this. Don't put on a show, and don't become intimidated, either. If you walk through that door as *you*, as just Gypsy, no one will be the wiser."

"Seriously? You actually believe I can pull off being your sub?"

"Not in a million years." He lightly traced his finger down the side of her cheek. "You're a natural Domme. Not in a sexual sense, no. But we're not here for that. You give off an air of confidence that will leave no question. You just stay by my side and be yourself. If you can do that, Gypsy, I can lead you through a piece of *my* world."

She breathed out a sigh of relief. "Thank you, Baron. That feels sooo much better."

He glanced down toward her hip. "The pain is gone?"

She nodded. "Okay now, if we're gonna pull this off like pros… you've got to give me a heads up on some of the details."

"This is something you have to see… explanations will not suffice. Just stay by my side. Don't get separated. And above all else, do not flinch or shy away. No matter what you see in there, remember this… *you* are an experienced Domme."

"Aww, hell." She shook her head. "Fine. No flinching. No screaming. No gagging. Got it."

He chuckled softly. "I'm certain it won't be as bad as all that. What's playing out in your mind…" He touched her forehead. "…is a thousand times worse than reality. I promise."

"Yeah, whatever. But won't they question two dominants showing up together?"

"Absolutely not. Most Doms are friends, or at the very least, acquaintances. If a Dom doesn't have a permanently contracted sub, they often go to these things together." He snorted. "We're not monsters, Gypsy. We're regular men and women. This is no different than meeting with an equal colleague for drinks or dinner… minus the drinking. No alcohol or drugs allowed."

"No alcohol? In a club?"

He nodded. "Let's not get too deep into all that at the moment. If you are truly curious, I will explain it all later. As for now, we have a party to attend."

He offered her his arm, but she faltered.

"…Baron?"

He silently waited for her to continue.

"When I found out you were a Dom, it didn't shock me in the least. You look the part."

"And just how do you know what *the part* should look like?"

"Well, I mean… the way I pictured a Dom would look— cold eyes, unwavering confidence, barking orders."

He half smiled.

"But look at *me*." She held out her arms. "I'm so vanilla I'm almost clear."

"Clear?" He chuckled softly. "Listen to me, Gypsy. When you stepped out of that dressing room… you looked as fierce as any Domme I've ever met. Like I said, don't think too much about *acting* the part. Just be yourself and you'll be golden."

"Alright." She sighed, finally accepting his proffered arm. "Why do I care? It's not like I'm ever gonna see these people again. If I make an ass out of myself, it's your reputation that will falter. Not mine. Lord Baron will be the one called into question."

"Master Baron."

Gypsy rolled her eyes. "Oh, excuse me. *Master* Baron."

He glanced sideways at her, smiling just before he leaned down and whispered in her ear. "You haven't even realized it yet, have you?"

"Realized what?"

"The ease with which you now say my name."

"Wha—"

"You have called me Baron since the dress shop. And, Gypsy… I like the way you say it."

His whispered words caused her to shuffle-step… just as he reached for the door.

Chapter 10

Gypsy released a relieved breath when they finally made it to the other side of the main club. It was too loud, too crowded, and all those flashing lights were giving her a headache. Calmness washed over her when she felt Baron's hand upon her lower back. She could easily picture how his long, elegant fingers must look... back-dropped by the dark silk of her dress.

Breathe, Gypsy.

I am breathing, Angel. And why are you just now chiming in? If you were truly doing your job, you would have talked me out of this nonsense.

The little demon chuckled. *This time... he was just as curious as I always am.*

"Always good to see you, Master Baron," a decidedly French-sounding man said as he opened the door at the bottom of the dark stairwell.

Gypsy hadn't looked directly at the speaking man; she was too busy taking in all the intricate carvings outlining the unusual doorframe. The twin jade dragons at each top corner, they were especially captivating... in a *magical* sort of way she had not expected.

"Marquis la Rune, this is Mistress Gypsy—my guest this evening."

Gypsy turned only when the stranger had lifted her hand to his lips, his dark hair falling around to hide his features.

"A truly lovely guest indeed, Master Baron," he said. "You always seem to pluck the rarest of blossoms."

When the man finally lifted his head and made eye contact with her, Gypsy was immediately smitten with the eerie image of a crow flying about in her mind. The man's eyes were like coals— black as was his long raven hair. Such a thing was not unusual in and of itself, no. But the milky white pallor of his fair skin—skin she would have sworn had never seen the light of day—was such a stark contrast, she was struck with a sudden loss for words.

The man noticed… and smiled.

"Perhaps you came with Master Baron, loveliest of rare blossoms, but one can always hope you do not choose to *leave* with him."

When Marquis la Rune reached for one of the loose curls hanging down to elegantly frame her lovely face, Gypsy quickly snatched his pale wrist, squeezing hard.

"Never… without my permission."

The man's smile returned only after she had released him. He closed his eyes, silently inclining his head toward her before Baron led her away.

"…Freak," she mumbled under her breath.

Baron only tightened his grip upon her waist by way of response.

"Allow me the pleasure of escorting you through this evening's scenes," he whispered.

Gypsy heard him, sort of. She was currently busy taking in the whole of the enormous underground arena they had stepped into, the floor of which was laid out with the many different *scenes* Baron had just mentioned. The spectators, for the most part, were sitting up in the stands—taking in several different scenes at the same time.

"It looks like the first one, here on our left, is a hardcore scene."

Gypsy glanced that way while he was still speaking.

"It's a bit much for a neophyte such as yourself," Baron continued. "Perhaps you shouldn't look."

"I am no neophyte."

"In *this* world… you definitely are," he whispered through a smirking smile.

"To describe me as such implies that this is the *beginning* of something. Of which, I can promise you, it is not."

"Ahh… Let a man have his dreams, Gypsy."

"This dream is rubbish. Never gonna happen. If you wish to dream of me, Baron, make it one in which I never get wrinkles no matter how many nights I sit up playing video games and drinking scotch."

"Ugh…" he mumbled. "And yet another fantasy… dashed against the stones."

She almost chuckled. Then, she noticed *the scene* he had just mentioned.

"Don't flinch," he whispered, holding her ever tighter.

Gypsy wasn't worried about flinching. She was more worried about losing the sushi they had only just shared at dinner.

The various scenes set up around the arena floor, being played out for all invitees to freely behold, were not actually *labeled*. If she were forced to give this one a name, it would have been… My Bloody Valentine.

The set was decorated to resemble an old Victorian style parlor—decorated all in red and gold—including the rugs, antique settee, and elaborate tapestries. What was distinctively *odd* in this otherwise picturesque setting, were the nude models strapped down in various places about the set.

Then, the smell hit her before the realization did. This scene wasn't as it had initially appeared. This scene… was all about body altering. Not just tattoos and extremely painful-looking body piercings, no. Those things were represented, yes, but they were not what caused her sudden unease.

What made Gypsy feel lightheaded… was the attractive couple displayed in the very center. The man was being branded—freehand style. The smell wafting over her as the hot soldering iron touched his tanned flesh, almost made her clamp her hand over her mouth.

Stop it, Gypsy, she kept telling herself. *No flinching. No vomiting. Oh dear lord… I want to vomit so bad.*

When the *artist* laid his sizzling tool on a tiny metal table—presumably to let the branded man catch his breath—he glanced towards Gypsy and winked. She didn't respond. She was certain the look on her face portrayed all the horror *this* particular Dom was looking for. Words were not necessary.

The thin, bald man then went over to sit beside his tattoo model.

"He uses the ancient art of bamboo inking," Baron said.

Gypsy didn't even get the chance to ask before the man picked up a finely sharpened piece of bamboo and began tapping it into the model's skin with a second piece of bamboo.

"Such skill," Baron whispered. "Look how fine the detail work is."

But Gypsy couldn't. She was having a hard time even *focusing*. Forget about being able to appreciate the highly intricate skills of this rather disturbing Dom… she was currently rendered incapable of such a normal thing as *looking* at the fine details.

When the eccentric artist heard Gypsy's tiny, yet sharp, intake of breath… he glanced back at her and smiled.

He eats people, her inner angel said. *I can tell by the look in his eyes… See it? There! Yeah… he eats people.*

The little devil could barely talk for laughing. *You watch too many horror flicks… idiot.*

Gypsy just concentrated on breathing.

"Are you ready to continue?" she finally managed to ask Baron.

Almost as soon as the half whispered words came out of her mouth, the tiny tapping noises stopped. Gypsy glanced back at the scene just as the artist approached the other model displayed in the very center of the set—beside the branded man. She was a petite woman with long black hair, medical bandages covering a large portion of her back.

When the bald Dom began to slowly lift the gauze, Gypsy had to suppress a scream. The body modification this particular model had undergone put all the others to shame. She was neither tattooed nor branded. The intricate heart pattern spanning from one shoulder blade to the other had literally been *carved* out of her pale flesh.

"When tended to properly…" the artist said in a soft voice, causing Gypsy to finally make eye contact with the man. "…the design will not heal in a raised scar." He motioned to the semi-charred skin of the branded man lying there next to them. "This lovely piece of art will heal as you now see it… *below* the natural skin line." He smiled. "A *true* carving."

Gypsy softly cleared her throat then. "I trust you will see to it personally… that it's *tended to properly.*"

"It is my greatest joy—caring for my living works of art."

When Gypsy inclined her head toward him, the bald artist responded in-kind.

Baron led her away. "I cannot believe you just questioned a Master concerning the care of his subs."

"What?"

Gypsy glanced back at the man. He was still staring at her. When he winked again, she smiled.

"I don't believe he was offended in the least," she said. "In truth, he seemed rather proud of the fact he could personally attest to their good health."

"Master Baron."

When the man called out after him, Baron growled under his breath.

"I can't believe we didn't even make it past the first scene," he mumbled. "I thought you would be better behaved than this."

"Liar," she said with a smile, as they turned back to face the waiting Blood Master.

"Apologies, Master Fuu," Baron said. "Forgive us for disrupting your scene and dishonoring you."

"What is your name?" Master Fuu said, ignoring Baron.

"Mistress Gypsy. I am so sorry. I'm not from around here—"

"No need in stating the obvious," he said, looking from her toes to her eyes and back again. "Is your flesh yet pristine?"

She nodded only once. "It is."

"If ever you are so inclined… come to me. I will see you in private."

"I am honored, truly."

Gypsy bowed toward him then. She wasn't actually sure *why* she did it, it just felt like the right thing to do.

"How in seven hells did you manage to pull *that* off?" Baron whispered as they turned to go.

"I have no idea. But get me away from here before he actually talks me into it."

"You mean… you would actually consider body modification?"

"Not in a million years. I'm just afraid… if that man told me to sit down and be still, I would. His presence is a powerful thing. I nearly pissed myself."

"Annnd… she's back." Baron sighed. "But you weren't wrong. Master Fuu is a Dom among Doms. I would steer clear of him for the rest of the evening, if I were you."

She snorted. "Done and done. Heck, I'll probably have trouble sleeping tonight. Definitely leaving the lamp on."

The next scene was a dungeon, complete with rack, stocks, and shackles hanging from chains. Someone was being flogged. Gypsy tried her best not to look *and* to squelch the shiver her reflexes were desperately trying to give in to.

The third scene was a doctor's office with a sexy patient... in the middle of a complete exam. Gypsy *did* shiver then.

"I said, no flinching."

"I wasn't flinching. I always do that when I see a set of stirrups and a paper apron. I hate the gynecologist."

Baron only smiled.

"Sooo... I thought this was all supposed to be about sexual fetishes or something."

"This is all supposed to be about pleasure," Baron said. "Sex isn't the only thing that brings on satisfaction. Although, by the time most of these scenes reach their end, sex will more than likely have taken place... in one form or other."

No sooner had those words left his lips... they came to the policeman scene. A woman was handcuffed and bent over the trunk of a staged patrol car. Gypsy picked up the pace and quickly rounded the corner.

When she came upon a set that looked like a classroom, she stopped.

You have got to be kidding me, she thought.

A smile crossed her face when she noticed the word DETENTION written in all caps across the black chalk board.

Her demon chuckled. *Not only school, but old school.*

Not just old school, the angel added. *Puritan old school. We may have had our fair share of spankings... but never with a cane.*

Baron stopped when he noticed the entranced look in her eyes. His chest tightened. Caning probably shouldn't be her first step toward his world, but a glimmer of hope was all he had wanted. He didn't bother watching the scene. Gypsy's ever-changing reaction was the only pleasure he needed.

The School Master made his willing student count out her deserved punishment. She was securely bound atop his desk, yet the woman didn't once fight against her restraints.

Gypsy watched, almost breathlessly, as the bright pink stripes seemed to glow across the woman's fair bottom. They grew closer together with every moan-inducing *thwack*, but they never crossed.

By the end of the scene, Gypsy was almost exhausted *for* the other woman. Yet, what happened next... touched her heart.

The demanding School Master was suddenly gentle and comforting. He released her restraints, lifting the petite woman to his chest and carrying her to the nearby bed. All the while... he was caressing her, whispering to her, treating her like the most precious person in the world. The Master lay down with his sub, brushing her hair back, gently rubbing lotion across her striped bottom. When the lady began to tremble, her Dom wrapped her up in his arms and held her until she slowly drifted off. The tender smile on the School Master's face as he gazed down at his sleeping sub—the worshipping look in his sparkling dark eyes—made Gypsy's breath hitch.

He adores her, the angel whispered.

I believe... Gypsy paused. *She adores him, too.*

The dark-haired young woman curled onto her side, snuggling into the bedding as a tiny smile turning up the corners of her pink lips. Gypsy couldn't look away. She watched the gentle rise and fall of the woman's relaxed breaths. It was then that she realized... she was jealous of what these two shared—the enormous trust each must have in the other.

Is that... love? she thought.

Twisted love... maybe, the demon answered.

Tell me, the angel whispered softly. *What love isn't just a little bit twisted?*

Gypsy was lost in her internal conversation—staring blindly at the satiated Asian beauty lying peacefully upon that small bed. She faintly heard Baron's deep voice, but it wasn't in any language she could understand.

"Mistress Gypsy." Baron touched her shoulder. "He was saying that you disrupted his scene."

"Huh?"

When she didn't actually turn to face him, Baron lightly brushed her cheek.

"Ahh..." the man said. "You speak English. Very good."

Only then did Gypsy focus on the handsome School Master standing at the edge of his set. Still, the current conversation hadn't yet sunk in.

"You distracted me," the man repeated.

Gypsy glanced down at the thin cane he was meticulously cleaning, almost forgetting the man entirely.

"Can you not understand me?" he said, smiling. "Is my accent truly that bad?"

Gypsy looked back up at the man's face, then quickly glanced toward Baron. He was staring at her, expectantly.

"Wha— Are you talking to *me*?"

The man smiled again as he laid the freshly sanitized cane down.

"I have been talking to you for quite some time now."

"Then would you mind starting over?"

"Heh." A dark glimmer flashed in the Dom's eyes. "I said, you distracted me—pulled me out of my scene. Were I a less skilled Dom, I may have injured her."

"Excuse me?" Gypsy narrowed her gaze. "You *do* realize you are performing in a public arena. Well, semi-public. If you can't handle a little attention, perhaps you should have left your tools at home."

She felt Baron tense beside her, but chose to ignore him.

How dare this man try to blame me! she yelled out internally. *He's the one beating on another human being.*

A stunning smile spread across the handsome School Master's face. "Ahh… Chikara, is your bite as painful as I believe it to be?"

She only glared at him.

"You distracted me, this is true. How could I concentrate properly when such obvious adoration was flowing from those enchanting honey-colored eyes of yours?"

"Pfft. You flatter yourself."

"Perhaps… and yet…" He reached for a long silk pouch hanging next to his other instruments. "…*this* treasure called out to me, only today."

Gypsy looked from the embroidered green pouch he was now holding—a pouch that could have been cut from the same bolt of material as was her new dress—back up to the sadistic School Master. She didn't speak.

"It has been ages since I felt such a pull. *This*…" He slid the ornately carved handle of a bamboo cane out of the silk. "…sang out to my soul. I wasn't sure why… until I saw you standing there."

"Me?"

He nodded. "When this beautiful instrument was crafted, the artist had *your* name etched upon his soul—Chikara. It was meant for you, from its beginning."

"Chikar— My name is Gypsy."

"Only to those who cannot read your essence. Yet... you were appropriately named while your soul still waited in the Great Temple. Before you took your first breath, the gods called you... Chikara—Power."

Baron sort of snorted out an amused laugh.

"I haven't purchased such a fine gift in quite some time," the man continued. "Well, not without already having the lucky recipient picked out."

Gypsy furrowed her brow. "Gift?"

He then handed her the pouch. "This enchanting piece of art has never tasted human flesh... for none but yours could be so sweet."

Gypsy slowly reached for the silk-wrapped cane, but withdrew when she heard Baron's breath hitch. She took a step back.

"Do not be afraid, Chikara. It was made for you. It was meant for you." The School Master smiled. "Come. I will train you how to properly use it."

"*Train* me?"

That dark glint returned to his onyx-colored eyes. "A dominant should never use an instrument on a submissive without first experiencing it for themselves. How else could you know with what strength to wield it? How else could you know the true joy you are gifting another?"

"Joy?"

"Yes, Chikara. This is not a weapon of torture. It is a tool of pleasure."

"And... you expect me to just bend over your desk and let you cane me?"

He smiled. "It would thrill me to no end, yes."

Gypsy crossed her arms and leveled her glare. "Well, Mr. School Master—"

"Please... call me Renji."

"Very well... Renji. I'll bend over for you right after the devil himself begs for my hand and we two-step through the frozen fires of hell." She turned to go. "So when that happens, I'll give you a call."

"Wait." The School Master leaned over the railing. "This *is* yours. Will you not accept it?"

She waved him off. "I have no idea how to use it, no intention of undergoing such training, and absolutely no use for it whatsoever."

When the School Master jumped the barrier and left his set, Baron quickly moved to stand between them.

Gypsy pushed past her new boss and faced the other man, but waited for Renji to speak.

"I will be gentle," he whispered. "I promise."

"If you so much as *touch* me with that thing, I will snap it over my knee and use the pieces to gouge out your beautiful black eyes. *I* promise."

"Let's make a deal then." He smiled. "If you have not reached the pinnacle of pleasure by the time I am done… my eyes are yours."

She looked deep into those beautiful dark orbs of his for a few silent heartbeats, before laughing softly.

"I like you, Renji. But trust me. It ain't ever gonna happen."

"Such a waste." He smiled again, sweetly this time. "Be that as it may, a gift is a gift." He held up the golden cord stretching from one end of the pouch to the other. "May I?"

Gypsy only stared at his handsome face as he drew nearer and gently placed the matching silk-wrapped cane across her back. She looked down; watching as he tenderly traced the golden cord now running between her breasts.

"Perhaps its tormented soul can find a measure of peace… lightly bouncing off your lovely bottom as you walk." He leaned in closer, whispering in her ear. "And promise me… if you ever decide to use it… find me, Chikara. I will gladly take your hand and lead you down the pathway of ecstasy."

When Renji didn't pull away from her—and Gypsy didn't make any attempt to move, either—Baron cleared his throat.

"Have you changed your mind, Mistress Gypsy? Are you going to take the School Master up on his offer? Or would you like to go on to the next scene?"

Gypsy quickly stepped away from the eager Asian Master and turned toward Baron.

"I am ready to go on."

After she had taken several steps, Gypsy became overly aware of the gentle tapping on her left butt cheek—caused by the *gift* now strapped across her back. She glanced back toward the last scene only to find Renji still watching her, smiling. When their gazes met, he winked.

"You handled yourself quite well, Mistress Gypsy," Baron whispered. "You are exactly Master Renji's type. Trust me. If you had given him only the slightest inclination, he would have never let you leave his side."

"You *know* him?"

"Of course I know him. Quite well, in fact." Baron smiled. "I cannot recall the last time I have been so entertained. These events are always curious, yes, but you have added a delicious amount of spice to this evening."

"Spice…" she mumbled. "Is that what you'd call it?"

He glanced sideways at her. "For a brief moment, I thought you were actually going to take Master Renji up on his offer. I must say, I would have enjoyed it much more than I should have."

Gypsy chuckled. "Yeah, because you are one seriously twisted dude."

"As far as twisted goes, I feel you will find I am one of the less twisted Doms here. *You* seem to walk an edgier path than I do. Two-stepping through the frozen fires of hell…" He snorted out a laugh. "Cute. Keep up with the way things are currently going, and you'll be accepting the devil's hand with a brand new tattoo and pretty pink stripes across your perfect little ass."

She only smiled and bumped him with her shoulder. Baron took the opportunity to gently clasp her hand. Gypsy didn't even flinch, only locked their fingers together even tighter.

"Come on," he whispered. "Let's take a seat in the stands. This next scene takes some time, but I think you will enjoy it."

"Ahh… What is *that?*" Gypsy whispered, amazed.

"It's called a Cyr Wheel. The model can use it as an extension of her own body."

"A Cyr Wheel…"

Gypsy stared, completely entranced by the beauty of the graceful dance playing out before her.

"It reminds me of Cirque du Soleil..." she barely mumbled.

Baron only smiled softly, spellbound by her enraptured gaze and sparkling eyes.

The model before them did indeed seem to be one with the giant silver hoop—spinning inside it, curving her body around it. The whole scene was exquisitely elegant. Gypsy was so captivated by the twirling woman, she didn't immediately notice the second model... the one meticulously bound in colored ropes. When she finally spotted *her*, Gypsy gasped.

"It's called Kinbaku," Baron whispered. "Translated in English it simply means... tight binding."

"...Kinbaku sounds much prettier."

"Yes. I agree. And the man standing with her..." Baron motioned with a nod. "...is a Bakushi—a Rope Master."

While Baron was speaking, the Bakushi finished binding the model and motioned for the dancing lady to join them.

"Wow..." Gypsy whispered to herself. "He... he is truly a beautiful man."

Baron tightened his hold upon her hand. "So... this is what Gillis was talking about," he mumbled.

But Gypsy didn't hear him; she was completely invested in the ongoing scene. When her breath audibly hitched, Baron nearly growled. He glanced back to the set just as the Bakushi reached for the Cyr Wheel.

Gypsy held her breath as the Rope Master began attaching the colored ropes—or *jute*, as Baron had explained—to the wheel itself. Only then could Gypsy truly see the genuine beauty of the Bakushi's artistic design.

When the beautiful Dom gently hoisted the large metal hoop up into the air, the bound model went with it.

"She looks like... an enchanting marionette," Gypsy whispered, mostly to herself.

When she felt Baron's gaze upon her, she sort of blushed and glanced at him sideways.

"Don't get any weird ideas, Sir. I think *she* is beautiful like that, not *me*. I mean, look at her face. Even though her eyes are closed, you can clearly see her obvious euphoria."

"But not you," he whispered. "You would not feel such joy, were your roles reversed."

Gypsy shook her head. "No, Baron. I wouldn't. You see… I have this extreme aversion to being bound. Even being pinned down while play-wrestling with Gillis—Ugh! It truly pisses me off to no end. Even when I see prisoners led into the courtroom in shackles, I cringe. Just the mere thought of a policeman binding my hands like that—no. I will never be bound. Never."

"All the instances you just mentioned… those were ones of being held against your will."

She softly snorted. "If I am ever *held* I promise you, it will be against my will."

"Fair enough," Baron whispered. "Would you like to move on, then?"

"No. I want to see the rest of it."

When Baron didn't respond, she turned to him and smiled.

"Just because I have no desire to experience it for myself, I will not deny that Kinbaku is truly fascinating. As long as I get to sit up here in the stands, I'm good."

Baron half smiled then. "When this scene has finished, I will introduce you to Jūshirō." He inclined his head toward the man on set. "He is a true Master of Kinbaku, the most esteemed Bakushi yet living."

"Yet living?"

Baron nodded. "His father was recognized throughout the world. And, truth be told… I believe Master Jūshirō will one day surpass even him."

"Yes, please." Gypsy giggled softly. "I *definitely* want to meet *him*."

"You have surprised me yet again," Baron mumbled, slowly releasing her hand. "This is the first time I have seen you act this excited over a man. I don't think I like it."

Gypsy didn't respond. She was already caught back up in the mesmerizingly sensual scene still playing out before them.

Chapter 11

"Oh… those look delicious." Gypsy grabbed Baron's hand. "Come on. I want a crêpe… drenched in chocolate."

He chuckled. "Are you a woman, or a child?"

She smiled. "Sometimes… I'm both."

"I blame this on Gillis," he mumbled. "He spoiled you."

"Damn straight, he did." She scanned the picture menu. "Which do you want? Let's get different ones."

"Why? So we can share?"

Gypsy shrugged her shoulders. "I don't know about *sharing*. But I'll be having some of yours, yeah."

"And… you don't mind eating food from a street vendor?"

"Why?" She furrowed her brow. "It's just dessert. How can you mess up sugar?"

"Very well. Have you decided?"

"I want the one with fresh strawberries and chocolate drizzle."

After Baron had ordered for them, Gypsy was nearly ready to jump up and down.

"What did you get?" she said through a giggle.

"I got what you asked for."

"No, I mean you. What did *you* get?"

Baron smiled with only one corner of his mouth. "Cheesecake with caramel sauce."

Gypsy giggled out loud then, clapping her hands. Baron rolled his eyes, but couldn't hide his smile.

<hr />

"Oh my gawd, Baron," she said after savoring her first bite. "*This* has got to be a slice of heaven. A *literal* slice of heaven."

"It's that good, huh?"

She nodded while taking her second bite.

134

"Then let me try," he said, taking a small bite of her pastry before she could protest. "Mmm... That *is* divine. Sweet, but tart and light at the same time. I like it."

"How about yours?" Gypsy eyed his honey-colored crêpe. "Does it taste as good as it looks?"

Baron smiled. "See for yourself."

When Gypsy bit into that flaky crust—all full of whipped cream, caramel, and a whole slice of cheesecake—her eyelids fluttered.

"Ahh... sooo good. I would totally lick that stuff right off the sidewalk."

Baron chuckled. "That's disgusting."

"I know. So you better make sure you don't drop any of it."

"Yes, it would be a shame to waste even a drop." He moved closer to her. "Hold still, Mistress," he whispered.

Gypsy did hold still, completely frozen as she watched his parting lips move ever closer. When Baron lightly licked the edge of her mouth, Gypsy gasped and held her breath.

"You had a little whipped cream on your cheek," he said, not withdrawing from their intimate closeness. "I believe it tastes even sweeter served up upon your soft flesh." He scooped some caramel sauce up with his finger and touched it to her lips. "Tell me, Gypsy. How does it taste served up upon me?"

She stared directly into his deep blue eyes as she slowly opened her mouth. His gaze left hers and lingered on her parted lips. When she finally opened them enough to lick his finger, he was trembling.

Baron groaned softly. The gentle sound soothed away all her inhibitions. Gypsy closed her lips around him, licking off every last drop of delicious sweetness.

Baron gasped. "...Stop... Gypsy... please."

When he moaned again, she released him.

"Stay as you are," he rasped. "Don't move an inch. Give me a moment to regain some semblance of control. Your affect upon me is currently visible to all."

Gypsy obeyed, quickly glancing around at the people passing by—some gaping, others intentionally looking the other way.

"Baron," she whispered softly. "I'm so sorry."

He half smiled. "How dare you apologize for one of the most erotic moments of my life? If we were alone—"

"Shhht." Gypsy quickly capped her hand over his mouth, then felt him kiss her palm. "Jeez. Stop it, already. We're making a giant spectacle of ourselves."

Baron took a deep breath then, and straightened back up. "Damn... That made me a little lightheaded, Ms. Rodden."

Gypsy blushed crimson. She didn't speak again until they had gone about a block and a half.

"I really am sorry," she finally whispered.

"For what?" Baron wrapped his arm around her waist. "For doing *exactly* what I had hoped you would do?"

When she didn't answer, Baron hailed a cab and ushered her in.

"Gypsy." He waited until she turned to face him. "You are the first woman I have ever met... that I would consider possibly being semi-vanilla with."

She bit her lip, then glanced at the back of the taxi driver's head before whispering, "And *you* are the only man I have met who I'd almost consider being a little... pralines-and-cream with."

He sucked in air through his teeth and pulled her closer. "Oh, Gypsy... I am *definitely* holding you to that one day. I promise."

<hr />

When the cab pulled up outside their new shared home, Baron helped her out and held her hand all the way up the walk.

Gypsy had butterflies warring like crazy in her tummy... until Baron opened their front door.

"What the hell?" she yelled, stomping up to Nasaka. "What do you think you're doing?"

Baron chuckled. "Told you."

"What?" Nasaka said. "I was just holding it up in front of the mirror."

She snatched the white dress from his hands. "You're sick. You know that, right?"

"Wow…" Nasaka looked her up and down. "Now that I see it on *you*, I don't have to wonder how sexy it would look. Damn, Doll Eyes. You make my mouth water."

Gypsy only rolled her eyes before stomping into her room, hanging the lovely blue dress alongside the others now filling her closet.

"Hey now… what's this?" Nasaka said, opening the silk pouch across her back and sliding the cane out. "Now *that* is one beautiful little tool."

Nasaka quickly swatted her bottom before Gypsy even had the chance to turn back around.

"Why you little shit," she hissed through clenched teeth.

Baron snatched the cane from Nasaka and moved to stand between the two. "That'll be quite enough of that." He glanced back over his shoulder at the smiling Asian man. "I should let her beat the hell out of you, but it's late… and I'm tired."

"I just bet you are." Nasaka's smile grew wider. "Now… where in the world could the two of you have gone? Hmm? It's not like you can find a treasure like *that* at the local convenience store."

"It was a gift," Gypsy snapped. "And I'd appreciate you keeping your grimy little hands off my stuff. And, Nasaka… if you *ever* do that again, I swear by every hair on my head I will throat-punch you so hard—"

Nasaka held up his hands. "I got it. I got it. I crossed the line. I'm sorry. I mean… Baron bought the gift, it's only right that he should be the first to use it."

"*I* didn't buy it," Baron said, slipping the cane back in its pouch and laying it atop her dresser.

Nasaka's mouth fell open as he turned to Gypsy. "You mean to tell me that Miss Creamy Vanilla Universe over there actually bought an instrument of torture?"

"I didn't *buy* it," she said. "It was a gift. And it is not meant to be an instrument of torture. Renji said it was a tool for pleasure."

"Renji?" Nasaka furrowed his brow. "Are you talking about Renji Yamamoto?"

Gypsy shrugged her shoulders.

"Yes," Baron said. "The School Master seemed quite taken with our straight-laced little doll-eyed friend. He said the cane had called out to him only today—named her Chikara and even offered to train her how to use it properly."

"Yeah, I just *bet* he did," Nasaka grumbled.

Baron narrowed his gaze. "...Taka Nasaka... You wouldn't happen to be kin to Jūshirō Nasaka, would you?"

Nasaka snarled up his nose. "He's my stepbrother. We share the same father."

"What?" Gypsy's eyes widened. "You mean to tell me that your *dad* was the greatest Bakushi that has ever lived?"

Nasaka didn't speak, only scowled.

Gypsy snorted. "Well... that explains that."

When she chuckled and left the room, Nasaka glanced over at Baron. "Why in the accursed flames of hell would you take her to a place like that?"

Baron smiled. "It seems your little doll-eyed beauty queen may not be as purely vanilla as you'd initially thought."

"Do not taint her," Nasaka hissed.

Baron patted the other man's shoulder as he made to leave. "I wouldn't dream of it, Dr. Magic Hands."

<hr/>

The trio flew to China and set up their apartment in Shanghi, then on to Bangkok to do the same.

"Ugh... it's so hot here, I can barely breathe."

"We should go shopping for some lighter clothing," Nasaka said. "Let's take care of that before we rest."

"You mean... *so* we can rest," Gypsy said. "There's no way I could lay down—all sweaty and sticky like this."

"*I* will take you shopping," Baron said to Gypsy, gently placing his hand upon her lower back.

"But you complain about everything I pick out."

"I do not *complain*. I simply try to advise. That's all."

"Advise a grown woman on how she should dress?"

Taka snorted out a laugh. "So blind..." he mumbled, shaking his head before walking out the door. "...So incredibly, ridiculously blind."

"Don't be upset," Baron whispered. "I simply enjoy watching you step out of the dressing room. I take pleasure in being the first to see you in your new clothing."

She blushed. "Umm… I'm not sure how I should take that."

"As an extremely high compliment." He smiled softly.

Gypsy just stood there, gazing up into his deep blue eyes… mesmerized by his perfect dimples. When Baron leaned down toward her, her breath hitched and her pulse quickened.

Baron's smile grew. "You're drooling, Ms. Rodden."

"Am… Am I?" she barely said, reaching toward her mouth to check.

"No." He lightly touched her cheek. "I was only teasing— embarrassed by the fact *I* was the one nearly drooling."

She felt her cheeks flame up. "*Now* you're teasing. Stop it."

He chuckled softly. "Very well, lovely lady. Come." He took her hand. "Would you prefer we ate *before* shopping, or after?"

"How about *during*? I want to get into some different clothes as soon as possible, but I'm starving as well."

"As you wish, Gypsy." He gently tucked her hair back behind her ear as he guided her toward the door, bending down as he reached for the knob and lightly brushing his nose against her neck. "Anything you wish," he whispered.

She froze… and then shivered. Baron only chuckled.

"This is where we shall say our farewells," Baron said.

Gypsy was staring out the large windows, watching the planes take off and land. "Yeah…" she said absently. "I guess it's time to get to work now."

"I'll make sure you have plenty of entertainment, Doll Eyes," Nasaka said. "I won't let you get homesick *or* bored."

Gypsy cast him a sideways glance and smiled. "I don't know if that's a good thing or a bad thing. With you, Taka, I never know *what* to expect."

"And how could *that* ever be a bad thing?" He winked at her.

"I can think of countless reasons why that would be a bad thing," Baron grumbled.

Nasaka only laughed and walked off.

"Are you sure you have everything you will need?"

"Yes, *Dad.* I'm sure."

Baron turned her to face him. "Stop saying that. It makes all those decadent dreams I've been having lately… feel horribly *wrong.*"

"Decadent dreams?" She smiled with only one corner of her mouth. "Tell me true. You been performing unspeakable acts with Taka when you close your eyes at night?"

Baron raised a single eyebrow, staring down at her but not speaking.

"It's okay." Gypsy glanced in the direction Nasaka had gone. "I won't tell him. He already has more confidence than any one human should. He's a doll, I'll give him that. As rare as you're gonna find, but—"

Baron pulled her against his chest, wrapping his arms around her and holding her there even though she struggled. "Don't fall in love with him. Promise?"

With his whispered words, Gypsy stilled in his arms.

"I cannot imagine sharing a home with you… just the two of us. I have never been one to be jealous, Ms. Rodden, not where any *other* woman was concerned," he mumbled softly. "But whether he knows it or not… Taka Nasaka is the luckiest man in the world."

Still, Gypsy didn't speak.

When Baron slowly released her, he tilted her chin up and gazed down into her honey-bourbon eyes.

They were still standing like that when the boarding call came over the intercom.

"*I'll* be taking over from here," Taka said as he approached. "We aren't scheduled to fly out for about another hour, Doll Eyes. You hungry?"

"Nasaka…"

Baron waited until the other man met his cold gaze.

Neither man spoke; they just stared at each other for an uncomfortably long time.

Finally, Gypsy cleared her throat. "Well, Mr. Bishop. Have a safe flight. I'll check in every week."

Baron turned back toward her. "I will hear from you daily, Ms. Rodden."

"O-okay…"

He held her conflicted gaze until the final boarding call.

Baron smiled softly then, letting her have one last glimpse at his perfect dimples. "I look forward to your return."

Gypsy swallowed hard. "Y-yeah… me, too."

When Baron had disappeared down the ramp, Nasaka gently took her hand. "Come on, Doll Eyes. Let's enjoy some Thai food while we still can."

"We'll be back in Bangkok before you know it," she said, craning her neck so she could keep her gaze fixed on the door Baron had just disappeared through, even though Taka was pulling her the other way.

"That may be true, but you can never have too much Thai food, Doll Eyes. Surely you can agree with *that*."

Gypsy rolled her *doll* eyes. Taka just laughed and tightened his grip on her hand.

From the enormous Suvarnabhumi Airport in Bangkok, Thailand, Baron flew back to the States while Gypsy and Nasaka once again headed out for Tokyo.

<hr/>

"Taka?" Gypsy dropped her head in her hands, letting her pen fall atop the mound of papers. "Can you ask her to bring me the rest of those files? I thought I told her to give me everything we had on Sato Enterprises. This can't be all of it. Huge chunks are missing. I don't have a single thing on March *or* September of last year."

"I told her to bring everything already." He freshened up her coffee. "If you ask me, she's not real happy with the change in bosses."

"Yeah, I get the same feeling." Gypsy placed her hand on her hip. "At least, that's what the fox says."

Nasaka chuckled. "Cute."

"I've been working a week on this crap. Enough's enough." She pulled up her email while she was still talking.

"You clearing it with the Pope?"

"Checking protocol," she mumbled.

Barely a minute had passed before she received a reply.

Nasaka leaned over her shoulder. "What's it say?"

"Do what you gotta do." She sighed. "Very well. Send her ass home, Nasaka. Or tell me what to say and *I'll* send her ass home."

"I'm on it, Doll Eyes."

Almost immediately, the attractive young woman came bursting into Gypsy's office.

"What the hell is she saying, Taka?"

Nasaka waited until the woman's tirade had slowed. "She said she doesn't answer to you, that Brad will be back soon and he will make sure you pay for mistreating her."

Gypsy furrowed her brows. "Brad?"

"Stevens." Nasaka glanced toward her. "The dude you replaced. Apparently... they must have had a *thing*." He motioned toward the teary-eyed woman.

When Gypsy stood, the other woman took a step back.

"Tell her every word I say, Taka. Don't miss a single thing." She walked to the front of her desk. "Men are pigs," she said, then waited for Nasaka to finish. "I don't know what Bradley Stevens told you. I have no idea what sweet promises he whispered in your ear."

When Nasaka finished speaking, tears welled back up in the young woman's eyes.

Gypsy sighed. "He lied to you, honey. That man will never step foot in this office again. I am here because of how loosely he ran the place."

Nasaka waited a moment before repeating the other woman's words. "He told her they were going to get married and move to America. He promised her."

"Did he even tell her when he found out he was leaving?"

Nasaka asked the woman, then glanced back at Gypsy and shook his head.

"Bloody hell." She rubbed her temples. "Didn't Baron say that Bradley Stevens was miserable here because he missed his wife and kids? That he was spending a king's ransom flying back and forth?"

Nasaka didn't answer. Gypsy sighed again. The woman started crying in earnest then.

"Ugh… I'm not equipped to handle this." Gypsy groaned aloud. "What was her name again? Sakara?"

Nasaka only nodded.

"Hey, Sakara."

The woman sniffed and wiped her eyes.

"You wanna go get some sushi?"

The woman didn't answer.

"There's a bar not far from here," Nasaka said. "Other side of the street on the next block."

"Hell, I could use a drink right about now." Gypsy grabbed her purse. "Let's lock up and call it a day." She reached for the other woman. "Come on, Sakara. Let's drown those tears then forget them, waddaya say?"

The woman didn't say anything after Nasaka had translated, just quietly followed them to the elevators.

After that day, Sakara came to work as a different person. She not only dug up all of the Sato files, she spent the next two weeks completely reorganizing the entire office.

Yet, even with her secretary's most capable help, it took Gypsy four months—instead of the planned upon two—just to fix what Bishop, Grey & Sweet *already* had going on in Japan.

⚬≪◆◆◆≫⚬

"What do you think awaits us in China?" Nasaka said, stuffing their carry-ons into the overhead compartment.

"If I find another distraught woman waiting in our office in Shanghi…" Gypsy looked out the window. "…I'm going to castrate Stevens when I finally get back home."

Nasaka sort of snorted. "I do believe our sweet little Sakara wouldn't mind being present for that horrifyingly grim little show. But I must admit, it does sound sooo like you, Gypsy."

"That's because I wasn't kidding, Taka." She glanced back towards him. "Even if Stevens didn't make a complete ass out of himself in the other two offices, I might just do it anyway… for Sakara's sake."

Nasaka smiled. "You like her, don't you?"

Gypsy just shrugged her shoulders and looked back out the window.

"That's nice," Nasaka said, taking her hand before leaning his seat back. "I'm glad. She likes you, too, Doll Eyes."

***

The original plan was to spend six months in Asia—two in each office—then six months back in America, such did not prove to be the case that first year. They spent four months in Tokyo, three in Shanghi, and almost two and a half in Bangkok.

Every office played out the exact same story—completely in shambles, files stuck everywhere, a brokenhearted young secretary, and more massages than Nasaka had ever given a single patient before.

"Your hands are gonna fall off, Taka."

He smiled. "Then, I guess I'll just have to rub you with my feet."

Gypsy snorted out a laugh. "So gross."

"What? I'll wash them first." He tickled her. "You excited about tomorrow?"

"Are you kidding? Jeez... I'm so homesick I can barely breathe. I never dreamed I would be so tired of looking at pretty Asian men."

"Well that's not going to change." He yanked on her ponytail. "Because *I'm* coming with you."

"Why did you follow me here, Taka? I mean... really? Tell me. Why? You are an accomplished physician with a thriving practice. You left your family. You put all your patients on indefinite hold. For what? A perfect stranger who offered you nothing in return? Why would you do something like that— something like *this*?"

"Perhaps because... I liked your colors."

"Stop teasing. I was being serious."

"I'm being serious as well. Just because *you* don't believe I can see auras, glean destinies, tame a nasty fox bite..." He tickled her again. "...that doesn't mean I can't. Besides, I am nothing if not an adventurer. I don't tie myself down stateside. Never have. Trace met me while I was on an enlightening walkabout in Australia. Remember?" He smiled and gently bumped his forehead against hers. "I came because I wanted to. I came because Baron

Bishop paid me a small fortune to. And also, I came because I wanted to watch you grow."

"Have I? Grown?"

"I thought your colors were breathtaking before. Now... Now, you positively glow." He shrugged his shoulders. "I'm just sitting back and enjoying the show, Doll Eyes. You know me... I'm all about the *experience*."

Chapter 12

Gypsy ran up the airport ramp and jumped into Gillis's waiting arms. She squeezed him so tightly he had to gasp for air.

"I've missed you so much, Gills. I thought about you every single day."

"Aye, Lass. I've missed ye more than there are words tae describe it."

When she finally released Gillis, he greeted Nasaka as well.

"Need a lift, wee ninja?"

"Nah. I've got things to catch up on—people to see. I might stop by the bar in a few days; see how things are coming along."

"Bye, Taka." Gypsy kissed his cheek. "Don't be a stranger. Okay?"

"Heh." Gillis snorted. "If he got much stranger, ye couldnae stand him, Kitten."

She punched Gillis and then hugged Nasaka before heading out to the truck.

"Did things go okay at the bar? Did my Vets miss me?"

"Aye, Lass, ye know they did."

"Did you find another waitress?"

"Aye."

"Girl or guy?"

"She's a lass."

"Do you like her?"

"Aye."

"Does she show up for work on time?"

"Aye."

"Does Sheila get along with her?"

"Aye."

"What's with all the one-word answers, Gills? Tell me the whole story. You know how I hate trying to guess. Show your cards, and quit acting so damn cryptic."

"I'm nae cryptic, Kitten. I'm just enjoying listening tae yer twangy wee voice. I've missed ye… even more than I realized."

"Gillis…"

She turned to face him, forcing the large Scot to stop and look her in the eyes. She didn't say anything, just waited until she had his full attention. Then, she pushed down her waistband and exposed her darkening birthmark.

"Yeah… *that* just happened," she said. "Only just."

"Damn…" Gillis closed his eyes, pinching the bridge of his nose. "Ahh… Kitten…"

"Just spit it out, Gillis."

"I like her. I do."

"Like who?"

"Becca."

"Becca? Who the hell's Becca?"

"The new lass I hired tae help run the bar."

"Help *run* it?"

"Aye." He opened his eyes. "She's good with numbers. Ye know how I hate that bit."

"I set it all up online, Gills. The purchasing, vendor payments, payroll—it's like a one-click gig. If you couldn't handle it you should've just called. As long as business is running along about the same, I could have ordered your supplies, paid the girls, and transferred the invoices in like five minutes a week."

"I know, Kitten. I just… I didnae want tae bother ye. I knew ye'd have yer hands full."

"…Bullshit."

"Wha— Why are ye calling bullshite? I'm telling ye the truth."

"Then why am I still in pain?"

Gillis didn't answer, only bit his lip and looked away.

"I would have never thought it," she said.

He glanced back at her when she started to speak.

"If someone had bet me a million dollars, I would have slapped my money down with a smile. I would have gambled my very last penny that you'd never turn on me."

"Gyps—"

"Now, here you stand—looking me square in the eyes and lying to my face. Hmpft." She snorted. "Feel that? Hell must have just frozen over. *That's* the day I would have picked that you would betray me."

"Ye've got it all wrong, Gyps. I'd nae betray ye, Kitten."

"Yet my hip says otherwise." She shook her head. "Just take me home, Gillis."

"But—"

She held up her hand. "Don't speak... just drive."

They were over halfway home before Gillis took a stab at a lighter conversation.

"I havenae seen yer wee laddie in a while."

"Who? Blaine?"

"Aye, Blaine, that was his name." He snorted. "Lad came intae the bar and asked for ye that first night ye left. When I told him ye were in Asia, he just aboot teared-up."

Gypsy remained silent.

"Ye didnae tell him ye were leaving, did ye, Lass?"

"Why would I tell him I was leaving? You knew. Trace knew. It was no one else's business."

"I think the lad loved ye—felt betrayed."

"Yeah, well... I know how he feels."

Gillis glanced sideways at her, bit his bottom lip, then drove the rest of the way home in silence.

⬥⬥⬥

"I'll get yer bags."

"It's only a carry-on, Gillis. I can handle it."

When he pulled open the door, Gypsy stopped and looked up at him.

"Why is the bar open? Did you forget to lock up?"

"Nah. I'm sure Becca is just getting started on the prep work. That's all."

"That's all? Are you saying... she has a key? To *my* bar?"

Gillis sort of froze up, but Gypsy stomped on in. When she tossed her bag towards the stairwell, the woman behind the bar turned toward Gypsy with a smile on her face.

"Ahh, you must be Ms. Rodden... the *Gypsy* in Gypsy's Kilt." She extended her hand. "I'm Becca Greyson. Nice to meet you."

Gypsy had to force herself *not* to grab her hip. The pain was intense, breathtaking.

Ho-lee-hell... that smarts! her demon cried out. *Oww! That hurts like a—*

Hey! her angel shouted. *Watch it before you say some really bad, bad words.*

When Gillis saw the two women—Becca with her hand extended, Gypsy looking like she was ready to devour the other woman—he quickly stepped between them.

"Umm, Becca... I'm sure Gyps is exhausted. She had a long flight."

"Don't be ridiculous, Gillis. I slept most of the way back." Gypsy pushed past him and gave the girl one seriously strong handshake. "Nice to meet you, too, *Becca*. Thanks so much for helping out around here during my absence, but I'm back. You can leave now."

"But... I..."

"But you what, honey? Forgot how to talk? Well, no need. You'll not be around long enough to have a proper conversation, anyway. Go on and clean out your locker now. Leave the uniform. You won't be needing it."

"Hey, Gyps, hang on a minute," Gillis said. "Yer just gonna be here a few weeks. Right? That means we'll be shorthanded again when ye go. Becca needs a job, and—"

Gypsy held up her hand. "Lots of people need jobs. Irrelevant of what will happen when I am gone, I'm here now. Becca, if your services are ever needed in the future, I'm certain Mr. McCullough will let you know."

As the obviously upset woman made to leave, Gypsy stuck her hand out, instantly halting the girl.

"Keys," was all Gypsy said.

When Becca looked toward Gillis, Gypsy snapped her fingers in the other woman's face.

"Keys!"

Becca jumped slightly before fumbling in her apron pocket. Her hands were trembling as she gently laid the bronze-colored key ring in Gypsy's outstretched hand.

"Leave the apron as well."

Becca wasn't in the locker room very long before she came running out, tears streaming down her face. She stopped in front of Gillis, but he didn't look up from his prep work.

"Don't be rude, Mr. McCullough," Gypsy said coolly. "The lady wishes you to see her out."

<hr/>

After she closed out the till and went upstairs, Gypsy headed straight for her room.

"Aye, Lass. Are ye really gonna act that way with me? Are ye just gonna keep ignoring me—stomping around in a jealous huff?"

Gypsy slowly turned back to face him, eyes narrowed. "Did you truly just say that to me? Gillis… did you somehow *forget* who I am? I know I've been gone a long time, but… damn. Have I ever *once* said anything about you dating or liking another woman?"

"Nae."

"And have I ever *once* acted jealous around you or anyone else?"

"…Nae." He glanced away and then back to her. "But I've nae seen ye act like *this* afore, either."

"So, you blame it on jealousy?"

It wasn't truly a question, and Gillis didn't answer.

"You do you, right, Gillis? That's the way we are. You do you, and I do me. I have never once placed demands upon you. Date whomever you want. Sleep with whomever you choose. You're a grown ass man and not bound to *me*. No, I am not jealous of Becca. I *loathe* the woman."

Gillis furrowed his brow, yet held his silence.

"I don't know what all happened between the two of you, and I don't really care to know. What I *do* care about… is this." She pulled her kilt down to reveal a purple bruise the size of her fist.

Gillis gasped. "Aye, Lass. When did *that* happen?"

"The moment *Becca* turned around and smiled at me. The tramp has been gone for hours and look how bad it still is."

"…Ye had tae work all night in that shape," he whispered to himself.

"It's not like I had a choice. I don't know what the two of you cooked up together that you're so hell-bent on hiding from me. But if you don't come clean soon, Gillis, you won't be able to stay here. I can't live like this. Hell, I can barely even *breathe* like this."

"We didnae cook up anything, Kitten. I swear it."

"Swear all you want. It's nothing but lies. The proof is in my birthmark."

She slapped the button on the elevator without another word, then slammed and locked the door to her room.

Gillis heard her scream, heard two different crashes coming from behind her closed door. Then the buzzer sounded, indicating someone was out in front of the bar.

"Bloody hell," he grumbled, before looking over at the little screen.

Taka Nasaka was standing outside the front door, waving at the security camera.

Gillis flipped the lock, but barred the other man's way.

"What are ye doing here in the middle of the blame night?"

"Perhaps you should tell me." Nasaka pushed past him. "We haven't been home ten whole minutes, and all hell has broken loose."

"What are ye talking aboot?"

"I was *trying* to have dinner with a few good friends when my cell started blowing up. Trace sent three messages, then called before I could even respond. As soon as I got the chance, I came over. What's up?"

Gillis didn't answer, only motioned Nasaka inside their home.

"Are you going to make me guess?" Taka glanced around the room. "Where is she?"

Gillis motioned toward her closed doors.

"I drove all this way." Nasaka turned to face him fully. "The least you can do is fill me in on the current crisis."

Still, Gillis didn't speak, just went to the fridge and took out a beer.

"This is perfect," Nasaka said sardonically. "The better part of a year on the other side of the planet—the girl is fine. Home a couple hours—she is forced into solitude."

When Nasaka headed toward the elevator, Gillis finally spoke.

"It's locked."

Taka turned back to face him. "And do you by chance have a key? Or do you believe I possess some strange magic that allows me to walk through walls?"

Gillis remained silent as he opened the wall safe and tossed the irritated *pretty* man a single key.

When Taka eased her door open, he heard her shower... then her whimpering, muffled tears.

Gypsy didn't even flinch when he gently touched her shoulder, before pulling her back against him.

"I've got you, Doll Eyes," he whispered. "You cry all you want. I'm not going anywhere."

But Gypsy didn't. When she felt Taka's warm skin pressed against her, she no longer felt the need to cry. There, in his healing embrace, all she desired was much-needed comfort.

She sniffed, wiped at her eyes, then turned to face him.

"Tell me what happened, Doll Eyes." He lightly brushed her cheek. "Let me try and fix it."

She didn't answer him, only glanced toward her left hip. Taka followed her gaze down to the enlarged fox bite.

"...Damn," he whispered, then kneeled down and kissed her there. "Don't worry, Doll Eyes. I'll calm the demon... if you'll let me." He stood and kissed her cheek, then smiled. "It's just the two of us here now." He kissed her forehead. "The lies can't reach you." He lightly kissed her other cheek. "I won't let them."

When Taka drew closer, Gypsy didn't respond. He lifted her chin, but the warm sparkle was absent her honey-colored eyes. She didn't move when he softly pressed his lips to hers... once... twice. Still, Gypsy remained as she was. When the tender, handsome Asian man kissed her a third time—pressing there a fraction longer then before—Gypsy hesitantly kissed him back. Their fourth kiss was mutual and warming, growing ever deeper with each rapidly passing heartbeat.

Taka pressed her fully against him, never breaking their intimate contact as he reached over and turned off the shower.

Gypsy returned his embrace, slowly sliding her hands around his neck.

He grabbed a towel as he continued kissing her, blindly guiding her into the other room.

When Taka gently laid her atop the bed, the towel fell loose from her hair. He tossed it onto the floor and brushed back her damp locks.

He kissed her ears, her neck, her chest. Gypsy moaned when he took special care at that sensitive spot where her neck and shoulder meet. She felt his lips part into a smile before he moved down to her breasts. She gasped with pleasure, mingled with the tiniest bit of delicious pain. But Taka wasn't finished. He continued his journey, gently kissing and caressing the large mark all but covering her hipbone. When his skilled attention took him further south, Gypsy clasped her hand over her mouth.

"No, Doll Eyes," Taka whispered. "Let me hear your sweet voice."

That night, in Nasaka's capable hands, Gypsy experienced her very first brush with mind-altering euphoria. She felt as if she was teetering on a precipice—the sky and stars spinning wildly out of control, melting and swirling until sanity was nothing but a distant dream. She wanted to scream, but her voice was caught in her throat. Her eyelids fluttered as even consciousness now toyed with her.

When the world finally stopped spinning and she slowly opened her eyes, Taka was softly smiling down at her.

"You are so beautiful," he whispered. "Was that your first?"

Gypsy barely nodded.

"So... I'm the only one who has ever been blessed to look upon you like this... see the warm glow spread across your cheeks... listen to the tiny noises your passion gave voice to."

She didn't respond, but felt her cheeks grow ever hotter.

"I am the luckiest man in the world," he whispered against her neck. "Will I be luckier still?"

When she felt him lightly pressed against her *there*, Gypsy pulled him closer and kissed him fully. Taka groaned when he pushed inside her. Gypsy's tender voice matched his. This was *nothing* like she had ever experienced before. She couldn't even put the incredible feeling into words. She drew her knees up to his sides, hungry for him in a way she had never thought possible.

Gypsy moaned out his name, couldn't help herself. Taka groaned at the sweet sound of it.

"Don't make me fall for you, Doll Eyes." He buried his nose against her neck. "Stop being so *utterly* perfect."

She gasped. "...Taka..."

"Just give in to it, Doll Eyes. Don't fight it."

When her voice went ever higher, Taka nearly lost control.

"Please, Doll Eyes," he barely whispered. "Stop being so utterly perfect."

⊰⟨●●⟩⊱

When Taka brushed her hair back and lightly kissed her shoulder, Gypsy cuddled back against him.

"I'm spending the night," he whispered.

"Mmm... It's probably already daylight out."

"I'm not leaving."

"Well, it's Sunday. You don't have to."

When he kissed her again, Gypsy felt his excitement growing between them. She reached back and lightly ran her hand along his hip and down his thigh.

"Stop being so utterly perfect," she whispered.

"I'm not leaving," he said again, wrapping his arms around her.

She smiled. "Good. I don't want you to."

⊰⟨●●⟩⊱

They didn't leave her room that whole day. Well, Gypsy didn't. Taka made a quick trip to the grocery store when she had fallen asleep once.

Gypsy woke to a large bowl of cut watermelon, some croissants, various sweets, cheeses, and bottled drinks.

"You need to keep your strength up, Doll Eyes." He winked down at her. "I will be requiring much, much more of you today..." He kissed her fingers. "...and tonight..." He kissed her shoulder. "...and again in the morning..."

154

Gypsy giggled when his lips finally found hers, but her playful laughter was soon transformed into sounds of growing pleasure.

"Can I try something new, Doll Eyes? A different position?"

When Gypsy barely nodded, Taka smiled.

"Nothing too extreme," he whispered. "I will slowly ease you into all the many different pleasures I can gift you."

Gypsy smiled and moaned when he sensually licked the back of her neck.

"Not everyone enjoys the same things." He placed tiny kisses down her spine. "Pleasure is the goal, Doll Eyes. If it doesn't *feel* good, let me know. There are so many other things that I *know* you will enjoy. This is all for you, Gypsy."

She moaned loudly when he finally took her from behind. Taka raised her up, locking one arm around her waist, gently grasping a handful of her long brown hair.

"I *knew* you would enjoy this. Just wait, Doll Eyes. I'm only getting started."

⁂

Taking a shower with someone, washing each other's hair... it was more enjoyable than she had imagined. The tender care they each took with the other was more intimate and bonding than any words they could have possibly shared. Getting dressed for work after such as that was an extremely hard thing indeed.

"Why don't you rest here while I'm at the office?" She glanced at him. "You *have* to be exhausted."

"No more so than you are." He winked at her. "Truth be told, I don't trust the Scot not to kill me while you're gone." He embraced her from behind. "Besides, I've got so much to catch up on; I don't even know where to start."

Taka waved toward Gillis when he glanced up as they came down to the living room. The Scotsman only narrowed his gaze, but didn't speak.

"You working the bar tonight, Doll Eyes?"

"Of course I am."

"If I can catch a break, I'll stop by and check on you."

"Don't push yourself," Gypsy said, dropping her high heels down beside the couch and reaching for her discarded apron. "We've both got rather full plates."

He winked at her then and smiled before leaving.

Gypsy dumped her apron out on the couch and started counting her tips.

"Is that what ye've been doing this past year?" Gillis grumbled. "Sharing yer bed with the Asian?"

Gypsy didn't turn to face him. "Taka and I have been sharing a house together. *This* was the first time we shared a bed."

"Ye slept with him, did ye nae? Dunnae lie tae me, Lass. Is that what ye've been doing up there for nearly two whole days?"

She raised a single eyebrow as she glanced his way. "Really, Gillis? Is this *really* a conversation you want to be having with me right now?"

The Scotsman only grunted and looked away.

Gypsy raised the lid on her coffee table chest and stared at the contents a moment before adding the neat little bundle she'd just counted. She sat back down before strapping on her heels.

"...Gillis?"

He didn't answer her.

"Are you *needing* something?"

"Nae," he grumbled.

She poured her orange juice before continuing. "You know if you need something, I'm here for you. Right?"

"Aye, I know. But I dunnae *need* anything."

She sat down across the table from him. "Are you good on money?"

He furrowed his brow. "Aye, Lass, I'm good. Why would ye even ask me such a thing?"

Gypsy shrugged her shoulders. "I don't know. I mean… what's mine is yours, Gills. You know that, right?"

"Aye, and what's mine is yers. What are ye getting at?"

She glanced towards her chest then back to him. "Just curious. That's all."

"Spit it oot, Gyps. Why do ye think I need money all of a sudden? Ye take care of my banking for me. Ye know how much I have."

He glanced towards the chest when she did, then furrowed his brow.

"I wasn't trying to imply anything, Gills. I haven't been home in a while and I was just checking. That's all."

When she glanced back at the living room a third time, Gillis jumped up and headed for her coffee table chest. He jerked it open and stared down at all the neat little stacks of bound paper bills.

"What is it, Kitten?" He looked sideways at her when she approached. "Is something wrong?"

Gypsy shrugged her shoulders. "Perhaps I just forgot, is all. I mean, it *has* been an awfully long time since I last looked in it."

"Aye, spill it, Lass. What's the problem? It's nearly full, is it nae?"

"...Yeah." She nodded.

"Gyps."

She sighed. "I don't know, Gillis. Just... something is off."

"Like?"

She pointed. "See how I line all of them up in a perfect row? I can get ten stacks across that way, and then twenty down this way—ten bundles per stack."

"Yeah. So?"

"Sooo... I was all but certain I only had room for a little over one more row down here." She pointed to the end closest to where they were standing. "Now... now there's enough space for two and a half more rows."

Gillis was furrowing his brow, staring at the empty spot while she spoke.

"But even if I am mistaken on how many rows I had... look here."

He looked to where she was now pointing.

"I *never* leave a bundle out of a stack. See? Every single stack—ten bundles. Now, see all these places? Nine bundles. Nine bundles. Eight bundles. Nine bundles."

Gillis chewed on his bottom lip.

"You *know* my weird tendency to need things to all be in even numbers, preferably in sets of fives. That's why I demanded to have *this* particular table. See? Ten stacks to a row, ten bundles to a stack, and twenty rows down this way fills it up completely." She sort of snorted. "I can't even *make* myself start stacking up the bundles until I get ten. See how I just toss them down there at the end? There's seven bundles now. When I get ten, I'll make a new stack. I may have been wrong about how many rows I had filled up, but I damn sure didn't leave any stacks minus a bundle or two. That would have made my eye twitch. I wouldn't have been able to sleep until I fixed it. Oh, crap!" She grabbed her purse. "I forgot the time. I'm gonna be late on my first day back." She quickly kissed his cheek and headed for the door. "See you by six, Gills."

"…Aye, Lass. Have a good day."

He had grumbled out the words, but his attention was still on the uneven stacks of money.

"…Dammit."

Gillis sighed before slowly letting the lid fall closed.

Chapter 13

She glanced at Baron. "What do you mean, he's a good lawyer?" Gypsy made an exasperated clicking noise with her tongue. "Would you call *me* a good lawyer if I left documents unsigned and unfiled—cases open for months on end—all because I was more interested in banging my secretaries than actually doing my job?"

"I don't know," Bradley said through a snarky smile. "Are your secretaries male or female? Either would be fine, but I will admit to enjoying one show much more than the other."

"Rot in hell, Stevens," she said, not even glancing his way. "Mr. Bishop, if you keep this man in your employ, he will cost you more money than he's even capable of being worth. Not to mention all the lawsuits he *should* have coming his way."

"What lawsuits are you talking about, Sexy Legs?" He took a step towards Gypsy, sucking air in through his teeth. "Damn… If you only—"

"Stevens!" Baron stood. "Mind what you say to Ms. Rodden. I am not ignorant to your unseemly dealings with clients and other employees alike. Currently, you still serve a purpose. But cross that line with *her* and your value will drop exponentially."

"Only with *her*, huh?" Stevens reached for her. "Why is she so special?"

When he touched her hair, Gypsy grabbed his wrist, bending his arm backwards before twisting it up behind him. She slammed Bradley Stevens against the glass wall of Baron's office.

"This is your only warning, you disgusting piece of human trash. If you *ever* touch me again, I'll break each and every one of these dainty little fingers of yours." She bent them back while still speaking. He cried out. "And I promise you… there will be no amount of therapy that will ever let you grip a pencil again, much less that puny little toy barely dangling between your scrawny legs."

She roughly released him then, but found that she was nowhere near able to stop grinding her teeth together.

Bradley spun towards Baron, cradling his right arm. "You saw that!" He looked at Gypsy. "I should file charges against you for threatening me with bodily harm."

"Do it." When she took a step towards him, he flinched. "I'll have plenty of time between you filing charges and them issuing a warrant, to do exactly what I just *threatened* I would do."

"I h-have a w-witness."

"I saw nothing," Baron said, taking his seat.

Bradley looked at the composed man behind the desk. "What do you mean, you saw nothing?"

"I saw nothing. I heard nothing. You're dismissed Mr. Stevens." Baron glanced then to Gypsy. "Ms. Rodden, there is yet business we need to discuss. Do you have the time?"

When Gypsy sat down, Baron looked over at the other man. "You can see yourself out now."

Bradley stomped across the room.

"Mind you don't slam my door, Stevens," Baron said coolly.

Gypsy rubbed her temples before resting back into the soft leather chair. "Why do you keep him here?"

"He serves his purpose," Baron said softly. "Now, tell me, Gypsy. How was your homecoming?"

She sighed. "It was… eventful."

"In a good way?"

"No. Not to start with. But my weekend ended on a rather pleasant note. So, I guess that makes up for the lackluster welcome."

"Want to talk about it?"

"Not even remotely."

"Hey, Gyps. Welcome home, Lass."

"Hey, Gills. You already finished with the prep?"

"Just aboot. Come here, Kitten. How's yer fairy saddle doing?"

"It's eased off a little." She tugged her skirt down on one side. "See? Not nearly as bad as Saturday."

"Aye, but nae nearly gone, either."

"Well." She shrugged her shoulders. "I guess I'll just have to suffer until you're ready to relieve my pain. You're the only one who can do it, Gills."

"...Gyps..." He gently wrapped his arms around her and pulled her to him. "I nae meant tae hurt ye, Kitten. Yer the most precious thing in the world tae me." He kissed the top of her head. "I thought telling ye the truth would be more painful."

"How could you possibly think that, Gills? You know that deceit is the trigger. No matter the truth, it will *always* hurt me less than the lie."

"I know, Lass. Forgive me." He sighed then and released her. "I just... I just cannae find the right words tae tell ye, Gyps."

Gypsy stared at his profile—his darkened countenance, the deep lines now creasing his brow—her heart sank.

"You love her. Don't you, Gillis?"

He bit his bottom lip, fighting back the burn of coming tears.

"Aye, Kitten," he whispered. "I fell for the lass. I truly did."

Gypsy had to fight back her own tears then. "Was it love at first sight?"

"Nae." He shook his head. "She grew on me. I fought it with everything I had, Gyps. I denied her advances for months. Then..."

"Then... loneliness set in," she softly said.

"Aye." He threw the hand towel down and wiped at his eyes. "Dammit, Gyps! Why did ye go and leave me? It's been naethin' but the two of us for the last several years. I dunnae feel right withoot ye, Kitten. I cannae handle being alone... nae anymore."

"Shhh, Gillis." She hugged him from behind. "I'm so sorry. Had you told me how you felt, I would have run home and never gone back."

"Aye, and that's exactly the reason I didnae tell ye. I'll nae be the mate who crushes yer dreams, Lass. I'll always support ye. I just didnae realize how weak I was withoot ye."

"And the one person who brought you comfort... I kicked her out."

"Nae, Kitten. Dunnae look at it like that. Yer fairy saddle can see what we cannae." He sniffed and turned around to face her. "I just hope the only thing Becca was hiding, was what I just told ye."

Gypsy glanced away. "...Yeah."

"Ye think there's more, Kitten, do ye nae?"

"I don't know, Gillis. I mean... that was pretty much the strongest reaction I've ever gotten before. Think about it. She *had* to know I would find out about the two of you before long. Why would she be trying so hard to hide *that*? Hell, for all she knew, you could have told me on the drive home. No... there was *something* else."

"Aye, maybe she just feared ye wouldnae want her hanging around the house."

"Hanging arou—" She narrowed her gaze. "Gillis, did you move her in with you?"

"Nae... but she stayed over quite a bit."

"Here? In *my* house? Without my knowledge?"

"Aye, it's my house, too, Lass. Why are ye getting so—"

"Gillis... *that* is the worst breach of trust I could ever imagine."

"What? Ye brought yer Pope here. And what aboot that damn ninja? *He* stayed the whole weekend."

"That's completely different and *you* know it!"

"How, Lass? How is ye having intimate company any different than me?"

"First of all, *Baron* wasn't intimate company. Second... *you* let Taka in, even gave him the key to my room."

"So what yer saying is... if *ye* had been the one tae grant Becca access, it'd be okay?"

"No. What I'm saying is... had I gotten to know her first, had my birthmark not reacted so violently, had I actually been home or even *asked*... things might have gone differently. Instead—in my absence—you hired a woman, gave her keys to my bar, allowed her to basically *run* my business, and then welcomed her into my home just like it was hers. Can you not see the difference there? Can you not see how my trust and my privacy were completely violated? Hell, Gillis, you didn't just replace me with *company*, you practically handed my whole damn life over... to a perfect stranger, no less."

When Gillis didn't say anything, Gypsy sighed and leaned back against the bar.

"Well, at least I know what you were trying to hide." She gently rubbed her hipbone. "Oh, and when you said you granted Becca access to our home, you better not have meant *granted her access.*"

When the Scotsman only glanced toward her and then quickly away, Gypsy grabbed her hip again.

"Dammit, Gillis!"

She ran up the steps two at a time. Gillis cringed when he heard that electronic voice come to life.

"Hello, Gypsy Rodden."

"Hey, House. Access files for all persons authorized to enter."

"Gypsy Rodden… authorized. Trace Spencer… authorized. Gillis McCullough… authorized. Becca Greyson… authorized."

Gypsy had to grit her teeth to keep her voice at a calm level. She took a deep breath.

"House, revoke authorization for Becca Greyson."

"Authorization for Becca Greyson… revoked by Gypsy Rodden. Do you wish the file deleted?"

"No. Flag as dangerous. If anyone tries to access file Becca Greyson, contact local authorities immediately."

"File, Becca Greyson… flagged as dangerous."

"House, all future access is denied for additional guests unless I personally authorize it."

"All additional access denied, per Gypsy Rodden."

When she came back down the stairs, Gillis opened his mouth to speak. Gypsy held up her hand, halting him.

"Don't. Don't speak. It's gonna take me a while to get over this one, Gillis. I don't care who you sleep with. I don't care who you love. But you'll not be doing it here. I didn't bar Becca from *your* life. I barred her from *mine*. She is not welcome here, now or ever. Date her all you like. Spend the night at *her* place. Hell, move in with her for all I care. But I better *never* see that cow's face around here again. Period!"

"…Gyps—"

"I said don't speak. I meant that."

Gillis swallowed hard when he noticed her left eye twitch. He suppressed his coming apology.

Naethin' I could say now would fix this, he thought. *I've seen that look on her face afore. Yet, I nae thought it would be directed taeword me.*

———⟨◆⟩———

"Okay, Sheila, you think you got it?" Gypsy pointed at the calendar. "This is backroom only. If someone calls, don't book a date until you check to see if it isn't already filled. Got it?"

Sheila nodded. "Got it. Dang, Gypsy, I'm going to miss you. Things run so smoothly when you're here."

"I won't be but a couple months this time. The new trainee is working out well, don't you think?"

Sheila glanced at the petite redhead. "Yeah, Ruby is doing fine. She already pulls in nearly as many tips as I do."

"And I've set everything up online, so I'll be running the show from Tokyo. You'll deal with the same delivery guys, your paycheck will draft into your account every Friday—"

"Oh, I just need to punch in our hours by Wednesday afternoon."

"By Wednesday *at* noon," Gypsy said. "It'd be easier just to remember to punch them in when you finish up on Tuesday. Okay? You'll be paid from Wednesday through Tuesday. Just think of Wednesday as your new Monday. That's when your week will start over. Got it?"

Sheila bit her lip and nodded.

"Don't worry about it. I'll call you the first couple of times and walk you through it. You did fine last week."

"Yeah, but you were standing right there."

"Either way—by phone or in person—I'll still be talking in your ear."

Sheila smiled. "Yeah, I guess you're right."

"It'll be fine. Trust me. If we make a mistake, no worries. We'll own it, fix it, and the world will just go right on spinning."

"I'm here to give you a lift," Taka said as he came into the bar, all smiles. "You packed and ready, Doll Eyes?"

"Almost. Give me a sec."

"A sec is about all you've got. You know what traffic is like from here to LAX."

"I'm coming. I'm coming."

Gillis stepped in front of her as she started out from behind the bar.

"Ye nae even gonna tell me bye, Kitten?"

"We said our goodbyes this morning." She smiled. "Goodbye, Gillis. I love you and I will miss you like crazy."

"Aye, and me as well, Lass."

When he hugged her, Gypsy tensed.

"Ye still cannae abide my touch, eh, Kitten?"

"Give me time, Gills. Rome wasn't built in a day." She smiled again. "And it wasn't *re*built in a day, either."

"Hurry up, Doll Eyes. I want to spend some time cuddling before you fly away."

"Put a cork in it, pervert," she mumbled, picking up her single carry-on. "Later, mates," she called out. "I'll be back before you know it."

—◄◄●◊●►►—

When Nasaka pulled out onto the freeway, he reached over and squeezed Gypsy's hand.

"I wish I could go back with you, Doll Eyes."

"It's just Tokyo, Taka. After four months living there, I know those streets about as well as I know these. Don't worry about it. I'll be fine on my own."

"If you'd just give me a couple more weeks, I could wrap things up here and join you."

"You know I can't. The Sato case is on the docket for Thursday. Even going now, I'll have to bust my ass to get everything in order before we appear in court."

Nasaka furrowed his brow. "Maybe it would be easier for me to let you go... if I'd gotten to spend more time with you. After the intense passion we shared, I can't believe you just shut me down like that."

"Stop trying to play the pouty card." She smiled. "You don't like to restrict your passions to just one partner. Remember?"

"I would... for you."

"Bah... You're so full of it."

He smiled. "I would *try*."

"If I thought you were actually capable of being monogamous, I'd *try*, too."

"You don't give me enough credit, Doll Eyes. With you wrapped in my arms... I was a different man."

She glanced out the window. "...Yeah... you said that before. I just had a lot of crap to deal with and only a few short weeks to sort it all out. I like you, Taka. I *could* like you a lot... too much, perhaps."

"But?"

"But I need the time to do it properly. I wouldn't want to halfass my time with you. Like I said... I like you."

"You like me enough to want to do it right."

"...Yeah. I wouldn't want to lose you just because my head was in the wrong place. Timing, huh?"

He squeezed her hand again. "My mom used to say... people we meet at the wrong time, are the wrong people." He glanced sideways at her. "If it's the *right* person... you make the time, no matter what."

She smiled. "...Yeah. Maybe she's right."

"No worries. I still love you, Doll Eyes."

"I love you, too, Taka. Never abandon me. Promise."

"I couldn't, even if it hurt me."

Chapter 14

"So? How did it go?"

When Gypsy heard his deep voice, butterflies began stirring in her tummy.

"Perfectly, of course," she said through a smile. "We won. Sato Enterprises is happy and set."

"And Ginzu Corp?"

"We've still got a few months to go before that one comes up."

"So... Gypsy... what did you wear to court today?"

"Wha— It doesn't matter, Baron. The judgment went according to the letter of the law."

"I am certain it did."

She could *hear* his smile. It irritated her to no end.

"Will there be anything else, Mr. Bishop?"

"You wore the green one, didn't you?"

Gypsy quickly glanced down at the lovely emerald-colored silk, but didn't answer.

"I knew it," Baron said, almost cooing.

"What I wore had absolutely no bearing—"

"Then why did you wear it? Gypsy... honey... the sooner you admit this, the better off you'll be. Sex sells, no matter the country. That's just the way of the world."

"Yeah," she grumbled. "Only because men still run it."

"Oh, really?" He chuckled. "Tell me what would change if *you* were in charge, Ms. Rodden. And before you answer, remember... I know you, Gypsy. I was blessed with a glimpse into your wicked little thoughts concerning men. By my approximation, nothing would change if women were running the planet. Sex would still rule it... only the dominant would change."

"Yeah, and you'd rather dine on broken glass than be dominated by a woman."

"...Perhaps," he whispered softly.

"So, is that the only reason you called? To see what I wore to court?"

"In part, yes. Tell me what you were thinking when you pulled that particular dress from your closet. What was running through your mind when you looked at yourself in the mirror?"

"I was thinking… this shade of green really makes my eyes sparkle."

"And it does…" He paused. "Is that *all* you were thinking?"

"That's all I'm going to admit to, yeah."

Baron chuckled. "That's my girl. Tell me. How are things going, otherwise? How are you getting on all by yourself?"

"Eh, it's fine, I guess. I mean, I have to eat at all the same restaurants as I did with Nasaka. I don't feel comfortable ordering anywhere else. Oh, but since he's not here with me, I get to ride the women's only train. So, that's good."

"Yes, it is. I'm glad to hear that. And what about your assistant?"

"Sakara? She's great. Sharp as a tack, that one. I couldn't do it without her. She has studied so hard. She almost knows more English than *I* do."

"I'm glad you're getting along so well. Why don't you get *her* to take you to new places? If you want to eat somewhere new, invite your assistant along."

"Yeah, that's a good idea. Then I can call it work—turn it in on my expense account."

Baron chuckled again. "As you wish, Gypsy."

"I was only kidding. I can afford to buy my own food. Hmm… Maybe I *will* invite Sakara, *treat* her every once in a while."

"Are you taking tomorrow off to celebrate your victory?"

"Tomorrow? No. Tomorrow is Friday, that's a celebration in and of itself." Gypsy leaned back in her chair. "This will be my first weekend not having to work the whole thing through. I'll celebrate then."

"Did you wear the shoes?"

"Huh?"

"The emerald heels. Did you wear them today?"

"Of course I did. They are the *perfect* shoes for this dress."

"Did you go back and buy more?"

She half smiled. "You know I did. Got a pair to match every single dress. The right pair of shoes can make or break an outfit."

"You're quite right. That's another thing I like about you. No tan-colored *safe* choice in footwear for my lovely little Gypsy."

"No way. I don't even own a pair of tan heels."

"I have noticed. I've mentally recorded every article of clothing you've ever worn. From the shoes to the dress to the jewelry... never have I seen a single thing I would change."

She snorted out a laugh. "Good thing, since it's not your job to be *changing* me in the first place."

"Is that so? Then... why is it you are constantly changing *me?*"

"Wha— I've never *changed* you."

"Oh, but you have, sweet Gypsy. You most certainly have."

<hr />

"Mondays suck," Gypsy said through a yawn.

Sakara smiled. "I agree."

"Why is that? I mean, we just had two whole days of zero responsibilities. Why is Monday like the biggest downer ever? Just because it's Monday?"

Sakara almost giggled.

"Hey, I'm gonna run and get some lunch. You want anything?"

"I'm good." Sakara pointed toward the bento box on her desk. "I packed plenty. I'll share, if you want."

"Naw. I appreciate it, but I'm in the mood for some onigiri from the convenience store downstairs."

Sakara smiled. "Yes, they have the best."

"Hey, you busy tonight?"

"No, Ms. Rodden. Do you need me to work over?"

"No. I was wondering if you wanted to go out and eat with me."

"Me?"

Gypsy nodded as she headed for the elevator. "You pick the restaurant. Anything you want. I'm ready to experience something new."

She was humming to herself by the time she made it down to the first floor. She had been in a good mood ever since she'd made it through her first court case completely unscathed.

Or... Her inner devil broke through her happy humming. *...are you this excited because Baron Von Dreamy called to check on you that day?*

He didn't just call, her little angel chimed. *He asked what she was wearing—made a confession.*

What confession? Gypsy snorted out loud. *You two are idiots. If everyone's conscious works like mine, no wonder the world's so screwed up.*

She was smiling when she walked over to the freshly packaged rice balls, but that happy smile soon faded.

"Aww... They're out of the kind I like."

They are rice squished into a triangle, her devil huffed sardonically. *How different can they possibly taste? Just pick one of the others.*

Yeah, her angel said, while apparently giggling. *You only just told Sakara you wanted to experience something new. Well... go on... get to experiencing.*

Gypsy looked from the onigiri in her right hand to the one in her left. The rice balls looked the same, yes, but they were a different flavor from the one Nasaka had picked out for her. She liked the pickled plum one.

What should I do? She glanced from the ones she was holding, over to the third unknown flavor still sitting on the shelf. *The little pictures don't make any sense. I have to be careful. They put mayonnaise on everything over here. Ugh! If I get a mouthful of mayonnaise I'd—*

"The ebi fumi is the best," someone said from directly behind her.

Gypsy glanced back. The handsome, elegant man was smiling, looking over her shoulder at the rice balls in her hands.

"...Ebi... fumi?"

The man nodded and pointed to the packaged onigiri in her left hand. "Yes. It tastes like shrimp. Do you like hot things? Spicy?"

She slowly shook her head.

"Then you don't want this one." He took the rice ball from her right hand and placed it back on the shelf. "That's wasabi fumi. Wasabi..." He waved his hand in front of his mouth. "Hot."

Gypsy chuckled softly.

"Do you like potato?"

"Yes," she said, still smiling.

The man picked the one up she had left on the shelf. "Seto fumi," he said. "Potatoes and soy sauce. It's kind of sweet, a little. You'd probably like it."

When he placed it in her empty hand, Gypsy looked from the ebi fumi to the seto fumi.

"Umm... do they have mayonnaise in them?"

"You want mayonnaise?" The man glanced back to the shelf.

"No!" she said, a little louder than she meant to.

A few people turned her way. Gypsy felt her cheeks warming up.

The man chuckled. "Don't worry. Neither one of those have mayonnaise in them."

She looked back down at the rice balls. "...Thanks."

"Do you like sushi?"

She glanced back up at the man. "Yeah. Why? Does sushi have mayonnaise in it?"

He smiled softly. "The nori fumi flavored ongiri tastes like sushi. It has extra seaweed in it. I thought if you liked sushi, you might like nori fumi."

"...Nori fumi?" She glanced back at the shelf.

"I got the last one," he said, holding it out. "Do you want it?"

"N-no. Umm, no thanks. That's very sweet of you, but I think I'll take these—see which one I like best. And if they don't have pickled plum, maybe I'll try the nori fumi next time."

"You come here a lot?"

"Yeah. My office is just upstairs—sixth floor. Coming here is convenient, and *much* easier than me trying to remember to pack a lunch."

Gypsy couldn't help but notice the handsome man's gentle seeming expression when she talked. There was something oddly familiar about him... comforting.

And definitely not bad on the eyes, her devil whispered.

"Do I know you?" She quickly bit her bottom lip. "Crap. That sounded really creepy—totally pick-up lineish. Sorry. It's just... you seem so familiar. Have we met before?"

Her mind started running through all the possible scenarios.

Maybe he works at Sato Enterprises. I could have seen him over there. Or court. Perhaps he works in the courthouse. No. I don't think so. But I swear... I could almost place money on the fact we have met somewhere before.

"That dress looks lovely on you," the man said, interrupting her frantic thoughts. "The color is perfect for your skin tone."

Gypsy glanced down at the embroidered red silk. "You think so? I always thought red washed me out too much. I don't normally go for this shade, but I loved the ornate buttons." She touched them as she spoke. "The way it looks like the little embroidered cranes are facing the button... it makes me think they are holding it up together. Two friends—one on each side—holding the world in their beaks."

She glanced back up at the man as she finished speaking. His gentle smile was reaching all the way up to his lovely brown eyes.

"Wow..." she whispered. "That was an oddly weird way to respond to a compliment. Apologies. That was really rude of me." She smiled. "Thank you very much, sir."

"It was my pleasure."

"Well..." Gypsy held up the two rice balls. "I think I'll take them both. Thanks for all your help. I better get back to work now."

"Are you going to eat both of them?"

"I probably can't hold them both." She half snorted. "But I'm a pretty good eater. I have to keep my caloric count a little on the high side, so I don't pass out at the gym." She furrowed her brow. "Although... I don't really get to work out while I'm over here. Not like back home. Maybe I should hold off on—"

"You don't like the way we exercise in Japan?"

"Oh, it's not that. I just... well... how *do* you exercise over here? I haven't seen a single gym."

"Mostly through martial arts, and probably not the kind that's running through your head right now." He laughed softly. "How do *you* normally workout?"

"Boxing." She smiled. "And probably not the kind that's running through your head right now."

They *shared* a laugh then.

"There's a wonderful dojo on the next block over. Back that way." He pointed. "The owner is a friend of mine. He is highly skilled—was even on the Olympic judo team. Yet he is kind and patient, especially with new students. You should stop by sometime... see what it's all about."

"Hmm... maybe I will. Now that my work is caught up and I won't have to pull anymore all-nighters for a while, I'd have time to join a gym. Umm... dojo."

"What kind of work are you in?"

"Oh. I'm a lawyer for Bishop, Grey & Sweet. I take care of their Asian clients."

"All of Asia?"

"Well, they don't have clients in *all* of Asia. We have an office here in Tokyo, one in Bangkok, and one in China."

"What part of China?"

"Shanghi."

"You must travel a great deal."

"...Yeah. Sometimes I forget where home is."

"And where is it—your real home?"

"California. Well, I've lived in California for several years now. Originally, I'm from Tennessee, but I went to law school in England."

The man smiled again. "From the United States to the UK to Asia... I think you're doing it backwards."

She chuckled. "Yeah... when you say it like *that*."

"Would you like to have dinner with me sometime?"

"Oh... umm..."

"You're not interested?"

"No. It's not that. It's just..."

"Just what?"

"It's a surprise, is all."

"A surprise? How so?"

"Well, I came to Tokyo nearly a year ago. I've not actually been *here* all that time, but out of the months I've spent in this city... not a single person has asked me out to dinner. In truth, you're the first stranger who's even started up a conversation with me. I just figured western women were invisible here, for some reason."

"I assure you that is not the case, Madam. I don't believe a single man here thinks you are *invisible*." He glanced around the store. "More often than not, they probably fear your rejection, so they simply don't ask."

"But not you?"

"If you decline my invitation, I will be heartbroken, yes." He smiled again. "But your gentle rejection will not make me less of a man."

She chuckled softly. "No. I'd be hard-pressed to think of anything that would make you seem *less of a man*." She blushed. "Oh, I just meant that... umm... you are... it's easy to see you don't have a problem with confidence."

"No," he said through a knowing smile. "Confidence is an area in which I have never been lacking." He reached into his pocket. "Here is my card. When you find yourself with a free evening, give me a call."

Gypsy immediately pulled a card from her purse to exchange with him. She didn't wish to offend him. She had made that mistake when she met with her Sato clients for the first time. It took Taka nearly ten minutes to straighten that meeting back out.

She glanced at the man's cream-colored card with the crisp black writing. The only thing she could make out in English was a single name, and a telephone number.

"...Nasaka?"

"Yes, Ms. Rodden. I am Nasaka."

Her eyes went wide. "...Master Jūshirō," she whispered, taking a step back.

He smiled. "So, you finally remember me. I must say... you landed quite a blow to my ego. I thought I was more memorable than that."

"But... how— How in the world did you recognize *me*?"

"How in the world could I not?" He took a step toward her. "Judging by your reaction... I doubt I'll be receiving your call anytime soon."

He reached for his card, but Gypsy hurriedly pulled it back. Jūshirō smiled, and then gently slipped it from her fingers and flipped it over.

"These are the kanji," he said, writing something on the back of the card before handing it to her.

Gypsy furrowed her brow when she looked down at it.

"For the dojo I was telling you about," he said. "*That* is what is written on the front. When you see the door that has those symbols on it, just go inside. Don't worry. He keeps long hours."

"Th-thank you."

"Do I scare you, Ms. Rodden?"

"N-no. It's not that. It's just…"

Jūshirō waited patiently for her to collect her words.

Gypsy glanced around before leaning toward him and whispering, "I think you are amazing. Your work… it is mesmerizing. Truly beautiful."

He smiled softly. "I am honored, Ms. Rodden, honored that you appreciate my art."

"It wasn't just your art. It was *you* as well—your grace, your elegance… your beauty."

"My beauty?" He smiled with only one corner of his mouth.

Gypsy nodded. "I couldn't get you and your scene out of my mind. I dreamed about it that night—all the colorful jute, the way you used it, the way you— Ugh… I asked Taka about a zillion questions—"

"Taka? You know my brother?"

She nodded again. "We live together. Well, *did* live together."

"Then you are very nearly family." He smiled again. "Now you *have* to let me treat you to dinner."

"Oh, no, Mr. Nasaka. It's not like—"

"And since you and my little brother are on a first name basis, I insist on the same courtesy."

"But I could nev—"

"Try it, Gypsy," he whispered. "It's not that hard."

"M… Master Jū… Master Jūshirō."

He smiled. "You can drop the Master. Or, if you prefer… drop the Jūshirō." He reached for one of her curls. "I would like that very much, Gypsy… very much indeed."

She swallowed hard. Her cheeks felt like they were on fire.

"It was so very nice to run into you again." He slowly released her hair and stepped back. "Tell my little brother not to be such a stranger. Oh, and when you *do* find the time to call… I would prefer our first dinner to be just the two of us. Taka won't get jealous. That's not his style."

"Oh, Taka isn't with me this time." She sort of shrugged her shoulders. "I had to come alone."

Jūshirō smiled with only one corner of his mouth. "You are a wealth of information, Ms. Rodden. A bit of advice... without even asking you directly, I have found out *where* you work, that you often work late into the night, where and when you normally take your lunch, that you are living all alone, and now I even have all your personal contact information." He slid her card into his pocket. "And that was all before you even knew my name. Well, before you remembered my name. Perhaps you should be a bit more guarded. You are as free and open as that little brother of mine."

"Oh... well... I knew you intended me no harm." She unconsciously reached for her hip. "There were no red flags, so to speak."

Jūshirō narrowed his gaze, watching her odd actions closely.

"But you're right," she said. "I just committed the number one faux pas in stranger danger awareness." She sort of snorted. "Good way to get a stalker, right there. Thanks for the warning, Master Jūshirō."

He smiled. "You are quite welcome... Mistress Gypsy."

"Oh..." She blushed again. "...Yeah."

"I must say, Master Baron always has the most exquisite taste in... friends."

"A-always?"

Jūshirō smiled before turning to go. "This has been the most delightful *lunch* I have had in ages. I'll be seeing you around... Gypsy."

"B-bye." Gypsy half waved before darting toward the register, then quickly jumping onto the open elevator.

Oh crap! Oh crap! What the— Holy crap!

Open mouth, her angel said.

And swallow foot whole, her demon added. *Oh, yeah, and remember this...* The internal voice went up a couple octaves. *Why do I care? It's not like I'm ever gonna see these people again. If I make an ass out of myself—*

Enough! Gypsy sort of grumbled aloud. *You don't have to remind me, Devil. I was there. I know what I said.*

When the elevator opened, she ran straight into her office and shut the door. Her heart was racing wildly. She had to steady her breathing, concentrate several long minutes before she could even sit down and enjoy her onigiri.

"Ugh... Mondays..."

Chapter 15

"That restaurant we went to a couple of days ago?"

Sakara glanced up at Gypsy when she spoke.

"Yes?"

"They had the *best* sake. It didn't taste like any of the other I've had. Why was it so good?"

"Ah, yes. I like it, too. They serve nigori sake. It is not as filtered. Makes it very sweet."

"It was certainly delicious. I could easily drink waaay too much of that stuff."

Sakara giggled. "Yes, that's very easy to do. If you like sweet things, you have to try Chuhai. Have you had it?"

"No. I've never even heard of it."

"Right now is the best time to buy it because they have apple-flavored. It's my favorite."

Gypsy furrowed her brow. "What is it?"

"A drink. In a can like beer, but sweet and light like a mixed drink. It's made from shochu."

When Gypsy only raised a single eyebrow, Sakara giggled again.

"Here, Ms. Rodden." She grabbed a notepad. "I'll write down the—"

"Just come with me," Gypsy said. "It's the end of the day, anyway. You were going to write down the kanji then tell me where to get it. Right?"

Sakara nodded.

"Is it on the way to the station?"

"Yes."

"Then let's just go. You can point out the store and show me what to get. That okay with you?"

Sakara smiled. "Yes. I want some, too."

"Alrighty then. My treat. Let's go."

"Oh… but you don't have to—"

"I don't *have* to do anything." Gypsy smiled. "That's what makes doing things you want, feel so good. Wouldn't you agree?"

Sakara only giggled again and grabbed her purse.

———◆———

With their purchases in hand, the two women walked out of the store still talking and laughing. Gypsy's cell phone rang.

"Oh. Hang on, Sakara. I gotta get this." When she looked at the screen and saw it was Sheila, she sighed. "Why don't you go on without me? This might take a while."

Gypsy waved goodbye while hitting the answer button. Shelia's frantic voice was so loud; she had to hold the phone out away from her ear.

"Alright. Alright. Just calm down. This is not a problem. All you have to do is…"

Gypsy leaned back against the building as she slowly walked Sheila through the payroll process, yet again.

When a man approached, stopping right in front of her, Gypsy realized she was leaning against the door to a business.

"Crap. Sorry. Sorry," she whispered as she moved out of the way.

With Sheila finally calm—and once the payroll system sent her a confirmation email—Gypsy hung up the phone and sighed. Only *then* did she notice the writing across that same door she had been blocking.

She quickly dug Nasaka's card out of her purse and flipped it over. She looked from the door to the card and back again.

"Looks the same," she mumbled. "Well, this is as good a time as any. If I don't start working off some of these calories, I'll have to go buy all new dresses."

Once inside, she slipped her pink heels off and stepped into the dojo. It was empty.

"…Hello?" She walked further into the room. "Hello? Is anybody here? …Are you open?"

Just as she turned to go, a man called out, "Be right there."

She walked toward the half-closed door the voice had come from and heard the man speaking in Japanese. She turned her back and waited for him to finish his phone call, not that she could have eavesdropped even if she had wanted to.

"Ah, so sorry about that," the man said as he came through the door. "I was already on the phone when—"

Gypsy turned toward him while he was speaking. They both froze.

"...Renji?" she half whispered, amazed.

"Chikara." He smiled. "I am honored you remembered me."

She shook her head. "This isn't happening. I should have *known* better. Jūshirō said it belonged to one of his friends. Why am I so surprised?"

"Jūshirō?" Renji's smile grew. "So, you are on a first name basis with the Rope Master, huh?"

"No. I mean... no, I'm not on a first name—"

"You threatened to gouge my eyes out when I gave you a gift. Yet, you are now taking advice and direction from a man who gets off tying women up."

"As opposed to *beating* them?" She snorted. "Hello, Pot. Meet Kettle."

Renji furrowed his brow. "...What?"

"Never mind. I should have known better. That's all. Sorry to have wasted your time, School Master."

When she spun around to leave, Gypsy nearly ran into a man standing right behind her. She let out a yelp and placed her hand over her chest.

"Holy jeez— You nearly scared the life right outta me." She took a deep breath. "So sorry. I didn't mean to yell like that."

When the bald man didn't answer her, Gypsy glanced back at Renji.

"He doesn't speak English?"

Renji smiled. "He does."

"Eep!" Gypsy yelped again when the other man gently ran his fingertips down her arm.

Get a hold of yourself, Gyps. Eewww. That feels so creepy. Don't flinch. Don't flinch. And for heaven's sake, don't gag.

"Is your lovely skin yet pristine?" the man asked.

At those words, Gypsy narrowed her gaze, then gasped. "Ah... the Blood Master."

The man's eyes lit up. "Blood Master?" He chuckled.

"This is Jimpachi Fuu," Renji said. "Master Fuu, this is Mistress Gypsy."

"Yes," Fuu said, smiling. "We've met."

"Apparently Jūshirō sent her down here."

"Jūshirō?" Fuu looked her up and down. "Do you have a taste for Kinbaku, Mistress?"

"No. I don't have a taste for anything. And please drop the Mistress part. My name is Gypsy Rodden. Feel free to address me as such."

"...Gypsy," Fuu whispered, still stroking her arm. "I must admit, I thought you were taller."

"I was. I mean... I'm barefoot now."

Fuu glanced down at her feet. "So you are." He smiled. "Tell me, Gypsy. Is your flesh yet pristine?"

She took a step back, relieving herself from his creepy-feeling touch. "Yes, Master Fuu. I am now as I was then—tattoo and carving free."

"Any piercings?"

"Only my ears." She touched them as she spoke.

"Wonderful. Wonderful," he said. "Do not forget my personal invitation."

Gypsy half smiled. "Yes. If ever I am so inclined, I shall contact you."

"Yes," Fuu said. "Skin like yours should be worshipped properly. I will take great care with you, Gypsy. The art I could create on this lovely canvas..." He moved closer, touching her again. "...would not be for public display. I'd wish to keep such an exquisite creation for my eyes alone."

"Umm... thanks?" She stepped away again. "Well, I gotta get going."

"But you never even said why Jūshirō sent you here," Renji said, following her to the door.

"Oh... I was just looking for a gym," she said nervously, trying to fasten the buckle on her heels.

"Let me help you with that," Renji said, kneeling in front of her as he easily fixed her shoe. "Now, the other foot, Chikara."

When she tried to obey, she almost lost her balance. Renji quickly stood up and steadied her.

"Careful, Chikara," he whispered. "If you are looking for a gym, Jūshirō sent you to the right place. I am gentle with beginners.

You don't have to trust me, but do me a favor. If you wish to go to a different dojo, take care you do not pick one of the rougher ones. Most of the ones around here, they treat women poorly."

"How will I know which one is a good one?"

"*This* one is a good one." He smiled softly. "My dojo is the perfect fit for you. And although this has definitely been an odd reunion, I promise you... this is not normal. I do not bring my *lifestyle* into my dojo. If you choose to train under me, Chikara, I will take great care with you. I promise."

"You promised the exact same thing when last we met."

"This is different. One has nothing to do with the other. Are you looking to learn martial arts?"

"Well, not really. It's just... I'm used to working out every day, but I don't have a gym in Tokyo. When I get back to Tony's, he fusses at me... says I've gone soft."

"Tony's?"

"Yeah. It's this smelly old boxing gym near my home in California."

"Boxing? You're a boxer?"

"No. I only train there. I don't compete or anything. But for burning calories and keeping your body fat down, you can't beat boxing. And, too... my dad always told me that a woman should never have to depend on a man to defend her. She should be able to defend herself. So, I learned how to box while I was still in high school."

"Please, Chikara. Please train in my dojo. It would be my honor. I won't even charge you for the first month—give you a chance to see if you like it or not, to see if I'm a good fit for you."

She half laughed. "Well, nobody can replace Tony."

"I wouldn't dare try," Renji said, smiling. "I might be a poor substitute for your American sensei, but I would like the opportunity."

"Well... you *are* on the way to the train station." She chewed on her bottom lip, mulling it over. "It *would* be convenient to drop in after work. What are your normal hours?"

"My door is always open. I will train you on *your* schedule. As for regular and specialized classes, all that information is in my brochure. Please. Just come sit down in my office and let's talk about it."

After that, Renji's place became a regular stop for her, every afternoon.

"I must say... I was surprised to get your call."

Gypsy shot him a sideways glance. "Oh really? Hmm. And here I thought the great Master Jūshirō had confidence enough to spare."

"This is true, yes," he said, smiling with only one corner of his mouth. "Still, my little brother is a rare creature. I feared you may be too smitten with him to even consider *my* company."

"Taka is rare, yes. He is a treasure I wasn't looking to find. Yet... you are rarer still. I wish I could have met your father. I bet he was the most beautiful man in all of Japan."

"A beautiful monster is still a monster," Jūshirō whispered softly.

Gypsy took his hand then, concern furrowing her brow. "Should we not have come to Osaka? Is this a painful place for you?"

He gave her a reassuring, closed-lipped smile and lightly touched her cheek. "Some of the most painful lessons in life... turn out to be our *greatest* lessons in life," he softly said. "Because of my father's poor treatment of the fairer sex, my little brother and I learned to treasure women above all else. Love—it is an amazing and glorious thing. Never take it for granted, precious lady. I can assure you... *we* do not."

"We?" She tilted her head. "You mean... you and Taka?"

Jūshirō smiled sweetly and leaned in to kiss her cheek. "Taka will love you always. As will I."

"...Jūshirō."

"From now on, lovely Gypsy, I wish you to call me Nee-chan."

"Nee-chan?"

He nodded. "It means older brother." He squeezed her hand as he led her into the famous noodle shop she had heard so much about. "I will take care of you in my brother's absence. I will treasure you in his stead."

"But, you don't have to—"

Gypsy almost squeaked when the elegant Rope Master lightly placed his finger to her lips.

"I *want* to." He winked at her before letting the waiting hostess seat them. "It will be my greatest pleasure," he whispered in her ear, before pulling out her chair. "This weekend... at the hot springs... with you..." He smiled again. "During your time with me, precious lady, I will treat you like the goddess you truly are. You will want for nothing... and little Taka will have no reason to worry about you."

Gypsy blushed brightly, but didn't speak.

"I would like to claim *all* of your weekends as my own. Will that be well with you, little sister?"

Gypsy swallowed hard before barely nodding.

Jūshirō smiled sweetly. "Very good. These next two days, I will show you all that Osaka has to offer. Then, a week from now, you will stay with me at my home in Tokyo."

It wasn't really a question, but Gypsy answered him, anyway. "I would *love* to see your home, Master Jūshirō."

He raised his brows and quietly waited for her to realize her error.

Gypsy blushed again. "I'm sorry. It might take me some time to get used to calling you... Nee-chan."

Jūshirō smiled again. "Practice makes perfect, precious lady."

Gypsy's shoulders stiffened when he fell silent and looked at her expectantly.

"Umm... It is as you say, Nee-chan. I will practice..." She smiled. "...every day."

"Very good." He inclined his head toward her as he gracefully draped his napkin across his lap. "I shall look forward to your continued growth... *and* to the day you will ultimately join our family." He lightly touched her hand. "When your bloom has reached its peak, dearest Gypsy, you will be the fairest blossom on the tree."

"My bloom?"

"When true love finally blooms across your fair cheeks... sparkles in your enchanting honey eyes..." Jūshirō paused. "I cannot wait to gaze upon you then, lovely lady. My brother is truly the lucky one of our pair."

"...Jūshirō."

Wait... Is he tearing up? her angel whispered. *He is. Oh my... that man is breathtaking. Simply... breathtaking.*

Yes, Gypsy. Her devil nodded. *This time... I have to agree with little-goodie-two-shoes over here.*

"But until that day..." Jūshirō continued. "...I will treat you as if you belong wholly to me." He smiled and squeezed her hand. "Will you let me spoil you, lovely goddess?"

Gypsy softly giggled. "Yes, Nee-chan. I would love that."

⚜

"When do you sleep?" Renji asked, while toweling off. "You work past five. When you leave here, you have to run to catch the last train. When do you sleep? When do you go out with your friends? When do you make time to go shopping?"

"I don't need *tons* of sleep." Gypsy took another drink of water. "I'm normally pretty hyper. As far as going out, I treat Sakara to lunch a couple times a week—exchange for her taking me to new places. And shopping... Taka used to keep the fridge stocked. It's pretty bare right now, but I ain't home much."

"Yes. Jūshirō mentioned that you were living with his little brother."

"Yeah, well... Jūshiro got it wrong. No matter how many times I try to tell him, he just won't let me explain. You see... Taka came here as my translator. That's all. We shared a company house... became good friends." She shrugged her shoulders. "He couldn't make it back for this last trip. So, I'm all alone. But it's only for a couple of months. No big deal."

"He doesn't miss you?"

"Who? Taka?" She snorted out a laugh. "I'm pretty sure he has plenty of other things to keep him occupied."

"And... you aren't worried about that, huh? Not jealous at all? Not even a little bit?"

"Why would I be jealous?"

"Are you not lovers?"

Gypsy strangled on her water. "N-no. Well, no, not really. I wouldn't call us *lovers*."

"But he *has* made love to you, has he not?"

"Jeez, you're getting a little personal there, Renji."

"I only say so because… I couldn't imagine sharing a house with you and not a bed. The torture would be unbearable."

She chuckled. "Yeah, well, apparently not. We were not intimate while we lived together. And we were both completely fine with that."

"But when you went back to America and had to separate… he couldn't bear your absence?"

"No. It wasn't like that."

"Then what was it like, Chikara? I am curious how a man can resist you, then obtain you, then just let you fly away and leave him. Do you not love each other?"

"Love? No… I don't think love had anything to do with it. Taka wasn't just my translator; he was my doctor as well, sort of. You see, I've got this weird birthmark that acts up from time to time. Taka calls it a fox bite, and… since he is this weird, hippy, guru doctor person who seems to be able to help me, we're close. I don't know *how* he helps me, but he does. He *cleanses* my aura, or something. Anyway, it was just a fluke that I needed a translator and he just happened to be right there. We're good friends. I like Taka."

"But you don't *love* him."

"We love each other, yeah. I don't know. It's complicated. Anyway, everything went great while I was here. The moment I get back home—bam."

"The fox bite?"

Gypsy nodded. "Taka rushed over to take care of me. But this time… this time there was really nothing he could do to make the pain go away."

"So… he comforted you."

She smiled. "I'd never been *comforted* like that before. Taka was exactly what I needed, when I needed it."

"You mean… you were a virgin?"

She shook her head. "Medically speaking, I haven't been a virgin since my freshman year at college."

When Renji furrowed his brow, Gypsy chuckled.

"I was in an accident—got hit by a car. The doctors had to remove all of my internal girly bits. They were destroyed." She sort of snorted. "I lost my womanhood to a motorcycle… and any chance of ever becoming a mother. Anyway…" She dismissively waved her hands. "The only man I'd ever *been* with was my best friend Gillis. We both got drunk one night, and... well, things just happened. Yeah, I know it was stupid, but that was *years* ago now— ancient history."

"You don't love Gillis, either?"

Gypsy turned to look Renji directly in the eye. "I love Gillis so much, I would never tie him down to a woman who can't even bear him a single child. Gillis is amazing. He deserves a wife who can..."

When she bit her lip and looked away, Renji began gently rubbing her back.

"So... I've had sex with two men who I wasn't *in love* with." She snorted and wiped her nose. "Guess that makes me a slut."

"Yeah. You've had sex twice in your life... real slutty."

She elbowed him and he laughed.

"I know what love is," she whispered. "I've got that in spades. I just don't know what *love* is. I love Taka, it's true. I'm just not real sure what *kind* of love I feel for him. Even though he tried... I kept him at arm's length. We get along well. I care a lot about him."

Renji smiled. "And what other *kinds* of love are you blessed with, Chikara?"

"Well, I love Trace, but I love him like I love myself... the same way I love my eyes or my legs or my lungs. Trace is a physical extension of me, as I am of him. Like I said... I love him like I love myself. Gillis... well, Gillis is a bit different. I actually almost fell in love with Gillis. At least, I believe that's what was happening." She took a deep breath. "I already knew how much he cared about me. Gillis was always quite vocal with his emotions in my regard. When I realized I felt the same way about him... I shut it down in a hurry. Eh, that was years ago now. We've remained best friends, but nothing more. So, even though I am surrounded by many different types of love... I don't truly know what *love* is. Not the lasting, 'til death do us part kind."

"I don't think that's true, Chikara. I think... I think you won't allow yourself to fall in love with someone because you believe you're not *worthy*, all because of some tragic accident. Maybe what you need to start thinking about is this... there are some men who don't *want* children. Have you ever asked anyone? Did you ask Taka? Gillis? You're only assuming you cannot give them what they truly want, but have you ever asked them? Me, personally... I never want to have kids. Think about it. How twisted would that little moppet be—growing up in *my* world?"

Gypsy snorted out a laugh.

"I don't want children, no. But what I do hope to have one day is a beautiful, intelligent, loving wife. A woman I can cherish. A woman I can grow old with. A devoted woman I can worship and share my life with." He smiled. "To me... *that* would be paradise. No kids to tie you down. No big family to suck your wallet dry. Just me and the woman I love—doing what we want, when we want, and waking up in each other's arms every single day."

"That's beautiful, Renji."

"I am not a rare find, Chikara. There are tons of men just like me. Who knows? Perhaps Gillis or Taka shares in this same dream. You'll never know unless you ask."

"Thanks for the pep talk, but I don't think so. Gillis... that ship has sailed. He's already found love. And Taka..." She chuckled. "Taka wouldn't be satisfied even if he had his own harem." She shrugged her shoulders. "Hell, he might already have one."

Renji brushed her hair back behind her shoulder. "All I'm saying is... give people a chance. Don't mark a man off just because you think you know what he wants. Quit closing yourself off from the world, from love. If you fall for the *right* man, your ability to have children will be irrelevant. Trust me. For the most part, women are the ones who want the babies. And if the day ever comes that the two of you wish to hear the pitter patter of little feet, there is no shortage of children who pray every night for a loving family. And like you said, Chikara, as far as love goes... you've got that in spades."

"Yeah, I guess." Gypsy paused. "Renji... that woman you were with that night."

"Yes."

"Is she your sub?"

"Yes."

"Do you love her?"

"I cherish her. She is very precious to me."

"But... you don't *love* her."

"Chikara, there is something about our world that you need to understand. What we do... it's completely mutual. A sub *offers* her collar to a Dom. If a Dom chooses to accept such a responsibility, it is no light matter. We treat our subs like goddesses. They are a *true* Dom's most prized possession."

"…Possession."

"It's just a word, Chikara. I promise you… my precious Jade wants for nothing. I make sure of it."

When Gypsy didn't say anything, Renji bumped her with his shoulder.

"Why the sudden curiosity? Were you hoping I was untethered? Did you wish to be my sub?"

Gypsy snorted. "Never gonna happen, Renji."

"Yeah. I could tell that the moment I first saw you standing there. I didn't know if you were truly a Domme or not, but I knew… you were definitely no sub."

"Nah, it just ain't in me."

"No, I suppose it isn't."

"Renji…" She paused again. "Could a Dom ever stop being a Dom?"

He chuckled. "Nah, it just ain't in him."

She glanced sideways at him. "…Smartass."

He laughed again. "I'm not really sure how to answer that, Chikara. A Dom is a man with a tendency toward a certain sexual pleasure. It doesn't negate the fact he is still a man. If you are asking me if a Dom could ever fall in love with a vanilla—sure, it happens. But what you need to remember is that love is a two-way street. He won't magically change his sexual preference just because he fell in love. Same as *you* wouldn't magically turn into a sub just because you fell for a Dom. We are all just human. We want what we want." He smiled. "So… tell me true. You're thinking about that gift I gave you, aren't you? Has hell frozen over yet, Chikara?"

Gypsy snorted out a laugh. "I thought it had, once… but the devil didn't ask me to dance."

Renji bumped her with his shoulder again. "Deep in your heart, you're wanting me to cane you. Aren't you, Chikara?"

Gypsy just rolled her eyes, then punched him.

Renji only laughed.

Chapter 16

"Hello, Ms. Rodden."

Gypsy looked up from her paperwork. "Mr. Bishop... Sir? What in the world are *you* doing here?"

"I came to take you out on a date."

"A date? You came all the way to Japan just to take me out to eat?"

"In part." He smiled. "The rest is a surprise."

"Ugh... Stop using your dimples. That isn't fair."

"I never said I played fair. Why would I do something so insane? If I am blessed with power, why not use it?"

No matter how she acted on the outside, Gypsy was truly happy to see a familiar face... especially Baron's.

"Sakara," Gypsy called out. "Take the rest of the day off. We're closing up shop."

Baron glanced at the smiling secretary. "Take tomorrow off as well. Consider it an early Christmas present."

"Tomorrow?" Gypsy furrowed her brow. "What kind of surprise lasts for two whole days?"

"The surprise kind of surprise." He smiled with only one corner of his mouth. "You hungry?"

"No. It's not even lunchtime yet."

"Well then, let's go home and get you changed."

"Changed? Changed for what?"

"How many times do I have to say it? It's a surprise."

"Wear the gold one," Baron said, handing Gypsy the dress.

"The gold one? Wow. This one makes me feel all fancy."

"You're an idiot." Baron chuckled as he pulled down the shoebox that had *golden* written on it. "These must be the ones," he said, lifting the lid. "Hmm... nice choice. I like all the sparkly rhinestones."

"See why I said the gold one made me feel all fancy?"

When she started putting on her gold hoop earrings, Baron said, "Wear the dangly ones." He handed her one of the chandelier earrings with diamond accents. "They'll look good with your hair up."

"You want me to wear my hair up?"

"Always." He smiled. "Gives me a better view of your sensuous neck."

"Pervert," she mumbled as she slid three golden bangles over her right hand.

"And the pièce de résistance." Baron pulled a thin box from his pocket.

Gypsy hesitated slightly before lifting the lid.

"Ahh... Baron..."

He smiled when her eyes lit up. "Golden chopsticks for my golden goddess."

She barely touched the jeweled tops. "Are those... diamonds?"

"Of course." He took them from the box and began twisting her hair up. "Only the best for my Gypsy," he whispered. "A treasure... for a treasure."

"Baron, I... I don't know what to say."

"Then say, thank you." He gently slid the second one in to lock her loose curls in place.

"Th-thank you, Baron." She turned from side to side, admiring her new hair ornaments.

"You're welcome, Gypsy. Do you like them?"

"Like them?" She smiled happily. "I *love* them."

"Good." He glanced over her shoulder at their reflection in the mirror. "They cost more than Stevens's bonus last year."

"Hmpft. That pig doesn't deserve a *job*, much less a bonus."

"...Gypsy."

She heard his deep whisper only a heartbeat before she felt his soft lips touch her shoulder.

"Baron?"

He didn't answer, only kissed her again.

"Mr. Bishop?"

He pulled her back against him then—running his hands down her sides, cupping her hips.

Gypsy felt his extremely large *bulge* now pressing against her backside.

"Baron... stop!"

At her strained, almost frightened sounding plea, Baron squeezed her tighter. He sucked in a sharp breath as he closed his eyes.

Gypsy remained quiet until Baron slowly released his held breath.

"Forgive me, Gypsy," he half whispered, half rasped. "When I saw how beautiful you looked, that mesmerizing sparkle in those gorgeous honey eyes... I forgot my place. I'm sorry."

Gypsy remained perfectly silent, perfectly still.

Baron sighed wearily, then grabbed her hand. "Come on. We don't want to be late."

"Late for what?"

"Gypsy..."

"I know. I know... it's a *surprise.*"

<hr/>

When they pulled up at the airport, Gypsy just stood there staring at the large building.

"Why are we *here?*"

"Why?" Baron chuckled. "Because this is where we get on the plane. I guess I could have asked the pilot to pick us up at the house, but there's not really anywhere to land there."

"Why do we need a plane?"

"Because we cannot *walk* to where we're going. Now, come on."

When Baron tugged on her hand, Gypsy refused to move.

"Where are we going, Baron?"

"...Gypsy."

"Where?"

"Bali."

"No!" She jerked her hand free.

"But you have to," he said softly. "You're the one who received the invitation. I'm just your plus one. I can't very well be showing up to Trace's wedding without *you*."

"I'm not going. I don't want to go. I had no intention of going. You can't *make* me go."

Baron grabbed her arm and forcefully pulled her against him. "Get. On. The. Plane," he said coolly.

She looked up at him, tears already filling her eyes. "But... why?"

He sighed and wrapped his arms around her. "Because, Gypsy... if you don't... you'll always regret it."

Once on the private jet, Gypsy kicked off her sparkly heels and downed a scotch.

Baron squeezed her hand. "I would never make you go through this alone."

"But isn't that *exactly* what you're doing?"

"No. And that is precisely why I came to Tokyo. This is something you *need* to do, Gypsy, and there was no way in hell I wasn't going to be here to support you."

"You know I hate you, right?"

"Perhaps you hate me today, yes." He smiled. "Yet, one day... you'll look back on this and thank me."

"Pfft." She turned to the window, shutting down any further conversation.

When her head started to doddle, Baron leaned her over against his shoulder.

"You sleepy?"

"Flying does that to me," she mumbled groggily. "...Baron?"

"Yes."

"Do you ever want to have children of your own some day?"

"Wha— Children? Why would you ask me something like that all of a sudden?"

She sat up and looked at him. "Just answer the question."

"No. I have never wanted children. Why?"

Gypsy shrugged her shoulders. "I don't know. Renji told me I should ask men. He said I shouldn't just *assume* I knew how they felt."

"Renji? How in the— Are you seeing Renji?"

She nodded. "He's my sensei. I see him every day."

"Your sensei?"

"Yeah. He has a dojo not far from the office. When I mentioned to Jūshirō that I missed working out at Tony's, he sent me down to Renji's."

Baron grabbed her shoulders. "Why are you going to Jūshirō?"

"I'm not *going* to Jūshirō. We just ran into each other and started talking. He has taken me out to dinner a few times—shows me new places."

"When did *this* happen?"

"I don't know. A while ago now. We ran into each other completely by chance."

"I highly doubt that," Baron mumbled under his breath.

"He thinks me and Taka have a *thing*."

"Who does? Jūshirō?"

Gypsy nodded. "I've told him over and over, but he just won't listen."

"Over and over? But... I thought you only ran into him by chance."

"That first time, yeah. We exchanged contact information then. Annnd... since the Sato case is now settled and my weekends are pretty much completely free—Jūshirō takes me places."

"Why have you not mentioned this before? What kind of *places* does he take you?"

"I didn't mention it because it's no big deal. And as far as where he takes me..." She shrugged her shoulders. "It's just normal places—out to eat, out shopping. Oh, he took me to Osaka one weekend. We stayed two whole days at a luxury hot springs resort. It was awesome."

"I just bet it was," Baron mumbled again.

"The weirdest thing happened that weekend..."

When she didn't immediately go on, Baron prodded her further. "Weird? Between you and Jūshirō?"

Gypsy shook her head. "No. Not between *us*. We were at this famous noodle shop in Osaka. Sakara had gone on and on about it, so I asked Jūshirō and he escorted me there. Anyway, we were enjoying ourselves—talking and laughing."

"Talking about what?"

"Just normal stuff—Taka, mostly. And *that's* what caused the odd looking couple to stop next to our table."

"What caused it? Talking about Taka?"

Gypsy nodded.

"What made you call them *odd* looking? Was something wrong with them?"

"No. That's just it. They were *ridiculously* gorgeous. So much so, they looked... odd." She shrugged her shoulders. "Anyway, I was telling Jūshirō a funny story about Taka. When they heard me say his name, the couple stopped right beside me and turned to each other—talking like we couldn't hear what they were saying."

"What *were* they saying?"

"The lady... she had the longest, blackest raven curls I had ever seen. She turned to the man and said... Dimples, did that woman just mention Taka?"

"Dimples?" Baron growled under his breath.

Gypsy nodded. "Yeah. He was super tall and had absolutely *stunning* dimples. Like I said... they were both ridiculously perfect."

"And... what happened?"

"Well... when the raven-haired lady asked him about Taka, the man she called Dimples grabbed her dainty hand and nervously looked around the restaurant before saying... Come, Lala. Let's get back to Jinn. We've been gone for far too long. Empress Naga will have our heads if she returns and cannot find you." Gypsy furrowed her brows. "Baron, where's Jinn? Is it in Japan?"

"I've never heard of it," he mumbled, obviously puzzled.

"Nor have I." Gypsy sighed. "Oh, do you know if the current Emperor's wife is named Naga?"

"No... it is not."

Gypsy shrugged her shoulders again. "Anyway, that's why I said the whole thing was odd. The fact they must have known Taka... talking about a town that's obviously not in Japan, or at least no one's ever heard of it... how their captivating beauty looked too perfect to even be of this world... and then mentioning an Empress that doesn't exist—beyond bizarre. Jūshirō thought so, too. I mean, didn't Taka say that Japan was the only country to still have Emperors?"

"Yes... I remember him saying something about that."

"Well, anyway... that was the only time something *super weird* like that happened to us. Mostly we just go to eat, then hang out at his house. Have you ever been to Jūshirō's house?"

"I have," Baron said coolly.

"Isn't his garden simply lovely? I could live in his back yard and be happy as a lark."

"Do you love him?"

"Who? Jūshirō?"

Baron didn't answer.

"You're joking, right?"

Still, Baron held his tongue, but Gypsy could tell he was grinding his teeth together. She lightly touched his clenched jaw.

"Hey... Baron... what's wrong?"

He didn't answer, only looked away.

"Are you worried about Jūshirō? Don't you trust him? I thought you were friends. He speaks highly of you."

"Do *you* trust him?"

Gypsy nodded. "I do... him and Renji both." She placed her hand on her hip. "I've never gotten a bad reaction from either of them."

Baron slowly relaxed his shoulders then, letting out a long, slow breath.

"Like I was telling you... Jūshirō truly does believe that Taka and I are lovers." She snorted out a laugh. "And Taka fuels this belief every time he talks to Jūshirō... he thinks it's hysterical. Anyway, Jūshirō promised Taka he would take care of me in his brother's absence... like I'm his little sister or something. That's why he demands I call him Nee-chan, because he believes I'll marry Taka one day. And like I said... Taka thinks the whole thing is hilarious—best trick ever."

"Taka Nasaka is a troublemaker."

Gypsy smiled. "Yeah, well, everybody already knows that. Anyway, it's nice hanging out with Jūshirō. He's kind and courteous and... I don't know... *regal* acting."

"He has never been inappropriate with you?"

"Nope. Never."

"And what about Renji?"

"Renji is my sensei."

"So?"

"So… I respect him more than I ever thought possible. He has sort of become my Japanese Gillis. We talk a lot. We're close."

"Is that right?"

Gypsy nodded again. "He knows about my fox bite, so he's always super honest and upfront with me."

"Upfront and honest in the fact he would like to cane you?"

"Yeah." She chuckled. "But that was just when we were first getting to know each other. Truth is… Renji is a Dom, through and through."

"So?"

"So… he knows me now."

"Meaning?"

"Meaning… he knows I could *never* be a sub… ever."

"So, he doesn't push the subject?"

"Nope. Never. Renji told me he wants to find a sub one day that he totally falls in love with. When he finds that *perfect* sub, he will marry her and spend the rest of his life worshipping and treasuring her." She smiled. "He makes his future sound so beautiful." She looked Baron in the eye. "I think that woman will be one of the luckiest in the world."

Baron smiled as he reached for one of her loose curls. "And what about working out? Do you only go to the dojo to talk about love and marriage?"

Gypsy almost giggled. "No. I'm already pretty good at Judo. Fuu is my sparring partner. Renji used to be, but the first time he left a bruise on me… he refused to spar with me anymore. Fuu doesn't mind. I actually think he likes to mar my *lovely flesh*," she said, trying to mimic the bald Asian man.

"Master Fuu? Jimpachi?"

She nodded.

Baron narrowed his gaze. "Hmpft… like one big happy reunion, huh?"

"Hey, you're the one who introduced me to that bunch of weirdoes."

He lightly yanked on the curl he was playing with. "But you weren't supposed to *like* them."

Gypsy chuckled. "Baron… will you fix my hair back when we get there?"

"Of course. Why?"

She pulled the golden chopsticks out and carefully slid them into the front pocket of his suit.

"Because, I'm sleepy."

Gypsy laid her head back then, and closed her eyes.

Baron gazed down at her angelic sleeping face. *What am I going to do with you, my dear? You run with wolves… and are completely oblivious to the dangers.* He wrapped his arm around her shoulders and rested her head upon his chest. *Men are pigs. Remember? We are all the same. No matter how sweet we pretend to be, we all want to claim you, dominate you… own you.* He sighed softly. *Gillis was right. You should be more wary, sweet Gypsy.*

"There," Baron said, putting her hair sticks back into place. "You look perfect." He took her by the shoulders and turned her to face him. "Gypsy, you are a beauty without equal. Not just on the outside. You are lovely to look upon, yes, but your inner beauty outshines every other woman I have ever known. You have this… *light* inside you, Gypsy. Sometimes, when I look at you… it's blinding. You *glow*, my love. Any man who has ever walked into your life and back out without snatching you up and making you his… that man is a fool."

"Stop being so sweet to me." She crossed her arms. "I'm still mad at you."

Baron smiled. "Be as mad as you want. As long as you stay by my side, *I* will be happy." He lightly kissed her cheek. "You'll outshine the bride, Gypsy. You are breathtakingly radiant. I can't take my eyes off of you."

"Thank you, Baron. I'm still mad at you, it's true. But… I appreciate what you're doing, what you are *trying* to do. It means a lot. Truly."

"Every word was the truth." He pulled her close. "The day you walked into my office, I had no idea the journey you would take me on."

"A magical ride?"

"Epic and heart-stopping."

She chuckled. "Okay. Okay. That's enough. You'll make my head swell if you don't stop."

"Shall we?"

She accepted his proffered arm, took a deep breath, then entered that tiny chapel with her head held high.

"Aye, Lass. Ye look like an angel," Gillis whispered when she sat down beside him.

"I feel like a princess," she whispered back.

"There's nae princess that can hold a candle tae ye, Kitten. I've nae seen ye look more beautiful."

Baron leaned over and softly whispered in her ear, "Told you."

The wedding was simple, yet elegant. The reception was small, but lavish. Baron and Gillis did an excellent job of keeping a smile on Gypsy's face, a gentle laugh spilling from her lips.

When the meal had been enjoyed and toasts were being made, Gypsy yawned.

"Aye, Kitten. When was the last time ye slept?"

"On the plane," she said through another yawn.

"And afore that?"

She blinked a couple of times, then turned towards the Scotsman. "I don't know. A couple of nights ago… maybe."

"Come now, Kitten. Ye know how ye get when ye go days on end withoot sleeping. Ye quit thinking straight—make poor decisions."

She yawned again. "I'm fine, Gills. They fed us too many carbs. That's all. Trace should know better. I mean, he *is* a doctor, after all."

"We should probably get going, anyway," Baron said. "I'm not sure about the traffic in this area, and it will be a major headache if we have to change the flight manifest."

"Okay." She covered her mouth through another yawn. "I'm ready."

Gillis pulled her towards him and kissed the side of her head. "I miss ye, Kitten. Come home soon. Okay?"

"Just a couple more weeks and I'll be able to wrap Tokyo up for a while."

"Good. After that, yer Pope..." He glanced toward Baron. "...should leave ye in the States for a bit. Let ye get acclimated afore he sends ye off again."

"I plan on keeping her there as long as possible," Baron said. "Now come, Gypsy. Let's say our farewells to the happy couple."

Gypsy put on her best smile and graciously hugged the glowing bride.

Hmpft... petite little bouncy blonde... figures.

Gypsy, her angel scolded. *Don't think like that.*

Accidentally yank her hair, her devil added.

"It's so good to finally meet you in person," Rose said, taking Gypsy's hands. "I believe I know more about you than even *you* know about yourself. You're all he ever talks about."

"It's all lies," Gypsy said through her pretend smile. "Don't believe a word of it."

"My Gypsy," Trace said, pulling her into his arms. "I'm so glad you came. This day wouldn't have been perfect without you here to share it with."

"I wouldn't have missed it for the world," she lied.

"I have a gift for you," he whispered. "I was just waiting for the perfect time to give it to you."

"A gift?" Gypsy chuckled. "But it's *your* wedding day."

Trace picked up the shallow golden box with an extravagant bow draped across the top.

"For you," he said, holding it out.

Gypsy slowly lifted the lid to find some folded-up documents. She quickly scanned them, then looked up to Trace.

"What's this?"

He smiled again as he wrapped his arm around his new wife. "It's a Quit Claim Deed for my half of The Kilt. She's all yours now, Gyps."

She looked down at the signed paper, and then back up to her dearest friend in the world. "You just couldn't wait, could you?"

"Gypsy, don't," Baron whispered.

She slowly closed the document, fighting with everything she had to keep her burning tears at bay.

"I want to thank you, Trace," she said, before looking back up to face him. "I want to thank you for saving my life that day. I want to thank you for your love, your support, and for the priceless gift of your own body that has sustained me all these years. I owe you more than I can ever repay."

"…Gypsy," Trace whispered.

She half smiled. "I don't think I ever put how grateful I truly am into words."

"You never had to, Gyps."

A willful tear slid down Gypsy's cheek then. She swallowed hard.

Rose smiled sweetly at their tender exchange… as she placed her hand over her own tummy and gently rubbed it.

Gypsy's eyes went wide at the sight. She staggered. Baron quickly wrapped his arm around her waist, steadying her.

"Gypsy?" Trace reached for her. "You okay?"

Baron felt her trembling. He held her tighter.

"This…" She slowly lifted the shaking golden box containing her *gift*. "This was the final tie. The last bond that needed to be severed before you could freely go on with your happy new life."

Silence fell over the small crowd.

"Was it easy?" Another tear escaped as Gypsy's steady gaze remained locked with Trace's. "Putting that pen to paper… did the ink flow smoothly? Did pain accompany each finely curved letter? Or… was it simply *relief* put into writing?"

"…Gypsy…"

Trace tried to take her hand, but she withdrew.

"You were my world, Trace." She could no longer contain her engulfing grief. "My whole… damn… world."

"As you were mine, Gyps," he whispered.

She swallowed hard, no longer bothering to wipe away her now constant tears. "Good-bye, Trace… Rose." She glanced at the other woman. "I hope that babe you now carry is but the first of many. I wish you well… all three of you."

Gypsy's knees would have buckled, had Baron not been holding to her so fiercely.

"I've got you, Gypsy," he whispered close to her ear. "I've got you."

"I want to leave now, Baron," she softly said, her trembling voice audible only to him.

"Yes," he whispered. "Anything you want."

"I just want to go home."

"Back to the States?"

"Tokyo. Just... take me back to Tokyo."

Gypsy just stood there, completely numb, as Baron carefully undid all the many buttons of her lovely golden dress. She quietly let him remove her jewelry, her gold and diamond hair sticks, and even remained still as he slipped her silky robe up over her shoulders.

"Feel better now?" he whispered softly, leaning down to kiss her cheek.

When he did, Gypsy placed her hand at the back of his neck and held him there. She didn't say a word, only moved so that their lips were all but touching. She felt his pulse race, heard his sharp intake of breath. She waited a moment more, several tortuous heartbeats. Then, she lightly kissed him.

Baron placed his hand on her lower back, slowly pulling her into him as the passion of their touch gradually escalated. When she gently ran her hand down the front of his tightening pants, Baron pulled away.

"No."

She ignored him, reaching for the buttons on his shirt.

Baron firmly grabbed her wrists. "Stop."

His smooth, gentle voice now carried the same ice Gypsy remembered during their first meeting... when Baron had told her to *sit*.

"Why?" She jerked her arms free. "Isn't this what you do? Have sex with lots of different women? What? Am I doing it wrong? Was I supposed to *ask permission* before I kissed you? Or do *you* have to be the one who initiates it?"

Baron made a disgusted noise. "You have no idea what you're talking about. Go to bed and sleep it off, Gypsy. You've have a rough day. You'll feel better in the morning."

"I don't want to feel better in the morning. I want to feel better now!"

When she reached for his shirt again, Baron slapped her hand away. Before she even realized what she was doing, Gypsy reflexively returned the action... slapping him across the face.

He didn't say a word. Baron remained as she had left him—head turned, cheek reddening.

"Oh my gosh! I'm so sorr—"

"Go to bed, Gypsy." His chilling voice swept over her like an arctic breeze. "...Now."

"I told you. I don't *want* to go to bed."

He turned back to face her then, eyes narrowed.

Gypsy gasped, a heartbeat before Baron purposefully slammed her up against the wall—tearing off her thin robe, kissing her violently.

"Is *this* what you want?" he said through a throaty snarl. "Do you want me to ravage you, Gypsy? Dominate you?"

"...Yes," she rasped.

With her heated admission, Baron pulled back. "No. I will not be your *pain-fix*, Gypsy. I won't let you use *me* to drown Trace out of your mind. I am not your toy and I am not your pretend lover. If you need *this* type of satisfaction, you will have to look elsewhere. Too bad Taka isn't here with you now."

"Yeah, it is," she spat, jerking her tattered robe closed.

"Perhaps you should call Renji. He could replace the pain in your heart with the one he would leave across your sweet little ass."

"Maybe I will," she snapped, pushing past him and snatching up her phone.

Baron grabbed her by the arm and shoved her back up against the wall. Gypsy began to struggle in earnest then.

"Let me go!"

"No." He pinned her wrists over her head. "I will not let you do something you will only regret tomorrow."

"Release me," she hissed.

"No." He tightened his grip. "I *won't* release you. Not until you calm down."

"Let go of my wrists." She squirmed and fought, but he had her pinned tight against the wall. "Don't bind me!" she screamed, pain-filled tears now streaming down her cheeks.

When she slowly gave in and went limp, tiny whimpers now shaking her shoulders, Baron scooped her up in his arms and carried her to bed. He snuggled up behind her and held her close.

"Shhh, sweet Gypsy," he whispered, stroking her hair and wiping away her tears. "I've got you now. I'll hold you while you cry it out. Let the pain go, my love. Let me be your strength… just for a little while."

———◆———

Her sobs eventually slowed. Her tears gradually dried up. Only her occasional tremors and swollen, bloodshot eyes remained as evidence of her pain.

"…Baron." Her voice cracked.

"Yes, Gypsy."

"Why didn't you make love to me?"

"How can I make love to you when you are not *in love* with me?"

She sniffed. "I wouldn't have stopped you."

"You wouldn't have stopped me from having sex with you, no. But… that is not the type of comfort you truly need."

When she didn't respond, Baron rolled her over to face him.

"Do you have any idea how hard that was for me, Gypsy? You know how badly I desire you. You felt the proof of that with your own dainty little hands." He took her hand in his, placing her palm against his mouth and kissing it. "I have wanted to hold you like this, like *that*, since the night I walked into your bar and met the *real* Gypsy Rodden. You have consumed my thoughts from that moment forth."

"Baron, you don't have to—"

"Shhh. Just listen to me. I may never be blessed with another moment like this one. Let me say what I have to say." He brushed her hair back behind her ear. "As badly as I desire it, as much as I fantasize about it… I cannot have sex with you. I cannot treat you like the other women in my life. You are special, Gypsy… precious."

"It's okay," she whispered. "You don't have to say anymore. I understand."

"Do you, Gypsy? Do you truly? Tell me. What is it you understand?"

"I understand I'm not like your other women. I'm not your *type*. I'm not *sub* material."

"Ugh… You truly are an idiot."

He gently rolled over on top of her, spreading her legs as he pressed comfortably against her. Baron pulled her knees up to his sides, wrapped his arms around her, and then cupped the back of her neck. Gypsy's heart raced as he slowly drew nearer, encircling the tip of her nose with his, before gently kissing her lips. When he pulled back and softly smiled, Gypsy melted inside.

"*This* is what I want from you, Gypsy. And... you are the only woman I have ever wanted this from." He kissed her again, a little stronger and a little longer. "I want this before I close my eyes at night." He kissed her again. "I want this when I wake every morning."

He moved down to her neck. She gasped.

"I want you wrapped in my arms. I want you staring into my eyes. I want us lost in each other."

She gasped again. "...Baron."

"What do *you* want, Gypsy?" he whispered. "Do you want these same things?"

She nodded her head.

"Do you want them with me?"

She nodded again. "...Yes."

"Gypsy..." He kissed her neck again, then looked her in the eye. "Can you say that you love me?"

She froze then, her lovely honey eyes growing a fraction larger.

Baron smiled softly. "When you can say those words, when you can feel what I'm feeling... only then can I make love to you. Only then will my kisses truly mean enough to heal you. And until that day happens, I will always tell you... No, Gypsy. I cannot give you what you want because... you cannot give me what I *need*. I will not enter you to help you forget Trace. It would hurt me too much."

"Why would it hurt *you*?"

"Because I love you, Gypsy. *Love* you. Tell me. How would you feel if the one person you desired above all... came to you and demanded sex? Bade you let him use you to get another woman out of his head?"

"Th— *That's* how it felt to you?"

He nodded. "Now do you see? Gypsy, you are the one woman I refuse to take that next step with, not unless your heart is in it. The pain of such a union... ahh, it would be more than I could bear. When I finally enter you, it will be because you *need* me to—body and soul."

"...I never knew," she barely whispered.

"And now... now you can never *un*know. I love you, Gypsy. And there's just no going back from that. Not for me."

She swallowed hard. "I'm sorry, Baron." A tiny tear trickled back to soak her hair.

"Sorry for what?"

"For making you feel that way. For acting like such an ass. I am truly sorry."

He kissed her forehead and squeezed her a little tighter.

"Can I ask something completely selfish of you?" she whispered.

He gazed down at her. "Anything, my love. Well, *almost* anything."

He smiled teasingly. Gypsy mirrored him.

"Can I— I mean..." She took a deep breath. "Baron... will you just hold me like this for a little while? Is that wrong of me to ask?"

He smiled warmly. "It will be my pleasure, Gypsy. I will be your comforter. Sleep safe within my arms... lovely goddess."

Chapter 17

"I have been emailing Marie," Sakara said. "The currier just delivered the final documents on *this* end." She laid a stack of files on Gypsy's desk.

"Oh... good. Thank you."

"Also, I have forwarded everything Marie needs in the States. She said she has the documents all printed up, and they now await your signature. As soon as *that* is done, she can have them notarized and filed within hours."

"Then... I'm finished here?"

"For now, Ms. Rodden, yes."

"So... I can go home then?"

"We were only waiting on these." Sakara tapped the files she had just brought in.

Gypsy sighed. "But my flight doesn't leave out until tomorrow night."

"That's why I booked this." Sakara handed her a printed confirmation page. "You fly out in four hours. That will put you arriving at LAX first thing in the morning. A full day before scheduled."

"Ahh, Sakara. If you weren't a woman, I'd kiss you."

"Please don't," she said through a laugh.

"Four hours? Holy Jeez... it takes two just to get to the airport."

"You better hurry then."

Sakara smiled when Gypsy jumped up and began frantically stuffing her briefcase.

"Good-bye, Ms. Rodden," she called out as Gypsy jumped onto the elevator. "See you next time."

Gypsy quickly looked up before the doors slid closed. She matched Sakara's friendly smile, and was waving like an idiot as her eyes began to tear up. When *would* she be back? Gypsy wasn't sure, and leaving in a mad rush like this... it just felt wrong.

"Bye, Sakara," she softly whispered within the empty elevator.

<hr>

Gypsy rubbed her eyes and looked at her watch. "Good." She yawned. "I should be able to make it in to the office by eight. That gives me the whole day to get the paperwork on this end filed. Then... vacation time. Whoo hoo!" She smiled to herself. "Baron promised me a whole week off. I'm gonna play video games until my vision blurs."

Gypsy came clicking down the hall while Marie was still pouring her first cup of coffee.

"M-Ms. Rodden? How— What are you doing here? You're not even scheduled to fly out of Japan until..." She started flipping through her day-planner.

"Not until tonight," Gypsy said. "Well, tonight in Tokyo. Which would be... Aww, hell. I don't know. What does it matter? I'm here now." She smiled.

"But... no one is expecting you back until Monday."

"And let's keep it that way, Marie." Gypsy put her finger to her mouth. "Mum's the word, love. Okay? As long as no one knows I'm here, I can stay locked in my office until I'm done... *undisturbed*. We're going to get this case filed *this* week, Marie. Because next week... next week I'm *free*," she half sang.

Marie almost giggled.

Gypsy tapped the corner of a file folder onto her smiling secretary's desk before heading to her office.

"Cream with two sugars. Got it?"

"Got it." Marie jumped up.

"And you better keep 'em coming," Gypsy said. "I've got some serious jetlag-hangover going on this morning."

"I'm on it, Ms. Rodden."

<hr>

Marie kept the coffee flowing right up until lunchtime.

"I brought you something to eat, Ms. Rodden—baked chicken and potato casserole."

"Ahh... you are a saint, Marie—Saint Marie." She chuckled. "Pull up a chair and eat with me."

"Are you sure?"

"Yeah, come on." Gypsy smiled. "Thanks to all your awesome prep-work, it looks like I'll be done in about an hour. I can have these filed by two, at the latest."

"As soon as you get *that* done, you go on home, Ms. Rodden. I'll run them to the courthouse for you. No worries."

"I knew I liked you for some reason."

The two women laughed and made small talk as they ate their lunch, then Gypsy went right back to work.

⸙⟨◆⟩⸙

"Does that wrap it up, Ms. Rodden?"

Gypsy dropped the file into the other woman's waiting hands, and sighed.

"Yes, Marie. I'm calling it a day." She plopped her bag down on her secretary's desk and started rummaging for her iPod. "Head on over to the courthouse, and don't come back. Grab your purse and go. Tonight, you're having a nice dinner with that gorgeous young man of yours."

Marie giggled as she switched off her monitor and draped her coat over her bent arm.

"Be at Treś Squared by seven," Gypsy said.

"Wha— Treś Squared?"

Gypsy smiled. "Yes, and don't be late. I made reservations for you guys, and that maître d' gets pretty snippy if you're not punctual."

"But... Ms. Rodden..."

"No worries, love. My treat—appreciation for a job well done." Gypsy sighed. "You have no idea the weight that was lifted off my shoulders when I closed that ridiculously thick case file, Marie." She winked at the stunned woman. "Trust me. You've earned it."

Marie gave her a big hug before heading toward the elevators.

"You're the best boss in the world," she called out just as the doors slid open. "Best boss ever!"

"Hush now. Go on and stop spreading such vicious rumors."

Gypsy watched as the doors slowly closed in front of the smiling—still waving—assistant she had hired nearly six months ago.

"Wow. Best boss ever, huh? You fishing for another title to add to your door?"

"Shut it, Stevens," Gypsy said, without even glancing toward the mocking man. "As of five minutes ago, I'm on vacation."

"Vacation, huh?"

"Yep. The next nine days will be a welcome slice of bliss." Gypsy sat down on the bench lining the wall and slipped on her tennis shoes, then dropped her high heels into her carry-on bag. "Nine days of bliss. Nine days of peace. Nine days of not having to look at *your* greasy little smile. Yes... nine days of heaven. I am sooo ready for this."

"Sounds magical." He tossed a marbled brown folder on the floor at her feet. "Too bad it was only a dream."

Gypsy jerked tight the bunny ears of her shoelaces and stared at the file, but dared not pick it up.

"Stevens... if you are yanking my chain, I swear by all that's holy, I will throat-punch you. Right here. Right now."

"Don't get mad at *me*. I didn't even know you were here. I was bringing this down for Marie—a nice little Monday morning surprise for you." He snorted. "Orders came straight from the Big Man. Seems you did such a bang-up job with the Toshima Corp. and Sato groups, he has entrusted your valuable *expertise* to handle Wallace & Gamble as well."

"Wallace & Gamble is John's case."

"*Was* John's case. It's all you now, babe."

Gypsy closed her eyes, sighing as she let her head fall back against the wall.

"I hate you, Stevens. I can truly say, and without reservation... I hate you."

"I know you do, sweet cheeks."

She slowly opened her eyes, focusing on that cocky smirk he wore so well. For more than a few heartbeats, she *seriously* thought about going ahead and just throat-punching the slimy little weasel.

"I know you hate me. Ahh, but those daggers in your lovely brown eyes... they make me sooo hard." He rubbed his crotch for emphasis.

This conniving man before her was truly the scum of the earth—not even worth the clean air he was freely breathing. Every time she looked at him, she had to swallow back the rising vomit.

"Truly?" Gypsy grabbed the folder and her bag as she stood. "And here I was almost certain you preferred batting for the other team." She smiled when he narrowed his beady eyes. "And seeing as how you totally *suck* with women, I was guessing some sweaty old dude probably showed you how to do it properly— suck, that is—because you do it so well."

"What did you just—"

"Oh." She slapped the elevator button and turned back to face him. "And if I thought you wouldn't be too intimidated to, you know... *try* and perform for me—sexually—I would slap you with a harassment suit so fast, that minuscule little ball sack you're playing with right now would suck back up inside you, like that." She snapped her fingers just as the door slid open. "Enjoy your weekend, lizard boy."

Gypsy playfully waved her fingers, before turning her hand around and flipping him a bird.

The doors slowly closed on his snarl, and her smile.

—⋘◆⋙—

Instead of going down, Gypsy hit the button for the next floor up and headed straight for Baron's office.

"Mr. Bishop," she said, opening the door without knocking. "What in the holy—" She glanced around. "Mr. Bishop?"

The office was empty.

"Well, hell."

Gypsy turned to go, but heard a muffled noise coming from the bookcase at the far end of the room. She moved closer. There was a tiny bit of light illuminating the side of the rich mahogany. When Gypsy lightly placed her hand against it, the large case pushed back with ease.

She looked through the tiny crack into the hidden room. There was a woman kneeling on the floor. Her wrists were bound. She had a ball gag in her mouth and tears streaming down her cheeks.

"What the hell?"

When Gypsy pushed the bookcase door open even wider, the woman glanced her way. The bound brunette's eyes went wide and she tried to call out.

That's when Gypsy saw him. Baron Bishop—on his knees, eyes closed, thoroughly enjoying the pounding he was delivering to his now frantic sub.

Gypsy's heart froze. She could have sworn it quit beating altogether. Her throat closed painfully tight and her feet were stuck to the carpeted floor. She couldn't scream. She couldn't run. She couldn't even turn away.

The woman must have finally gotten his attention, Gypsy wasn't sure since there was nothing but a loud ringing in her ears, but Baron slowly opened his eyes and glanced her way. He froze as well.

"…Gypsy…"

At the sound of his regret-filled whisper, the horrible spell cast over her was suddenly broken. Gypsy ran from his office, slinging the large case file Stevens had given her across the room.

"Gypsy, wait!"

But she couldn't. In truth, Gypsy was shaking so badly she wasn't even certain she could step onto the opening elevator. She let the doors slowly close as Baron ran toward her. She watched him disappear, and hoped she would never see his handsome face again.

⋅⋅⋅⋅⋅◈⋅⋅⋅⋅⋅

Gypsy walked all the way home, but not on the main sidewalks. She ducked into alleys, cut across the park. She didn't want to be seen. She wanted to be invisible… invisible and numb. But the world just kept speeding on by—children playing, sirens in the distance, a dog barking.

At least her normally active inner voices were giving her a bit of needed peace.

When Gypsy finally made it back to The Kilt, the place was deserted. She was truly thankful. Gillis was gone, and there was still another hour to go before anyone showed up to do prep work.

She opened the fridge, took out a beer, and downed it with one go.

"Ugh... I'd love a Chuhai right about now," she mumbled, before clicking on the TV... and then flipping through every channel without stopping.

She thought about having another beer, thought about going down to the bar and mixing up some watermelon margaritas. Instead, Gypsy slowly walked up the curved staircase and plopped down in front of one of the large metal windows.

She stared out upon the city, but saw nothing. The only scene now playing out in her mind was the horrific one she had only just witnessed.

He said he loved you, her angel whispered softly.

Yeah... Even the little devil's voice sounded kind. But she never said she loved him back.

"No... I never told him," she whispered. "Now... now he'll never know."

<hr />

Gypsy heard the front buzzer sound and glanced over at the little screen just in time to see Gillis open the door and let Sheila in.

"Hmm... I didn't even know Gills was home. He must not have come upstairs. Strange."

She sat down at the table and started on her second beer, then noticed the bar's ledger book underneath a pile of last month's invoices.

"Well, might as well work as to worry. It'll do me some good." She grabbed an ink pen and switched on the adding machine. "My mind needs *something* else to concentrate on right now."

Her phone started vibrating then. When Gypsy dug it out of her purse, she had twenty-seven missed calls... all from Baron Bishop.

"Freak," she mumbled as she turned the power off and tossed it aside.

Adding up the daily deposits was easy, mind-numbing work. Gypsy whizzed through the columns without much thought, until she came to the total line.

"What the—"

She checked the numbers again.

"Nope. No mistakes."

Then she flipped back through the previous months. They all fell short. For nearly a year, the bar had been losing some serious money.

"All but three months ago," she mumbled, looking at the total *then* and the total *now*. "Why didn't Gillis tell me business had dropped off so much? I would have adjusted the ordering."

She snatched the invoices up and started scanning them, then checked the ending inventory sheet.

"How in the hell are we buying, and apparently *using*, the same amount of liquor... and still going in the frickin' hole?"

She began flipping further back through the ledger.

"It's the same damn thing for a whole year. A thousand wonders we ain't broke by now."

Yeah, her angel said. *We thought we'd make money going to Asia, not lose it.*

"Going to Asia..."

Gypsy flipped back to the month she and Taka had first left California. A little over halfway through the month, sales took a sharp dive and never recovered.

"I wonder what happened."

Low deposits were consistently recorded for the next eight months.

"Then, bam," she mumbled. "Right back to normal."

Yeah, for one whole month. Her angel snorted. *What was so special about that month?*

Well... the writing's different, her devil said.

"The writing?"

Gypsy looked back to the prior year and compared them, month for month.

See? her devil said. *Different writing.*

"But that's not Gillis's penmanship. Who else could have made out the deposit?"

She snatched up the timesheets and looked at the first month in question.

"Blood. Dee. Hell!"

Wait. No… that can't be right, her angel said. *It can't be Becca. You fired her when you came home last time.*

The writing doesn't lie, her devil said. *Apparently, our dear friend went behind our back and unfired her.*

"No." Gypsy furrowed her brow. "I've been running the payroll through Sheila. I haven't paid out a single check to Becca Greyson."

Her devil snorted sardonically. *Just because you haven't been cutting her a check, doesn't mean she hasn't been helping her boyfriend out around the bar.*

Gypsy grabbed the ledger and stormed downstairs.

"Gillis McCullough, I ought to rip your damn balls off!"

By the time she made it to the bottom of the stairs, Gillis and Sheila were both staring in her direction, mouths agape.

"…Kitten, when did ye get back—"

"Don't *Kitten* me!"

Then, Gypsy noticed Becca's golden hair peeking out from behind the Scot.

"No. Frickin'. Way!"

She slung the book down on the bar and marched toward Gillis.

He held up his hands. "Hang on, Lass."

"Let me at her, Gills." She shoved the Scot out of the way.

Becca was standing there like a deer caught in the headlights.

"Why you little lying, thieving, skank-saw-whore-bag!"

Gypsy grabbed the other woman's golden hair and slammed her pretty little face down against the bar. Blood squirted everywhere.

"I'll kill you!" Gypsy screamed, jerking the addled girl back upright.

Gillis forcibly tore Gypsy off the bleeding blonde.

"Get outta here, Becca," he yelled. "Go! I cannae hold her."

As Becca ran past them, Gypsy kicked her square in the back, sending the other woman flying out from behind the bar and sprawling across the floor.

"Let... me... go, Gillis!"

She jerked free as the blonde made it to her feet and ran for the door. Gypsy snatched up a bottle of whiskey and hurled it at Becca's head. It missed her by no more than a couple of inches and exploded against the far wall. Becca was still screaming when she shoved open the door and raced out into the parking lot.

Gypsy spun around on the Scot. "Why did you stop me, Gillis?"

"If I hadnae, ye'd a killed her, Lass."

"That's bloody well better than she deserves."

She yanked up a bottle of scotch and flung it against the wall before he could stop her.

"What's gotten intae ye, Gyps? Have ye lost yer bloody mind? She could have ye arrested for that."

"Let her try. We'll see whose ass ends up in jail." Gypsy narrowed her gaze. "Are you taking her side, Gillis?"

"There's nae side tae take, Gyps. Yer jealousy—"

"Jealousy?" She stared at him a couple heartbeats, then shook her head. "You know what... screw you, Gillis McCullough." She slammed the ledger down on the bar. "Does *this* look like jealousy to you?"

He looked then to the open pages she was pointing to.

"Look at this... March of last year—March of this year. Notice anything strange?"

"The total money is way down," Sheila whispered, before taking a hasty step back.

"See there?" Gypsy pointed to the scared woman. "Even Sheila saw that something was off, with just one little peek. Now, look at this... April last year, and April now. Or should I say... April when I was home, and April when I was in Tokyo."

Gillis furrowed his brow and leaned closer.

"May when I was here..." she continued. "...May when I was gone. June—June. July—July. All the way up until December, then look."

"They're nearly the same," Sheila said.

"Yes." Gypsy nodded. "And would anyone like to venture a guess as to why?"

"Aye, Lass… because *ye* were home this last December."

"Ding. Ding. Ding. Give the man a prize. And what did I do when I got home in December?"

"Sent Becca packing," Sheila said.

"We have a winner, ladies and gentlemen." She flipped to January then. "Now… what I'm having a hard time figuring out is this." Gypsy looked at Gillis. "If I threw Becca's ass out into the street in December, how in the bloody hell is *her* handwriting here in my ledger for January and February? Right along with these *amazingly* low deposit amounts."

Both Gillis and Sheila held their silence.

"And *why*, might I add…" Gypsy slammed the book closed. "…was that frickin' whore in my bar just now?"

Gillis swallowed hard and looked away.

"By my calculations, Gills… that filthy skank has stolen over two hundred thousand dollars from us. Two. Hundred. Thousand. Dollars! Not to mention all my tips that seemed to *magically* disappear out of my own home. Those were *my* tips, Gillis! I worked my *ass* off for that money!"

He turned back to face her then, pain and guilt creasing his brow.

"Countless nights of me having to put up with drunk men's bullshit… the thousands of times I circled around this bar with my feet and back killing me… all the pain… all the crap… all the sleepless nights. And for what? Huh? So your thieving little slit could *take* it from me? Huh? Do I work for *her*, Gillis? Do I work my ass off so that *Becca* can have what *she* wants?"

"Nae, Gyps. I—"

"Just shut up! You don't give a shit about me, Gillis McCullough. While you were busy trying to figure out how to keep your dick wet, your whore was walking out *my* door with *my* life's savings in her front pocket. Did you think it was funny? Did you laugh about all the mornings I could barely crawl up those damn steps, while she was stuffing my tips in her frickin' purse?"

"Nae, Gypsy! I swear. I didnae know—"

"No," she said coolly. "You didnae *care* to know. And that's the difference. I told you when last I was home. I *told* you my tip money was going missing. I even showed you, Gillis. And still…

still, I come back to my own home and find that worthless piece of trash behind *my* bar. If *you* weren't the one taking the money, Gillis, then you knew it had to be her. You knew it! Still… you bring her in here the moment I'm gone." She shook her head. "If that isn't complete disdain for me as a person, as a human, as your supposedly *best* friend… then I don't know what is."

Gillis didn't answer. There was nothing he could say.

"Tell me one thing, Gills. Did you let her go back upstairs?"

"Nae, Gyps. I swear it."

"Fine. Fine." She nodded. "I thank you for that, Gillis. Now… get the hell out."

"Wha— What do ye mean, Lass?"

"I *mean* exactly what it sounded like I meant. Get the hell out of my home. Go upstairs. Get whatever shit you're gonna need, then get the hell out. You don't live here anymore, *Mr. McCullough.* If there's anything you can't haul off tonight, I'll make arrangements for you to come get it later."

"Gyps—"

"Now, Gillis. Out."

He didn't even go upstairs. Gillis gently kissed her on top of the head before walking out the door.

Gypsy turned when she heard the wooden bar chairs being scooted around.

"Don't worry with that, Sheila. It's my mess. I'll clean it up."

"I don't mind, Ms. Gypsy. I got it. I wouldn't want you to get cut."

Tears filled Gypsy's eyes then. Her knees gave out and she sat right down where she was standing.

Sheila ran behind the bar and knelt down beside her.

"What happened, Ms. Gypsy? Did you get hurt?"

"I've lost everybody, Sheila. Every single person in my life… they're all gone now."

Sheila wrapped her arm around Gypsy's shoulders and held her while she cried out her words.

"First it was Trace… then Taka. And today I've lost two huge pieces of my heart in a matter of hours. I saw Baron doing… I don't even want to talk about what I saw Baron doing. And I just kicked Gillis out of my life as well. Gillis… I can't believe it. I thought *he* would be sitting beside me when I died." Gypsy had to blow her nose before she could continue. "I went to the wedding, Sheila. I went to Trace and Rose's wedding."

Sheila patted her arm and continued to rock her.

"She's pregnant. She's already pregnant. Can you believe that? Rose is carrying Trace's child."

"Oh, Gypsy… honey."

"And look at me, Sheila. Look at me. I'm sitting on my ass in the middle of the floor, bawling my eyes out… and I don't even know how to say *I love you*. A man asked me, and I couldn't even spit out the words. Can a person even *get* any more worthless and pathetic than this?"

"Shhh…"

Sheila wrapped both arms around her and held Gypsy as tight as she could.

"I'm all alone now, Sheila," she cried. "I am completely… utterly… alone."

The bell rang when someone opened the door.

"Crap. We forgot to lock it back. Don't worry, Ms Gypsy. I'll get rid of them. You stay right here." Sheila rounded the bar. "I'm sorry. We're closed. There's been an accident and— Oh, it's you."

Gypsy stood, wiping her eyes and trying to straighten out her clothes.

Taka slowly approached the bar and looked at her.

"What can I do, Doll Eyes?"

"Did Trace send you?"

Taka nodded. "He's frantic—thought you'd been in a car wreck or a plane crash."

"As you can see, I am fine."

"Oh, I can see you alright, and you look anything but fine. What were you doing sitting in the floor?"

"I was having a meltdown. What do you think?"

Taka didn't answer.

"Are you *reading my aura?* What does it say? Pathetic? Destroyed? Alone? Well, it's not lying. Do me a favor, Taka. Call Trace and tell him to stop worrying about me. If he *feels* anything else, tell him to ignore it. If he does that long enough, he'll probably quit *feeling* me at all. That'd be best… for *both* of us."

Gypsy glanced up in time to see Baron coming across the parking lot.

"Aww, hell no. I can't do this right now. Stop him. Somebody go out and stop him!"

When Taka ran out to intercept Baron, Gypsy said, "Lock the door, Sheila. And flip the closed sign."

Both men ended up banging on the door, but Gypsy wouldn't budge. Eventually, they gave up and left.

"You stay here, Sheila." Gypsy headed up the stairs. "I'll be right back."

⚬

Sheila was sitting at the bar when Gypsy reemerged from the stairwell. She mixed up a batch of watermelon margaritas and placed a full glass in front of the only waitress who had stuck with her since day one.

Gypsy held up her glass. "Here's to The Kilt."

"The Kilt."

When they had nearly finished their drinks, Gypsy sighed loudly.

"I'm closing down the bar, Sheila."

"For good?"

Gypsy nodded. "My heart's not in her anymore. I can't do it." She sat five bundles of money down on the bar. "This is for you, Sheila—tide you over until you find another job."

"I can't take your money, Ms. Gypsy. You worked hard for those tips."

"Hush now, and do as I say."

"But—"

"Yes, I worked hard for this money, Sheila, and I can damn well do with it what I want."

The other woman bit her lip and held her tongue.

"Now, here's five thousand dollars. Your last check will draft into your account as usual. I'm giving you this in cash for a reason, Sheila. Don't turn it in to the IRS. That means don't deposit it all at one time, either."

Sheila nodded her understanding.

"Now, I want you to go to Studio." Gypsy pulled a business card from her pocket and started writing on the back of it. "Ask for Dominic. He's a friend of mine from the gym. Hand him this card and tell him I sent you down there. Got it?"

She nodded.

"He manages Studio. He'll give you a job. Go on down there tonight and get the ball rolling, but go online and sign up for unemployment... just in case."

"Yes, Ms. Gypsy."

"Thanks for everything, Sheila. And don't be a stranger, you hear?"

Sheila ran around the bar and hugged her. "I love you, Ms Gypsy. Life's not going to be the same without you."

"I love you, too, Sheila. Pop back in from time to time; let me know how you're doing. Who knows? I might even manage to get dressed and have a few drinks with you."

"Don't lock yourself up in this big old place, Ms. Gypsy. Don't turn into a hermit."

"But, Sheila, honey... that's the only dream I have right now."

"Please don't say that, Ms. Gypsy." The young woman leaned across the bar, a serious look darkening her normally timid expression. "Just because you've lost your way... doesn't mean you're actually lost. Remember that."

Gypsy smiled softly. "I will, love. I truly will."

<hr />

Gypsy was balancing out the bar's accounts when Gillis came back. She tore a check from the book and handed it to him.

"Aye, what's this, Lass?"

"Your half of the money."

"Money for what?"

"Half of the bar's assets. It's not nearly as much as it *should* be, but I want you to have it."

"Nae, Lass. I cannae taking yer money."

"It's your money, too. We worked it together."

"What are ye saying?"

221

"I'm closing her down, Gills. I'm beat down and broken right now. I just don't have it in me."

He plopped a large shoebox down on the bar and hugged her.

"I cannae be sorry enough, Lass. I know I cannae fix what I broke, but I'll nae be the same again."

"Neither will I," she whispered.

"Where's all yer men? I thought at least that pretty ninja and yer Pope would be hanging around here."

"They are no longer a part of my life, either, Gills. I'm all alone now."

"Come now, Kitten. Ye'll nae be able tae shake *those* two."

"It's already done."

"Ye mean… ye quit being a lawyer?"

She nodded. "Earlier today—before I ever made it back to the bar."

"What happened, Lass?"

Tears filled her eyes. "I don't wanna talk about it."

"And the ninja?"

"That ended before I left this last time. Well, I don't know if you could say it *ended*, seeing as how it never really *started*." She shrugged her shoulders. "Either way, we parted on good terms."

"Let me stay, Lass. If yer nae going tae the office, nae going back tae Asia, and nae running The Kilt… what are ye gonna do? If ye stay here by yerself, ye'll shrivel up and disappear."

"That's what I want to do, Gills. I want to be alone for a while. I *want* to disappear."

He held her for a long moment. "I brought ye something, Kitten."

Gillis flipped the lid off of the large boot-sized shoebox. It was stuffed to the brim with bundled money.

"Where'd you get that?"

"The skank's," he said, snorting out a laugh. "That's where I went when I left here. She denied everything, of course. But I tore her place apart until I found this. Recognize it?"

"Is it… my tip money?"

"If I had tae bet. At least, the bundled part probably is. It's nae all ye lost, Kitten, but it's close tae half. I wish I could have found it all." He bit his bottom lip before continuing. "I wish I could go back and change this whole last year."

"Me, too, Gills…" She squeezed him one last time. "Me, too."

—❦—

Gillis was leaned up against the front of his truck—staring back into the bar, watching the only woman he had ever truly loved as she kept wiping down clean tables—when Baron Bishop pulled into the parking lot.

"How is she?" Baron said as he walked up.

Gillis nodded toward the lighted, empty bar. "Destroyed," he said. "And I helped make it so."

"As did I," Baron whispered.

"What did *ye* do tae her? Let's compare the wounds we left upon the lass."

"The day of Trace's wedding…" Baron leaned up beside Gillis. "…I confessed my love for her. I couldn't believe it, couldn't believe what I was saying. But more than that, I couldn't believe I was actually *feeling* it. I told her that day, but… she couldn't tell me back. She didn't love me in return."

Gillis snorted. "Tae be a learned man, ye sure are an idiot, Pope."

Baron turned to look at him. Gillis just smiled and shook his head.

"My Kitten fell for ye that first day. She's been trying tae fight it ever since, sure. But make nae mistake… she loves ye. She just dunnae know how tae say the words. Ye can see it in her eyes, Pope. Hell, even *I* can see it in her eyes."

"…Damn," Baron whispered.

"So… that was over two weeks ago. Why did she wait until now tae quit? What happened today?"

Baron swallowed hard. "She caught me with a sub."

"Just with her? As in… walking around town?"

Baron shook his head. "No. She caught me *with* her. It was the last day of our contract, the last time I would… you know."

Gillis nodded.

"Everything was going to change tomorrow," Baron said. "When Gypsy stepped off that plane tomorrow night, I was going to *make* her love me back. No more subs. No more *Master.*

Tomorrow I was going to start a brand new life. I was going to be a changed man. And... I was honestly looking forward to it."

When Gillis didn't laugh or even have a smart come-back, Baron looked over at him.

"Aye, I tore the lass's heart open as well," he said. "I fell in love with a thief. While she was gone this past year... Becca nearly robbed my sweet Gypsy blind."

"What?"

Gillis nodded. "Stole over two hundred thousand dollars... right oot from under my nose. Nae a fool has been born that's as big as me. She'll nae be able tae forgive me—forgive my betrayal of her... of *us*. Ye should have seen the look in her eyes, Pope. I'll nae be able tae forget it. I crushed my wee Kitten... same as if I'd stomped her with my own boot heel."

"First Trace, then me... then you."

"Aye, all within a two week span. Taka's oot, too. Happened before she left this last time."

"What will she do now, Gillis?"

"Well, first... she's closing Gypsy's Kilt. After today, she'll probably lock herself away in that big old empty house... stay right there 'til there's naethin' left of her."

"You can't let that happen, Gillis. You can't let her waste away all alone like that. You have to do something."

"Aye, did ye look in her eyes? When she learned of yer betrayal... did ye see the look in her eyes?"

Baron bit his lip and turned back towards the bar.

"Aye, ye did." He sighed. "I saw it as well, Pope. I watched her soul crumble... right there in front of me, and it was all my fault. Nae, if anyone can help the lass, it'll nae be me... nae anymore."

Gillis pulled the check she had handed him from his pocket and slowly started tearing it in two, then again, and again. When it was in tiny little pieces, he held it in his palm and watched as the wind carried it away, bit by bit.

"I'm going back home, Pope," Gillis said softly. "Going back tae Scotland afore the lass realizes she hates me." He snorted. "I am nae strong enough tae weather *that*. I dunnae deserve her forgiveness... nae any more than the lass deserved my betrayal." He slapped Baron on the shoulder. "Good luck tae ye, mate. I'm headed back across the pond."

Baron watched until the red glow from Gillis's taillights faded from view, then... he turned back to Gypsy's Kilt.

———⟨◆◆◆⟩———

She slowly walked up the steps, pausing on each one. She sighed softly when she finally reached the small entryway.

Gypsy had made up her mind. The hardest decision she'd ever had to make. Well... the most painful, most final one.

"Hey, House."

"Welcome back, Ms. Rodden."

"Yeah... House, pull up data for all authorized users. Delete everyone *except* Gypsy Rodden."

"Retrieving data for Gillis McCullough... Confirm delete."

"Confirmed."

"Data for Gillis McCullough... deleted by... Gypsy Rodden. Retrieving data for Trace Spencer... Confirm delete."

Gypsy faltered. She bit her lip and tried to will her coming tears away.

"Data for Trace Spencer. Confirm delete."

Gypsy swallowed hard, and then cleared her throat. "Confirmed."

The computer voice paused. "Place palm on space provided."

"It's me, House," Gypsy said. "Confirmed."

"Place palm on space provided."

Gypsy sniffed, cleared her throat again, then placed her hand on the small screen.

"Hello, Gypsy Rodden. Please proceed with voice activation."

"Hey, House. I'm home."

"Welcome back, Ms. Rodden."

"Delete data for authorized user, Trace Spencer."

"Data for Trace Spencer... retrieved. Confirm delete."

"Confirmed," she quickly said, before her voice could crack again.

"Data for Trace Spencer... deleted by... Gypsy Rodden."

Then, Gypsy walked back down to the bar... and cried.

Chapter 18

Gypsy cleaned the bar from floor to ceiling, rewashed all the clean glasses, organized the liquor bottles, flipped the chairs up on top of the tables, and scooped out the ice machine before going back upstairs.

She hit the button on her phone to check the time and saw that she had over fifty new missed calls, thirty-eight text messages, more than forty voicemails, *and* Taka had completely blown up her social media pages and streams. She sighed as she thumbed through all the new emails. Trace, Taka, Baron—they had all texted, tagged, and voice-messaged her into delirium. Gypsy didn't open a single email, didn't read even one text, didn't listen to the first message.

She was blindly staring at her phone when it started vibrating—Trace's smiling picture popping up on the screen. Gypsy walked over to the sink, ran a glass of water, then dropped her still-ringing phone down into it.

She slept on the couch that night, didn't even *try* to make it up to her room. The bad thing about sleeping downstairs in the commons room—no way to block out the morning sun. It didn't matter, though. Had the sun not woken her way too early, the numerous buzzes coming from the front door would have. Mostly it was Taka, but Gypsy had many unwanted guests drop by that day. She didn't speak to a single one of them. She just laid there on the couch, staring at the muted Weather Channel on TV, and occasionally glancing at the small security screen. Every time that buzzer would sound, she would automatically glance toward it, then back to the flatscreen up on the wall.

When Taka started using the two-way talk feature, Gypsy rolled off the couch and headed up to her room.

"I know you can hear me, Gypsy… I'm not doing this for me. I'm doing it for Trace… If you don't open this door, he's flying in tomorrow… Gypsy, please let me in… I won't say anything, I promise… I'll just listen—"

She slammed her bedroom door and fell across the large, soft pillow top.

"Ugh… Just go away," she mumbled into her silky bedding.

———◈◈◈———

Gypsy didn't know if it was day or night when she woke, didn't really care, either. With great effort, she dragged herself out of bed and trudged to the shower. Her toothbrush was still hanging out of the corner of her mouth as she slipped on her t-shirt and some yoga pants. She pulled her still-damp hair back into a ponytail, then headed downstairs.

Instead of going down to the living room, she let the elevator stop on front of Trace's door. Gypsy turned the knobs and let the large double doors slowly swing open. Her lone shadow fell across the empty room. An unsettling silence filled her heart, crept deep down into every hidden spot within her. It was an eerie silence… the silence of her future.

"…Damn," she whispered softly.

Just like Taka said. Her little angel sighed wearily. *We did this. We set ourselves up… to be all alone.*

I thought you were supposed to be the good one, her devil huffed. *Enough with the gloom and doom. Don't listen to him, Gypsy. We don't need anyone else. We're strong. We're tougher than hell, and you know it. We can do this on our own.*

"…Thanks," she mumbled aloud.

———◈◈◈———

The orange juice was out of date. The bread had long since gone stale. Gypsy took another drink of beer as she stared into the empty fridge.

"I miss how convenient the house in Japan was," she said, to absolutely no one.

The door buzzer sounded again. Gypsy rolled her eyes, but walked over to the little screen anyway. It was the UPS man.

She gave him a halfhearted smile when she let him in.

"Sorry you had to wait."

"No problem, Ma'am." He smiled. "This one just needed a signature, is all."

She handed his little electronic tablet back, but he wasn't paying attention. He was gazing around at the bar.

"Great place," he said. "I didn't even realize this was here."

"New route?"

"Yeah." He looked back to her then. "Oh. Sorry."

He hastily retrieved the tablet, but knocked the little stylus off onto the floor. They both bent down to retrieve it at the same time, and nearly bumped heads.

"Oh. Sorry, again." He blushed.

"You smell good," she said, leaning closer to him. "Like… salt water, seaweed, and…" She sniffed again. "…board wax."

He smiled. "You caught me. I like to hit the waves first thing in the morning. But this day… ahh, this day woke up as an amazing sunrise—completely showing off, bursting full of color. I stayed and enjoyed it, stayed longer than I should have. I didn't get to shower before changing into my uniform."

"Well, I like it." Gypsy smiled. "So, you're a surfer?"

"Yes, Ma'am. Do you surf?"

She shook her head. "Not anymore. Too old and too tired."

"Too old?" He lifted a single eyebrow and gave her a funny look.

She chuckled. "Yes. Too old. Ahh, but I used to love the way it felt… the way it smelled… the way the sun would leave tiny streaks of light auburn in my hair."

"Why did you stop?"

Gypsy focused back on the brown-clad delivery man as her fond memories flitted away.

"I don't know. Life, I guess. Life just got in the way." She sort of snorted. "Hell, it's been so long since I've been to the beach, I don't even know if I remember the way."

"…Life?" The young man glanced back around at the bar. "How can you call it life… if you quit doing what you love to live it?"

Gypsy stared at him a moment—the innocent look in his questioning blue eyes. She smiled.

"Sage advice, Brother. Make sure you always follow it."

"I know you were joking about not knowing how to get to the beach—seeing as how you can almost throw a rock to it from here—but if you're ever up before sunrise, walk down there. Walk right out into the water, far enough that the world around you is gone from your peripheral. Far enough so that it's just you and the sea and the gentle breeze. Then... be still. Be still, and wait. When that first tiny hue of color inks slowly across the sky, when the dark waves begin to lighten and the first ray of dawn sparkles to life atop the water... there's no other feeling like it. No high that can even match it. And if you still have your board, even better. Sitting atop it, rocking with the gentle movements of the sea, watching the sun slowly wake up in all her radiant glory... damn. It's almost better than sex."

Gypsy chuckled softly. "Sex was what your description put me in mind of. You spoke as if you were talking about a lover."

He blushed again. "I have a burning passion for the sea, yes."

"Good for you." She walked him back to the door. "And I hope your mistress always treats you well. Take care out there, you hear?"

"Yes, Ma'am. I always do."

Gypsy flipped the lock on the door, then rounded the bar and picked up the phone.

"Hello. Lucky Locks," the man said.

"Yes. Hello. This is Gypsy Rodden down at Gypsy's Kilt. I need to schedule an appointment to get some locks changed out as soon as possible. Do you know when you can have a man drop by?"

Gypsy was leaned back in one of the tall barstools, her feet propped up on the bar, all the shiny new keys laid out beside her, eating the vegetable lo-mein the take-out guy had only just delivered. If her mouth hadn't been full, she would have been singing along to the catchy Scottish drinking song wafting from the old jukebox.

A Scotsman clad in kilt left the bar one evening fair... She hummed along. *And one could tell by how he walked that he'd drunk more*

229

than his share... She glanced out the window, and her humming ceased. She had to swallow hard to get her last bite of noodles down.

Baron was standing by his parked car, leaning against it with his hands in his pockets. He made no move to come to the door. He was just standing there—silently watching her, his long silhouette stretching across the parking lot with the sinking evening sun.

Gypsy's throat tightened, hot tears burning the backs of her eyes. When their gazes met, Baron smiled with only one corner of his mouth, displaying a perfect dimple. Every time he did that, Gypsy melted inside... even though she tried to deny it aloud.

She slowly walked over to the large window, gently placing her hand upon the sun-warmed glass. Baron stood up straight, lifting one hand in a small wave. Gypsy never broke eye contact with the handsome man she had truly loved as she pulled the little string... and slowly let the shade fall down between them.

Why did you do that? her little angel asked.

You know why, her devil responded. *We saw him... plain as day.*

"Yeah," Gypsy whispered. "How can I ever *un*see that? The look on his face... the look on *hers*... the way he—"

Stop it! her angel shouted. *Just stop it! I wanna think about something else now.*

Yeah, me too, her devil added. *Let's watch a movie... or read a book.*

Oh! Oh! her angel happily chimed. *Let's play video games!*

Gypsy half smiled, shook her head, and was singing aloud to that funny old tune before she made it to the stairwell.

"And there, behold, for them to view beneath his Scottish skirt, was nothing more than God had graced him with upon his birth. Ring-ding didle idle i de-o. Ring dye didly i oh..."

That certainly is a catchy little tune, her angel said.

Yeah... Kinda gets stuck in your head, don't it? Her devil started humming along.

"...As a gift they left a blue silk ribbon, tied into a bow, around the bonnie star the lad's kilt did lift and show..." Gypsy dug through her gaming drawer. "Ring-ding didle— Where is that dern CD? I *know* I put it in here..." She finally jerked out the tattered old plastic packaging. "Here we go," she said aloud, smiling. "Time for a little bit of action around here."

Wait. Sing the rest of the song first, her angel whined.

Oh, I'll do it… you big baby, her devil snapped. *And in a startled a voice he says, to what's before his eyes…*

"Oh, lad, I don't know where ye've been, but I see ye won first prize."

When Gypsy giggled, her angel and devil both joined in.

———⊰⟨•◆•⟩⊱———

"Aww! Dang it! Shoot! Shoot! Shoot!" Gypsy growled before hitting the restart mission button again. "I *always* miss that stupid orb over there on the water. I hate that dern thang!" She bit her lip and leaned along with the character onscreen.

Umm… Why are we playing Jak and Daxter?

Her devil sort of shrugged his shoulders. *Guess she felt like going old-school today.*

"Ugh!" Gypsy threw the controller. "I hate you!"

She collapsed back onto the couch and grabbed her electronic tablet. Just as she started to hit the Audible icon, she received a chat message from an email address she didn't recognize.

"Ms. Rodden… you there?"

Gypsy thought about not responding, but curiosity and boredom won out.

"…Yeah. Who is this?"

"Ms. Rodden? Thank goodness! I was so worried." There were three little crying emojis after that. "It's Sakara."

"Sakara? Wow… I didn't expect to hear from *you* like this. Where are you?"

"An internet café. Ms. Rodden, what happened?"

"I don't want to talk about it. Really… I don't."

"Then, we won't. Can I call you?"

"No. I drowned my cell."

"…" Then more crying emojis.

"I miss you, too, Sakara."

"Are you coming back to get your stuff?"

"Not anytime soon. Whoever replaces me will probably just toss it. Why don't you go get it, Sakara? Anything I left over there… if you want it, it's yours. I'd much rather you have it than some stranger… or a dumpster bin."

"Will I ever see you again?"

"Buy a plane ticket and come to America. If you can get to LAX, I'll pick you up and keep you as long as immigration will let me have you."

"That's very sweet, but I wouldn't want to impose."

"No imposition. Sakara, I live in a place nearly as big as our whole office building in Tokyo. And I'm all alone. If you can swing the ticket and time off, I'll feed you and put you up for free."

Sakara's next message was three whole lines full of crying emojis. Gypsy chuckled.

"Keep in touch, you hear?"

"I will, Ms. Rodden. And… you need to check your email sometimes."

"I will. I will. Talk to you soon, love."

"…Bye." Followed by even more teary emojis.

***

Gypsy spent the next two weeks reading, listening to audio books, running laps around the fifth floor landing, and tossing pieces of that stale bread out the window to the birds.

She went up to the rooftop every night to watch the sunset, even thought about that whole *walk out into the ocean at sunrise* thing. She thought about it, yes, but didn't actually do it. She swept up all the little gravels that were scattered about the rooftop. *Thought* about sweeping the parking lot as well, but felt sure one of her *stalkers* would stop by for a chat. She sighed… a lot. Whistled… every now and then. Yet, never once did she glance into the mirror, not even as she got out of the shower. In truth, Gypsy was afraid of what she might see staring back.

The stillness of her new life was slowly driving her to the brink of madness.

She showered, changed, and tossed her gym bag over her shoulder. Just as she started for the door, the front buzzer sounded. Gypsy froze. That sound almost never happened anymore. Even Taka had finally given up and quit coming by.

"Hello? You in there, surfer girl?"

Gypsy leaned back and looked at the little security screen. The UPS man was waving into the camera.

"Glad I caught you here, Ma'am," he said as she opened the door. "You've got a ton of them today."

"A ton of what?" Gypsy looked toward the back of his open truck as she spoke.

"A ton of boxes."

"From whom?"

"They've got international stamps on them. Looks like… Japan."

Gypsy furrowed her brow, then held the door wide so he could push the trolley inside.

"You wanna just prop it?" he said. "I saved you for last. Everything left on the truck is yours."

She glanced back at the nearly packed truck. "All of those… are for me?"

"Gypsy Rodden. Your name's stamped on every one of them. Careful with *this* load. There's some heavy ones on the bottom, there."

She cut the tape on one box and found it full of shoeboxes. "What the—"

She opened another box. It was full of colorful dresses.

"…Sakara." Tears quickly filled her eyes.

"One more load after this one, Ma'am. Hey… you okay?"

Gypsy wiped her cheeks. "Yeah." She sniffed. "These are the remains of a life I walked away from. That's all."

He watched as she pulled the emerald dress from the box.

"You mean… these are personal things? Not for the bar?"

She shook her head. "No… not for the bar. This is stuff from my home in Tokyo."

"You lived in Tokyo?"

She nodded.

He snorted. "Heh. I would have pegged you for definitely Southern."

"I *am* Southern… goofball." She half chuckled. "I just worked in Asia for a while."

"And… you had all your stuff shipped to a bar?"

"I live here."

"In a bar?"

"Upstairs." She motioned toward the steps at the other end of the room, before lifting the opened box.

"Wait... you gonna carry all these up, one at a time?"

"Two at a time might be pushing it." She snorted. "My arms are *that* long."

"Wait. I'll help you. Let me finish unloading and I'll use the two-wheeler."

Gypsy stopped. "You don't mind?"

"I told you this was my last stop of the day. Short route, too—seeing as how most of my load was being delivered to the same address. You can only stretch a truck so big."

She returned his friendly smile. "Thanks. I'd appreciate that."

"Not a problem, Ma'am—all part of the job."

⚬⟨◆⟩⚬

"Whoa... this place is amazing!"

"I know, right?"

"Standing on the outside... you'd never imagine it."

Gypsy smiled as she kept unpacking.

"That's a totally messed up front door, though. Did you swipe that from some spy movie set?"

"Nope. I stole it from Alfred. Welcome... to the Bat Cave."

The man laughed. "You're funny. I like you."

"I like you, too, umm..."

"Skip." He held out his hand. "Skip Johnson."

"Nice handshake, Skip."

"Thank you, Ma'am. You, too."

"Drop the Ma'am bit, please. You make me feel like a rocking-chair granny."

"Oh! Is that the new xBox?"

"Sure is."

"*And* a new Playstation?"

"Yep."

"Awesome. Do you have— Oh. My. God! You actually have Diablo: Reaper of Souls."

Gypsy smiled. "Ultimate Evil Edition. It's one of my all-time favs. The graphics *rock* on that version. If you wanna talk about awesome, you should play the new Assassin's Creed."

"Hmpft..." He looked back to her. "I never would have pegged you for a gamer."

She chuckled. "Skip, dude, you've met me like *one* time."

He glanced down into the open box at his feet. "What's this?"

Gypsy turned just in time to see him slide Renji's *gift* out of the green silk pouch. Skip's eyes went wide.

"So... you know what it is then, huh?"

Skip blushed and shook his head.

"Pffts. Liar."

"Wait." He quickly grabbed a box before she could. "That one's heavy."

"Heavy? Wonder what it is?"

Gypsy sliced the tape.

"Towels?" Skip furrowed his brow. "Why were towels so heavy?"

She smiled when she unrolled one of the familiar looking towels. "Ahh... Sakara, I love you."

"What is it?" he said, looking over her shoulder.

"Skip, my new friend, I'm about to introduce you to the most amazing thing to ever hit your young taste buds." She held up the can and smiled. "Welcome to the wonderful world that is Chuhai."

"Is it alcoholic?"

"Deliciously so, yes."

"You can't ship that into the US that way."

"Apparently... you can. Want one? The apple is the *best*."

"I can't. I'm on the job."

"I thought I was your last stop."

"You are. You were. But I've still gotta take the truck back to the loading dock."

"Aww... I'm sorry. Well, thanks for helping me get all this stuff upstairs. To show my appreciation, when you find yourself *not* on the job, feel free to stop by and take Assassin's Creed for a spin."

"And Diablo?" He glanced over at the large flatscreen.

"Yep," she said. "You're welcome to it."

"How about tonight?"

Gypsy looked up at him and chuckled. "Well, it just so happens I'm going to have my hands full this evening." She motioned toward the surrounding boxes. "So if you wanna play, the system's all yours."

※

"You are sooo right, Ms. Rodden. This game is amazing!"

"Skip, you call me that one more time and I'm gonna punch you."

"The set-up you've got here is totally rocking my face off."

Gypsy glanced over at the smiling man. "Glad you like it, Skip. Let me take a wild guess… you moved up here from Venice Beach, right?"

"Straight out of Dogtown," he said, keeping his eyes fixed on the game. "You ever been there?"

"When I first moved back from England…" She scooped up another armload of shoeboxes. "…that's where I learned to surf."

"No way."

"Yes way."

When Gypsy came back downstairs from her latest shoe-run, she noticed the action playing out on the screen.

"Hold up, Skip. Let me show you something right there." She grabbed the game controller. "If you go right over here… hit this… turn and fire… Boom! *That* just happened."

"How did you do that?"

He jumped up and stood beside her, closely watching which buttons she pushed.

"Okay. One more time…" She walked him back through the gameplay again.

"Sweet." He laughed. "How'd you figure out how to do that?"

"It's a game-hack some dude posted on YouTube."

"Sweet. Know any more?"

"Not in this area. There's some further along in the game, though. I'll shout at you if I notice you're near one."

"Hey. Can I have one of those chew high things now?"

"Chuhai. Sure. They're in the fridge. You want apple or peach?"

"Are they real sweet?"

She chuckled. "Like drinking glitter infused unicorn sweat."

He scrunched up his face. "Naw… I'll just have a beer."

She tossed him one. He barely caught it.

"You saw where that came from, right?" Gypsy said.

Skip nodded.

"The first one was on me. You know—hostess and all. You're on your own from here on out, Skippy. I ain't your damn maid."

He smiled and took a drink. "I swear… you're the funniest *grown-up* person I've ever met."

"Oh no… you did *not* just say that."

"What?"

"Did you just call me old?"

"Wha— No!" Then he started laughing.

Gypsy punched him. He only laughed harder.

After that day, Skip came by three or four times a week for the next few weeks. Gypsy didn't mind. That young man provided the only happy voice in her now solitary life.

———◆———

"Thanks for letting me bring my bike inside the bar."

"No worries, Skip. It's not like I'm using it for anything else. Besides, I'd feel responsible if you left it outside and somebody stole it."

He sat his helmet on the bar. "I'd never be able to afford another one like her, that's for sure."

"Just be careful on that thing, okay?"

He smiled. "Safe as a baby in his mother's arms."

Gypsy snorted.

"Let me take you for a spin some time, Ms. Gypsy."

"Ain't gonna happen, Skippy."

"You'd love it. It would make your heart race. Your blood would run *screaming* through your veins."

"Naw. Thanks, but… I don't have the best history with motorcycles."

"How about with your heart racing?" He suddenly pulled her close to him. "You got a good history with that?"

"Skip... what are you doing?"

"I haven't seen you for the last couple of days. I missed you." He buried his nose in her hair. "I missed the way you smell. I missed the sounds of your giggles... the twangy, messed-up way you speak."

"Okay, Skippy. Cool your jets. You've gone far enough." She tried to pull back from him.

"Just a little more," he whispered, lightly running his nose up the side of her neck.

Gypsy's stomach clenched. A deep, burning ache started growing within her.

"Why are you—"

"Just let me touch you, Gypsy." His sweet hot breath tickled her ear. "I haven't been coming here this last month, only because I think you're way cool." He moved to the other side of her neck. "I like you, Gypsy. I have since the first time you opened that door—all ponytails and yoga pants."

"Please don't do this," she barely whispered.

"Why?"

He tipped her chin up so that she was looking directly into his sky-blue eyes.

"Because, Skip, you're the first *fun* company I've had in ages. Don't mess that up. Please."

"I have no intention of messing it up." He bent down toward her. "I plan on making our time together much... more... *fun*."

"...Skip..."

Baron had decided he had given her about enough time to calm down. It had been over two months since Gypsy had walked in, caught him, then walked out of his life. He wanted to talk to her. He was going through hell. He decided to stand outside and ring that damn buzzer all night, or at least until she got pissed enough to come down and yell at him. He didn't care *how* he got to see her. Only that he did.

When Baron pulled into the parking lot, both front doors of Gypsy's Kilt were propped wide open. His heart leapt. Then as he got out of his car, he noticed some guy was walking his motorcycle inside the bar. Baron suddenly slowed his steps. His breath hitched when Gypsy stepped out and popped the latches, letting the doors slowly close before she locked them again. She was smiling, talking to the guy in the vivid green helmet.

"Who is that? Taka?"

Baron waited until the man removed his helmet, revealing his sun-streaked, light brown hair and boyish features.

"Who the hell is that?"

He moved closer, suddenly halting when the handsome younger man grabbed Gypsy by the waist and began nuzzling her hair. Baron froze. This couldn't be happening. How? She never left her home.

How in the hell did she meet a man… locked up all alone inside that damn place?

Baron may not have known *how* it had happened, but the fact that it *had* happened was becoming painfully obvious.

When the man started kissing her neck, Baron's stomach twisted in on itself. When the boy moved to claim her sweet lips as well, the previously cold Dom's reality began to fracture around him—falling away like broken shards into an endless abyss. When Gypsy wrapped her arms around the other man's neck, the ground opened up beneath Baron's two thousand dollar Italian shoes. He couldn't move, couldn't breathe… couldn't look away.

Gypsy pushed back from the man and Baron felt his heart begin to beat once more. She went behind the bar then, and scooped ice into her blender.

"Watermelon margaritas," he whispered. "…She's upset."

As the other man followed Gypsy behind the bar, he killed the lights on his way. Baron gasped, but then realized… from where he was now standing, he could still make out the couple within.

I should go, he thought. *Walk away and leave right now.*

Yet, he did not. He knew he wouldn't. There was no way he could leave. Not without knowing what might happen, no matter how painful.

The man walked up behind her and kissed her shoulder. Gypsy squirmed and pushed him away. He didn't stop. He pulled

239

her hair back and kissed her neck. Gypsy resisted, but not nearly as much as before. Baron held his breath when the other man slid his arms around her waist and pulled her back against him. When he kissed her neck that time, Gypsy slowly rested her head back against his chest.

"Do not succumb, Gypsy," Baron whispered.

Then the man slowly slipped her t-shirt off over her head.

Don't touch her, Baron thought. *Don't—*

The brown-haired young man was cupping her breasts, gently running his hands across her lovely skin. He smoothly hooked the tips of his fingers into the waistband of her pants, slowly sliding them down her legs. The man then lightly kissed her perfect ass… before standing back up and spinning Gypsy around to face him. She looked scared, half frozen.

Throat-punch him, Gypsy. Why don't you fight him off?

When they shared their next kiss, Baron knew there was no fight left within her. She melted against the young man. After several pain-filled moments, Baron gasped aloud when the man lifted her up upon the bar. Tousled-hair, motorcycle guy slipped off his shirt before slowly parting her legs and kissing his way down her stomach.

Gypsy cried out. A painful lump rose up in the back of Baron's throat. He could hear her. Just barely, but… he could *hear* her.

"Oh god… no…" he whispered.

She leaned back, tiny whimpers escaping with each breath. She suddenly cried out again and sat straight up, running her fingers into the young man's wavy hair. Her voice grew louder and louder until it abruptly stopped, catching in her throat. She jerked, then visibly shivered. The man kissed his way back up her trembling body, reaching her lips as he stood up between her legs.

"No, Gypsy. Don't let him—"

Baron heard her low moan as the man's hipbones slowly disappeared behind her bent knees. She let her head loll back while the man kissed her neck, his movements slow and steady. Her voice began to rise with the gradually increasing speed of his thrusts—rising and rising until Baron was certain she could be heard all the way out to the street. When she reached her peak, Gypsy went silent… slowly curling into the man's chest, tightening her knees about his waist. The man lifted her chin and kissed her again, tenderly, deeply. He smiled down at Gypsy, brushing her disheveled hair back behind her shoulders, gliding his fingertips down her lovely cheek. Then he scooped her up in his tightly defined, tanned arms, and they disappeared upstairs.

With her absence, Baron felt his breathing slowly return to normal. He felt sick. Had he just witnessed her first surrender? Did he just stand there and watch that handsome young man's initial claiming of *his* Gypsy?

Baron bent over from the waist, bracing himself against his knees.

That had to be their first time, he thought. *Otherwise, why would she have resisted? Why the terrified look on her sweet face... the trepidation? Thank god I couldn't see her beautiful eyes. I don't think I could have handled that.*

Then... as his numbness receded, his anger began to rise. Why hadn't he stopped it? Why had he just stood there and let it happen? He could have made a noise... drawn attention to himself... banged on the front door.

Why? Do you think she would have let you in? he thought. *Let you trade places with the boy between her legs? No. She would have kicked you out, cursed you... then let sexy-tan-motorcycle-guy comfort her all night.*

Then another thought hit Baron, bringing fresh pain along in its wake.

Is this what she felt like? When she saw me in the office... did she completely shatter inside?

He closed his eyes as the first tear trickled down his sculpted cheek. This level of grief had not occurred to him—this gut-wrenching, soul-destroying pain. Baron had seen thousands of people having sex before; some scenes were even beyond proper description. He had watched other people having sex. Other people had watched him having sex. He had shared partners... at the same time, even. Sex was a huge piece of his life, but never had it felt like *this* before. Never. If what Gillis had said before had been right, if Gypsy truly did love Baron but just didn't know how to say it...

"...Damn," he whispered.

He felt the bile rise up in the back of his throat. Only now, only after he had witnessed *this* night, only in this very moment did he finally understand. Gillis had understood immediately. He *knew* how badly he had crushed her. That's why he went back to Scotland without another word. Because... how do you come back

241

from this level of betrayal? How do you ever make it past this degree of pain? How can you ever feel the same way towards that person again? Baron didn't have the faintest idea.

I deserve this, he thought. *Gypsy deserved her revenge, and I deserved to be standing right here... feeling exactly the way I do, feeling exactly what she did.*

"I deserve this," he whispered. "Dear god, Gypsy... what have I done?"

Chapter 19

The next couple of months seemed to fly by for Gypsy. Skip was exactly what the doctor ordered. They laughed. They played. They had sex... *lots* of sex. He helped her see the world through different eyes, helped her to realize... she didn't have to take herself, and life, so seriously all the time. She got to experience the overpowering sensation he had described to her that first day they'd met—the way it feels to stand in the ocean and watch the sun come up... the warming heat of it upon your back, tiny black ripples sparkling to vibrant life all around you... amazing.

They went swimming, surfing, played volleyball on the beach. And after a few weeks of constantly begging, Skip finally talked Gypsy into riding his bike. He had been right. It was a thrill like no other—completely freeing. The sex *that* night was beyond incredible, lasted until nearly dawn. Exactly the way Skip had hoped it would.

The happy couple didn't fight, didn't have a single fight. If Skip wanted to do something, go somewhere, Gypsy was up for the challenge.

"Want to go hiking this weekend?" he whispered against her sweat-soaked skin. "We can camp out. I've got all the gear."

Gypsy caught her breath and rolled away. Skip pulled her back to him, snuggling her from behind.

"If the weather's good—sure," she rasped. "As long as there ain't no skeeters. I'm catnip for skeeters."

"Pffts... skeeters..." Skip laughed into her hair. "What the hell is a skeeter?"

"Oh, excuse me... mosquito."

"No, Babe... don't change it. I *love* the way you talk. Say it again... skeeters."

She giggled when his tiny kisses began to snake down her spine. He pressed against her and she gasped.

"Mmm... Looks like I'm not done with you yet, Gypsy," he purred. "Damn, Babe... do you even realize how sexy you are?" He turned her to face him. "The way you walk—that unconscious twist to your hips. I love to walk behind you, watch your delicious womanly sway. The way you talk—that accent coupled with how you smile through half your words. I hate when you talk to other men."

"Why?"

"I'm a dude, Gyps. I *know* what's going on in their nether regions."

"You're an idiot."

"And you're sexy as hell." He kissed her. "I love watching you get dressed in the mornings, the way you *shimmy* into a t-shirt instead of just pulling it down." He growled against her neck. "Just thinking about it makes me so hard. I've never known a woman like you before, Gypsy... one who can cuss out a video game and punch my arm, then just melt beneath me when I push you back onto the floor." His little kisses trailed down her neck. "How many times has that happened, Gypsy?"

She gasped when he reached her breasts. "I... I've l-lost count."

"Mmm... You smell so good... taste so good. Let's greet the sun together, Gypsy. We'll take my board, paddle out even further. I want to watch the sunrise with you pulled back against me."

His attentions began to grow in intensity. Gypsy moaned.

"Ohh... I love it when you make that sound, Babe. I wanna hear more."

<hr />

"I'm going back home this weekend, Gyps. Come. Go with me."

She snorted. "I don't think so, Skip. I'm not sure our relationship is one you'd take home to Mama."

"What are you talking about? Mom will *love* you."

"Not happening, Skippy."

"I want to see what you think of the place."

"Venice Beach? Skip, I told you I've been there. Remember?"

"I'm talking about the town, Gyps. You went there to learn to surf. I want to know what you think about where I grew up."

"Why?"

"Cause that's what couples do, right? Share not only their futures, but their pasts as well. Especially since I hope my past will also be part of my future."

"What are you talking about, goofball?"

"Venice Beach. When I took the job at UPS nearly four years ago, it was in hopes that I could work my way up to bid on the route I wanted. That time has finally come. I put in a bid for Dogtown this week. Hopefully, I'm going back home."

"What? But... what about your friends up here?"

"Gypsy, you *are* my friends up here."

"What?"

Skip nodded. "Before you... I surfed at sunrise, drove a truck all day, then crashed when I got home. That's it. I didn't branch out here because I had no intention of staying."

Gypsy just stared at him, silently, a tide of dread slowly rising within her.

"Now..." Skip shrugged as he continued. "...things are finally going the way I had planned. So, whaddya say, Gyps? Come back home with me this weekend, see if there's a house that catches your eye."

"...A house? Skip... *this* is my home."

He snorted out a laugh. "Christ, Gyps, you've lived all over the world. *Anyplace* can be your home."

"I'm not moving to Venice Beach. *This* is my home."

He stopped cracking pistachios then and looked up at her. "What are you saying? That you'd just let me leave... on my own? But... I thought you cared about me."

"I do care about you, Skip. But I never said I'd move away with you. Hell, I didn't even know *you* wanted to move."

"Yes... you did. I shared my dreams with you, Gyps. I told you I wanted to move back to Dogtown someday."

"*Some*day, yeah. I thought you meant like when you retired or something. Not *right now*."

He glanced away. "Don't do this, Babe. Please?"

"Do what?"

"Don't shut me down like that. Let's talk about it. You can't just say no without *talking* about it. I've never had anything like this before, Gypsy." He took her hand, gently squeezing it. "No other woman has ever torn my insides up like you do. I'm not ready to lose what we've got. Hell, I don't think I'll *ever* be ready to lose what we've got. We're together, right? We stay together, right? No matter where the waves take us."

"…Skip, I—"

"What's here for you, anyway? *I'm* the only person you're ever with. *I'm* the only one you let in that door. How can you say you'd rather stay with an abandoned old bar than come with me? What will you be losing? We'll still have the ocean. We'll still have each other. We'll still greet the sun drifting atop the sea. Is this empty old building better than all that? I'm talking about the rest of our lives together, Gypsy. I'm trying to be open with you, like always. You're shutting me down when I'm just trying to be real."

"Skip… if you're going to be real with somebody, you have to expect real in return. *This* is my home. I feel the same way about this *empty old bar* as you feel about Dogtown. I have no intention of leaving… ever. And I've never given you reason to think otherwise."

Skip fell silent.

Gypsy watched his Adam's apple slide slowly up and down his neck. She knew he was trying to swallow back the hurt.

"Skip…" She squeezed his hand. "Save tomorrow's worries for tomorrow. You haven't even gotten the transfer yet, right?"

He shook his head.

"Our paths are what they are. Maybe ours have just crossed… maybe they'll continue on together for a while. I don't know. But until we come to a definite crossroads, let's save the hard decisions for when they *have* to be made."

"That'll be in about two weeks," he whispered. "We'll hear back from the bids by then."

She smiled. "Okay. We'll save this conversation until *after* we hear back on your route transfer."

"Yeah." He kissed her knuckles. "No heavy stuff until then."

"That's right. And perhaps… no heavy stuff then, either."

"Yeah… we'll just wait and see." He pulled her onto his lap.

"That's always best," she whispered, leaning over against his strong chest.

"We trust each other." He squeezed her. "We care about each other. Things will work out. I just know they will."

"That's right, Skip. Things will work out for the best… for both of us."

❦

Gypsy had spent the entire day reading. She had gotten so lost, so sucked into that make-believe world, she had completely lost track of time. When she closed the book and glanced at the clock, she shot out of bed so fast she almost got dizzy.

"Crap. Skip will be home any minute. I wanted to make supper tonight. Looks like it'll be takeout again."

She jumped in the shower before the water got completely warm. She yelped, but grabbed the bottle of shampoo and got to work. By the time the bathroom was nice and steamy, Gypsy was squeaky clean and belting out an old Stevie Nicks tune. She placed her razor on the rack just as she hit a high note and turned around. She screamed.

Skip was standing in the shower with her, completely naked and smiling from ear to ear. She hadn't even heard him come in.

"Holy jeez!" She grabbed her chest. "You nearly scared the life right outta me."

He pushed her up against the cool, tiled wall and was kissing her before she could even catch her breath.

"Do you have any idea how sexy you are?" he said between kisses. "Ahh… Gypsy… the things you do to me on the inside, especially when you're not even trying… I never thought I would be this lucky."

She half moaned, half chuckled. "Skip, honey… we can't do this right now. I promised to make you a home-cooked meal, but I laid in bed all day, reading. I know you must be starving."

"I am. That's why I stopped and picked up dinner for us. But right now… I'm only hungry for you, craving what only *you* can give me. I want you so bad right now, Gypsy, I want to hurt you in my claiming. Ravage you until your strength is gone… and keep going even when you beg me to stop."

"Skip—"

He covered her mouth with his, and started making good on his words before they even made it out of the shower.

Skip had told her true, he was starving for her. He was almost animalistic in his lovemaking. She cried out his name twice before he covered her wet hair with a towel, carried her out of the shower, and all but threw her onto the bed. When she giggled, he growled and pinned her down.

Gypsy was well and truly exhausted when Skip finally ceased in his claiming of her, so exhausted she couldn't even nod her head when he asked if she was okay. She only lifted a single finger to acknowledge him, didn't even open her eyes. If there was a single spot upon her body where it was possible to ache, it did, but in a deliciously satisfied way.

"Are you sure?" he whispered.

She didn't respond.

"Are you even here with me, Gypsy?"

She sort of lifted her eyebrows via response. At least, she *thought* she did.

He scooped her up in his arms. "Gypsy… Babe… are you okay?"

She tried to smile.

"Open your eyes, Gypsy."

She couldn't.

"Do you remember your safe word?"

Her lips parted, but no sound came out.

"Gypsy, come back to me, Babe. You're scaring me."

When she started to tremble, he wrapped a blanket around her, kissed her forehead, then grabbed the bottle of water on the nightstand.

"Here, Gypsy. Take a drink, Babe. Come on."

She did, only a tiny sip.

"Come back to me, Gypsy. Fly back into my arms and let me see those lovely bourbon-colored eyes of yours."

She tried to smile again. Maybe she did, she wasn't sure. Her eyelids fluttered before she finally got them half opened.

"…Skippy," she barely whispered.

He smiled. "There you are, my enchanting little lover. How was your first trip into subspace?"

"…Into what?"

"They call it subspace. It's sort of a semiconscious state, a place your mind drifts to."

"W-why?"

"Pain takes you there... pleasurable pain."

"Pain?" She swallowed another tiny sip of water. "What did you do?"

"It'll all come back to you, Babe. Take one more drink, then just relax for a minute."

She did.

"Gypsy?"

"Hmm?"

"What is your safe word?"

"Apple."

"That's right." He smiled. "And why didn't you use it?"

"...I didn't want to."

"But I could have really hurt you."

"You didn't."

"Only because I realized you were slipping away from me. When I saw your eyelids go to half-mast, then your body just went limp... no more flinching, no more moaning... I put the cane away."

She smiled as she closed her eyes again. "Where did you learn how to use it?"

"You can learn lots of useful things in college, right?" He chuckled. "Naw... my uncle on my dad's side is a Dom. Well, he used to be, before he married my aunt. I guess he still is... with her. But I don't like to think about that." He shuddered. "I asked him about it one day. I was nineteen, and completely full of myself. Uncle Gene said... If you want to learn how to wield it, you have to learn how to take it first. That day, I learned what it meant to be caned. And... my training went on for the next couple of years. My Uncle Gene taught me something I could never learn from a book. Not in how to be a *Dom*, per se. That's not what I was after. He taught me a lesson *all* men need... how to take a woman where she *truly* wants to go."

"You are a very... bad... boy," she barely mumbled.

"Did you like it, Gypsy?"

She smiled again, but didn't open her eyes. "I swore to stab Renji's eyes out... if he ever touched me with that thing."

"So... you want to stab me?"

She barely shook her head. "I *will* punish you, yes. But that felt way too good, Skip. Way... too... good."

He smiled, then kissed her again. "I look forward to my punishment, Gypsy. If it is by *your* hand... I can take it."

She half opened her eyes. "Don't be so sure, Skippy."

He gently hugged her. "As long as you're with me... I will take what you dish out, and beg for more."

"Stop being so perfect," she barely whispered, before drifting back off... with a contented smile upon her lips.

"Oh my gosh." Skip groaned and rubbed his tummy. "That sushi hit the spot."

"Yeah. It *was* pretty good. I'd never had any from that place before." She glanced sideways at him. "So... are you gonna spill it, or not? You're practically about to burst. What's gotten you in such a good mood?"

"A couple things."

Gypsy giggled when he pulled her onto his lap, then grimaced at the dull pain that followed.

"Sorry, Gyps. I guess I was a little too rough, huh? I'll have to remember to control myself better next time. It's just... Ugh!" He squeezed her. "I just want you so... damn... bad. I can't get enough."

She kissed his cheek. "It's okay. How many times do I have to say it? I'm fine."

"There's something else I'd like to hear you say." He brushed her hair back behind her shoulder and waited for her to face him. "I love you, Gypsy Rodden."

Her happy smile slowly faded.

"I've wanted to tell you for weeks now. You were right... I was about to burst. I love you with every cell that's in me, and nothing will ever make me regret it."

When she didn't say anything, only looked down and away, Skip took her chin and turned her back to face him.

"Hey, Gypsy. Listen to me. I didn't say that to put any kind of pressure on you. I love you, Babe. That's just the plain and simple truth. My love is not contingent upon your reciprocation.

It's there. It's real. And it's not going anywhere. I love you whether you love me back or not. That's not gonna change, Babe."

"I'm sorry." Hot tears filled her eyes. "You know how much I care about you, Skip. It's just—"

"Shhh…" He touched his finger to her lips. "Look at me."

She did.

"I love you, Gypsy Rodden." He softly smiled. "And I'm just tickled to death to finally have the courage to tell you." He gave her a quick kiss. "And there's more."

She furrowed her brow.

"The bids came back in today." His smile grew impossibly wide. "I won the route in Dogtown!"

———◄◆►———

They had midnight margaritas—Gypsy's specialty—to celebrate the realization of one of Skip's dreams.

"I'm not even going to ask," he said, finishing off his second drink. "I know how you feel about moving. And… now you know how I feel about *you*." He hugged her from behind. "My invitation remains. I want you to come with me. But I also need you to understand that just because I'm leaving, doesn't mean we're over. You are mine, Babe. I'll carry my love for you down there, and come back up here every chance I get. No worries. No stress. Just the way we've always been."

Gypsy turned to face him then, and smiled. "Thank you, Skip. You have no idea how much that means to me."

Chapter 20

Baron was driving by The Kilt late one afternoon. Without even truly thinking about it, he turned into the parking lot and stepped out of the car.

He had no intention of ringing the buzzer, knocking on the door, or bothering her in any possible way. He just felt like he needed to be near her. His *heart* needed to be near her.

You are pathetic, Master Baron, he thought. *Look at you. What has happened to you... to the cold Dom? Are you becoming a stalker? A pining, pitiful excuse for a man? Where is your pride, Baron Bishop?*

No matter his internal berating, he knew full well where his pride had gone. It had followed his heart down into the abyss that was now his insides. He was hollowed out, well and good.

"She undoes me," he whispered to himself. "Even her memory gives me hope... and crushes me in the same instant."

Baron's feet froze when he heard faint giggling. He quietly made his way around to the side of the building. He waited a moment, then heard a tiny pinging sound... followed closely by her heart-stirring laughter. He ventured a few steps more.

There it was again... ping... then giggles.

He glanced up to the fifth story fire escape. His breath caught.

Gypsy was lying on her back, a pillow propping her up, cushioning her head from the hard brick wall. She had her feet dangling off the side of the rusted metal structure, and that large pink bowl sitting atop her tummy.

He silently stepped into the shadow of the building, terrified she had noticed his presence. Soon, he heard the sounds again—ping, then giggles. He dared to venture closer.

When Baron had finally made his way along the wall to where he now stood directly beneath her, he sat down on the dirty pavement in his designer business suit... and smiled as he watched the watermelon seeds bounce off the dumpster across from him.

She was lounging on her fire escape, eating watermelon from a giant bowl, and spitting the seeds to the ground below. Every time one would make contact with the metal dumpster lid, it would ping... and Gypsy would laugh.

Had she not already owned the whole of him, this peaceful little scene would have solidified her within his heart forever.

Baron stayed until the only woman he could ever imagine loving, finally filled her belly with sweet watermelon, then crawled back through her metal window and left him alone once more.

"I cannot stop loving you, sweet Gypsy," he whispered to himself. "One day... one... day..."

<hr />

Gypsy turned off the blender and poured her drink, before grabbing the hand towel and wiping down the already sparkling bar top. She sighed before licking some of the large sugar crystals off the rim of her glass. Just as she put the sweet, pink drink to her lips, someone banged on the front door.

She turned to find Sheila standing right outside—smiling, waving, and holding up a bag of Chinese take-out.

"Hey, Ms. Gypsy. Please don't get mad at me. I just stopped by to see how you were doing, and... because I miss you."

"Dang, Sheila. I could never get mad at you."

Sheila raised a single eyebrow.

Gypsy snorted. "Well, I could never get mad at you for stopping by and bringing food. Get in here, girl."

"Oh... watermelon margaritas," Sheila mumbled, before turning back to face her old boss. "Something bothering you, Ms. Gypsy?"

Gypsy looked from the drink back to the normally smiling young woman. "Ya know, Sheila... sometimes I just make them because I like the taste."

"Uh huh. So... what's happened?"

"Nothing. Jeez." Gypsy motioned toward her glass. "You want one or not?"

"Are you kidding?" Sheila smiled. "If the boss-lady's serving, I'm drinking."

"Pffts... idiot."

"I brought your favorite lo-mein," Sheila chirped, sitting the containers out on the bar.

Gypsy smiled. "Between you and Skip, my ass is gonna rip these yoga pants in two."

"Skip?" Sheila furrowed her brow. "Who's Skip?"

After giving Sheila an extremely encapsulated version of her time with the young, hunky surfer, Gypsy finished off with, "So, needless to say, I haven't been back to Tony's since I closed down the bar. And now, with Skip all the way down in Dogtown, I don't know... I just went back to sitting around, staring out the window."

"So you haven't seen Dreamy Dude in over two months now?"

"Dreamy Dude? Pffts. Jeez, Sheila... I miss you. Yes. I see him. Skip comes up a couple times a month. We spend every other weekend together."

"And after he goes back home?"

"After one of his weekend visits... I spend the next couple of days trying to recover."

When the other woman furrowed her brow, Gypsy chuckled.

"Dreamy Dude is intense, Sheila. I could barely keep up with him when we were living together. Holding in all that pent-up passion for two weeks, let's just say... he doesn't come through that door *talking*. Hell, I barely know if it's daylight or dark the whole time he's here."

"He's in love with you," Sheila said softly.

Gypsy shrugged her shoulders. "*Thinks* he is, yeah."

"Ms. Gypsy, if you don't mind me saying... take your armor off sometimes."

"My armor?"

Sheila nodded. "You are one of the most beautiful people I have ever been around. Not just on the outside... you're even prettier on the inside. Oh, and it's not just me. You have a gift, Ms. Gypsy. Some sort of *light* inside you or something. I don't know. You make people smile, make them feel good about themselves. That's why the Vets always wanted to come here. They came through that door with lines marking up their foreheads, and walked back out with smiles turning up their lips. Everybody sees your armor, Ms. Gypsy, but everybody also sees that big heart shining through those lovely honey-colored eyes of yours. Every man in your life… they wrap their arms around that armored shell and squeeze tight, just hoping one day you'll take it off and let them hold the *real* you."

Gypsy swallowed hard. "Shut up, Sheila." She cleared her throat. "Enough about me. What's going on in your life?"

"Well… when you closed up shop six months ago, I did exactly what you told me to do. I went to Studio and gave Dominic your card. He called me in the next week. I've been there ever since."

"You like it there? They treating you right?"

"Well… it's not The Kilt, but they treat me alright."

"Seen Gillis?"

Sheila shook her head. "Not even once. I *have* seen… What did you call her? Skank bag?"

Gypsy snorted. "Skank-saw-whore-bag."

Sheila almost strangled on her margarita. "Yeah… her."

"She was alone?"

"Nope. She came with one dude… left with another."

"I should've stomped a mud hole in her ass."

Sheila chuckled. "You broke her nose and cracked two of her teeth. She had to have surgery."

"Pffts. And I'm sure she used *my* money to pay for it."

"So, you haven't seen the Pope?"

Gypsy shook her head.

"Your pretty little ninja?"

"No, Sheila. Besides my Dreamy Surfer Dude, you're the only other person I've let in."

"So… you've just been hiding out here for the last six months?"

"Yep. Pretty much."

Sheila blushed. "I met someone."

"At Studio?"

"No. He's not really the Studio *type*."

"Then what *type* is he?"

The other woman's cheeks grew even redder. "The biker type."

"Biker?" Gypsy chuckled. "Hell-oh-nelly, girl. You better watch your ass."

"Whaddya mean?"

"Is he a drug dealer?"

"No."

"An arms runner?"

"A what?"

"Does he sell illegal guns?"

"No."

"Well, what's he do?"

"He's a mechanic."

"Oh, I'm certain he *is*." Gypsy smiled. "Does he wear a black leather jacket and ride a Harley?"

"Yeah."

"Does he hang out with a bunch of shady-looking dudes that all go by strange nicknames?"

"Not *all* of them."

"Does he call it a motorcycle *club* instead of a motorcycle *gang*?"

"That's because it *is* a club."

"Is his name Jax?"

"Aww, hell, Ms. Gypsy. You've been watching too much TV."

Gypsy laughed. "I was bored. I've been burning Netflix up."

"Sons of Anarchy?"

"Yep." Gypsy smiled. "Binge-watched the entire series in one go. All seven seasons."

Sheila giggled. "It's not like that in real life, ya know."

"No. Actually, I don't know. What's it *really* like?"

"They're just normal people, doing normal stuff."

"Nothing exciting?"

Sheila blushed. "The sex can be, yeah."

"Don't I know it? A man with a wild side... duh-am."

Both women shared a smile before finishing their meal.

⊰⟪◆⟫⊱

"Damn." Sheila sighed. "I wish this old place was still open."

"Some days... I do, too."

"Sooo many memories."

"Yeah." Gypsy snorted. "We had a ball here, didn't we? Lots of good times…"

"Then why don't you do it, Ms. Gypsy? I'd help. There's nothing *wrong* with the place. Just start unlocking the doors."

"To be honest with you, Sheila… I've been thinking about it. I'm seriously starting to get bored."

"Then just do it."

"No. I can't go back to the way it was. That'd just be too painful. I've suffered through a lot to put my past to bed. I'm afraid if I open The Kilt back up, I'll start spiraling again."

"Then don't do it the way it was. Change it up. Make it new. You own it. Make it *your* place… the way *you* want it to be."

"I'll think about it."

"Well, let me know what you come up with." Sheila sighed then stood up. "I've gotta get going."

"Thanks for the food, love. Thanks for the company, too. Bring Jax around sometime and let me meet him."

"His name is Mark. And… I will." Sheila smiled and waved as she headed out the door.

As soon as silence once again filled the empty bar, Gypsy picked up the phone.

"Hey, Tony. How's life been treating ya?"

"Better now that I've heard *your* twangy little voice. Get your butt back down here, Gypsy girl. You're my only little ray of sunshine. All these men keep the place pretty stunk up."

"It stunk when I was there, too."

"You're joking, right? Jeez, girl. When you breezed in and out my door, your lingering scent made every jarhead that walked through here, smile for the next thirty minutes."

"Liar. You like me too much."

"Now that's the truth of it, Gypsy girl. You been keeping yourself in shape?"

"That's what I'm calling about. Can you give me the name of the company that installed your equipment?"

"Why?"

"Well, I just thought maybe I would—"

"No, you won't. You'll get out of that damn bar and come down to the gym. Wait until all the morning guys have gone to work and all the evening guys are still on the job. The place is normally dead, oh… around say ten o'clock."

Gypsy smiled. "Okay, Tony. I'll think about it."

"If I don't see you in here by ten tomorrow, I'm going to work you so hard you puke."

"Seriously, Tony, I'll probably puke, anyway."

"So… tomorrow at ten?"

"I'll think about it."

"Gypsy girl…"

"Fine. Fine. See you at ten tomorrow, you hateful old codger."

Tony was still laughing when he hung up the phone.

"After two weeks back, you can almost punch as hard as you did when you first started coming here… almost."

"Bite me, old man."

Tony laughed. "I figured you'd show up here all fat and soft. You been cheating on me?"

"No." Gypsy smiled. "No man could ever replace *you*."

He mussed her hair. "Really, Gypsy girl, how've you been staying in shape?"

"I ain't. I still get winded way too quickly. But I haven't just been idle, it's true. While I was in Japan, I joined a dojo."

"Style?"

"Judo."

Tony nodded.

"And since I've been back, I've kept up with my daily Kata. Also, I have a friend whose been keeping me pretty active… but he moved recently."

"So I'm your last choice, huh?"

"Naw. It ain't like that. You know better."

Tony laughed and mussed her hair again before she headed to the locker room. The workout today had left her feeling awesome. Tony's was *exactly* what she had been needing.

I feel like amazing things are on the horizon, she thought, smiling and waving as she headed back out into the beautiful California sunshine.

"You've lost weight."

At the sound of that mesmerizingly deep voice, Gypsy slowly turned toward Baron Bishop.

He was standing there on the sidewalk, a drink container in each hand, smiling with only one corner of his mouth.

"No. I think I've gained," she barely mumbled.

"Whichever the case... it suits you. You are lovely, Ms. Rodden."

Gypsy didn't speak, just stood there staring at his amazing dimples and trying to figure out the best route to make her escape.

"Mango smoothie?"

When he handed her the drink, Gypsy glanced down at the cup and back up to his dark navy eyes.

"It's your favorite, no?"

When she made no move to accept it, Baron took a step closer.

"It is terribly hot today. I knew you would be walking home... you always do. I thought I would give you something to keep you cool."

"What do you want, Baron?"

"Just to look at you... hear your voice... make sure that you're happy."

"Happy is relative," she said, starting past him.

"He doesn't make you happy?"

Gypsy stopped. "What did you just say?"

"The boy... the one with the motorcycle... does he not make you happy?"

"H-how did you know about *him*?"

"I saw you."

"Saw us where?"

"At the bar... the night he kissed you in your bar."

A huge lump rose up in Gypsy's throat. She didn't know whether to get angry or just run away.

"It was not my intent, I assure you," Baron said, holding the smoothie out again.

Gypsy numbly accepted.

"I was simply checking in on you—see if you were doing well. The front doors were propped open when I pulled in. At first, I was afraid something might be wrong. As I made my way over... that's when I saw the young man rolling his bike inside."

"Baron—"

"*You* stepped out then." He smiled. "My first vision of you in over two months... you were breathtaking. I had nearly made it to the door when... when that handsome brown-haired boy took you in his arms. You looked... uncomfortable... scared. I couldn't look away, Gypsy. Forgive me."

"How long did you stay?"

"...Until he carried you up the stairs."

Gypsy turned to go, but paused. A war was waging within her, and she didn't even know why. She swallowed down her coming tears and turned back to face the man she had wanted so desperately to whisper those *three little words* to.

"Baron..." She looked deep into his darkly stunning eyes. "...I'm sorry you had to see that." She bit her bottom lip, but her tears ignored the pain. "I would never have done that to you on purpose... I know how bad it hurts."

"...Gypsy..." he barely whispered.

She turned to go then, *literally* running away from a pain she had struggled so hard to forget.

Chapter 21

She was cutting up some fruit, trying out different drink mixtures, when she heard a tiny rapping on the front door.

Gypsy was smiling when she let Sheila in, then her heart nearly stopped when all the loud motorcycles started pulling into her lot.

"What the hell?"

"Hey, Ms. Gypsy." Sheila smiled. "I've brought someone to meet you."

"Aww, hell, Sheila." She sighed and popped the door locks. "Well... come on in."

Gypsy was already back behind the bar when Sheila and *the gang* came in.

"This is Mark." The petite young woman giggled, pointing to a man as he approached. "Mark, this is Ms. Gypsy."

He extended his hand. "I've heard a lot about you, Ma'am."

"It's all lies. Every damn word of it." Gypsy smiled. "Nice to meet you, Mark. Nice handshake you got there."

"And you as well, Ma'am."

Gypsy picked up the knife she had been using and pointed it toward the handsome, sandy blond man her sweet friend was happily hanging onto.

"Cut the *Ma'am* crap. You hear?"

"Yes, Ma'— Uh... Ms. Gypsy."

She smiled and gave him a little nod.

"Whoa... Who's the wildcat with the blade?"

About six or eight men had entered, Gypsy glanced toward them.

"Take a seat, boys. My name is Gypsy Rodden, and this is my bar. No need to stand on ceremony—seeing as how I'll probably forget your names anyway—but it just so happens, you fellas have caught me in a rare mood. Pick a stool and tell me what you think."

She began pouring the colorful drinks and sitting them up on the bar.

"What? You expect me to drink this frou-frou shit?"

Gypsy coolly glanced at the jeering young man with raven black hair. "Does that sign on the door say OPEN?"

He glanced toward the entrance, then back to her.

"...No."

"No... that's right. It doesn't. Do you normally stroll into someone's home and immediately make an ass out of yourself?"

"N-no."

"This is my home, boy. Take a seat. Shut your mouth. Act gracious. Or I'll drag your skinny ass right back out the way you came in. Are we clear, you and I?"

"Y-yes, Ma'am."

She glared at him.

"It's Ms. Gypsy," Mark whispered.

"Y-yes, Ms. Gypsy."

Gypsy smiled then. "Very good. Now... take a drink and give me your honest opinion."

The skinny man strangled. Gypsy glanced down at his glass and smiled.

"What's wrong, boy? Too frou-frou for you?"

"What the hell *is* that?"

"Blueberry Moonshine." She smiled. "My uncle makes the best you've ever tasted. Here, try the apple pie. If you can't stomach that one, I've got cinnamon, wild raspberry, or... just straight up Shine."

"You got a new shipment today?" Sheila asked.

"Naw. This ain't the legal stuff. It's a gift from back home. Uncle Bill wanted my opinion on his latest creations. This is for *home*... not the bar."

"Sooo..." Sheila said, smiling. "What do you think?"

Gypsy glanced at Mark. "He's good-looking. A little rougher than my tastes tend to lean, perhaps. Hmm... I don't know, though. I like that close shave he's got going on there... nice, smooth jaw line—"

"No!" Sheila half screamed.

Gypsy looked toward the blushing girl. "What?"

"I meant about the bar. What do you think about reopening the bar?"

"Oh..."

Gypsy glanced toward Mark. He was smiling, blushing, and looking down.

"My bad, love," she said to Sheila. "Actually, I've been thinking a lot about it."

"Oh, yeah? And... what did you come up with?"

About that time the door opened and Skip came strolling in. He didn't bat a lash at her leather-clad company as he walked behind the bar and gave her a tender kiss.

"Damn... I've missed you, Babe," he whispered.

"I've missed you, too. Safe trip?"

"As always. Hey... you got a new shipment from Uncle Bill." Skip chuckled. "One day, you guys are gonna get caught."

Gypsy smiled. "Hope not."

"Who delivered it?"

"I didn't know him. Some trucker down out Nashville way. Said he had it in his cab for nearly two weeks." She pointed toward the now empty pink box with the large glittery ribbon adorning it.

Skip chuckled again. "Love the way Bill packs it. No way in hell someone would ever believe that actually contained anything other than a make-up gift for the old lady."

Gypsy giggled.

"Hey! Who's the surfer with the crotch rocket? What? Can't ride a real man's bike?"

Gypsy stabbed the large knife down into the cutting board and turned to the skinny raven-haired man again.

"What did I just say about manners?"

The man swallowed hard then, his sardonic smile quickly fading.

"Everyone... this is Skip," Gypsy said. "You will treat him with the utmost respect, seeing as how he was the only one actually invited here. Skip, this is Sheila, Mark, and Mark's lovely friends."

After handshakes and greetings were shared around the bar, one of the men leaned over towards Gypsy.

"Is he your... what? Lover? Roommate? Bestie?"

Gypsy smiled at the teasing man. He wasn't being sarcastic, she could easily see. And... she had never minded a bit of good-natured ribbing.

"What's your name?" she said.

"I'm Raymond. Everyone calls me Shark."

When the man smiled, he displayed a whole mouth full of shiny white teeth—more than what looked to be normal. He was handsome, in a total bad-boy way.

"Well, Shark." She returned his smile. "This man right here is all three of those things. And as far as lovers go… he makes me scream out his name multiple, multiple times."

Skip popped a pistachio in his mouth, then wrapped his arms around her from behind. "She means, I make *sure* she screams out my name. Ladies first. *That's* the difference, gentlemen."

With Skip's words, comfortable laughter filled the room. Thus began a long evening of drinking, talking, and bonding.

After the pizza delivery guy had come and gone, Gypsy sighed.

"If I eat that, my tummy is gonna hurt."

"Want me to run up and make you a salad, Babe?"

A collective "Aww…" went around the bar. Gypsy rolled her eyes at the teasing men.

"No. What I really want is a burger and fries. Or… a big juicy steak."

"Wow." Skip kissed the side of her head. "You turning into a carnivore on me?"

She chuckled. "No. I just… want something different."

"You craving red meat?" Mark asked.

"I don't know. Maybe."

"Got a grill?" the skinny man asked.

"No."

"Ben makes the *best* steaks," Sheila said, motioning toward that same skinny guy.

"Is that right?" Gypsy smiled. "Well, he may *make* the best steaks, but it doesn't look like he's eaten very many of them."

Ben blushed when everybody started laughing.

"So… tell me what you've been thinking," Sheila said. "I *know* it's been eating away at you."

"Well…" Gypsy tossed a pistachio shell into the trash. "To be honest… I've thought of little else. If I'm going to open her back up, I want to make some big changes. The bar itself is only about one fourth of this floor, the back room is half. I'd like to use the other fourth—that unfinished storage part over there—to put in pool tables, dart boards… games of some kind."

"And food," Ben said. "Make part of it a kitchen. You *have* to serve some kind of food. You know… just small stuff—chips and salsa, potato skins, hot wings."

"Is food all you think about, Skinny?" Gypsy teased.

He smiled. "I like food."

"What's the back room for?" Mark asked.

Gypsy shrugged her shoulders. "Parties, get-togethers. The Vets used to have their monthly soirées back there."

"Can I see it?" Mark stood as he spoke.

"Sure. Come on."

Gypsy led him to the back room.

"Wow. This is a lot bigger than I'd thought."

"It seats eighty, *with* the dance floor, a hundred without."

"You two sneaking off together," Shark said, coming into the room. "Whoa… This would be the perfect place for the club meetings and rallies. We've got that toy ride and the poker run coming up. Plenty of parking." He elbowed the other man. "What do you think, Mark?"

"Well, since this isn't *Mark's* bar…" Gypsy smiled. "…you're asking the wrong person."

"Please, Ms. Gypsy." Shark turned on his thousand watt smile. "The toys are for kids in foster care, and the money raised from the poker run goes to Coats for the Cold this year. Whaddya say?"

Gypsy smiled. "Do you always get your way when you do that?"

"Do what?"

"Smile like that. Turn on the sparkling charm. Beg."

"Does begging work with you?" Shark smiled again.

"…Sometimes."

Shark took her hand and kissed it. "Please, Ms. Gypsy. Please let us use this room. We'll pay you for it."

Gypsy rolled her eyes. "Jeez… we'll see."

Mark softly chuckled.

As she made her way back into the main bar, Gypsy heard the old Scottish folk song playing on the jukebox.

Ben grabbed her just as she came through the door and started spinning her around to the catchy tunes. Gypsy *would* have gotten angry, had the skinny man not looked so darn happy. Instead, she just giggled.

Ben passed her off to a tall, silent man with graying hair and a long beard, then grabbed Shark and started spinning *him* around as well.

"Get your hands off me, ya runt," Shark said.

"Oh, come on," Ben said. "We don't have enough partners."

"Well, *I'm* not your partner. Let go."

Everyone else was laughing and enjoying themselves.

Skip rested his elbows on the bar and leaned over towards Sheila. "You've got some interesting friends," he said through a chuckle.

"I want to be just like her," Sheila said, eyes trained on Gypsy. "She has this... *warmness* to her. Don't you think?"

Skip glanced over as Gypsy was passed to another biker. "...Yeah," he softly whispered.

"I don't know how to explain it," Sheila said. "She's got this... inner glow. This... loving strength. She makes people smile... and can scare the hell out of them when she wants to."

"I know what you mean."

Sheila chuckled. "Just watch her. She's got a magnet in her heart; I just know it... draws people to her."

"She is amazing, yes," Skip whispered.

"Amazing, energetic, warm, nurturing... that's it." Sheila smiled. "She's nurturing—nurturing in a soft *and* strong way. You can tell how much she cares about people. And they can tell it as well. I love her. I always have. One day... I want to be just like her."

"Well, Sheila, keep it up... and I'm sure you will be."

Skip and Mark exchanged nods as the handsome biker came over and took the smiling young woman in his arms.

"May I have this dance, Milady?"

Sheila giggled. "It would be my pleasure, Milord."

"Aww... Ain't that cute?" Shark said through a smile, as he leaned back against the bar and laughed with his old friends.

Skip popped another pistachio in his mouth and continued to watch the woman he loved… being happily twirled all around her normally empty bar.

———◆———

The next time Baron drove by Gypsy's Kilt, there were about a dozen Harleys in the parking lot. The double doors were standing open. He pulled in—his heart racing.

When he neared the door, Baron heard the sound of hammers and saws… then laughter. *Her* laughter.

"No, Chipper," she was saying. "Those go over there."

Baron quietly stepped inside. Her laughter returned. The sound lifted his heart, caused his dimples to show.

"Skinny, if you do that once more, I'm gonna punch you. I ain't kidding, neither."

Baron stepped into the room just as a slight man with scruffy black hair yanked on Gypsy's ponytail. She whacked him across the stomach with her free hand and kept painting with the other.

"Damn, Ms. Gypsy. That sorta hurt."

"I warned you. Now, get back to painting or I'll send you in there to work with Blade."

"His name is Slade. He's just too scared to correct you."

"Scared?" Gypsy stopped painting. "I've never been mean to Blade—Slade. I'm going to go talk to him."

"No! Don't do that," the skinny man said. "He's real shy. You make him nervous. He'll just mess up what he's doing if you go in there and try to talk to him."

"Be that as it may," Gypsy said. "I don't like making people nervous and uncomfortable. I want Blade to like me—Slade."

"He *does* like you. That's why he's so nervous."

When the arguing duo turned to leave the room, Baron was standing in the doorway.

"Hello again, Ms. Rodden," he said, dimples ever present.

"…Baron," she whispered, startled.

He took his hands out of his pockets as he approached her, still smiling.

"Wha— What are you doing here?"

"Your doors were open. I was curious."

He slowly reached for her. Gypsy didn't move.

"You have some paint..." Baron licked his thumb before touching her cheek. "...just here. All better now." He smiled again. "You look enchanting, Gypsy. Beautiful, as always."

She glanced down at her ragged t-shirt and cut-offs.

"You lie," she whispered.

"I would never lie to you, Gypsy... even if it caused me pain." He waited until she glanced back up at him. "I've missed you. Missed seeing your smile, hearing your twangy voice. And I did not lie. When I walked through that door... you took my breath away."

They were standing there, quietly gazing into each other's eyes when Shark came into the room.

"Is there something I can help you with, Mister?"

Baron casually glanced toward the broad shouldered man, then back to Gypsy. "No." He smiled. "There is nothing else I could possibly need."

Shark moved to stand beside Gypsy, arms crossed over his muscular chest.

"This man bothering you, Ms. Gypsy?"

Baron looked Shark in the eye. "Are you trying to protect her? ...From *me*?"

"If I need to," Shark said.

Baron looked back to Gypsy, giving her that gorgeous half smile of his, using his dimples in a way he knew always melted her inside.

"Answer the man, Gypsy," Baron said softly. "Am I bothering you?"

"No." She smiled and glanced up at the large sentinel of a man. "We're fine here, Shark. This is Mr. Baron Bishop of Bishop, Grey & Sweet. Baron, this is my friend Shark."

The two men shook hands.

"A lawyer, huh?" Shark said.

"Business law, yes," Baron said, his gaze now locked back with Gypsy's.

"The motorcycle club is helping me to revamp The Kilt. I've hired them to do all the heavy stuff," Gypsy said. "Sheila introduced me to them. She's dating Mark. You'll meet him in a bit, I'm sure."

"You're reopening the bar?"

"Yeah." Gypsy stuck her hands in her pockets. "Thought I'd been lazy long enough. I wanted to change her up, though. Turn over a new leaf, a new chapter in my life. New Gypsy—new bar."

"A new Gypsy," Baron whispered, mostly to himself. "I would love to meet her sometime."

She smiled. "Is that so?"

Baron nodded. "I'd love to introduce her to the new Baron. He's not the same man she met that day in the office… the one who demanded she *sit*."

Gypsy blushed. "I don't know. I kind of liked *that* Baron. It was the one I saw the last time I came to your office… *him* I'd like to forget."

"Ahh, but they were one in the same," Baron softly said. "Two sides of the same old coin."

"What then?" Gypsy said. "Has the currency changed?"

"Entirely." Baron gently pulled her ponytail around and draped it over her left breast. "As different as the yen is to the dollar."

"I don't remember them being all that different," Gypsy said, glancing at her hand when Baron took it in his. "Japan— America… it seemed like the same old money to me."

"Then you weren't looking closely enough. Tell me, Gypsy. Is the exchange rate not worth another glance? Will you count it a loss before you've even added the difference?"

Several other bikers came into the room then, led by Ben. Gypsy hadn't even noticed the skinny man had left. She cleared her throat and motioned toward them.

"Baron, I believe you know Sheila."

The young woman smiled and waved. Baron acquiesced.

"That is Mark, there beside her. This is Ben," she said, touching his shoulder. "I call him Skinny. You've met Shark. This is Slade." The young man blushed when she gave him a quick wink. "And that's Rachet, Tiny, Phil, and Patches."

"Just Patch," the man said, shaking Baron's hand.

"The others are around here somewhere," Gypsy said. "I'll introduce you to them later."

"And… where's the surfer?" Baron said, glancing around.

"Pffts."

When Skinny chuckled, Gypsy elbowed him.

"He'll be back this weekend," Shark answered in her stead. "He rides up from Dogtown, every other Friday."

"Is that so?" Baron said, turning back towards a blushing Gypsy.

She cleared her throat. "Thank you, Shark. That'll do for now."

"Does Skip know about him?" Shark said, motioning toward Baron. "The way he looks at you—does Skip know?"

"They have never met, no," Gypsy said.

"Well, I don't like it," Shark said. "He looks like he wants to devour you."

"That's because I do." Baron smiled. "Gillis said almost the same thing."

"...Yeah." Gypsy glanced down. "I remember."

"Hey, Ben!" someone called out. "Steaks are here."

"Hot damn!" The skinny man ran out of the room.

"Looks like he's getting ready to fire up the grill," Shark said. "I better give him a hand. You gonna be alright, Ms. Gypsy?"

"Yeah, Shark. I can handle myself."

"She's not kidding," Baron said through a half smile. "She has never had a problem putting me in my place."

"She's tough as nails," Shark said, patting her shoulder before turning to go.

When the room had emptied, Baron casually pulled her ponytail back around to the front.

"Why do you keep doing that?" Gypsy said. "It drives me crazy, hanging down that way."

"I was only trying to help," Baron said softly.

"Help with what?"

He leaned down close. "You really need to start wearing a bra," he whispered.

"What? You can't tell."

She glanced down at the hard peaks showing prominently through her old t-shirt.

"When did *that* happen?" she mumbled to herself.

"When I walked into the room." Baron lightly touched the side of her face, letting his finger glide along her jawbone and down her neck. "When you turned to look at me."

Her stomach clenched. The soft t-shirt material was now becoming almost painfully abrasive. She knocked his hand away and covered her breast.

"It wasn't you," she half pouted. "It was your dimples. Don't take it the wrong way. They are my weakness... regardless of the man."

"Forgive me, Ms. Rodden. It must have been my mistake."

Gypsy rolled her eyes. "Had lunch yet?"

"I have not."

"Want to join us?"

Baron smiled. "It would be my pleasure."

Chapter 22

"The place looks great," Skip said, kissing the top of her head. "You are amazing. You know that, right?"

"Yeah." Gypsy leaned back against him. "I guess I am pretty awesome."

"You guys ready?" Shark called out.

"Yep," Gypsy yelled. "Let her rip."

They slowly pulled her new awning tight. Tears immediately filled her eyes.

"It's perfect," Skip whispered.

Gypsy nodded her head. "I love it."

When her voice cracked, Skip squeezed her closer.

"Gypsy's Place... it suits you."

"Yeah," she whispered. "It does."

When all the cheers had settled down, Gypsy hollered, "Drinks are on the house, boys!" Which only caused the ruckus to get louder again.

After Gypsy had finished off her second Chuhai, a truck pulled up in front of the bar. Two men got out and started carrying bouquets in—one for every table and a large one for the bar itself. She slid the pink card out of the tiny envelope, her heart racing.

Congratulations on your new life, dearest Gypsy. As lovely as these flowers are, they pale under the beauty that is your smile.
~Baron

She glanced up just in time to see him walk through the door, all smiles and dimples, carrying a case of champagne he then handed off to Shark.

"So... that's Baron Bishop?" Skip whispered into her hair.

"Yeah... that's Baron Bishop."

He walked right up to her, his intense gaze never wavering. Gypsy smiled.

"You brought alcohol to a bar?" She chuckled.

Baron lightly kissed her hand. "The last time I checked, you didn't serve champagne. The occasion would call for nothing less."

"Hi, I'm Skip," he said, stepping in front of Gypsy.

"Yes. I know who you are." Baron glanced around the smiling young man. "Would you like the honors, beautiful lady?"

Baron handed her a bottle of the exquisite champagne. When Gypsy popped the cork, everyone cheered.

Taka came in amidst the shouts. He grabbed Gypsy, kissed her full on the mouth, then took a big drink from her glass. Gypsy giggled.

"Everyone, this bold-ass man is Taka Nasaka—my friend, doctor, translator, and ninja extraordinaire. Get used to seeing his pretty mug. He's like a bad case of the itch. He just won't go away."

"I've been waiting for the lights to come back on in here, Doll Eyes. Good for you. The place looks great. And your aura…" He kissed her forehead. "…it is sublime."

"Thanks, Taka. And thanks for holding back and letting me breathe a bit. How's Trace?"

"Trace is fine. I bent his ear a little… convinced him to let go. You need to fly on your own, Doll Eyes. By the way…" He winked at her. "…your wings are beautiful."

She blushed.

"Wait. Hold that pose." Taka snapped a picture with his phone. "That makes number two. Oh, I got one of your enchanting smile, just as I walked in," he said, fiddling with his phone.

"What are you doing?"

She tried to look at the screen. Taka jerked it away.

"Texting Jūshirō." He smiled.

"Texting Jūshirō what?"

"Your pictures."

"Why?"

"To make him jealous."

"Jealous of what?"

"He needs to get off this whole *sub* thing," Taka said. "Ever since he caught Sakara out and questioned her concerning your sudden absence, he's been hoping you would come back to Tokyo."

"Why?"

Taka shrugged his shoulders. "He thought perhaps you were broken *just* enough to let him talk you into sceneing with him."

"*Sceneing?* You mean… let him tie me up? In front of people?"

Taka nodded. "I'm certain he wouldn't be *too* choosey. Public or private—he'd take what he could get."

"Not bloody likely. I'll never be broken enough for *that*."

"That's what I told him, but he wouldn't listen. I hope these pictures do the trick. Oh, wait… here's a text from Renji… He wants to know if you ever got to properly enjoy his *gift*."

Taka looked up at her just as Skip wrapped his arms around her from behind.

"Renji? Is that the cane guy?" Skip asked.

Gypsy didn't answer.

Skip smiled at Taka. "Tell him, thanks. She loves it. It suits her *perfectly*."

Baron strangled on his champagne. Taka just stood there, slack-jawed, staring at the young man now kissing Gypsy's neck.

"…Well, hell," Taka whispered, mostly to himself.

"Toast! Toast! Toast!"

Gypsy turned toward the cheering bikers and lifted her glass. "Here's to my new friends. I couldn't have done it without you. Here's to my precious Sheila. You have enlarged my tiny world in an amazing way."

"Especially with me," Skinny called out.

Everyone laughed.

"Especially with *all* of you." Gypsy smiled. "I will hold you each in my heart, always."

"Here. Here," Shark said.

After they had lowered their glasses, Gypsy held up her arms. "Listen up! There are two cardinal rules here at Gypsy's Place." She held up as many fingers.

Sheila started giggling at what she knew was coming next.

"Rule number one: Keep your pecker in your pants. Rule number two: Keep your hands to yourself. Break either one of those rules and I will stomp your ass, right before I toss you out that door. Got it?"

"Umm…" Skinny raised his hand. "Can we keep our hands on our pecker?"

Muffled chuckles filled the room.

"As long as your pecker's in your pants and you ain't on cooking duty, put your hands all over it, Skinny."

The man blushed crimson.

❧

After over half the case of champagne had been consumed, Gypsy said, "No one leaves here tonight. I will not have your death or dismemberment on my conscience. I've got a couch, two extra beds, and plenty of sleeping bags."

"Don't forget the air mattresses," Skip whispered.

"Yeah," Gypsy added. "And two full-sized air mattresses."

"Bring one down here," Shark said. "I'll keep an eye on the bikes."

"That won't be necessary," Gypsy said. "Walk them around to the side and bring them in the back room. We'll just scoot the tables back. There'll be plenty of space."

"I'll get the door," Sheila said, heading into the back as all the guys filed out the front door.

"It's like I'm looking at a whole new you," Taka said, smiling.

"No," Baron said. "I've seen her like this before. The night we first met. I was in awe of her, then... and now."

"So..." Taka took another drink. "The youngster took you to new heights with the cane, huh? How did *that* come about?"

"I don't know." She shrugged her shoulders. "It just *happened.* He waited until I didn't have enough strength left to resist him."

Baron growled under his breath.

Taka smiled. "Oh, yeah? Well, I would've put money on you leaving it back in Tokyo."

"I did. Sakara packed all my stuff up and shipped it here."

"On *my* dime?" Baron grumbled.

Gypsy chuckled. "On the Firm's, yeah. At least, she better have." She furrowed her brow. "I might need to check on that. If she didn't, I owe her a pretty penny for that postage."

"And where did you meet the surfer?" Taka prodded. "What is he? Like... twenty-four? Twenty-five?"

275

"He's twenty-seven. He was the UPS guy that delivered all those boxes from Sakara."

Taka smiled. "Ahh… serendipity at its finest."

"He offered to carry them upstairs for me."

"Did he now?" Taka smiled even bigger. "Did he help you unpack as well?"

Gypsy nodded. "I was his last stop. He said he had the time."

"Yeah, I just bet he did," Baron mumbled.

"So…" Taka waited until she glanced back at him. "Did he see Renji's *gift* while helping you unpack?"

She blushed.

Taka chuckled. "Brave boy. A little on the young side, though."

Gypsy shrugged her shoulders. "I don't think so. We've got lots in common."

"That's more than ten years difference."

"Bite me, Nasaka. You saying I look old?"

He held up his hands. "Not a day over twenty-five, Doll Eyes."

"Liar," she grumbled.

Taka chuckled. "Hey, if it works for you, who am I to complain? The boy took you where I could not."

"What's wrong, Taka." She smirked. "Jealous?"

"Madly. Are you kidding?" He smiled. "Ahh… to be the first to place pretty red stripes across that lovely ass of yours… *jealous* is too small a word, Doll Eyes."

"Nasaka…"

Gypsy and Taka both looked toward Baron when he spoke.

"Could you *please* shut up?"

Taka smiled again. "Looks like I'm not the *only* one jealous. Watch out for *that* one, Doll Eyes. He's a man used to getting what he wants."

"Naw," Gypsy said. "Baron's got more than enough to keep him busy. I'm yesterday's news. Besides, I was only being honest. Don't ask the question if you can't handle the answer. My thoughts are… if you have to lie about something you've done, you shouldn't have been doing it."

"Well said, Doll Eyes." Taka kissed the side of her head, then whispered to Baron as he turned to leave. "If you want someone to be real with you... they need to know that you bleed, too."

When she heard the pretty Asian's soft words, Gypsy turned to Baron, furrowing her brow. He swallowed hard, but held her questioning gaze.

"When you have the time..." Baron said. "...I'd like to talk to you."

"Bikes are all tucked away," Skip announced as he came back into the bar. "Ready to head upstairs?"

"I'm outta here," Taka said. "We'll do our sleepover when it's not so crowded, Doll Eyes."

"Taka." Gypsy grabbed his arm.

"Calm down, lovely lady." He placed his hand to her cheek. "Don't worry. The only sips I had came from *your* glass. I'm good. I promise. Besides, you know I don't need a reason to sneak into your room. If I was inebriated, I'd stay and have my way with you."

"Not while I'm here, you won't," Skip said, smiling.

"Keep telling yourself that, lover boy." Taka kissed her again. "I'll see you soon, Doll Eyes."

"Call me when you get home. Promise?"

Taka waved as he headed out the door.

"Well..." Gypsy clapped her hands together. "Let's put you boys to bed."

"You all set down here, Babe?" Skip wrapped his arms around her and kissed the top of her head.

"Yeah. I think we're good." She glanced around at her already snoring company.

"Then I'm hitting the sack." Skip kissed her again. "You coming up?"

"Yeah. I'm gonna go down and double check all the locks, wash up the dirty glasses, wipe down the bar. I'll be there as soon as I'm done."

"I'll try to wait for you, but I'm seriously drained."

"Aww... you're so cute when you're sleepy." She chuckled. "Get on up to bed." She swatted his bottom. "Get some rest. Don't worry about me."

"You'll be there when I wake up, though, right?"

She smiled. "Right there beside you."

When Gypsy bounced back down to the bar, Baron was emptying glasses and gathering up trash."

"Oh…" She paused. "I thought you were upstairs."

"I was. I couldn't watch the sickeningly sweet nightie-night the two of you were sharing."

"But… you don't have to do that." She grabbed the trash bag he was holding. "Go on up and get some sleep."

"If you don't want my help… then I guess I'll just get going."

"I'm not letting you drive home. Didn't you hear what I said about—"

"Gypsy… I had one glass of champagne. One. And that was hours ago now."

"Oh…"

"You didn't notice because you couldn't take your eyes off of Skip and Taka."

"That's not true, Baron. I'm sorry I made you feel that way."

"Stop it, Gypsy." He grabbed her arms and squeezed tight. "Stop playing so nice with me. Stop acting like we are little more than strangers."

"I'm sorry, Baron. I don't know how else to act. I wasn't trying to hurt you. I *was* trying to keep my distance, but—"

"Why? Why would you ever try to distance yourself from me?"

"Because I don't want to get in the way. Listen, Baron. You told me how you felt, and at the time… I wasn't able to reciprocate that. At least, not out loud. That's all on me. I own that. And… I have spent these last many months coming to terms with your decision. And I have… mostly."

"What decision?"

"The fact that you moved on. The fact that you found someone else. I mean, I don't blame you. You offered. I declined. Like I said, that's on me. I guess… I guess what hurt so bad… was how *fast* you moved on. I mean… it had only been two weeks. I may not have ever told anyone that I loved them before, but I'm pretty sure I wouldn't be over it in two weeks. Hell, I wasn't even the one to *say* the words, and I've been a frickin' basket case for months now."

Baron just stared at her, brows furrowed.

"Maybe I truly don't understand *that* kind of love," she said. "But, to me... to me, when I finally say the words, they are going to carry meaning... power. When I tell someone I love them, it will come from the very core of my being. I will be saturated with it. Consumed by it. Once the floodgate is open, I won't know how to close it back. I guess that's why I was so shocked to see you with another woman. Well, *that*, yeah... and *how* you were with her."

Gypsy shuddered.

"Shhh..." Baron wrapped his arms around her and pulled her close. "Don't go there, my love. Stay with me in the here and now. Push that dark stuff away."

"I have." She pried herself free from his embrace. "That's what I've been doing. And because I know *exactly* how bad it hurts, I will never do that to another woman. So please, if you don't mind... keep your hands to yourself. I don't want whatever-her-name-is to go through any pain on my account."

"Oh, Gypsy..." Baron rubbed his temples and sat down. "Did you forget who I am? Who I was? Did you completely disregard the snippet of my private life that I introduced you to?"

"What are you talking about?"

"Doms and subs, Gypsy. Do you not understand how that works?"

She looked at him for a moment, then shook her head. "No. Not really."

Baron sighed. "It is a world I'm not certain you would understand even if I tried. But I want to, Gypsy—try. Will you let me?"

"You opposed to washing dishes?"

He furrowed his brow. "No. Why?"

"I'll wash. You talk and dry. Deal?"

Baron smiled before following her behind the bar.

"And don't leave any spots," she said, over her shoulder. "When you dry them, you have to make sure they sparkle. No one wants to drink from a spotty, dull glass. Got it?"

"Yes, Ms. Rodden. I understand completely. Sparkling stemware—satisfied boss lady."

She glanced back at him, then rolled her eyes.
"…Smartass."

Baron only smiled.

"I have been a Dom since I was in my early twenties," he started. "In that time, I have collared many subs. The way it works is by mutual contract. A sub must offer me her collar—submit to me. If I am interested, I will accept."

"Who wouldn't be interested?" she said. "Free sex."

"No. It's not like that. Sex is there, yes, but it involves a whole lifestyle. If I accept a sub's collar, I am completely responsible for her. I see to *all* of her needs. Same as she sees to what it is I require from *her.*"

"You mean… you take care of her *completely?*"

"Yes. She submits herself—her care—to me. If I take on a sub, I am completely responsible for her wellbeing. I feed her what will keep her healthy, maintain her energy level, keep her hydrated. I take care of her medical needs, her housing, her clothing."

"Why?"

"If I wish her to be waxed, manicured, clothed a particular way—all for me… how can I ask *her* to pay for these things? She is submitting herself to me. Therefore, all of these things are my responsibility."

"Like a pet, then. Like someone would treat their cat or dog—pick one out from the pound, buy them treats, certain foods, toys, take them to the groomer."

"Gypsy… please."

"What?"

"Let's just move on."

"…Fine, then."

"Gypsy…" Baron softly sighed. "A sub is not a pet, they are a human. And such being the case, a Dom must respect their time with the sub. That is why we do initial contracts of six months. Less, if it's decided upon in advance. At the end of the contract period, we have a get-together. There, the sub is given her collar back and can then choose whether she wishes to offer it to another Dom or not."

"Can she not just keep the same Dom?"

"If the Dom and the sub agree, yes. But for the sub's benefit, the same Dom can only accept her collar the second time *if* the Dom promises the sub a more permanent contract."

"Meaning?"

"Meaning… if a Dom was allowed to keep using a temporary contract over and over with the same sub, minus any promise of long-term commitment, then that Dom could potentially use up the best years of that sub's life and then just leave her high and dry and all alone."

"…That's awful," Gypsy whispered.

"Yes, it would be. So, for the sub's benefit, certain rules like the one I just mentioned are set into place."

"So… do *you* have a long-term contract with your sub?"

"No. I never have. I have never contracted with a sub past the initial six months."

"Why?"

"Because, I have never found the one who is right for me. A long-term contract *should* end with a lifetime commitment."

"Marriage?"

"Usually, yes."

"Why are you telling me all of this?"

"To explain to you who I am… who I was… who I have been for the last twenty some odd years. I'm trying to explain what you *saw*."

Gypsy flinched.

"That was my sub. Not my girlfriend. Not someone I loved. That woman was my contracted submissive." Baron paused. "I have not taken another. I'm not certain I ever can."

"Why? Did you sign a second contract with her?"

"No." He turned her to face him. "That was the last day of our contract. The last time I—"

Gypsy pulled away.

"What I'm trying to say is this… that was me closing the book concerning *that* part of my life. I had finally found what I had been searching for. I would never be able to accept anyone else's collar. I knew that. I told my sub that." He sighed. "She begged me to own her one last time before I took her that night and released her. I'm not blaming her. It was *my* fault. I shouldn't have done it. I didn't even want to. But, I was weak to her tears and her reasoning."

"Her reasoning?"

He nodded. "I had ignored her sexual needs for over a month. I was not holding up my end of the contract."

"Why not?"

"Because I couldn't. I didn't want to. I wanted only one woman. And that woman... she was not my sub." He inhaled deeply and bit his bottom lip before going on. "My contracted sub... she thought she had failed me. She begged me not to release her after so many weeks of neglect. She feared I was displeased with her and would tell the other Doms—such a thing could destroy a submissive's reputation; keep any other Dom from accepting her collar. When you walked in on us that day, Gypsy... when you ran out like that... she knew. She knew why I no longer had interest in her. She could tell by the look on your face... by the look on mine. I uncollared her that evening and left the party. I've never been back."

"So... where are you getting your subs from now?"

"Gypsy. Dammit." Baron grabbed her up and carried her into the other room. "Have you heard *nothing* I've been saying? Can't you get it through your thick skull? I don't want another sub. I don't want *any* other woman. I only want you."

"Let me go, Baron. That hurts."

He loosened his grip, but didn't release her.

"I know I got mad at you that day," she said. "I know I stormed out and refused to even speak to you. But I couldn't help it. I was in pain... such pain. I couldn't breathe, couldn't walk straight, couldn't even eat for days. I almost went mad. I was really, *really* close. But even if we could both take it all back, even if we could use magic to go back to that night in Tokyo... I still couldn't give you what you want. I couldn't say it then, and I can't say it now."

"Damn your stubbornness, Gypsy Rodden."

He kissed her. She pushed him away.

"Stop it, Baron. I don't want this. I don't want *you*. I have Skip now. After all these months, I am finally happy."

"Have you told him you love him?"

"No. Of course not."

"Then you are not happy, Gypsy. You are merely content."

"Well, whatever it is, it's a helluva lot better than what I had with *you*."

"You have no idea what you had with me." He kissed her again. "What you *still* have with me," he whispered against her neck.

"Baron... please, stop."

Baron didn't stop, nor did he see the tiny tears now escaping the corners of Gypsy's tightly closed lids.

When he cupped her breasts, her stomach clenched and her breathing became shallow. Gypsy ran her fingers into his thick, dark hair... and jerked his head back.

"Stop it, Baron! I can't live through this again. You have the power to destroy me. Please... have mercy."

He kissed her lips then, soft and tender and loving. He didn't stop, didn't let up... until he felt her melt against him. He laid her back atop the large pool table as his kisses grew deeper and ever more passionate. When he parted her lips with his tongue— consuming her, devouring her—Gypsy moaned.

Baron slipped off her t-shirt, then his.

He smiled down at her. "I will never be that foolish again, Gypsy. You may not *want* to say it, but I can see it in your lovely bourbon eyes... hear it in your tiny, passionate moans."

"...Baron..."

He kissed her again, lost himself in the warmth of their touching skin. "...Gypsy," he whispered softly as he pressed himself between her legs, grinding his hipbones into her supple thighs.

Gypsy started crying then, tiny whimpers replacing her previous moans. Baron froze.

"...Gypsy? What happened?" He quickly stood up. "Did I hurt you?"

She put her hands over her eyes and shook her head.

"Then, what is it? What's wrong? Are you truly in love with Skip? Did you only just realize your feelings for him?"

She shook her head again, her bitter tears streaming back to soak her hair.

"...Baron."

"Yes, my love. What is it?"

"I can't... I can't do this. I can't..."

"Shhh. Shhh. Shhh. Don't cry, Gypsy. I cannot handle your tears. I'm sorry I pushed. I didn't mean to—"

"I can't say it. I just…"

Baron's breath caught. He feared her next words, and longed more than anything else in the world to hear them.

"I don't love Skip. I don't even know…" She sniffed.

"Let me see your eyes, Gypsy."

She shook her head again. "I just… Baron, I just…"

"What is it? You can say it. You're safe with me, Gypsy. I promise. No matter what, I will always protect you."

She sniffed again, but her tears only increased, her shoulders jerking with her sobs.

"I… I lose myself in you, Baron. When you're around… when you smile… when you touch me… I can't breathe… I can't think. I just… *lose* myself." She drew in a deep, haggard breath and pressed down against her burning eyes. "I love you, Baron. I have loved you since… for as long as I have known you. I fought it at first because I wasn't *supposed* to love you. But after our time in Tokyo… after we shared those crêpes on that busy sidewalk… all I could think about… was you."

"Oh, Gypsy…"

Baron reached for her, but his hands were trembling so badly, he wasn't sure he could even hold her properly. He gently pulled her into his arms, then cradled her in his lap, tenderly stroking her soft hair.

Gypsy kept her hands over her eyes as she rested against his warm chest. "When I walked into your office that last day…"

"No. Don't say it. Please."

"Oh… my… god. I had never felt anything like that before. I felt like my insides completely hollowed out. Like—"

"Like the world fractured around you," he whispered. "Like the earth opened up… but refused to swallow you, refused to cease your pain. You were standing there—nothing but a shell—yet your damn heart just wouldn't quit beating, wouldn't just *stop*… and let you move on from your wretched reality."

She sniffed, wiped her eyes, and then finally looked up at him. "Yes… exactly like that."

"I know, my love. I know how you felt because that was exactly the same way I felt… when Skip sat you up on that bar and—"

Gypsy clamped her hand over his mouth. "Shhh... Please forget you ever saw that. I never wanted you to feel such pain."

Baron gently took her wrist, lowering her hand. "Only if you will forget you saw me as well. Gypsy, I will spend the rest of my life, right up until my last breath, trying to make up for the hurt I have caused you."

They both just fell silent then—holding each other, comforting each other—wrapped up together in their past pains, and their present love.

And there... they healed, each as best they could.

Chapter 23

The sunrise found Gypsy and Skip astraddle his surfboard, as far out into the ocean as she would let him paddle.

"Look at it, Babe. Today... it's particularly breathtaking."

"Yeah... the most beautiful one yet."

"Feels like we're floating atop heaven, doesn't it?"

Gypsy softly smiled.

Skip wrapped his arms around her and kissed her shoulder. "You gonna tell me what's wrong?"

She didn't answer.

"Is it that handsome man with the cold eye?" He kissed her shoulder again. "Did you sleep with him?"

"No. Of course not. I'd never cheat on you, Skip."

"Thanks, Babe." He rested his chin on her shoulder and looked back out at the beautifully sparkling waves. "Is *he* why you can't love me back?"

"...Yes. I don't know how to love more than one person. Not *this* kind of love."

"And that's because you shouldn't be able to." He hugged her tighter. "How late was I?"

"About a year."

"Damn. What sucky timing."

Gypsy smiled. "A friend once told me... the timing is only wrong when the person is wrong. Or... something like that."

Skip chuckled. "If you're gonna impart sage wisdom, Babe, you can't add... *or something like that.*"

Gypsy's smile grew.

"Damn, Babe. Getting over you is gonna hurt like hell."

"You don't have to get over me, Skip. You helped me when I didn't have another soul in this world. You pulled me out of the darkness and made me laugh again. I may not be able to love you like I love Baron, but I will never leave you... never cheat on you."

"Wow... That's super selfish, Gyps."

286

"Selfish?" She glanced at his smiling profile. "How so?"

"What if *I* want that? What if I want to know what being loved like that feels like? How am I ever gonna find a woman who worships the ground I walk on, if *you're* always hanging around? Jeez."

Gypsy chuckled. "Maybe I *do* love you."

"Too late, Babe. This ship's done sailed."

She laid her head back against him and continued smiling.

"Can I take it slow?" he barely whispered. "Give me time to wean my heart off of you, Babe."

"Anything you want, Skip." She placed her arms over his about her waist. "Anything you want."

He squeezed her tighter, kissed her cheek, and smiled as they enjoyed their final sunrise together.

<hr />

"Rise and shine, my sweet petunias."

Gypsy slapped Slade's butt as she walked by. He groaned and curled up on his side.

"I've let you guys sleep 'til half past noon. It's time to get up. We have lots to do. It's Grand Opening Day!" she sang. "Come on, boys. I've got a foolproof cure for a hangover. It's waiting for you downstairs."

Sheila and Mark came down on the elevator then, still yawning as they strolled toward the door.

"Hello, lovebirds. Sleep well?"

They both nodded to her before heading downstairs.

"Let's go!" Gypsy clapped her hands. "Up and at 'em."

"What the hell is wrong with you, woman?" Shark mumbled into his pillow. "Are you the damn energizer bunny or something?"

"Yeah," Slade said. "I love you, Ms. Gypsy. But that damn accent of yours is piercing my brain like a hot poker. Tone it down, girl."

Gypsy chuckled. "Well now, Slade. Look at you. You haven't said ten words to me in the last two weeks. Glad to see you've got a little bark in ya."

"That ain't all I got in me," he mumbled.

Ben chuckled then.

"Ahh, so you're awake, Skinny. I heard you giggling over there. Get your ass up." She slapped Shark on the butt this time. "Come on, big guy."

"Stop, Ms. Gypsy," he said through a moan. "You strolled in here around four this morning, then you and surfer boy headed back out while it was still dark outside. What's *wrong* with you?"

"I'm naturally hyper. So? What are *you* gonna do about it? Come on. Get up. I ain't gonna let you be until you open your eyes."

Shark sat up quickly, growling as he grabbed Gypsy around the waist and pulled her down, tucking her in front of him, spooning her.

"This'll calm your hyper little ass down for a minute. Now be quiet and quit struggling. I just need fifteen more minutes. Please, Ms. Gypsy."

"I wouldn't do that if I were you," Skip said as he walked into the living room. "She don't like to be—"

Gypsy spun out of Shark's muscular embrace, straddling the large man as she pinned his arms above his head.

"*Never* try to hold me down," she hissed. "Never."

"She was trained by an old boxing champ *and* an Olympic gold winning Judo Master," Skip said as he poured his orange juice. "If she doesn't *want* to be held down, she won't be. Trust me."

Shark smiled then. "Oh, yeah? Well, maybe this is *exactly* what I wanted." He flexed his pelvis, pressing himself up against her. "I'm *up*, Gypsy. You happy now?"

When she felt his large morning arousal beneath her, Gypsy jerked away. "Ugh! That's disgusting!"

"I've never had any complaints. What's the problem? It's still in my pants. I haven't broken any rules."

"You didn't keep your hands to yourself," she snapped.

"Yeah, well you didn't, either." He jerked his pillow up and whacked her in the head. "I said I need fifteen more minutes."

Ben and Slade sat up then, eyes wide. But instead of going ballistic like they thought she would, Gypsy started laughing.

She jerked Tiny's pillow out from under his head and slammed it down on Shark. The big man sat up and glared at her.

Gypsy gave him a sardonic smile. "Don't *start* nothing, and there won't *be* nothing."

He growled just before grabbing her around the waist and tackling her. Skip watched them for a minute before shaking his head, smiling, then heading downstairs.

—⊰⟨•⟩⊱—

"Squeee! I'm sooo excited!" Gypsy said, squeezing Shark's huge bicep.

"Jeez, Ms. Gypsy. You're acting like a little kid."

She smiled. "A little kid that totally whipped your ass this morning."

He snorted.

"Hey, Skinny!" she yelled. "You got everything fired up and ready to go back there?"

Ben stuck his head out of the kitchen. "Just waiting for the orders to start pouring in."

"Okay, boys, listen up. For those of you who now work for me—Shark, Skinny, Tiny." She nodded toward each as she spoke. "No drinking on the job. Period." She turned to the rest of them. "And for those of you who do *not* work for me, this is no longer my home. It is now a bar. You want something, you pay for it. I love you all, but I can't have you drinking up my profits. Oh, and for those of you with honeybuns waiting on tables…" She pointed at Mark and Ratchet. "…tip your waitresses. Those girls are working their asses off for you. Treat them like you would like *other* men to treat them—tip wise. Fair enough?"

They both nodded.

"Alrighty then… Tiny, you got the door. Skinny, you're my awesome chef. Make this place smell good. And you, big boy." She slapped Shark on the butt. "You're behind the bar with me." She smiled. "Hope you can keep up."

"Now that I'm working for you…" Shark glanced at her sideways. "…isn't that called sexual harassment?"

Skip chuckled and then popped a pistachio in his mouth.

"Yeah, it would be *if* you could make it stick," Gypsy said with a wink.

"I've got witnesses." Shark looked towards Skip.

Skip held up his hands. "I didn't see *anything*."

Shark just cocked his eyebrow at the smiling young man.

"*I* will testify," Baron said, coming into the bar with Taka. "That was clearly inappropriate behavior between a boss and her subordinate."

"Thank you," Shark said. "I'll go press charges… when this damn headache goes away."

"I'll testify, too," Taka said. "But only if I get to *watch*."

"Freak," Shark and Gypsy said in unison.

Taka chuckled. "So… what's with the cheerleader get-up?" He pointed to Gypsy's uniform. "Fetish night?"

"Nope." She smiled. "College Game Day. I'm sporting my Tennessee orange. Sheila chose Southern Cal. And Barb is wearing…" She looked around for the little blonde. "What's Barb wearing?"

"Ohio State," Sheila said.

"That's right. Ohio State."

"And this is what you chose to be your regular uniform?" Baron asked.

"Only on Saturdays. Monday's are College Rules. We wear schoolgirl uniforms."

"Sign me up for Mondays," Taka said.

"Freak," Skip and Shark said at the same time.

Taka only laughed again.

"Tuesdays are Biker Night. We've got jeans, chaps, and leather vests."

"And you ought to see her ass in those jeans," Shark mumbled.

When Skip cleared his throat, Shark looked away.

"Anyway…" Gypsy rolled her eyes. "Where was I?"

"Wednesday," Baron said, glaring at the two men behind the bar with her.

"Oh, yeah. Wednesdays are Ladies Choice, and Fridays are unthemed. We will wear our old kilt uniforms on those two nights."

"You skipped Thursday," Baron said.

Gypsy smiled. "Thursdays are Asian Delight. We'll wear cheongsams on that night."

"Jeez, Doll Eyes," Taka said. "You have *any* idea what you're going to be putting these men through?"

"She knows *exactly* what she's doing," Baron said coolly.

"Oh, come on. Really?" Gypsy sighed. "It's a bar... *Hello.* Sex sells. Right, Baron?"

He sort of growled and looked away.

"Fine. Tell me this. If you two had to pick a bar, would you go to the one where the waitress wore cute little outfits? Or would you choose the place with matronly, sloppy looking women taking your order? Hey, this is just good business."

"Just watch yourself," Baron said. "Don't take any unnecessary chances."

"Are you kidding me?" Gypsy grabbed Shark's arm. "Check out this gun show right here. Just look at this hulk of a man I've got standing beside me."

"Yeah," Skip said. "And if anyone tries to pick on him, she'll beat them up for him. Right, Shark?"

Shark only chuckled and kept doing his prep work.

"And it's not just the outfits," Gypsy said. "Our menu will be themed around it as well. College Rules and Game Day will be chips and cheese, hot wings and the like. Biker's Night and Fridays will be burgers and fries. Ladies Choice will be chicken fingers and veggie plates. Then Asian Delight will be egg rolls and sushi."

"And Skinny Guy can handle all that?" Taka asked.

"Ben is amazing," Gypsy said. "He knows about anything that has to do with food."

"Can't tell by looking at him," Shark said.

"Yeah." Skip snorted. "Dude has got to have one *serious* tapeworm."

"It's almost six. You guys staying?"

"That's why we're here, Doll Eyes," Taka said through a smile. "You never know what opening night is going to be like."

"Whoo hoo!" Gypsy clapped happily. "Free labor. Can't ask for better than that."

"Looks like we've got a line starting out there," Skip said. "I'll go tell Tiny to start letting them in."

<hr/>

Gypsy leaned over the bar, groaning as Taka massaged her lower back. "Ho... lee... hell." She jumped, sucking in a sharp breath when he hit a particularly sore spot.

"Sorry, Doll Eyes."

"That shift kicked my ass," she mumbled

"You ready to admit you're getting too old for this gig?"

"Bite me, Nasaka."

And, he did… right on her bottom.

"How did you do?" Baron asked.

"The till is five times what it was on our best night in The Kilt." She groaned again.

"And your tips?" Baron asked.

Taka reached around and felt of her apron. "Spilling out on the ground."

Gypsy didn't move.

"You've got a good business head on your shoulders. I've always known that," Baron said softly. "You think you've bitten off more than you can chew?"

"Nah." She propped up on her elbows. "It'll slow down when the new wears off. I'm definitely going to need another waitress, though. And maybe some help for Skinny. Least 'til things start to chill."

"Save your money, Doll Eyes," Taka said. "I'll hang around and fill in until you see how it's really going to go."

"I can't ask you to do that, Taka. You're a doctor, for goodness sake."

"Doctor's orders then," he said.

"He just wants to wear the uniforms," Skip mumbled under his breath.

Gypsy and Taka both chuckled.

"I'm going to be hanging around anyway, might as well use me while you can." He lightly kissed her back. "Any problems with your fox bite?"

"Nope. He hasn't acted up in months."

"Good girl. Let's hope things stay that way. Have I ever told you just how amazing I think you are, Doll Eyes? Just watching you… it makes me smile."

"…Thanks," she said, her eyes slowly closing.

"Better get her upstairs, Skippy," Taka said. "She's about ready to hit the wall."

"I'll lock everything up," Baron said. "See that she gets a good night's sleep."

"I will." Skip scooped her up in his arms. "Come on, Babe. Time to put you to bed."

When the two had disappeared upstairs, Taka turned to Baron. "What do you think?"

"I think… if I had a tenth of her energy and stubbornness, I would already be ruling the world."

"What about surfer boy?"

"She won't hurt him. He helped her when neither of us could. I dare say, without Skip… we wouldn't be standing here right now. She will let *him* decide. I'll leave it to her."

"You're a stronger man than I could ever be," Taka said, shaking his head.

"No," Baron whispered. "No… I'm not."

Chapter
24

Two weeks had passed, and if anything... business had only gotten better.

"I'm drag-assing, Ms. Gypsy," Shark said.

"Not used to going from first shift to third, yet?"

"Not used to *any* of it." Shark slumped over across the bar.

"Here's some coffee, big guy," she said. "Extra strong."

"Babe!" Skip came busting through the door, yelling her name.

"Aww, hell," Shark muttered.

"I can't do it, Gyps. I tried. I *really* tried." Skip rounded the bar and wrapped her up in his arms. "I just can't do it, Babe. I missed you sooo much. I can't eat. I can't sleep— What are you wearing?"

Gypsy glanced down. "A dress."

"Barely, if even. Where's your uniform?"

"What? It's an a-line dress. It doesn't touch me anywhere, just hangs from my shoulders. Besides, Fridays are unthemed. And as far as uniforms go, I don't really like wearing my kilt anymore... too many memories."

"Go change," he said.

"Skip..." Gypsy furrowed her brow. "What's gotten into you? You've never said one thing about how I dress. Not one. In fact, you like me to look good. I can tell by the way you act when I'm dressed particularly cute—chest all puffed out, strutting like a show rooster."

"That was when you were all mine. That was back when I had nothing to worry about. Now... you're constantly surrounded by guys, I'm hours away, and you refuse to admit that you truly love me. It's killing me, Gypsy. I'm not playing. Now, run upstairs and change before the bar opens."

Gypsy rolled her eyes. "Pffts. Like *that's* gonna happen."

"Aww, hell," Shark muttered again. "Here we go."

Skip crossed his arms over his chest. "Gypsy, it barely comes down to mid thigh."

She glanced back down. "Yeah… but my socks come all the way up above my knees. And look…" She flipped up the bottom of her dress. "…hot pants—so no one can catch a peek, even if I bend over. What's the big deal? The only skin showing is my arms and the couple of inches between my socks and dress tail. See?" She spun around. "It's not any shorter than my kilt. And look… you can't even tell I'm not wearing a bra."

"Oh, for the love of Pete," Shark said. "I don't need to know *any* of that."

"Then don't listen. And you, Skip… quit acting weird." Gypsy grabbed her apron and tied it on.

"Oh, no, no, no," Skip said, lifting her up and sitting her atop the bar. "Every excuse you just used went flying out the window when you put the apron on. You're killing me, Babe. I haven't seen you in two weeks, and you do *this* to me? No. I can't do it. I can't let you go, even if you aren't *in love* with me. I just can't walk away from you."

"That's your decision, Skip. I told you that already. If you want to keep things between us as they are, I will gladly stay with you. It's your call. You know how much I care about you. I would never hurt you."

"No. I mean, yes… I want to be with you, but I don't want things as they are. I go crazy every time I have to leave. I don't trust Baron."

"You don't have to trust Baron. You only have to trust me."

"I know that, but…" He wrapped his arms around her. "Marry me."

"What?"

"If you don't want to move to Dogtown, that's fine. You can stay here. Just… marry me, Gypsy."

"No way, Skip. You know how much I care about you and that I would never do anything to hurt you, but I won't marry you just so you can feel more secure in our relationship."

"But, I love you."

"I know you do. You trust me, too. Right?"

Skip nodded.

"Then trust me when I say, that is one majorly *bad* idea."

"Hold up," Shark said. "Wait just a minute. Are you saying that you and surfer boy have been trying to call it quits?"

"No." Skip squeezed her tighter. "I *won't* call it quits."

"Well now." Shark chuckled. "I didn't realize you were about to be a free woman, Ms. Gypsy. Now *I've* got a shot in there."

She glanced over at the big guy with the blatant smirk. "Never gonna happen, Shark."

Shark just chuckled.

When the front door opened, Gypsy tried to push Skip away.

"People are coming in now. You have *got* to let me down off the bar."

"…No."

"Skip, please."

"Hello, Shark… Gypsy… Skip."

Baron's voice was icy, as cold as she had ever heard it.

"I've brought someone by to see you *if* you can let go of your *boy toy* for a minute."

When Skip loosened his hold, Gypsy quickly jumped down off the bar and spun toward Baron. Her eyes went wide, soon followed by her smile.

"Sakara!" she sang, running around to hug her old friend. "How in the— I mean— What in the world are you doing here?"

"Mr. Bishop said you were in need of an assistant. He flew me over to help you."

"Help?" She quickly glanced toward Baron, then back to the pretty, smiling Asian girl. "Oh, who cares? I'm just glad you're here. Let me introduce you to everyone. This is Shark."

When Gypsy walked behind the bar and touched his shoulder, the large man waved at Sakara.

"And this is Skip."

"H-hi," he barely choked out.

Skip blushed brightly. Sakara did, too.

"And that's Sheila." Gypsy pointed. "Mark, Tiny, Barb, and that's Skinny back there in the back."

Everyone threw up their hands and Sakara half bowed to each of them.

"It is very nice to meet you all." Sakara reached into her purse. "I have a gift, Ms. Gypsy. From Renji."

"Renji?" Gypsy took the card, opening it as she glanced up to see Taka coming into the bar.

"Hello, Sakara. Long time, no see."

"Hello, Mr. Nasaka."

Baron had been watching Gypsy silently move her lips as she read the card. Then, her eyes went impossibly wide.

"Ho… lee— Mother of— Oh, dear lord."

"What is it?" Baron asked.

When Gypsy didn't answer, he turned to Sakara.

"What is it?" he repeated

Sakara shrugged her shoulders. "He said it was private. I did not look."

When Baron glanced back to Gypsy, he could tell she was holding up a picture… her mouth was hanging open. He bolted behind the bar and gazed down over her shoulder. It was a picture of Renji, nude down to the waist. His long dark hair was in a loose, tousled braid hanging down over his right shoulder. He was looking down and sort of to the side. The School Master had the string of his Judo pants in his right hand, tugging it down so that his hip and the whole of his V were prominently displayed.

Baron snatched up the card.

I miss our time together, Chikara. If you had only stayed just a little longer… I could have taught you sooo many things. Come back to me, lovely goddess. Let me take you to heights that only I can. I will be gentle with you, Chikara… always will I be gentle. I can heal that troubled heart of yours, beautiful lady. Let me show you what real love and worship truly feel like.

~Renji

"Why that little…" Baron reached for the picture, but Gypsy pressed it close to her chest. "Give it to me, Gypsy."

"…No."

"Now." The word dripped with ice.

"N… no," she barely whispered. "I want to keep it."

Skip and Shark exchanged a nervous glance.

"Why?" Baron hissed. "I thought he was only your *sensei.*"

Gypsy didn't answer.

Baron was almost trembling when she turned further away from him and slid the picture into her apron pocket.

"Jūshirō couldn't find Sakara before she left," Taka said. "He mailed his, but he went ahead and texted you the pic."

"Texted?" Baron spun her around to face him. "You got a new phone? When?"

"Only a few days ago."

"Only a few days?" Baron narrowed his gaze. "And yet, Jūshirō has your number and I do not."

"I gave it to him," Taka said. "What? Don't look at me like that. He asked me for it. What was I supposed to do?"

"You gave Taka your number, but not me?"

"Don't get mad at *her*," Taka said. "She didn't have a choice. I went with her to pick out the phone." He smiled. "So... she didn't actually *give* it to me. I took it."

"You went with—" Baron closed his eyes and rubbed his temples. "We'll talk about this later. It's nearly opening time. You better hurry up and change."

"She already is changed," Skip said. "That's what she's wearing tonight."

Baron glanced down at her. "No, it's not."

"Yes, it is." Gypsy glared up at him. "I'm a grown ass woman and this is *my* damn bar. I can dress myself all on my own, without any help from the likes of you two."

"I thought she looked great in it," Taka said. "I talked her into getting it in pink and white as well."

Gypsy slowly turned toward the smiling Asian man, daggers shooting from her eyes.

"You're not helping," she said through gritted teeth.

"You took Taka shopping?" Baron asked coolly.

"No," Taka said. "I took her. She needs to get out and cut loose every once in a while."

"No, she does not," Baron and Skip said in unison.

Taka chuckled.

"Excuse me," Sakara said. "Where should I put my bags?"

"I'm sorry, honey," Gypsy said. "I'll carry them upstairs."

"They're heavy," Baron said. "I'll get them and you get the door."

"Okay. Skip?"

The man glanced at her when she spoke.

"Will you take care of Sakara for me?"

Skip's eyes widened. "...Sure."

"Show her around, get her something to eat, something to drink. I'll be back down in a flash."

"It would be my pleasure," Skip said, smiling and blushing again.

Sakara giggled, her cheeks flaming like crimson lotus blossoms.

"Aww, hell." Shark shook his head, then turned towards Taka. "You are a frickin' tsunami, aren't you, little guy?"

Taka shrugged his shoulders. "I try my best to keep things interesting."

"Uh huh." Shark snorted. "You're mad, that's what *you* are."

"You have to maintain a *little* spark of madness." Taka smiled. "If you lose that... you're nothing."

Gypsy stomped up the stairs with Baron close on her heels. When they reached the landing, he tossed the luggage to the side and pushed her up against the big metal door, pinning her wrists high above her head.

"Let me go." She squirmed, but didn't escape.

"Stop resisting, Gypsy." He forcefully rammed his pelvis against her backside, holding her in place. "I said, *stop*."

The chill now flowing through his words—absent any warmth or play—made her breath hitch. She stilled.

That's the man we saw in his eyes when we first looked into them. Her angel shivered.

Yes. Her devil smiled. *I do believe we are finally meeting The Dom.*

"Give me the photo, Gypsy. I will release you if you promise to give it to me of your own free will."

"But... I really do want to keep it. It was a gift."

She whimpered when his grip on her wrists tightened. He lifted her arms until she was on her tiptoes.

Gypsy's breathing suddenly increased, she was almost panting. The feel of his large bulge pressed against her bottom, the smell of his sweet breath against the back of her neck, the way his hard chest rubbed against her shoulder blades... she grew heavy with want, desire filling her foggy mind.

What the hell is wrong with me? she thought.

That man behind you now. Her devil groaned. *That man can make you mind... force you to willingly submit to those dark desires you claim not to have.*

Shut up, her angel whimpered softly. *He's scary.*

Yeah, Gypsy thought. *In an oh-my-gawd-could-you-get-any-sexier kind of way.*

"You *will* freely give me the photo. Then... you will go inside and change."

"Why? This dress doesn't show anything. It isn't even tight around my boobs."

"This dress is *seduction* at its finest. Why do you think Taka picked it out? It hints at modesty, while it teases you with desire." He pressed his hips deeper into her. "Were you tending the bar nude, you could not draw any *more* attention. The couple inches of skin that's showing, only pulls the mind up your thigh, causing delicious fantasies about what lies *just* out of reach. And those socks—while covering your legs—only make even *more* lurid thoughts arise. Oh, Gypsy... visions of those sock-clad limbs wrapped tightly around my waist, highlighting where I am connected to you... moving within you."

She felt his desire, his enormous growing desire, now pressing into her as he buried his nose into her hair and noisily sucked air through his teeth.

Ho... lee... hell, she thought. And not in a completely sexy way, no, in a tiny bit terrified way.

He's gonna devour us, her angel whined.

Her devil groaned again. *Mmm... I can't wait.*

"And what if you have to bend over, hmm? You only do that about a thousand times a night. Does everybody get a free show?"

"H-hot pants," she barely managed to whisper.

"What?" He thrust against her with the word.

She whimpered again. "Shorts, Baron. I have shorts on underneath. No one can see anything."

He took a tiny step back and lifted her dress. He almost purred as he ran his hand up her inner thigh and grabbed her left butt cheek.

"Mmm, Gypsy... dammit." He slammed himself back against her with even more force. "You have become hyper-sexualized. I blame Taka and Skip, but you are not innocent in this. We will talk later. As for now... give me the picture of Renji."

"I don't understand why you're so upset, Baron. *You* were the one who introduced me to him. And if my memory serves me correctly, and it does, you were ready to hold my purse and watch him bend me over his desk—"

The slap on her ass was so sudden, Gypsy squeaked. Baron held his hand there for a moment before he slowly began rubbing little circles across her butt, spreading the heat from the blow out across her entire cheek.

"You have no idea the points you are racking up right now, Gypsy."

"Points?"

"Marks against you. I will not forget them. Soon, you will have to pay."

"Pay?"

"Yes. I will extract payment for each infraction. Much I let slide with you. This... this I cannot."

"Stop it, Baron." She began to struggle again. "I won't be *paying* for anything. I've done nothing wrong."

He pushed her again with his hips, but what he pressed against her that time made her breath hitch.

Oh... my... gawd. I can't handle this man. He will tear me in two.

"Oh, but you will pay, Gypsy," he whispered into her hair. "You just can't imagine yet exactly *how*."

"Everything alright up there?"

Baron hissed before calling back down the stairwell, "This doesn't concern you, Taka." He turned back to her. "You won't give it to me?"

She shook her head.

Baron growled, then slid his hand down her side and into her apron pocket, removing the photo.

"And your phone."

She shook her head again.

When Baron grinded into her, Gypsy began to tremble all over. He noticed, and smiled.

"One last time," he whispered.

She paused, then shook her head again.

He reached into her other pocket and pulled out the new phone. She heard him pressing buttons, then his sharp intake of breath.

"That son of a—"

More buttons were pressed before he dropped the phone back into her pocket, then slowly released her.

Gypsy immediately rubbed her wrists.

"Now, open the door."

She glared at him. His cold eyes never wavered.

Only when Gypsy reached toward the little screen did she realized how badly her hands were shaking.

"Hello, Gypsy Rodden."

"Hey, House. I'm home."

When the internal tumblers began to move, Baron grabbed her arm, pushing her inside as soon as the door came open.

She stumbled a few steps before spinning back to face him. "If you *ever*—"

Her words were cut off when Baron shoved her up against the wall, wrapping her legs around his waist as his passionate kiss found her. Within a heartbeat, Gypsy was moaning. He cupped her ass and pressed himself against her.

"…Baron…"

When she barely whispered out his name, Baron suddenly released her.

"Wh-what happened?" she half whispered.

He straightened his shirt and smiled down at her, his prominent dimples causing her heart to race even faster.

"You succumbed," he said, clearly satisfied.

She glared at him, slowly balling her hands into fists.

"I did *not*."

"Yes, you did. And in record time, no less. What was that, Gypsy? Three? Four seconds?"

"You are a major ass. You know that, right?"

He pulled her to him. She started to struggle, but he held her chin and looked deep into her eyes.

"My beautiful little Gypsy," he whispered. "You are so good at troubling me. What am I going to do with you? Spank you? Bind you? Flog you?" He gently kissed her lips. "Or will I simply spend days upon days, claiming you? Making love to you until all those other men are but a pale memory. I promise you this, beautiful lady… you have yet to know *true* pleasure. I look forward to teaching you that." He kissed her again. "Now, run along back downstairs. You've got about half an hour before your adoring fans start to pour in. I'll take Sakara's things up. Which room?"

"You mean… I can wear the dress?"

Baron raised a single eyebrow, but didn't speak.

"It's okay, then. Right? Can I wear it?"

When he smiled, Gypsy's tummy clenched. Her throat grew strangely dry and a deep burn started to grow within her nether regions. She shuffled uncomfortably.

"Since you ask so nicely..." He tucked her hair back behind her ear, lifted her chin, and kissed the tip of her nose. "...then, yes. You can wear the dress. Now, which room?"

"Put her in Gillis's."

Before Baron could turn from her, Gypsy ran her hands up and over his chest, admiring the feel of his defined pecks beneath her palms.

Baron held perfectly still, staring down at her dainty hands upon him... the lust now filling her bourbon-colored eyes.

"You have yet to know true pleasure, either," she whispered. "Being with a woman who not only worships your incredible body, but also treasures the heart within... being with a woman who loves you without rules, without exceptions, without limitations... I look forward to teaching *you* how pleasurable *that* will be." She lightly touched his cheek before turning to go.

When the door closed, Baron sucked in a deep breath. He was lightheaded, bordering on dizzy. That tiny woman consumed him, undid him. It was beyond thrilling... and utterly terrifying.

Taka met Gypsy at the bottom of the stairs.

"You okay, Doll Eyes?"

She snorted. "Like *you* care. Damn, Taka. It's like you enjoy causing *epic* waves."

"That's because he does," Shark said.

"Where's Sakara?"

Gypsy glanced over at the corner table when Shark motioned toward the couple. They were both smiling, both blushing. When Skip would lightly touch the back of her hand, Sakara would giggle softly.

"Well... I'll be damned," Gypsy mumbled.

"Amazing, isn't it?" Shark said.

Taka smiled. "...Serendipity."

"Ugh... I need a Chuhai."

"Which one?" Shark asked. "Apple or peach?"

"One of each."

"I thought you said no drinking on the job." He popped the first can and handed it to her.

Gypsy downed half of it with her first gulp. "*You're working, I'm owning.* There's a difference."

Shark chuckled.

"So... what happened?" Taka asked.

Gypsy began filling the salt and sugar dishes for their margarita special. "He took Renji's picture." She didn't glance up as she spoke. "He took my phone, too—deleted Jūshirō's message before I even got to see it."

"Damn... Props to the Pope," Shark said. "You've got to admire a man who can set *your* fiery little ass straight."

She glanced sideways at the large, buff bartender, then just rolled her eyes.

"Don't stress over it," Taka whispered. "Here."

He slid his phone across the bar. Gypsy didn't touch it, but she couldn't pull her eyes away from the screen.

"Th-*that* is Jūshirō?"

"What?" Taka furrowed his brow. "Of course that's Jūshirō. Don't act all innocent with me, Doll Eyes. You guys went out every weekend for months."

"And whose fault is that?"

Taka only smiled and winked at her.

"And it wasn't *months*. Five or six times—tops. And he only did that because he thought I belonged to *you*."

Taka chuckled. "Yeah. You should've heard how he cussed me when I finally told him the truth. He was livid."

"Why?"

"*Why?* Because he wanted you. That's why. And... that's also why I told him you were mine." Taka shook his head. "I know my brother... and I know you as well, Doll Eyes. If Jūshirō had been given a green light where you are concerned... we would never have seen you again."

Gypsy blushed. "Yeah... you might be right."

"I know I'm right." Taka leaned back in his chair. "Admit it, Doll Eyes. Go ahead and tell me the truth of it."

She bit her bottom lip, keeping her gaze locked on the picture before her. "Jūshirō is amazing." She smiled. "As regal and elegant as any prince. He treated me like a goddess—handled me like fragile spun glass." She swallowed hard. "The time I spent with Jūshirō—in his home, especially—those are my favorite memories of Japan. It felt like... like we were royalty or something. He loved spoiling me... and I *loved* being spoiled."

"He treasured you," Taka whispered.

Gypsy nodded, then took a deep breath. "That was back before I actually knew how Baron truly felt about me." She glanced up at Taka then. "Thank you."

"For what?"

"For lying to your brother. He withheld the truth of his desire because of you, right? Had that not been the case, had Jūshirō shared with me his true feelings, I definitely would have reciprocated them. I mean... if that man had asked it of me— asked *anything*—I don't think I could have denied him."

"Thus, why I lied, Doll Eyes. When I laid eyes on you that day at Tony's, the first thought that popped into my head was... Jūshirō would love her... love her *too* much."

"Yeah, well... like I said, thanks."

Taka smiled as he leaned toward the bar. "He told me you let him braid your hair."

"Only because he let me braid his first." She blushed. "I just gave him a simple, elegant braid. But Jūshirō... he took great care with mine. It felt so good, so soothing. The man pampered me, *that's* for sure. He spent nearly two hours on my hair that day—did some intricate basket-weave over the entire back... complete with colored ribbons and everything."

"Well, he *is* a master of Kinbaku, after all."

"Yeah... I couldn't even get it loose—had to go to work like that the next day. When I finally made it to the dojo that night, Renji undid it for me... laughing his ass off all the while."

Taka chuckled. "So, you went on a bunch of dates with my brother, spent entire weekends alone with him in his home, even let him play with and bind your lovely hair... yet you act like this picture is the first time you've ever seen him."

"This is the first time I've ever seen him look like *that*. I went out with him, yeah—fully clothed every single time. I had no idea he was so... so perfect."

Shark looked over her shoulder then. "Damn, Ms. Gypsy. You sure have *interesting* friends."

She didn't answer, just kept staring at the picture of the Rope Master on his knees, completely nude except for the silky robe barely hanging from his shoulders. He was leaning back slightly, looking off to the side, one hand lightly touching his flawless neck, the other splayed out… barely covering what was hanging there between his legs. Jūshirō was physical perfection in Asian glory. Not an ounce of body fat. Skin the color of an autumn moonbeam. Every single muscle of his tightly defined body stretched taut for her viewing pleasure.

"You're drooling," Taka said. "Stop it. You're starting to even make *me* jealous. And you know me, Doll Eyes. I don't do jealous. So quit lusting after my brother."

"Why, Taka?" Gypsy glanced back up at him when the screen finally faded to black. "Why did Renji and Jūshirō do this?"

He shrugged his shoulders. "I was as shocked as you. Believe me. I've never seen them photographed like *this* before. Especially Jūshirō. He always stays *behind* the lens. He said he did it for you, Doll Eyes. After he talked to you in the store that first time, he couldn't get you out of his mind. He didn't take you on all those dates for *my* sake. He did it because he desired you for himself. He wants to bind you so badly he can barely breathe. Apparently, when you left… he spiraled into some dark, lonely place. He sent *this* in hopes it would pull your desire up to match his—bring you back to Japan." Taka smiled. "I confided in him, told him how you *truly* felt about Japanese men. But… I think he took it to a whole new level. And judging by the sweat popping out on your chest… I believe it worked."

Gypsy glanced down, then back up. "But… didn't you tell them about me and Baron? Didn't you tell Jūshirō the truth?"

"Yeah. That's why he sent *this*… in part."

She furrowed her brow again. Taka chuckled.

"He wants you to desire him above all, that is true, but there is another reason as well." Taka leaned closer. "Jūshirō and Baron and Renji… they have all been friends for *years*. And, their exquisitely discriminating *taste* in women runs along the same path as well. They… share, sometimes."

"Share?" she whispered.

Taka nodded.

When they heard Baron coming back down the stairs, the three quickly separated. Taka jabbed his phone down in his pocket. Gypsy grabbed a towel, turning around to dab her chest. And Shark became real busy sorting out glasses.

Baron stopped short, glaring from one to the other.

"Anything you would like to share?" he said coolly.

"Oh. Hi, honey." Gypsy turned to him and smiled. "I didn't hear you come back down."

"Is that so?" he said, walking straight up to her and taking her in his arms. "Then… why is your heart racing?"

Shark cleared his throat and coughed. Taka sent the overly buff man a vicious glare.

Baron didn't turn toward either of them. He kept his gaze locked with Gypsy's.

"He showed you, didn't he?"

Gypsy didn't answer.

Baron leaned down closer. "Did Taka show you the picture of Jūshirō?"

She bit her lip, before barely nodding.

Baron kissed her then. Right there in front of everyone. It was a firm, yet gentle kiss. He cupped her cheek in his hand, pulled her close to him, and completely melted her in every possible way.

When he finally released her, Gypsy was dizzy. She grabbed the bar to steady herself.

"Are you thinking about Jūshirō now?" he whispered.

She shook her head.

"Do you wish a picture of *me* as well?"

Her eyes went wide, but she didn't answer.

"No matter what that smiling little troublemaker over there told you…" Baron motioned toward Taka. "…*you* I will never share. Never."

Chapter 25

The next several weeks went by in a blur.

Sakara proved not only to be invaluable in helping run the bar, she also became as close to Gypsy as any sister could have. Gypsy loved the younger woman way past friendship. She counted her as treasured family.

They went to the gym together, shopping together, sat up and watched sappy movies together. Gypsy showed her how to play video games, and Sakara taught Gypsy how to make her own lo-mein instead of always eating take-out.

The two women moved all the stuff Gillis had left behind, up to Trace's old room. Within the first couple of days, Sakara had truly turned it into her own, comfortable little home.

"I never want to go back, Ms. Gypsy. I never want to leave you. I love it here. I love your friends, your bar, your house. I can't think of a single thing that I truly miss about Japan."

"Chuhai," Gypsy said through a smile. "I hate having to ration out what you smuggled over here for me."

Sakara laughed. "Then, we should fly over once a year and ship back more."

"We might just do that."

"Is that all you miss from your time overseas?"

"Pretty much. Being a lawyer... well, you already know... I didn't really have time to sightsee. I miss the blooming cherry trees, and the sento baths. Other than that, I prefer California."

"I have never seen Mr. Bishop act the way he does when he's around you. Every time he had to come overseas to the branch offices, he was cold and distant and... scary."

"Tell me about it." Gypsy snorted out a laugh. "I know *that* Mr. Bishop all too well. I, too, am surprised at just how different he is today... compared to when we first met." She softly sighed. "I was *physically* attracted to him, yeah. I mean... who wouldn't be?"

Sakara giggled.

"But I also wanted to rip his icy cold eyes out." Gypsy sighed again. "Then... I fell in love with the man. Now... no matter what he does, I love him more every day."

When Sakara fell silent, Gypsy squeezed her hand.

"You don't have to put it into words, Sakara," she whispered. "And you don't have to try and hide it, either. I already know. I saw it in your eyes—in *his* as well—the night you walked back into my life. It's okay. Trust me. I will never have hard feelings toward you concerning Skip. If you think you might like him... go for it."

"Are you sure?"

"I care about Skip. I want him to be happy. The only reason we were still together was because he was trying to find a reason to let me go. *You* gave him that reason. I'm happy with Baron. I want Skip to be happy, too."

"I don't know," Sakara whispered softly. "He is always very nice to me, but he has never even asked me out or anything. In my heart, I fear it would be a one-sided relationship. Why would he want me... when he had someone like you?"

"You're joking, right? Jeez, girl. You are gorgeous. How can you not see that? Trust me. That cool acting surfer dude, he's *crazy* about you."

Sakara only blushed.

⚜

When Skip stopped by the bar a few days later, he came to Gypsy—head bowed and blushing brightly—and asked if he could take Sakara out on a date. Gypsy's heart sang. Two of her favorite people, stumbling clumsily into what Gypsy could only hope was a lasting love. She couldn't stop smiling.

"Yes," she said sternly. "You may ask her if she wishes to go out with you. Yet, do *not* pressure her. If she is interested she will say yes, minus your begging and whining."

"Thanks, Babe."

Gypsy noisily cleared her throat.

"I meant... Thanks, Ms. Gypsy."

She smiled. "Now listen to me, Skip. Don't you dare do anything to hurt that girl. You hear me? No spanking. No caning.

No... any of that other stuff. She isn't innocent, no, but she has been hurt... been lied to. You take special care with her. *Talk* to her. Ask her what she thinks, what she loves, what her interests are. Get to know *her*, Skip, before you even think about climbing into bed. Got it?"

He nodded.

"You'll not find another one like her, I can promise you that. And... I'm pretty sure she loves sunrises, even more than I do."

When she winked at him, Skip blushed again.

"Thank you, Ms. Gypsy. I won't let you down." He started to leave, but paused. "Umm... you know that thing you told me about wrong time—wrong person, or right time—right person?"

"Yeah." Gypsy chuckled. "Something like that."

"Well... I think you were right."

"Yeah, Skip. I think I was, too."

When the smiling young man ran towards the back room, Shark leaned over and bumped Gypsy with his shoulder. "Who the hell are you? I mean... are you like *perfect* or something?" He snorted. "No one would believe all this crap, even if I told them. What *are* you to those two now? Their mother? A couple months ago he was in here begging you to marry him. Now you're setting them up? And smiling about it?"

"It's hard to watch them grow up and sprout their own wings," she said softly.

"Pffts." Shark snorted again. "I take it all back. You're not amazing *or* perfect. You're an idiot. Just like that Taka fellow."

"I didn't *do* anything, Shark." She smiled. "It's just... serendipity."

"Yeah. Whatever *that* means."

—⟨◆⟩—

"Hello, my luscious little friend," Taka said as he entered.

"Uh-oh," Shark grumbled. "Here comes trouble."

"Hey, Taka. What's up?"

"You tell me what's up. Did you ever get Jūshirō's letter?"

"I did."

"And?"

"And... he looked even more delicious in the 8x10 he mailed."

"8x10?" Taka chuckled. "He never did do anything small. That's Jūshirō for you."

"No." Gypsy sighed softly. "There is nothing *small* about him."

"Stop fantasizing over my brother while I'm sitting right here. That's... disturbing."

She shrugged. "You're the one who brought it up."

"So... did you tell Baron? Or did you hide it?"

"I kept the letter. It was beautiful. I kept the picture for a few days, too."

"Then what?"

"My conscience started bothering me. I laid it out on the kitchen table when I knew Baron was coming over."

"And?"

"And... he never mentioned a word about it. But when he left, the picture was gone."

They both turned toward the door as it opened.

Gypsy smiled. "Hello, Baron. You look even more handsome than usual. How *ever* do you do it?"

He was smiling with only one corner of his mouth as he made it to her side. Baron wrapped his arm around her and kissed her forehead.

"I figured *you* would be here," he said to Taka.

"Of course I'm here. It's Thursday—Asian Delight. I never tire of seeing her in those dresses. Besides, Skinny still hasn't mastered sushi... not properly. I've got to help out where I can."

"Uh huh." Baron turned back to her. "Gypsy, when the bar closes tonight, you need to pack a bag."

"Why? What's wrong?"

"Nothing is wrong. We're going on a little trip."

"But... I can't. I can't leave the bar."

"You can, and you will. Haven't you been training Sakara to do everything?"

"Yeah, but—"

"No buts."

Chapter 26

Flying always put her to sleep. Always. Gypsy smiled to herself as she nuzzled back against the big roomy chair.

"So... where are we going?" She covered her mouth and yawned.

Baron smiled. "It's a secret."

Gypsy pulled the blanket up over her shoulders and closed her eyes.

"Before you drift off into dreamland, beautiful lady, we need to talk."

"Mm hmm." She didn't open her eyes. "Talk about what?"

"Our future."

"I'm not going anywhere, Baron. You know that."

"I do, yes. Yet... we have not *progressed*."

She slowly opened her weighted lids. "Is this about the sex thing again? I told you I was sorry. But what with Gypsy's Place being so crazy still, and then getting Sakara settled in... when I wasn't completely exhausted, we haven't been *alone*."

"No." He softly chuckled. "This isn't about the sex thing. This trip will rectify that."

Her eyes opened a little wider. Baron smiled.

"Are you flying me out of the country so you can sleep with me?"

"Partly, yes." He tucked her hair back behind her ear. "But there is another reason as well. That's what we need to talk about."

"Okay. Go ahead."

"You know the packet we worked up?"

She sat up a little. "Our What-If/Maybe-Someday packet?"

He smiled softly. "Yes, our What-If/Maybe-Someday packet that contained all of our personal files."

"Yeah. What about it?"

"Do you still agree with everything in it?"

"...Yes."

"Do you even remember what all it contained?"

"Of course I do. It's only been a couple months. There were deeds to everything we own—your house, my house, the bar, the office, ya-da ya-da. And all our financial crap, living wills, dead wills, blah, blah, blah. Why are you bringing this up now? I agreed to everything. You agreed to everything. We both signed and notarized the whole packet. Right? Wait…" She furrowed her brow. "You wanting to back out on all that stuff? I mean, we didn't even file it yet. It would break my heart, yeah, but… if you want out, all you *legally* gotta do is tear it in half."

"Ugh… lawyers." He tapped the tip of her nose. "No. I don't *want out*. Not now. Not ever. I just wanted to make sure you were still okay with it."

"Yeah. Of course I am. I signed every document in there, and I stand by them." She snorted. "Like you said, I'm a lawyer. I didn't take a single piece of that file lightly."

"Yet… you failed to mention *one* document in particular."
She furrowed her brow again.

"Our marriage license," he said softly. "You mentioned everything else, but not that. Have you changed your mind?"

"No." She snorted. "Without that, the rest of the file would be worthless."

"True." Baron took her hand. "I know we combined our lives strictly by the book, almost sterile like."

"Being who we are, that only makes good business sense."

"And yet… I never actually got down on my knee and asked for your hand in marriage."

"Aww… is that what you're doing? How sweet."

He chuckled. "No. I'm never going to ask you because I don't want to take a chance on you saying no. You freely signed your name to the dotted line. All I have to do is file it. I've got you, Ms. Rodden. You can't say no now."

Gypsy softly chuckled. "I wouldn't, even if you begged me to."

"Well, that's never going to happen."

She smiled and closed her eyes again. "Was that all?"

"No," he whispered. "I have to make a confession."

"Umm hmm… 'bout what?"

"I took that file down to the courthouse yesterday."

She yawned. "That's sweet."

He chuckled. "Yes. It *was* sweet. Do you understand what I'm telling you, Gypsy?"

"…You filed your paperwork. Right?"

"I filed *our* paperwork."

She slowly opened her eyes. "What paperwork?"

"Our What-If/Maybe-Someday packet. I took it to the courthouse yesterday, right before I came by the bar. I met with Judge Broker in his office and he signed off on every single page."

She tilted her head to the side, brows furrowed.

"As of 5:27 yesterday afternoon, you officially became Mrs. Gypsy Bishop… with all the benefits and angst that goes along with it."

Gypsy didn't speak; she just stared at him, bewildered.

"Are you mad at me?"

A single tear slid down her cheek just as her bottom lip began to quiver.

"Gypsy? You alright?" He cupped her cheek. "Are those tears of joy? Oh, Gypsy, please tell me those are tears of joy."

"We're… *married?*"

Baron nodded. "Are you mad because I didn't tell you?"

She pursed her lips and shook her head.

"Say something, my love," he whispered softly.

"I'm—" Her voice cracked. "…I'm the happiest woman in the whole world."

<hr />

"Paris?" She giggled. "I've always loved Paris."

Baron frowned. "Thinking that *I* would be the first to stroll down these streets with you—I knew it was too much to hope for."

Gypsy wrapped her arm around his and squeezed. "I lived in England for what felt like half my life. I mean, it's just… right over there." She pointed.

He softly snorted. "You're an idiot."

She smiled up at him. "Well, you're the first man I've strolled down these streets with, whom I loved."

"How much?"

"How much do I love you? Pffts… as if such a thing could possibly be measured. Let me see… when you pass through a room and your scent lingers, ahh… Baron. When I walk in where you have been, my insides do a little flip. When I hear your deep voice, even if you're in a different room talking to someone else… I automatically smile. When you stand in front of me with your hands in your pockets, smiling with only one corner of your mouth, gazing down at me through those smoldering blue eyes…" She shivered. "I get this strange tightening feeling deep down in my belly. When I feel the tip of your nose touch the back of my head, or my neck, or anywhere… my breath catches in my chest—feels like I'm gonna explode."

He wrapped his arm around her waist. "Is that all?"

"Well… while I *have* seen and touched your chest—ran my fingertips down all those impossibly delicious abs—I can't really speak as for what the rest of you does to me."

"Dear heavens… Me, Baron Bishop, I have just married a woman whom—not only have I not had sex with—she has never even seen me completely naked."

"That's because you're so sweet and innocent." She smiled up at him. "Saving yourself for the honeymoon and all."

"Smartass."

He lightly popped her butt with his hand. She giggled.

"In truth… I'm sorta nervous, maybe even a little scared," she half whispered.

"You do not have to fear me, Gypsy. I would never hurt you. Well, I would never hurt your *heart*. My mouth waters thinking about all the other different hurts… the ones you will soon be enjoying."

Gypsy swallowed hard then—didn't even notice when Baron held open a door for her.

"After you, beautiful lady."

Only then did she realize they had stepped inside a posh jewelry store.

"I am here to see Jacque," Baron said. "We have an appointment."

When the attractive young woman walked into the back, Gypsy leaned over toward Baron and whispered. "Jacque? As in… Cousteau?"

He smiled. "…Idiot."

315

She was still chuckling when the pasty man with the raven hair walked in.

"Ahh… it's *you*," she half whispered, half gasped. "The doorman in Tokyo."

Jacque bowed graciously. "The pleasure is all mine, Madame… for a second time." He smiled. "Please, follow me."

As the odd man led their way into the back, Gypsy whispered, "Do you have freaky connections everywhere?"

"Yes. I do. Remember that, if you ever try to run away. I can find you… no matter where you plan to hide."

"Pffts. Like I'd ever run away."

Baron leaned down close to her ear. "We've yet to have our wedding night, my love. Perhaps you will feel differently with the sunrise."

"Why? Are you that bad in bed?"

"Points, my love. You continue to rack up marks against yourself. Marks I will soon see *here*." He popped her bottom again, a little harder this time.

They walked into the plush, private showroom and Jacque opened a blue velvet box sitting atop a glass table.

"Per your request, Master Baron."

When he turned the box to face them, Gypsy gasped.

"Oh, it's sooo lovely." She reached toward it. "May I?"

"It is yours," Baron whispered softly. "Created *especially* for you, my love. There is not another like it in the world."

"For me?" Gypsy delicately touched the platinum pendant. "It's a heart," she whispered to herself. "It's a heart *lock*. Oh… it's so beautiful."

"With your permission," Jacque said as he reached toward her.

Gypsy jerked back before the man could touch her hair.

"No," she snapped, a little louder and a little harsher than she meant to.

Baron chuckled softly.

Jacque smiled and bowed again. "I learn my lessons well, Madame. I did *ask* this time."

Gypsy looked back to the sparkling pendant. It had a smooth, matte finish with little dark stones swirled across the front. The lock was in the shape of a heart, slightly larger than a quarter, with a tiny little keyhole on the front left side. The chain that held the enchanting pendant looked to be of woven platinum—solid in form. When Gypsy touched it, she was surprised it was flexible.

"Byzantine, Madame," Jacque said.

She turned to Baron. "May I wear it?"

"That is my greatest wish," he whispered softly.

Gypsy picked up the velvet box and held it out to him. Baron's eyes widened slightly.

"Will you put it on me?" She lifted her hair.

He smiled. "And *that* would be my greatest honor."

Baron took the necklace and draped it over her from behind as Gypsy watched in the mirror.

She couldn't contain her smile. Her cheeks were aching by the time he had clasped the lovely masterpiece in place. She gasped softly as she moved closer to the mirror.

The beautiful byzantine chain draped like sparkling fluid atop her skin. The pendant rested comfortably at the base of her throat, the black stones across catching the light, shining with a breathtaking glory she had not noticed while it lay within its box.

"Does that…" She leaned closer. "Do the stones spell out something?"

"Those *stones* are black diamonds," Baron said, pulling her hair back and lightly kissing the side of her neck. "And, yes. It says… le mien."

"Le mien," she whispered. "What does it mean?"

Baron met her gaze in the reflection and smiled. "It means *mine* in French."

"Mine…" she whispered softly before looking back up to him. "Why French?"

"It is the language of love, Madame," Jacque said as he approached her. "With your permission."

Gypsy looked at the pale French man, but he wasn't speaking to her. His gaze was fixed above her head. Gypsy glanced up at Baron just as he gave one quick nod of his head. Then she felt Jacque take her hand in his.

"Madame… to be present during your collaring…" He swallowed hard. "…I do not feel worthy."

"My… *collaring*?" She glanced back at her image in the mirror.

Baron placed his hands upon her shoulders and looked down at her through moistened eyes.

"The man who holds you now," Jacque said. "He has searched the world over, waited his entire life for his perfect match to come along. I am no fool, Madame. I know you are not of our world, not accustomed to our rituals. Alas, the only way for you to truly understand what it is you have done for Master Baron this day… is to mirror *our* custom with one of your own, one you are far more familiar with."

Gypsy was more confused than ever.

The raven-haired man stepped back. Then, Baron turned her to face him.

"My beautiful Gypsy."

When a single tear trickled down his cheek, Gypsy's breath caught painfully in her throat. She watched—numb and stunned— as Baron knelt down before her.

"I have never wanted another woman," he said softly. "I have waited, not so patiently, for you to find me… for you to love me." He kissed her left hand, held her fingers to his lips for several heartbeats. "Now, let me honor *you*… as you have so graciously honored me."

Gypsy gasped when she felt the cold metal slowly sliding up her finger, encircling her there. Baron kissed the ring, and then her hand again.

"All that I have… all that I am… is forever yours," he whispered.

When her knees buckled, Baron quickly stood and held her to his chest.

"Do you understand now, my love?" He kissed the top of her head. "*This* is how I felt when you offered me your precious collar."

Gypsy couldn't speak, could barely even breathe. All she could do was stare at the large diamond on her left hand, hold to the man she loved more than life itself, and quietly cry.

<hr />

How did I get so lucky? Gypsy thought.

She was lounging in the warm bath, gazing happily at her stunning diamond ring—smiling, elated, blissful—when Baron came into the room.

"How is it you take my breath away anew, each time I look upon you?" He knelt down beside the tub. "Admiring the symbolic, tangible proof of our bond?"

"Yes," she whispered. "It is almost *too* extravagant."

"Is such a thing even possible?" He chuckled. "I wanted to make sure it was easily noticeable."

"Well, I don't see *that* being a problem."

He smiled down at her, gently running his fingertips out the length of her collarbone. "I want the men of the vanilla world to instantly realize that you are mine. Same as the ones from my world can tell with but a single glance at this." He touched her necklace as he spoke. "Le mien," he whispered. "…Mine."

"Oh, yeah? Then what marks you as mine?"

"Every action I take. Every word that spills from my lips. Every single thought that crosses my mind." He pulled her hand up to his lips, kissing it before whispering, "Come, Gypsy. I need to hold you. I have waited for this moment… for far too long."

<hr />

When Gypsy stepped from the bathroom—still tying her robe—Baron was undressing. She quietly gasped, not entirely certain if the tiny sound was audible or only internal, seeing as how her heart was racing loudly in her ears. There before her stood a man that was physically *her* perfect. No matter how uncool and star-struck she appeared right now, Gypsy couldn't possibly pull her gaze from the visual feast before her.

Is he real? She tried to swallow, but found the task almost impossible. *Is that truly my husband?*

Yeah, he's real alright, her devil purred. *Deliciously so.*

As Baron moved, the tight definition of his abs stretched around to his sides, highlighting his thin waist. He had the sculpted chest of an old Greek god—hard and muscular.

I'm glad he's not all hulkish and pumped up, her angel whispered. *I hate it when men look like they have muscle boobs.*

Yeah… me too, she thought.

Baron was facing the closet, hanging up his shirt. His taut muscles rippled under his flawless skin with each tiny movement.

A burning pressure was fast building inside of Gypsy, pulling an ache from deep down in her gut.

I want him, she thought.

Then take him, her devil said through a smile. *He's all yours.*

Baron hadn't yet registered her presence. When the jingly noise of his belt buckle made her gasp, he glanced sideways at her as he slid down his pants. She swallowed hard.

Holy Mother of Jupiter, she thought.

Who's Jupiter? her angel asked.

She's not thinking straight, her devil answered. *But who cares? Look at the size of—*

"Gypsy…"

Baron's deep voice interrupted her lurid, internal dialogue.

"Huh?" she barely managed to say, as her wide gaze slowly drifted back up to his smiling face, and ahhh… those tummy-twisting dimples.

"See anything you like?"

She only nodded.

He slowly approached her and placed his finger underneath her chin, pushing up, closing her gaping mouth.

"You look like you could devour me," he whispered as he bent to kiss her neck. "I would love to hear what's running through that pretty little head of yours right now. Are you nervous?"

"I wasn't until…"

She felt his lips part into a smile against her neck, just before he kissed her again.

"Until what?" he whispered.

"Until… you *know* what." She blushed.

Baron slid his hands inside her robe and slowly pushed it off her shoulders.

"Baron… are you going to hurt me?" She gasped when he kissed her on that sensitive spot where her neck and shoulder meet. "Are you g-going to make me pay for the m-marks I have against me?"

"Not tonight, sweet Gypsy. Tonight I will claim you as my own, erase any other's touch from your mind. Tonight… I will truly make you le mien." He touched her pendant as he said the word.

"I already *am* yours… unequivocally."

Baron slid his arm around her waist and pulled her against him. "If I lose control... forgive me."

Gypsy nearly stopped breathing.

———❦———

She could barely keep her eyes open. The sensations brought on by his slightest touch kept washing over her in tiny, tingling waves. Simply the feel of his weight pressed atop her was nearly maddening.

"Look upon me, Gypsy."

She tried.

"Gaze into my eyes, beautiful lady. I want you fixed in the here and now."

"But..." She barely opened her eyes. "Your kisses burn like the sweetest of fires. I can't... I only want to enjoy them."

"Ahh, but I wish our gazes locked at all times. I don't want you thinking about Renji."

"Wh-who?"

"I don't want you closing your eyes and picturing Jūshirō touching you."

"P-picturing who?"

She released a sweet, small moan. Baron smiled.

"That's right. Eyes on mine, my love. Let me see what I do to you. Look at me and gaze upon the heaven I am now in."

"Baron... I can't take much more." She softly groaned. "I am swollen with desire."

He smiled. "Yes. That was my intent."

"I need..."

"What do you need, Gypsy?"

She looked deep into his eyes. "I need to feel you within me, moving within me. I need you to make love to me."

At her gentle, whispered confession, Baron smiled. "I have waited over a year and a half to hear those words. There were days, week, months even... when I thought the possibility merely a dream." He lightly touched her chest, gently sliding his fingertips down to her navel as he spoke.

"Baron... are you... are you trembling, my love?"

"How could I not be?" he whispered. "This is my first time, Gypsy. The first time I have *made love*, yes, and also the first time I have been completely vanilla."

"Don't you like it? Do you want to do something else? If you want—"

He pinned her wrists down atop the silky sheets. "It's the most amazing, satisfying feeling in the world. Touching you, kissing you, hearing your sweet voice when I master each tender place... I was simply savoring the joy."

He kissed her then—consuming her, exploring her, melting her from the inside out. When he felt her completely relax, Baron slowly entered her.

Gypsy gasped, grabbing the sheets, twisting them up in her fists. Baron filled her on a level she had not thought possible. Not only physically, he filled her spiritually and emotionally as well. With each movement, the gorgeous man pressed atop her now filled in all her empty places, crept into every tiny wound in her heart, healed every single fracture left upon her trembling soul. He drowned her mind with nothing but elated happiness... a love she could never measure.

When Gypsy cried out, her back arching with her first wave of euphoria, Baron smiled down at her.

"I love you, Mistress Bishop," he whispered.

Gypsy smiled and tried to catch her breath. "I love you, too... Master Baron."

He growled—low and deep and feral. Gypsy gasped again.

<hr />

Baron grumbled when she rested her book atop his head. He squirmed, then nuzzled quietly back between her breasts.

"Are you always gonna sleep like this?" Gypsy asked.

"Always," he mumbled against her bare skin.

Gypsy chuckled and looked down at her impossibly handsome husband. Her knees were bent—feet flat on the bed. Baron was lying between her legs, his head resting between her breasts and his chest atop her tummy.

She smiled and ran her fingers through his dark, tousled hair. "Do you have any idea how much I love you?"

Baron only mumbled again, then wrapped his arms around her.

"We fly back tomorrow," she said, playing with his hair as she absently stared at the opposite wall. "We have been in Paris for a week, and haven't even taken in the first sight."

"Paris will look exactly the same on our next trip. If you are trying to talk me into leaving this bed, nothing you say will convince me to move."

She smiled again as she glanced back down at him. "What if I told you I wanted you? What if I asked you to ravage me this very moment? Would you move then?"

He pulled her all the way down under him. "Yeah," he whispered against her neck. "That'll work."

Gypsy giggled happily, but those giggles didn't last long.

Baron liked when she called out his name, loved it when he took her to the point she could barely rasp out *Master*.

She was panting—completely spent—when she felt the tip of his sharp nose gliding down her spine. She shivered. Gypsy was already grasping at the pillow when he made the same sensuous journey back up.

Her breath hitched when he buried his perfect nose into her hair, touching the back of her head before whispering, "Again…"

Chapter 27

"We'll make it back before opening time." She turned to Baron and smiled. "I'll still have a couple of hours to get ready."

"You're not wearing that black dress," Baron said.

"Which one?"

"The one with those *socks.*"

She chuckled. "But that dress looks so cute on me."

"Yes. It does. You can wear it at home—every day, if you want—but not tending the bar."

"How about the pink one?"

Baron glanced at her sideways, then rolled his eyes.

"If you insist on working the moment we get back, it's Friday... wear your kilt."

"Yeah. I guess you're right. I wonder how Sakara did."

"You know exactly how she did. You called her a dozen times a day."

When they pulled into the parking lot, Gypsy furrowed her brow.

"What's going on?" she mumbled.

The lot was packed and the doors were propped open.

She glanced down at her watch. "It's only a quarter past four. I hope something hasn't happened."

"Let's go see."

Baron helped her from the car and had to keep a tight grip on her hand to keep her from breaking into a run.

When they stepped through the door, Gypsy gasped and placed her hand to her chest.

"What *is* all this?"

Flowers filled the entire room. Splendid arrangements adorned every flat surface.

"Welcome to your wedding, my love," Baron whispered into her ear.

"My… my wedding? But how?" She reached for her hip. "How were you able to hide it from me?"

"I didn't." Baron smiled. "I knew that would be an utter impossibility." He wrapped his arm around her waist and placed his hand over hers covering her fox bite. "I *may* have mentioned aloud what I had done—filing our paperwork and booking the plane. And… I *may* have mentioned it where Taka could hear."

"Yes. He *may* have," Taka said as he approached and kissed both her cheeks. "Awesome collar," he whispered. "The finest I've ever seen. Jūshirō will go into mourning."

"*You?*" She looked her dear friend in the eye. "*You* did all of this?"

"With a little help from your friends," he said.

"Are you surprised?" Baron asked.

"Are you kidding?" Tears started filling her eyes. "I've never gotten to be surprised in my life. Then… you go and start surprising me at every turn. How?"

"I took your little Asian friend's advice." He motioned toward Taka. "As long as I didn't think about it, as long as I planted the seed but left all the details up to someone else… I wasn't hiding anything from you."

Taka winked at her when Gypsy glanced over at him.

"We had openly discussed all of our paperwork before hand," Baron said. "Even the marriage license. When I filed it at the courthouse that day, I wasn't *hiding* anything."

"Yeah, but…"

"But what, my love?" Baron smiled down at her. "We had already agreed to do it… someday. And as far as our honeymoon goes, I told you the moment I walked through the door to pack a bag and get ready for a trip."

"Yeah… I guess you did…"

Baron gently touched her heart-shaped lock, and smiled. "I mentioned to Jacque what *I* thought the perfect collar would look like. The perfect wedding rings as well. I simply mentioned it in conversation. That's all."

"Then… how did he know—"

"I trust Jacque, implicitly," he said through a half smile.

Gypsy stared up at him for a moment. "Pffts… lawyers."

"Yes. Lawyers." He gave her a little wink. "I love you, Gypsy Bishop."

She swallowed hard. "I love the way that sounds," she barely managed to whisper. "And I especially love the way it sounds in *your* voice."

Baron smiled again, before gently kissing her forehead.

"Come with me, Doll Eyes," Taka said softly. "You haven't seen *anything* yet. Let's get you ready. Let's dress up the goddess who's the star of this party. What do you say?"

Gypsy giggled then, and quickly followed him upstairs.

"You picked this dress out, didn't you, Taka?"

"You got me, Doll Eyes." He fastened the last rhinestone button and turned her around. "A vision in white, if ever I've seen one. What do you think?"

"It takes my breath away... all this lovely beadwork." She chuckled. "It weighs about twenty pounds."

"And it fits you like a glove," he said, before kissing her shoulder and glancing back up at their reflection. "This dress is so *you.*"

She smiled. "I know, right? It's exactly what I would have picked out."

"I double-checked your size when we went shopping that day. But I already had your measurements seared into my memory... from our brief *time* together."

Sakara and Gypsy both blushed, but Sakara didn't say a word, just kept curling up Gypsy's long hair. She *did* glance at her in the mirror, but she only smiled, didn't speak.

"Now then," Taka said. "Let's see if we have everything. Something old..." He picked up a shiny silver hair ornament with tiny little flowers dangling from it. "This was my mother's," he whispered. "It is my wedding gift to you, Doll Eyes."

"...Taka."

He slid it into the curls piled at the back of her head. "...Perfect. Just like an angel." He quickly turned his head before wiping his eyes. "That covers the something old. Something new would be... everything else you've got on. Now for the something borrowed."

He lifted a lovely tiara from a box and turned back to face her.

"Where'd you get *that?*"

Taka raised a single eyebrow. "It's mine, and I want it back. Thus the whole *something borrowed* bit."

"Yours as in... you *wear* it?"

"I have," he said, adjusting it atop her head. "There... perfect, of course."

"Taka?" She chuckled softly. "How in the hell did we ever end up in bed together?"

He met her smiling gaze. "I'm not gay. I'm *try*sexual, Doll Eyes. I told you that." He lightly touched her cheek. "But for you, I would have gladly gone just straight." He smiled softly. "Yet... you didn't ask."

She swallowed hard before clearing her throat. "Straight, maybe. But you definitely wouldn't have gone vanilla."

"Ain't that the truth?"

When he chuckled, Gypsy was relieved that the tension from a moment ago was suddenly lifted.

"And from what I recall," Taka went on. "You wouldn't have wanted me to go *completely* vanilla, anyway." He sucked in a quick breath. "Wait... Are you saying that Master Baron—"

"All I'm saying is... he's definitely trying. But I gotta tell ya, if he adds any more *flavor*, I don't think I'll be able to handle it. The man's insatiable."

"As are you, if my memory serves me correctly." Taka lightly circled the tip of her nose with his before whispering, "And it does."

Gypsy glanced toward Sakara. The poor girl's cheeks looked like they could burst into flames at any moment.

"Uhh... Where were we?" Gypsy quickly said. "Something old... something—"

"Ah, yes." Taka stepped back. "Something old—check. Something new—everything. Something borrowed—tiara. Oh... something blue." He went over to her bed and opened a new shoebox lying there.

"Hey... Taka?"

He turned back to face her.

"Are you ever going to tell me what happened to the Slight Samurai? I'm curious."

"Ahh... Musashi." Taka smiled. "Well... as I said before, he was very thin—not much muscle to show. And, mostly because of his build, but also because of his upbringing... he was passed over by the great Feudal Lords of his time."

"What was his upbringing?"

"Musashi was raised in the wild. No parents, no siblings, no other human contact. Such a thing left him minus manners, minus common decency, minus proper speech. He was skilled, yes, but he was *wild*. And because of that, a retainment—the *one* thing he desired above all else in the world—forever eluded him."

"That is so sad." Gypsy bit her bottom lip. "What in that tragic story... What in it reminded you of *me*?"

"Because of how it ends, Doll Eyes." Taka smiled softly. "One day... surrounded and threatened by drunken, dishonorable samurai... his back against the wall, *literally*... Musashi found the *one* thing hidden deep within him that no one else had—couldn't even come close to."

"Wh-what was it?"

"His *passion*—a fierce determination to never give up, to never give in, to never back down or surrender. Musashi owned a ferocious *will*—a vicious, undeniable *fight* that would always see him through. On that day... Musashi, the Slight Samurai... defeated all who opposed him. On that day, he did not receive a retainer, no. On *that* day... Musashi claimed a Lordship—*took* it... by the tip of his sword, with the edge of his beloved blade."

Gypsy swallowed hard, but remained silent.

"And that is what you brought to mind, Doll Eyes." Taka smiled again. "That day... in that smelling old boxing gym... I was blessed to behold the aura of a woman who would one day make it... no matter what."

Sakara quickly dabbed away Gypsy's tears before her mascara could run.

"I fell in love with you, then and there. I'd never seen anyone with colors like yours before. I *had* to find a way to accompany you on the magical journey I knew your life would be. And it has been, hasn't it, Doll Eyes? ...Truly magical."

She barely nodded.

"Yes... Jūshirō was right. Now that your glory has finally bloomed in full... you are the rarest blossom upon the tree." Taka sighed through his lovely smile. "Now… what was I— Oh, yes… something blue."

Gypsy silently watched as he gently pulled out pale blue, rhinestone-covered high heels.

Her eyes went impossibly wide. She squealed.

"Here's your something blue, Doll Eyes. Custom made… just for you." He knelt down in front of her as she slipped them on. "Perfect." He stepped back. "*You*, my love, are a vision. An absolute vision. You are the masterpiece I have dreamed about for my own wedding day."

She glanced toward him and half smiled. "For your bride… or for you?" she teased.

He gave her a quick kiss on the cheek. "Either one."

Gypsy giggled.

Taka walked behind her and met her gaze in the mirror. "I like to keep my options open, as you know. But today… today I will live vicariously through you, Doll Eyes. I got to make all the arrangements. I picked out the flowers. I was the first to get to gaze upon your glory. Except for the part where you take another man's hand… I will hold this vision of *our* wedding in my heart… always." When a single tear trickled down his cheek, he quickly stepped away. "Better Baron than Jūshirō." He cleared his throat. "If you were walking down that aisle to meet my brother, I wouldn't have been able to stand it. Come on, Doll Eyes." He reached for her hand. "There is someone waiting downstairs for you."

⚜

When Gypsy made it to the bottom of the steps and released her long dress, she looked up and yelped. She would have stumbled had Taka not been holding her.

"Aye, Kitten. I miss yer wee screams." Gillis smiled, tears spilling down from the corners of his eyes. "I'm here tae do the one thing I swore I'd nae do… give ye away. But now that I've seen ye, I dunnae think I can do it."

"Buck up, big guy." Taka slapped his shoulder. "I had to bite my lip and dress her up for him. The least you can do is walk her down the aisle."

"Aye, but how do I release her once we make it all the way down?"

Taka glanced away and didn't answer.

"Gypsy, Lass… ye've nae looked more beautiful. Nae woman ever has. My heart swells for ye… and shatters at the same time."

"Mine, too, Gills." She sniffed. "Mine, too."

"I know yer Pope will nae again let me near ye. So I want tae tell ye now… I'm sorry, Kitten. I'm sorr—"

Gypsy placed her fingers to his lips. "I forgave you that same day, Gillis. Of course I did. You are my best friend. I could never stay mad at you. I love you too much."

"I love ye more, Kitten," he whispered. "I love ye so much more."

"Alright," Taka said, handing both of them tissues. "Pull yourselves together before *her* mascara starts running, and *you* turn into a swollen-eyed mess. Come on. Everyone's waiting."

When Taka disappeared into the back room, Gillis held his elbow out toward Gypsy.

As they reached the door, the wedding march started. Gypsy sniffed.

"Aye, Lass. What are ye worried aboot? Yer already married tae the man of yer dreams—dimples and all. Look at this as naethin' more than an extravagant party in yer honor."

She chuckled then. "We've done it all backwards."

"Tell me aboot it, Kitten. Ye've always been like that—headstrong, going against the grain."

She glanced up at him. "I didn't know there was any other way."

Gillis was still chuckling when they stepped into the back room.

Gypsy heard all the gasps, all the chairs scooting back in her honor, but she couldn't glance to the left or the right. Her gaze was locked with the smiling man standing underneath that flower-draped arch, awe and wonder clear upon his face. If Gillis wasn't beside her, tugging her along, she wasn't even sure she could move her feet at all. She was floating through a dream, drifting along inside a surreal fairytale.

When Baron took her hand, neither of them could turn to face the judge. They just stood there, gazing upon each other. Surrounded by everyone they knew, yet completely alone.

Judge Broker had to clear his throat twice, then physically grab Baron by the arm when it came time to exchange rings. Everyone chuckled.

The sparkly diamond band looked like someone had draped tiny lights around her finger. Coupled with the breathtaking ring from Paris, there was no way anyone could mistake her for unwed.

"Too much?" Baron whispered.

"You know me." Gypsy smiled. "*Too much* isn't in my vocabulary."

"Good, because mine is the same."

Gypsy furrowed her brow, then felt a small tapping on her right arm. She turned to see Sakara holding out a matching band.

She almost cried when she slipped it on Baron's long, elegant finger. "Mine," she whispered.

Baron's tears escaped then, and they kissed before the judge could even tell them to. Thunderous cheers rocked Gypsy's Place.

The drinking and dancing soon ensued. Gypsy was passed to so many people she lost count. All of the veterans were there, her new biker friends, and even a few people from the office. Tony was talking to her when someone held a fresh champagne glass out to her.

"I'll quit hogging the bride now," Tony said. "Don't be a stranger, Gypsy girl. I'll see you at the gym tomorrow, right?"

"I'll be there with bells on."

"If you can still walk," Baron whispered.

Gypsy strangled on the champagne he'd just given her.

"You have a few guests who have been holding back all evening," Baron said softly. "They wish to speak to you now."

Gypsy turned toward the men as they approached. Her knees nearly buckled. Baron wrapped his arm around her waist.

"M-Master Fuu?"

"Ahh, Mistress Gypsy."

He took her hand. Gypsy didn't miss the fact that the bald Blood Master looked toward Baron and waited for his consenting nod before kissing her hand.

"You are as rare as a winter lotus blossom." He leaned in closer. "Is your flesh yet pristine, my dear?"

"It is." She smiled. "And if that should ever change, it will be by *your* hand."

"Only in my dreams, lovely lady. Now that *this* man has collared you… I dare say he will never let *any* other Dom touch you." He winked then. "We missed our chance."

"As did we," Jūshirō said, taking her hand from Fuu, kissing it without even glancing at Baron.

He tightened his grip around her waist.

"Did you get my letter?" Jūshirō whispered.

Gypsy blushed.

"The first, last, and most inappropriate gift she will ever receive from you," Baron said coolly.

Jūshirō smiled. "It was the first, yes. *Perhaps* the most inappropriate… yet, certainly not the last."

"It was lovely, Jūshirō." Gypsy softly smiled. "I was truly honored."

He leaned in closer. "You made my heart sing, beautiful lady," Jūshirō whispered. "A song it had never known before."

"Thank you, Nee-chan," she barely whispered.

The Rope Master kissed her hand again, and then stepped back as Renji took his place.

"Hello, Chikara. My sincerest congratulations to you both."

Baron nodded when Renji looked him in the eye. The School Master smiled as he took both of her hands in his.

"I would have put money on never seeing such an exquisite thing about your flawless neck. It pains me to say it, Chikara, but that collar makes you all the more enchanting. I envy my cold-eyed friend, there. To think that a man could tame you… to think that a woman could finally live up to the extremely picky Master Baron… I am in awe of you both. I would have held you most precious, Chikara, most beloved of all. Yet, even with my greatest of care, my worship of you would pale in comparison to the man who won you. I will go to the temple—pray that the gods will always smile down upon you."

"Thank you, Renji. That is the sweetest thing anyone has said to us all night." She lightly kissed his cheek. "I will miss you, Sensei."

He jerked slightly when her lips touched him, but the silent nod Baron gave the stunned Dom put his heart at ease.

"I will miss you, too, Chikara. Come visit when you can. I will buy you all the Chuhai you can drink."

"That's a deal." Gypsy smiled. "How's next week sound?"

Renji chuckled. Baron only rolled his eyes.

Gypsy stepped out of her magical-looking fairytale shoes and sighed. She glanced over to the elevator doors when she heard Skip's unmistakable laughter.

Sakara was blushing when she lifted her head

"Ms. Gypsy," she said sweetly. "We're heading down to Dogtown. You two need your privacy tonight..." She glanced up at Skip. "...and I'm really looking forward to seeing his hometown."

"Oh... okay. Well, you guys be careful. And call me when you get there."

"We will," Sakara said. "The bar is closed tomorrow. All of your regulars were at the wedding, but I also hung a sign on the front door."

"That means you're free to do whatever you want until Monday night," Skip said with a smile.

"Two whole days all to ourselves." Baron wrapped his arms around her from behind. "I hope you can handle it, Mrs. Bishop."

When Gypsy giggled, Sakara blushed again.

"About that..." Sakara said, then looked to Skip. "I hope you don't mind if I cut back to part-time, Ms. Gypsy."

"Part-time?"

Sakara nodded. "It's too far to drive every day. I thought perhaps I would come back up to help on Fridays and Saturdays."

Skip smiled happily. "After begging and pleading and crying my eyes out, she's finally agreed to move in with me."

Gypsy took the younger woman's hand. "...Sakara."

Sakara blushed again. "I know this seems a bit fast, but... I love him, Ms. Gypsy. I can't explain it. It just *happened*. When our eyes first met... I couldn't even breathe."

"I know the feeling," Baron whispered.

Gypsy was still in shock when the happy young couple left the bar together.

"Well… I'll be damned," she mumbled under her breath. "Magic must be in the air."

"Yes," Baron softly said. "I was just thinking that very thing."

Gypsy smiled up at him. "I love you, Baron Bishop."

He gently kissed her. "I know you do, dearest Gypsy," he softly whispered against her lips.

Baron scooped her up in his arms then, and carried her to her room. It took him almost ten minutes to unhook all the buttons down her back.

"Taka did this on purpose," he grumbled.

"Most likely, yes."

When he lightly kissed her between her shoulder blades, Gypsy shuddered.

"My beautiful wife," he whispered. "We've already had our honeymoon, but the *real* fun is only starting."

Baron led her to the bed, melting her with heated kisses. He reached for Renji's gift then, smiling as he slowly slid the beautiful cane from the dark emerald silk.

Gypsy's eyes widened. Then… she giggled.

About the Author

Jennifer Kaye Ensley is a native Tennessean by way of Missouri, born there and quickly ushered down South. A product of public school and private college, she spent her early twenties bouncing across the country. Fascinated by rich culture, ancient customs, and thick accents, she's compelled to drink in the many exquisite differences humanity is gifted with. A self-described, happily divorced mother of three with a black belt in sarcasm and an über common minivan, she does little to hide her wicked wit, advanced sarcasm, and extreme shoe addiction. "At the core of me, I'm one slightly twisted, pink haired, sword wielding, invisible ninja with a laptop, an imagination, and very little *me* time. That's just who I am. I'm comfortable in my skin and I love my life. Totally not kidding about the hair, the swords, or the laptop, but I might've stretched it just a little with the invisible part."

You can find Jennifer at the following locations:
www.facebook.com/ADancewithDestiny
www.JKEnsley.com
www.twitter.com/JenniferEnsley

Made in the USA
Charleston, SC
08 August 2015